THE PAINTED LADY

Maeve Haran

WINDSOR
PARAGON

First published 2011
by Pan Books
This Large Print edition published 2012
by AudioGO Ltd
by arrangement with
Pan Macmillan Ltd

Hardcover   ISBN: 978 1 445 87203 2
Softcover   ISBN: 978 1 445 87204 9

British Library Cataloguing in Publication Data available

Printed and bound in Great Britain by
MPG Books Group Limited

Author's Note

In the will she had drawn up on 7th October 1702 Frances Stuart provided the funds to acquire a house in Scotland, which was to be named 'Lennoxlove'.

Almost three hundred years later I was married in this wonderful romantic house and we included a portrait of Frances in our order of service. Even though I knew nothing about La Belle Stuart, I was already intrigued.

I would like to thank her and dedicate this book to her. I hope she would have approved.

*For Alex, Georgia,
Holly and Jimmy*

The Painted Lady

You think you know not my face or name, and yet, good people, you have carried me in your pocket for more than three hundred years. For I am Frances, called 'La Belle Stuart', and was loved by a king (and pursued by him for five years), and it was I that posed for Britannia, stamped on the copper coin of England.

This is my tale, and I will leave you to tell whether it be high romance or tragedy.

Prologue

Paris, 1659

Frances Stuart reached down, unlaced her worn shoe and scratched the painful redness of her toes. Her mother would certainly not approve of so vulgar a gesture, for a lady feels no pain, exhaustion, hunger, and certainly no itching.

The chilblains had been with her since November, and nothing—neither scratching nor wearing two pairs of stockings, nor her old nurse's remedy of potato rubbed into the fiery skin—had made a scrap of difference. Her mother's dresser had argued for egg white and honey, and a passing scullion threw in that his master used the halves of lemons squeezed onto his itching fingers and toes. Yet what use were such counsels to her? Where would she get honey or lemons in these lean times?

In the old days, the days before the troubles over the Channel in England, when the King still had his head, they would have had honey and lemons aplenty. Here they got only soup to eat (and not much meat in that), old bread, and certainly neither honey nor lemons. And yet she did not live in the poor quarters of Paris amongst the lepers and the plague-afflicted. No, she, Frances Teresa Stuart, of noble Scottish lineage and a distant cousin of King Charles, lived at the Court of his widow, Queen Henrietta Maria, in the Palais Royal—and almost starved there.

And froze also. The great echoing apartments they had been grudgingly lent by the French king

1

were rarely heated and they had little money for fuel to warm themselves, let alone the hordes of tattered Cavaliers and starving soldiers who flocked to the Queen's side. When, a year ago, the tyrant Cromwell was struck down by God, they had danced in their cold rooms and hoped things would change, but still their meagre state persisted.

Like any young girl, Frances longed for ribbons and silks and pretty gowns, when instead they were forced to make their clothes from the very hangings of their beds!

A strong desire to scratch came over her once more and to distract herself she turned to her commonplace book, in which she kept her dreams, her plans and her most secret thoughts. Today she did not write, but drew. Her favourite subject was a fine manor house with a tower and eight tall chimneys built of herringbone brick. Why did this self-same house always come into her mind whenever she picked up her pen? Was it because she never had a home to call her own, no fields to run in, no passageways in which to play Hide and Seek, no mellow arms of golden stone to fold her inwards, nor garden full of roses and gillyflowers to remind her that she was in England's gentle embrace? Instead she had lived here, amongst strangers, speaking French before she spoke her native tongue, for as long as she could remember.

She heard steps and guessed it was her sister Sophia, and hid the commonplace book beneath a threadbare cushion, pretending instead to make a castle out of cards.

Practice had made her fingers nimble and she had built it to the third storey before Sophia burst into the chamber, followed by her mother, and

2

accompanied by a maid of honour to the Queen, one Mary Villiers, whom all called by her familiar name of Mall.

Her sister regarded the castle of cards, her head cocked like some silly hen wondering if the rooster will deign to mount it, then, noticing that their mother and Mall were preoccupied with some discourse of their own, she quietly knocked it down.

Their mother, Sophia Stuart, continued conversing unchecked, but Mall, chestnut-haired and quick-eyed, known in her younger days for her own pranks and japes, caught Frances' eye and smiled in sympathy. Mall had been a beauty at twenty and saw in Frances' fair, willowy elegance a reflection of her own younger self. When French heads turned in admiration of Frances, Mall took more pleasure in it than her own mother did.

'Frances,' Mall requested, 'run and fetch my copy of the Psalms. You will find it in my closet near to the coffer that holds my combs. And there is a sweetmeat next to it you may have for a reward.'

Her sister shot her a look of venomous envy, for sweetmeats in this place were as rare as hen's teeth.

As she began to leave the room, a swish of silken skirts announced the arrival of Her Majesty Queen Henrietta Maria and her youngest daughter, the Princess Henriette-Anne.

Henrietta Maria walked across the room and stood next to the great window looking over at the north wing of the Louvre Palace opposite. Their apartments were to the side, facing the palace colonnades, which had a symmetry and grandeur unknown in buildings in London, with the exception of the great Banqueting House, whose name none could mention to the Queen since it was the site of her beloved husband's execution.

Despite her many sufferings, Frances noted, the Queen's dark hair had kept its lustre, and her eyes showed no sign of defeat. Until her son, Prince Charles, regained his throne and was crowned Charles II, she vowed that the gleam of battle would never die from her eyes. Even in the plain black clothes she always wore since her husband's death, she still resembled the noble queen, glowing with regal dignity, so often painted in silks and satins by Master Van Dyck.

And yet it seemed to Frances that it was a quality of mind that marked her out, for her physical appearance could be small and plain. Indeed, years ago, her own niece had declared herself shocked that the beautiful lady of the portraits was in fact a little woman with long lean arms, crooked shoulders and teeth protruding from her mouth like guns from a fort.

Frances hung back. The Queen was so tiny of stature that she herself, at five feet eight inches, felt like the giantess her sister so often rudely called her.

At the back of the great empty room a page arrived. Frances saw on closer study that it was one of the Queen's liveried dwarves. Grinning, he handed a letter to the Queen. 'From His Majesty Prince Charles.' He bowed low, kissing the Queen's feet with surprising agility for one of his sturdy bulk.

The Queen tore open the seal with excited fingers. 'He comes here! My son is on his way to visit me!'

Of a sudden, for no reason but that the Prince was popular, and they knew that with his ease and

4

charm he would lighten all their spirits just when they needed it, all in the room began to clap.

The Princess Henriette-Anne looked happiest of all.

'My dearest brother comes next week,' she exclaimed. 'And indeed I have not seen him once these five years. Hurrah!' And taking hold of the dwarf's small hands, she began to spin around the room until at last, exhausted, they collapsed in a dizzying heap.

'Henriette, you forget yourself!' reproved the Queen. 'You will have to learn to behave like a princess again.'

Henriette laughed. 'Not for my brother's sake. He is the least stuffy prince in all of Christendom!'

'He too is going to have to learn to conduct himself as a king. Even if he is in exile.'

Frances smiled sadly at Mall. For she knew how the French scorned our Charles and called him the 'Threadbare Prince'. Henrietta Maria had tried to repair their fortunes with a grand alliance, but no eligible princess or great lady thought our Prince Charles a promising catch.

Frances took her leave and went to search for Mall's book of Psalms, the thought of the sweetmeat quickening her steps.

In the Great Gallery outside their apartments she came across a sight so sad that she could only stop and stare. A scruffy band of ex-soldiers, dirty, disordered and desperate for a few sous, was in the act of chipping the gilding from the palace ceiling in the hope of selling it. At the far end of the gallery another man leaned out of the window to break off a pane of glass, eager for the price of the lead that latticed it.

5

Frances felt a deep shame flood through her that so noble a cause should be laid so low as this. 'Stop!' she commanded, forgetting her youth, and trying to draw herself for once to her full height. 'Where is your honour that you strip this palace like a marauding army?'

The leader of the men, as swarthy and unkempt as a privateer on the high seas, pushed towards her, leering. 'Like a marauding army, is it, my fine lady?' he demanded, thrusting his face right up to hers so that she could smell his rank breath. 'And you know how armies act when they've been in the field for months without wine or women?'

His filthy fingers grabbed at her dress.

Frances froze, fighting back the bile that rose in her throat, urging herself the while to stand up to this coward who dared to prey on young women.

While his rabble of men shouted encouragement, a sudden voice cut across their exhortations. 'Release the lady, you stinking vermin!'

Frances found herself forcibly wrenched from her attacker's grasp and flung aside by a tall young man with flaming russet hair, and a look of murderous rage in his grey eyes. 'Are you so reduced that you would violate the innocence of this young woman? Was our fight, and loss of life and country, for nothing that you behave so?'

The soldier eyed the stranger's fine brocade doublet. 'Fine talk from one who can afford to eat! If we have no food nor warmth, at least we can . . .' He gestured crudely at Frances, his eyes resting hungrily on her torn chemise.

'Prince Charles is on his way here. How do you think he will like to hear of virgins ravaged and this palace looted—and by his own men?' The stranger's hand strayed menacingly to his sword belt. 'Leave now, or you will pay for this insult with your blood!'

'So this is why we fought a war?' the soldier reluctantly signalled to the men to leave. 'To starve and find ourselves banished without even a roof over our heads.'

'Just as well,' her rescuer retorted. 'For it seems you would sell it, if you had one!'

As soon as they had gone he turned to Frances, taking in the torn silk of her dress, which she was vainly attempting to disguise. 'Are you recovered, mistress? I hope you took no hurt when I laid hands upon you?'

He reached out a hand to help her up.

For the briefest of moments their gaze locked and she saw that a look of desire darkened his eyes also, though he strove to hide it.

She did not know if it was relief, the intensity of the moment or some deeper swirling emotion, yet far down within her she felt an answering leap of longing and wished that he would lean down and kiss her lips.

To cover her confusion at so strange and shaming a reaction she answered him more stiffly than she meant. 'I could have defended my own honour without your intervention, sir.'

His crack of laughter took her by surprise. 'By God, I'm sure you could. That ruffian would have been on the floor and his cronies also, floored by one glimpse of that stern gaze of yours. No doubt in the late troubles you could have slain whole battalions with a glance.'

Frances felt obliged to curb this flight of fancy. 'Well, not whole battalions. Besides, I was not born

7

until the great battles were already fought.'

'I am sure such a detail as that would not have held you back.'

Seeing that he was well and truly laughing at her, she pulled herself up to her full height, which dwarfed many men. Yet not this one. He stood at least six feet tall.

'So,' he bowed low, his grey eyes teasing, 'which avenging goddess do I have the good luck to be encountering?'

The sound of girlish laughter told Frances that her sister Sophia, possibly with Mall's daughter Mary in tow, was fast approaching, no doubt wondering about the fate of Mall's book of Psalms and the sweetmeat. She glanced behind her. When she looked back her deliverer had all but taken his leave. 'Fear not,' he kissed his hand to her, 'I will make it my business to find out. For now I shall call you fair Diana, chaste Goddess, who defends her honour not with a bow and arrow, but with sharp words and sombre glances.'

To her great relief, since she did not wish her sister to turn this incident into a much-bruited anecdote, by the time Sophia hove into view the stranger had already gone.

'Frances?' her sister asked, her nose for gossip twitching like a dowser scenting water. 'Why have you been so long? And who was that young man just departing so precipitously?'

'I came across some soldiers stealing lead and gilding and had to persuade them to desist.'

Sophia shot her a look. 'Was that not foolhardy in one so young as you?'

An odd smile curled Frances' lips as she answered. 'Do not worry. We goddesses know how

8

to defend ourselves.'

Sophia shook her head. 'What foolishness is this? True, you are as tall as the Giantess of Bermondsey, but a goddess? That sounds a pagan fantasy to me—and blasphemous to boot.'

Frances hid her smile and took her sister's hand. Just like their mother, whose name she shared, Sophia had never had a sense of humour. Frances had almost forgotten the pleasure of dallying with one who did.

And now, just as he would do, she would make it her business to discover who he was.

Mall was her usual source of information, especially information she did not wish her sister Sophia to stick her nose into, but all were so busy with preparations for the arrival of Prince Charles that it was hard to find Mall, let alone pin her down even for a short moment's confidence.

They might have little fuel or food, yet the Queen wished to put on the best possible show to welcome her son, and such was the high esteem in which he was held that despite the harsh winter that had descended on Paris that December, it felt to all like the sudden coming of spring.

The anticipation at Prince Charles' visit brought a smile to the face of all, from the humblest turnspit boy to the highest Lady of the Bedchamber. The Queen decided to receive him not at the Palais Royal, where he might notice the depredations of the soldiery or the poor state of her furnishings, but at the smaller chateau at Colombes, an hour's ride away. Rooms were cleaned, curtains and rugs shaken out, and a feast of sorts—lean though it might be—prepared to welcome what all hoped was the King-in-waiting.

9

The cook was grateful to have at least game for the pot. And the courtiers made sport of hunting rabbits so that, though there would be nothing to rival the ten or fifteen courses that a royal banquet would once have offered, the Prince could at least have a choice of meats. Marchpane, made of almonds and too expensive for their reduced budget, was but a distant memory, yet the cook's artistry made a great pie out of apples saved from autumn and some preserved plums, which he cooked in a fine tart adorned with a tiny crown made of gilding begged from King Louis' confectioner.

The most excited of them all was the Princess Henriette-Anne. Though the fourteen-year age-gap between Charles and herself made him almost an uncle rather than a brother, she waited for his arrival with childish impatience.

'Will he have changed greatly since I saw him last?' she demanded of her ladies. 'Is he still that laughing black-haired man I remember, who used to dandle me on his knee when I was a little maid and sing "Ride a Cock Horse to Banbury Cross"'?

*　　　*　　　*

Frances thought she had rarely seen Henriette look so lovely. She had always been tiny, a doll of a girl, so fragile-looking that a puff of wind might blow her into the Seine, but now she beamed with happiness and anticipation. Frances had never met the Prince herself, yet she could not miss the powerful effect he had on all around him, especially his little sister.

'Almost like getting ready for a bridegroom,'

10

commented Sophia, with her customary want of tact.

'She has time enough for that yet,' corrected their mother. 'Let her enjoy the pleasures of a wedding without its tribulations.'

'Think you she means the marriage bed?' enquired Sophia, ever ready to pick up any insinuations in that department.

Frances looked away, overcome by the memory of the strange sensation of the other day, when she had longed to be kissed, and knowing that her mother, with her narrow disapproving ways, was the last person on God's earth she could ask about it.

'Fancy, it is five whole years since last we met! Do you think he will know me?' Henriette asked coyly, enjoying the fact that all told her she had transformed from a gawky child into a lovely young woman.

At this, Mall clapped her hands. 'I have had the most diverting thought. Let us play a jest on him!'

Mall was famous for her pranks, but none of them were sure they wished to join her in one. However, when Henriette laughed and heartily endorsed the plan, they had not much choice but to agree to Mall's madcap thought.

'Frances!' Mall took her by the elbows and pulled her sharply to stand by the great fireplace, which, for a rare occasion, was actually filled with blazing faggots. 'You are almost of an age with Her Highness. You shall pretend to be she.'

'I am three years younger,' Frances protested.

'Well, you are nearer in years than any of the rest of us.'

'Yet I am five inches taller!'

Mall seemed much struck by this.

11

'You shall sit then.' Behind them was a carved wooden footstool, inside an alcove, next to a fading tapestry of David and Bathsheba, half-hidden by the sweep of a threadbare curtain.

'The very place!' Mall clapped her hands delightedly and pulled forward the stool.

'But I cannot remain seated when His Majesty arrives,' Frances protested. 'It would go against every rule of precedence.'

'Faugh! The Prince is the least ceremonious man of my acquaintance.'

Frances sat on the stool and nervously arranged her gown, wondering what Prince Charles would be like.

Had he kept his spirits and his faith during his long exile? Many men in his position would have given in to the promptings of despair.

There was no further time for such thoughts as Prince Charles of England strode into the room, a smile of anticipation lighting up his long, lean features. Had he been in his own Court, he would have had trumpeters and Court musicians to announce him. Here it was simply the Queen's dwarf shouting that the Prince was here.

Frances' first impression was that our Prince looked more Spanish or Italian than the son of old England. Black brows and a thin moustache the colour almost of a raven's wing, his skin tinged not with the milky paleness of English nurture, but with the olive of a distant sun-scorched clime, together with thick black hair tumbling down to his shoulders, lent him a foreign and exotic look.

Here he stood before them, the 'black boy' born when Venus was high in the sky at midday—a strange fact greeted by all as an omen of his auspicious future, when instead it presaged the death of his father and the loss of his kingdom.

Although she tried not to stare, Frances was startled at how plain his clothes were. Accustomed to the magnificence of Louis XIV's Court, she could hardly believe that his coat was a simple black, adorned only with the merest sprinkling of lace. And as the sun shone in from the great window, her heart went out to him, for if his coat were not actually threadbare, it shone with continual pressing and in one corner she was sure she spied a darn. It was true then, the gossip that Mrs Chiffinch, who managed the Prince's household in exile, had not the money even to send clothes to the washerwoman and had to wash and darn them with her own hands.

That England's hopes had come to this!

And yet the friendly good humour of Prince Charles' manner belied any promptings of dejection at his lot. Instead he clicked his fingers and from the room beyond appeared his chief advisor, Edward Hyde, heavy and hobbling with his gout, followed by a yapping band of spaniels and, to the delighted amazement of all present, by a monkey dressed in a black suit, with its own feathered Cavalier's hat. Lastly came a courtier bearing on his arm a greenish-grey parrot.

'My sweetest sister.' The Prince knelt at Frances' feet. 'I wish to present this gift as a token of the love I bear you.' He handed her the parrot with great ceremony. 'I hope you might teach him to speak, for I and all my courtiers have failed to do so.'

Behind them the giggling began, a tiny wavelet growing into a tinkling river of laughter as the

13

monkey pulled back the curtain behind which Henriette-Anne was hiding.

For a moment Prince Charles looked dumbfounded.

But Henriette ran forward, seized his hand and kissed it. 'Dearest brother! Forgive us for our trickery. We wanted to see if you would know me after so long an interlude.'

A slow grin spread across Charles' dark features.

'So to whom, then, did I have the pleasure of offering this parrot?'

Henriette laughed. 'May I present Mistress Frances Stuart to Your Majesty?'

The King bowed low. 'I had heard how lovely my sister had become, and Mistress Stuart as her substitute was no disappointment.'

His gaze rested on Frances so long that she began to feel uncomfortable. He was so powerful, even in exile, and so much older than she was. He seemed more of her father's age than her own, and yet the interest that glinted in his eyes—if she mistook it not—was anything but fatherly.

She had heard that in the spotlight of his blackbird-keen gaze each woman felt that only she existed in all his universe. But none had told her that his desires would be so evident, even for one as young and green as she.

'So, Mistress Minx,' Prince Charles looked away from Frances at last and slipped his arm around his sister, 'you thought you would deceive your poor dunce of a brother, did you?'

'It was Mall's idea,' Henriette accused.

'Odds fish, and so it would be!' Mall emerged from behind the curtain and curtseyed to Prince Charles. Since she had been six or seven years old they had been brought up together as brother and sister, ever since the assassination of her father, the Duke of Buckingham.

Feeling she ought to withdraw from the intimacy of the tender reunion, Frances tried to hand the parrot to Henriette. It began to squawk loudly in protest.

'See, Frances, how he has taken to you,' laughed Henriette. 'You must keep him. Brother, could I not have the monkey instead?'

As if he approved of the suggestion, the monkey took off his hat and bowed to her.

'He is my prize possession!' protested Prince Charles. 'I have been offered a hundred crowns for him by the Ambassador of Muscovy.'

Henriette smiled her winning smile.

'Take him then!' Charles picked up the monkey and placed him in her arms. 'I never was able to refuse you, even when you were the tiniest child.'

His sister laughed. 'I was not a taking infant, I know. It was only you who paid me any mind.'

'I knew already what a beautiful and accomplished young woman you would one day become. And I was right, was I not, Ned?'

Charles turned to Edward Hyde, his most trusted advisor. Hyde bowed stiffly.

'So, what news from England?' Henriette demanded. 'Now that Cromwell is dead, surely the people will demand you back soon enough?'

Charles shrugged, a careworn look clouding his face. 'Sure enough there was dancing in the streets when Cromwell died. Yet now the people are strangely quiet. Not even a dog wags his tongue in London, or so our friends tell us.' Though he was trying to make light of his position, Frances could hear the edge of disappointment in his voice. 'If the people want me back, they are being mighty quiet about it. They have not raised the Maypole in the Strand for me yet.'

'When it happens, it will happen fast, Majesty,' Edward Hyde counselled, shifting from one swollen leg to the other. 'For my money, General Monck's the man to watch, not that ninny Cromwell's son whom they have put in his father's place as Protector.'

'Aye, Tumbledown Dick they call him,' Charles mused. ''Tis often thus with the son of an over-strong father. My own father would not have made such a mistake.'

They all fell silent, struck by the awful memory of King Charles stepping out onto the roof of the Banqueting House, bravely and gallantly walking to his death wearing two doublets against the chill, so that none thought him shivering from fear instead of cold.

'Come—' Charles looked around at the small group, now disconsolate—'let us cheer ourselves with a glass of wine. Another thing denied my people too long.' He noticed for the first time the gay gown that Henriette wore to greet him. 'Gold becomes you, Sister, it makes you look like a little cat I once possessed, who loved nothing better than to unravel my sash.' He laughed gaily. 'Indeed, you are very like her. I shall henceforth christen you Minette, little puss, in her memory.'

They all joined in the much-needed laughter. None of them had seen Henriette so light-hearted as she was today. 'Thank you, sire,' she curtseyed low and hid her dimples behind a pretty fan. 'The gown you so admire has an interesting history.'

16

'And what is that, pray, little puss?'

'My clever nurse fashioned it from my old bed curtains.'

A shadow cast itself over Charles' dark features like a cloud that crosses a sunny hillside. 'Indeed, that it has come to that.' He shook his head sadly. And then, being of an optimistic disposition, he shrugged it off. 'It becomes you, all the same.'

'I see you made an impression on His Majesty,' teased Mall when the Prince had departed to pay his respects to his cousin Louis, and they were walking back to visit her children Esme and Mary, before their nurse sang them to sleep.

Frances flushed, building up the courage to speak to Mall of private things.

'Mall . . .' she began, suddenly shy. 'You have had two husbands, the first when you were younger even than I. Did you ever feel a strange stirring . . .' she searched for the right words '. . . so that, at a certain person's look, your body soared and sang?'

Mall pealed with laughter and then, repenting of her levity at such a moment of disclosure, made herself be serious. 'It usually takes more than a look! And is it His Majesty who caused these waves to rock your calm harbour? I saw that he talked with you as if none existed in this wide world save you two.'

Frances shook her head. 'No, it is not he, but quite another. Indeed, I wished to ask you who the gentleman might be, since no one comes to Court but you know all about him, from bonnet to spurs.'

'Describe this paragon to me.'

Frances smiled. 'He is tall with hair as burnished almost as the setting sun when it sinks down in winter.'

'Bless the Lord, I am in love with him myself . . .

17

Did he give you no clue of his name, then?'

'Mama! Mama!' Mall's nine-year-old daughter Mary ran up, fit to burst with excitement. 'Prince Charles says I may ride in front of him on his great white horse and be grander than any queen in Europe.'

Mall laughed, seeing in her daughter the wild child she had been herself, and promised to come and watch.

'That power you felt,' she said softly to Frances so none could hear. 'It can be a part of your armoury. You can make others feel it also. Indeed, I have seen men watch after you with a look of longing when you leave a room. It is time I taught you to use your gifts, especially now that you have found these longings in yourself. Have you ever seen a woman make a gentleman open a door for her, using just her eyes?'

Frances laughed and shook her head.

'It is easy when you have the skill. I will find you a gentleman, that you may practise your art on him. Indeed, my husband's brother, Ludovic, comes this very afternoon with his dull and dutiful charge, my nephew Charles, who will succeed him as Seigneur d'Aubigny. Let us be ready for them. I will teach you to open a door using only your eyes. And now I go to see my daughter riding astride a king. My Mary is a solid child, rather than a thing of beauty. She should enjoy it while she can, for I do not think the experience will be repeated when she is grown.'

'Mall! Shame on you! What kind of mother says such a thing as that?'

And so, later that day, Frances Teresa Stuart was instructed in the art of lowering her grey-blue eyes and looking upwards through thick lashes, and thence towards the door, which to her amusement Mall insisted would be opened without her uttering a word.

Frances was trying to teach the silent parrot, now a firm gift to her from Minette, to speak either in English or in French, with a signal lack of success, when their guests arrived.

'Mistress Stuart,' Mall bowed formally to her brother-in-law, 'may I introduce my kinsman Ludovic Stuart, the Seigneur d'Aubigny?'

'The pleasure is entirely mine.'

Frances was surprised by the strong Scottish burr in so French a title, as a lean and ascetic gentleman with short red hair and piercing blue eyes leaned over her hand. But this was naught to the shock she felt when he introduced his companion.

'And this is my ward and nephew, Charles Stuart, who rejoices in the King's name, yet without any of his wealth or trappings!'

The tall, russet-haired young man who had rescued her from the ruffians stepped forward and kissed her hand with detached formality, making no reference to the circumstances of their previous meeting and certainly none to the look of frank desire that had so stirred her.

'Good afternoon, mistress. I am delighted to make your acquaintance.'

'Do you live here in Paris?' Frances enquired, keeping her voice steady. He seemed so different today, so stiff and formal. She would never have suspected the fire beneath this patrician exterior, if she had not seen it with her own eyes.

'I have been staying with my uncle. Yet I intend to return to London as soon as I can.'

'Will that not be dangerous?'

'I am convinced it will not be many days before our King is restored to his rightful throne.'

'I hope you are right.'

Frances saw Mall gesture towards her nephew and the door beside them, which was firmly closed. For a jest she followed Mall's instructions, glancing coyly downwards, then back up at the closed door.

Charles Stuart watched with amusement.

Suddenly, without warning, the parrot left Frances' arm and launched itself onto the young man's padded shoulder.

He held up a hand and the parrot obediently hopped onto his second finger. 'Good day, Charles Stuart, heir to the Seigneur d'Aubigny,' it greeted him cordially.

'Good heavens,' Mall marvelled. 'The creature talks.'

Frances dissolved in laughter, all thought of Mall's instructions in the art of coquetry forgotten. 'You are to be congratulated,' she told him delightedly. 'He has said not a word to us, before your arrival.'

'I am told I have a way with God's creatures,' Charles informed her, with a wink that transformed his stiff manner. 'The less attractive they are, the more they like me.'

The parrot squawked in protest.

'And by the way . . .' he trailed off tantalizingly.

'Yes?'

'I would be happy to open that door without you batting your eyes so obviously in my direction.' He turned, smiling to himself, the parrot still attached to his finger as if it had been welded there by an iron shackle, while Frances fumed and concluded that, whatever the stupid bird had decided, Charles

Stuart, son of the Seigneur d'Aubigny, was rather too pleased with himself for her liking.

And yet, in the coming days, it was not the newcomer's confidence or his teasing manner that persisted in invading her mind, but the wolfish smile that had lurked briefly in his grey eyes. More than once she found herself reliving that rescue with a very different outcome, where he lifted her into his arms and carried her to safety—if safety could indeed be the word to describe what she imagined happening afterwards in the privacy of her chamber.

Some of this forbidden delight must have been manifest in her expression, since Mall bore down upon her relentlessly. 'So, Mistress Innocence, I hear from your sister that you were rescued from marauding soldiers—and by none other than my nephew Charles. I wondered if it might be he, when you mentioned the russet hair, yet I thought it not possible. I could not imagine him in such a role. Surely it was not he who ruffled your waves so?' She fixed Frances with a penetrating gaze that was not without kindness. 'If so, you had better calm them. Nephew Charles needs a rich wife. Since the family scandal, Ludovic Stuart has been forever telling him that he must be honourable and fulfil his duties by marrying well. Ludovic has even found him a wife.' Her face softened at the shock she saw in Frances' eyes. 'He is betrothed to one Elizabeth Rogers, eighteen years old with a portion of ten thousand pounds. Whether he likes it or not.'

The unfairness of it all cried out to Frances. Like so many others who supported the King, her family had lost all. She would have no portion to bring to a marriage. The thought of a bleak future—marrying some old man who would take her beauty in place of wealth—or of remaining unwed, little more than an unpaid servant in some distant relative's house, so clouded her mind that she forgot even to discover what scandal it was that had engulfed the family of the reportedly dull and dutiful Charles Stuart, heir to Ludovic Stuart, the Seigneur d'Aubigny.

Chapter 1

At last she stood, the wind whipping her hair from beneath her hood, on the deck of *The London* on her way to the city of that name, her heart soaring with excitement at what might await her.

The weather was fair, with but one brief squall, and it took no more than seven hours to reach the longed-for English shores. It had been almost two years now since the monarchy had been restored and Prince Charles had at last been crowned King of England.

They were bound for the Queen Mother's residence at Somerset House, where they would stay until Catherine of Braganza, the King's intended bride, arrived in a month or two, and Frances would move to Whitehall to be her lady-in-waiting.

In the end it had all been thanks to Minette.

Frances was far too lovely, she decreed, to moulder away in some French palace. She must go to London and shine in the setting of her brother's restored Court. And so, armed with a letter to the King insisting that she was the prettiest girl in the world and the most fitted to adorn a Court, Frances had set out for a new life with Mall and little Mary to bear her company.

The only sadness that had marred their joyful preparations was the death of Mall's dear son, Esme, at eleven years old, of typhoid fever. Mall had been so prostrate with grief at the loss of her sweet, chestnut-haired boy, the image in miniature of his mother, that she would see no one for two weeks. It had been the Queen Mother, Henrietta Maria herself, who insisted that Mall go with Frances to London, away from the scene of such unhappiness. It was the needs of Mary, her sweet daughter, that finally lifted her from her despair.

'What a strange thing is life,' Mall mused to Frances as they readied themselves to depart. 'Now my sweet Esme is gone and will never inherit his father's title, and Mary may not, for being a woman, it must go to the next male heir.'

'And who is that?'

'My nephew Charles. Your rescuer is about to become the Duke of Richmond.'

Frances turned away, not wanting Mall to see the pain in her eyes. Not only was he married to another woman by now, but that woman was about to be his duchess.

Mall had chosen for them to arrive quietly, via Lambeth, and from there to go by water past the reddish brick of the Palace, where lived the Archbishops of Canterbury, then towards Westminster Abbey and the warren of Whitehall Palace and thence to Somerset Stairs.

The first thing that struck Frances about London was the noise. Paris, though a great city, was not so great as London. Everywhere bells rang continually, day and night. Street vendors with trays of vegetables, flowers or China oranges cried their wares; huge drays pulled by four horses rumbled through the cobbled streets, barely missing street children and sometimes getting stuck in the narrow roadway. A forest of signs creaked, nine and a half feet up, so that the horses might pass beneath, advertising all manner of trades. Yet what surprised her most of all was the blackness of the air, and

24

the layer of soot that settled upon everything and everyone, tearing at your throat and bringing tears to your eyes.

'You will become accustomed to it,' Mall shrugged, leaning forward to cover little Mary's mouth with her veil. ''Tis the sea-coal burned by all. The soot stopped only once when the coal ships could not make their way through icy weather, and suddenly the city was clear as dawn on a dewpond.'

They rounded the final bend in the river and threaded their way through dozens of wherries, passing a great building on their left. Frances asked Mall what it was.

'Westminster Hall where Noll Cromwell had himself decreed Lord Protector and sat in the Coronation Chair in his purple and ermine. Much good it did him in the end.' She pointed to a small smudge high on the roof. 'That's his head. The King dug him up from the Abbey, with the other traitors Ireton and Bradshaw, and hanged them from Tyburn Tree, then cut off their heads and stuck them there for Londoners to admire.'

Frances shivered. 'I had not thought His Majesty so barbaric.'

'Barbaric!' Mall turned on her angrily. 'The King is too tender by half!' Frances had never heard such anger from her. 'He only punished a handful of those traitors who put his father to death. I would have hanged the lot! But the milk of human kindness overflows in our King. He shrugged and said he was weary of hanging.'

They rowed onwards, struck silent now, past the Palace of Whitehall towards their destination at Somerset House.

'There it is,' Mall pointed out, her breath

spiralling upwards in the freezing air of afternoon. Before them was a great square building of yellow brick, adorned in the centre by a clock tower and two graceful wings, fronted by ornamental lawns and a vast garden laid with trees to one side.

'It is a fine building indeed,' Frances said in admiration.

''Twas not so when Cromwell's scum of soldiery took it as their barracks!' Mall almost spat. 'They sold off every picture, carpet, piece of plate and hanging they could lay their filthy hands on. It has taken the Queen two whole years to make it habitable again so that she can return and live here. It will be our job to finally ready it for her.'

'I will do so gladly.'

'And be not squeamish. You see those windows?' She pointed to the long gallery that fronted the river. 'That is where they hanged Cromwell's effigy—and good riddance—for this is where he dared to have himself laid in state, just as if he were as great a man and monarch as the saint he had slaughtered.'

Frances could not repress her horror at so much violence. 'Cousin, I did not know you were so bloodthirsty.'

'Do not speak of that which you do not understand!' was Mall's angry reply. 'My husband lost all because of Cromwell. His two young brothers, the flower of Charles' Court, strode into battle in their silks and were cut down before they had ever lived.'

'I am sorry. I spoke out of turn.' Her own family had also suffered grievously, yet she felt more in tune with the King who had wearied of hanging his enemies. Revenge did not bring back the dead.

Yet she must respect Mall's loss. This world, where injury was still so fresh, was new to her after so long across the Channel. 'Mall, beloved cousin, I have much to learn.'

'Yes,' Mall's voice was cold and hard with pain. 'You do.' The boat glided in towards the stairs leading from the river up to the great house. 'I am sorry, Coz. You will find that, despite the King's restoration, wounds still fester. Yet I will help you understand.' She took her daughter's hand and held onto the boatman as she climbed down. 'Come, it will not be sad. London is like no city on earth for fun and laughter. What we lack in cultivation, compared with Paris, we make up for with merriment!'

Mall was telling no less than the truth. After so many years of repression there was a giddy, breathless sense of adventure in the sooty air of London, as if everyone had to prove that life was vital, pleasure-filled and free of all restriction.

They walked up the grand stairs from the river, through the gardens and across a wide terrace overlooking the Thames, where a crowd of finely dressed people watched their progress curiously. As they passed, each lady nodded her head to Mall while the men bowed. Frances followed, amazed that Mall seemed to know each and every one of them.

Once inside Somerset House, a Groom of the Bedchamber was summoned, who took their belongings to their chambers. Used to sharing with her sister, Frances had expected a dormitory or some little nook, tucked away in a corner of the great house. Instead she was allotted a large square room in the east tower, with a fine view of the lawns with their great marble statues of Thames and Isis.

As she unpacked her clothing and hung her gowns on pegs and laid her petticoats and chemises into the press provided, she wondered where to put her parrot. Attached to one wall, in the furthermost corner, was a sconce once destined for a candle-holder. Frances hung the bird's cage on it. He squawked and ruffled his feathers angrily, hopping from one foot to the other in comical protest.

'Where then?' Frances demanded.

In the other corner of the room a dressing table with a Turkey rug draped over it stood near the great window.

'So you want to look out at the river, do you? Yet it is too grand for the likes of you, bird. What if you drop your seed on that fine stitching or spoil its glorious colours?'

Nevertheless she placed the cage upon the dressing table.

'God bless Charlie Stuart!' commented the bird in approval.

'Aye,' Frances shrugged. 'God has blessed him all right. He has wed his heiress and, for aught we know, has the son he needs to keep his uncle happy. And now he is a duke!'

She had no time to dwell on Charles Stuart's domestic arrangements, for she heard Mall calling to her that they were going out to explore the city while the sun still shone.

'We shall not see much—a little taste only of the delights to come.'

Across the Strand from the back of Somerset House stood the hackney-coach stand, next to the greatest maypole in London.

28

'Just think,' Mall marvelled,' it took twelve sailors to pull it back up after Cromwell felled it. Old Noll banned maypoles, along with play-acting, wassailing and even Yuletide. Imagine the poor citizens of London. All those years without any festive cheer. No wonder they were glad to see him go!'

Frances, Mall and little Mary clambered into the coach for a tour of the city. On every street painted signs swung high above them, announcing the tailors, shoe-makers, linen drapers, mercers, felt-makers, hatters, hosiers and button-makers that thronged London. Frances learned that if she wanted ivory combs, she must seek a sign that showed a painted elephant; Adam and Eve offering apples meant a fruiterer; apothecaries' shops sported unicorns or dragons; a sign with a row of coffins reminded Londoners that one day the purchasing would have to stop.

But for now she could see the citizens were mad for getting and spending. Deprived of any luxury during the years of Cromwell, lavishness was now the order of the day. And, unlike Paris, where rich and poor were somewhat separated, here they lived cheek by jowl in each other's pockets.

Down each narrow street, so cramped they were almost alleys, the unsuspecting walker might, with equal ease, stroll into a tippling house packed with costermongers or the hidden mansion of some rich merchant.

Frances' head was whirling with the new sights and sounds of London. What it lacked in elegance, she found, it more than made up in energy.

'Tomorrow we visit Whitehall,' Mall announced, 'and meet the other ladies who will wait upon the

Queen.'

The Palace of Whitehall! Later that night Frances was so excited that she could hardly sleep in the huge bed she had entirely to herself. She was so used to sharing with Sophia that it had seemed strange at first, but now she luxuriated in the fine linen, the hangings of brocade tied up with golden tassels, and the rich velvet covering on her bed. Not long ago she would have looked at them with thoughts only of turning them into a gown. Now she had dresses aplenty, and Mall, with only little Mary to clothe, seemed to be taking great pleasure in adding to that growing wardrobe.

Next day, the weather being balmy, and it being but the skip of a pebble from Somerset House to Whitehall, Frances had thought it would be easy to walk there.

'Walk!' Mall laughed at her innocence. 'My dear girl, your gown would be mired before you took two steps. The filth from the channels down the middle of the street would choke you; you would be pushed untimely to the ground by the gallants who keep to the wall for fear of ordure being thrown from the windows and spoiling their silver lace. And no doubt your purse would be stolen into the bargain! In London we travel by wheels or water.'

Impressed though she was by Mall's superior knowledge, it struck Frances, as they hailed a wherry, that for two ladies dressed in satin gowns, petticoats and mantles and holding fans, climbing in and out of a wet craft that bobbed disconcertingly in the late spring breeze, travelling by water was not a method much to be favoured over walking in the street, no matter how hazardous the roadway.

Mall had completed her own outfit with a black

silk vizard, which covered half her face, giving her a rather frightening appearance, like the harbinger of some dread fate. It was, she explained, simply to ward off the damaging rays of the sun, and she advised Frances to do the same.

Frances laughed and said she would take her chances.

They made good speed and reached Whitehall in only fifteen minutes.

'Well, mistresses,' asked the wherryman as they approached the muddy shore, 'be it Whitehall Stairs or the Privy Stairs you're desiring?'

'What think you, doddypol?' Mall snorted.

The Whitehall Stairs were public and used by all manner of people. The Privy Stairs, on the other hand, went only to the Palace and were used solely by the noble.

The wherryman looked them up and down and dutifully rowed towards the latter.

On arrival they climbed carefully from the craft, picking their way past a post to which a dozen small boats were made fast, onto a rickety plank wall, which curved out over the mud like an arthritic finger. The tide was low and half the river was solid mud almost across to Lambeth Palace. The stairs led to a small jetty from which Whitehall Palace spread out before them.

Frances, used to the elegant palaces of the Louvre and the Tuileries, built in graceful squares or curves, stared in shock at the vast collection of houses and buildings that made up the Palace of Whitehall. 'In truth,' she declared, 'it is not so much a palace as a village or town.'

The warren of Whitehall, comprising hundreds and hundreds of small rooms and large

31

apartments—some tall, others humble—stretched back from its river frontage, through four acres, past the Bowling Green and Privy Garden and the King's tennis court, the Horse Guards parade ground and the Banqueting House, almost as far as St James' Park.

'A heap of houses, my mother always called it,' Mall looked round affectionately. 'Fifteen hundred rooms, and can house six hundred courtiers. The largest—and ugliest—palace in Europe. Knew you that I grew up in York Place, which the King has since made part of his palace? So, I live at the Court, but still I live at home.'

With a thrill of nervous anticipation Frances wondered if they might see the King and, if they did, whether he would remember her or no.

'Is the King in residence?'

'At this time of year?' Mall laughed at her ignorance. 'He is at Newmarket. He visits twice, in spring and autumn.' Her expression blackened. 'And takes My Lady Trollop with him.' Even though she had been at Court so short a time, Frances had already heard much of the scandalous Barbara Castlemaine, born Barbara Villiers, and another of Mall's numerous cousins. Barbara had shocked the nation by spending the very first night that the King returned to London lying in his arms. The fact that she already had a husband of her own had not stopped her. The King, for his part, had tried to mollify the unfortunate Roger Palmer by making him Earl of Castlemaine, and thus Barbara became Lady Castlemaine. Yet everyone at Court, Frances knew, simply referred to her as The Lady.

'Dearest Barbara is breeding the King's bastard,' Mall continued. 'Though they do say the last

32

one much resembles not His Majesty, but Lord Chesterfield, my lady's previous lover.'

Frances bit her lip, taken aback at Mall's indiscretion about one who was her own cousin.

'Oh,' Mall laughed, 'I am too generous to her. There are those who speak much worse of her than I do. Ned Hyde, the Chancellor, loathes my lady so much he will agree to no money or privileges being accorded to her. When the King wished to make her husband Roger an earl, so that Barbara might call herself a countess, he had to do so in the Irish peerage, so that his own Chancellor need not affix the great seal to it!'

'But cannot the King do whatever he will?'

'Where have you been sleeping these last years? It may make my blood boil, but the King must not overstep his mark and be seen to act as his father did.'

They had arrived within the Palace and a liveried servant led them to the apartments that were being readied for the Queen.

'So, lad,' Mall quizzed him. 'Are you looking forward to a new mistress taking charge of the household?'

The servant nodded. 'Yes, indeed, my lady.'

'No doubt he feels he has one already,' Mall commented in a low voice. Once inside, they were led through a labyrinth of passageways until they reached a large suite of rooms panelled in English oak, finely carved and pilastered, the panels gilded and painted with fleurs-de-lis. 'The Queen's Apartments,' announced the groom who was accompanying them, bowing.

From the adjoining room they heard a sudden chattering, like a flock of starlings gathering at

33

dusk, preparing to find a roost. A door opened and the flock descended, led by a lady of middle years.

'Mall Villiers! Come here and kiss my hand like a good niece ought.'

Mall smiled and ran to her side. 'Good day to you, my aunt Suffolk, I was happy indeed to hear of your appointment. First Lady of the Bedchamber no less!'

'Aye. And Mistress of the Robes and Keeper of the Privy Purse,' confided her aunt.

Frances looked from one to the other, taking in the deep, polished brow and intelligent hazel eyes that both ladies shared.

'Not forgetting Groomess of the Stool!' breathed an elegant young woman, who far outshone the others in style and elegance.

'Silence, Cary Frazier! You are ever gossiping like a wench at a wassail.'

'My lady aunt,' Mall curtseyed, acknowledging her greater precedence. 'May I introduce Mistress Frances Stuart?'

Frances curtseyed too, finding the appraising gaze of six young women fastened upon her.

'So is all decided for the Queen's household?' Mall enquired.

'Indeed, no.' The Countess of Suffolk shook out her elaborate dress like an anxious hen. 'We are a very unsettled family as yet. The Queen will be here in a month, and only the dressers are fixed: Lady Wood, Lady Scroope, Mrs La Garde,' she gestured to a shy-looking young lady.

'And Cary Frazier here. If she can allow us the time from her dress-maker. The maids of honour are also chosen: Mrs Wells, Mrs Price, Mrs Warmestry, Mrs Boynton.' Each lady nodded in

turn to signal her presence. The title 'Mrs', Frances
had learned, was given even to unmarried ladies,
since 'Miss' denoted not an unmarried but a kept
woman. 'And of course Mrs Stuart.' She curtseyed
in acknowledgement of the honour. She knew
how closely these posts were sought after. Much
jockeying for position, and even outright bribing,
would have led to this list. Being as near to the
Queen as all these ladies would be brought with it
great influence.

'And which ladies will be of the Bedchamber?'

This, of all the roles, was the most sought after
and influential, since it brought the most intimate
access of all to the Queen. And with it, great
opportunities to forward any suits that needed
pressing and the possibility of profiting by doing so.

The Countess dropped her voice. 'None are
named. It is a mystery.'

'Why so?'

The Countess looked over her shoulder. 'We
wonder if it is in connection with The Lady.'

Frances had rarely seen Mall so shocked.

'She would not dare! Expect to be a Lady of the
Bedchamber to the Queen, when she is the King's
mistress? Not even she!'

The Countess shrugged and signalled with her
head that Mall should follow her to a discreet
corner of the room, where they continued talking in
low voices.

'Mistress Stuart . . .' Frances found three of
the ladies gathered round her. The boldest, Cary
Frazier, began touching the sleeves of her dress.
'Tell us, mistress, how these sleeves are wrought.'
She pointed to the way Frances had rolled back the
blue satin of her oversleeve, by means of tying it

with ribbons to expose the chemise beneath.

'Oh, it is just some little trick the ladies in Paris do.'

'Is it indeed?' asked Cary Frazier. 'Too difficult for all of us poor Englishwomen?'

Frances could see her attempt at modesty had been taken for pride.

'And you show so much of your chemise beneath your gown, you could be in the boudoir rather than in company,' Jane La Garde, another of the Queen's dressers-to-be, pulled at the soft cloth Frances wore under her gown. 'Do you not give scandal that you wear your underlinen on display so?'

Frances shrugged. 'It is the fashion there.'

'And the colour of your hair,' chipped in Catherine Boynton. 'I have seen naught like it here. What shade hath your hair-dresser wrought it?'

Frances' chin went up at this, conscious this was no friendly inquisition. 'The colour of nature, mistress. The one I was born with.'

'Well said, Frances!' Mall congratulated. 'Come, ladies, cease this interrogation. In Paris, Mistress Stuart is famed for the artlessness of her beauty.'

A ripple of laughter ran through the group of ladies and Frances wished Mall had left her to her own defence.

'Ah,' quipped Mary Scroope. 'You could not expect us to know of artlessness at this Court!'

'For myself,' Jane La Garde added quickly, 'I admire your hair greatly. Will you show me how to braid it thus, and still have some fall softly over your shoulder?'

Frances smiled eagerly. 'Indeed I will. Though the French ladies thought me as unpolished as a

36

country wench compared to their fine beauty.'

'Since we are not as polished as you, then we must be ladies of the hovel rather than the Bedchamber.' Catherine Boynton's voice was dipped in vinegar.

'Now, now, ladies!' Mall had finished her private conversation. 'We will spend much time together in the service of the Queen, we must be friends.'

Her words reminded Frances of her old nurse abjuring Sophia and her to stop quarrelling. To her surprise, of a sudden she missed sorely her sister and their apartment in the Palais Royal. Yet this was her home now, in England, and, despite these unwelcoming ladies, she intended to be happy here.

'How soon comes Queen Catherine, my lady?' Jane La Garde asked the Countess of Suffolk.

'The end of May. Then they go to Hampton Court to do their honeymooning.'

'Is it true my lady Castlemaine plans her lying-in there with the King's bastard?' asked Catherine Boynton.

'If she does, she will get a flea in her ear from me, as well as a squalling child to care for,' snapped Lady Suffolk, who was Barbara's aunt as well as Mall's.

'If only it were true that my aunt could truly send my lady Castlemaine away with a flea in her ear,' whispered Mall as they walked back towards the water, having taken their leave of the assembled ladies. 'But where my cousin Barbara is concerned, the King is as blind as a newborn puppy.'

'And what gives her such power over the King?' Frances enquired. She knew the King to be kind and tolerant—a man as much as a King—someone to be admired in so many ways, and could not

37

comprehend the hold this lady seemed to have on him. 'Is it her great beauty?'

'Oh, Barbara Castlemaine is beautiful all right. Like a ripe peach, caught when it is fullest and juiciest, just at the moment before it begins to corrupt. Yet that is not the attraction she holds.'

'What is it then?'

'Her appetite. Barbara has an itch as strong as any man's. I remember, when she was a child, she used touch herself down below, in full view of the company, as if for all the world there were nothing to be ashamed of in it.'

Frances looked away, shocked and yet intrigued.

She would never in a thousand years admit as much to Mall, yet she also felt a fascination for this outrageous creature who dared to flout every convention laid upon virtuous women.

Barbara Castlemaine might be the Devil incarnate, yet compared to the ladies amongst whom Frances had grown up, whose chief delight was spending pious hours upon their knees, she sounded exotic indeed.

They spent the afternoon playing with Mary in the gardens in front of Somerset House, where there were square lawns to run on, bordered by straight gravel walks on each side and by three avenues of trees leading down to great stone steps to a lower garden, bordering the river. Through a locked iron gate they glimpsed a strange craft, which Mall explained was modelled on a boat called a gondola, all the way from Venice.

'I would like to go on it,' said Mary.

'And I also,' Frances nodded.

'Not today, sweeting.'

Mary looked so distraught that Frances had to

38

cheer her by chasing her over the lawns and hiding behind a statue of Triton, before jumping out to say 'Boo!'

When they climbed back up to the house it was to find a gentleman, rather stout and florid, yet richly attired in black velvet, with dozens of brass buttons lining his coat, sporting a fair-coloured wig.

'Are you a soldier?' Mary asked him.

'No, indeed—well, not at the moment, and never if he can help it,' laughed Mall. 'This is my brother, George Villiers, the wicked Duke of Buckingham. Mary, meet your uncle.'

'Are you indeed my uncle?' Mary asked.

'Odds fish, Mall, what a way to introduce me to this charming pair.' He bent down on one knee, but succeeded, owing to his rather heavy bulk, in looking ridiculous instead of romantic. 'I am indeed, young lady.'

'I am Mary, Lady Stuart,' the child said, suddenly important. 'Yet I will not become Her Grace of Richmond, even though my brother died, because I am a girl.'

Frances shot a look at Mall, fearful that this reminder of Esme would bring her pain. Yet Mall smiled at the child's prattle.

'True indeed. The Duke of Richmond is now my young cousin Charles.' This time it was Mall's turn to shoot a look of amused enquiry at Frances.

She pretended to ignore it. 'Come, Mary, let us run up those great steps and beat your mother and her brother back to the house.'

At that, Mary picked up her skirts and dashed towards the steps, with Frances after her.

'So, Butterfly,' she heard the Duke enquire of his sister. 'How do you like being back at the English

39

Court?'

Frances could not hear the reply, but at the top of the steps behind the statue of a Nereid she had to stop because the lace of her shoe had come untied. She bent down to fasten it. The words she heard next froze her to the spot.

'Congratulations, Sister!' the Duke said in a low voice. 'She is perfect in every way. What innocent beauty, and such artless charm! You could not have found a fitter contrast to the over-ripeness of our Barbara, or a better answer to our prayers. How could the King resist so tempting a morsel as that?'

Frances waited for Mall to fire up at such demeaning words, but instead her answer chilled Frances to the bone.

'Indeed, I think you are right, George. Like a water ice, she will clear his palate after so long a diet of over-rich food.'

'What a clever Butterfly. And tell me, how is your scandalous poetry progressing?'

Frances did not stay to hear the answer, but ran on, her heart racing in the wake of little Mary. She had been naive and a fool. Mall had seemed so much her friend—indeed, her only friend—and now she saw that she could not trust Mall any more than those poisonous ladies-in-waiting.

She had never greatly believed in her own beauty, though others told her of it, and now she heartily wished she did not possess it. Perhaps she had been naive to trust Mall so completely. Mall had lived at courts all her life, and had learned to make judgements over what would be useful and what not. Frances had thought herself a friend— almost a daughter, since her own mother was not given to natural affection. Now she suspected that Mall had coolly weighed up her charm and innocence not as qualities in themselves, but for their use in furthering the cause of the Villiers' interests.

It was time she fought her way out from under Mall's wing and made some friends she could trust.

When she reached the graceful arches and porticoes of Somerset House she found that a Groom of the Bedchamber awaited her, holding a small posy upon a silver salver.

'Pretty flowers!' exclaimed Mary. 'Are they for me?'

The man smiled at her childish prattle. 'You are a little young, my lady, to be sent posies. They are for Mistress Stuart from Mrs La Garde,' he announced gravely, handing Frances a letter. 'This note accompanied them, and her apology that she could not come and present them herself.'

Frances tore open the letter. It was a short missive, littered with misspellings and liberally decorated with blotches of ink, apologizing for the unkind treatment Frances had received from the maids of honour. 'Whom, if their name meant aught, should know to behave better.'

It seemed that she had one friend at least.

Chapter 2

As the arrival of Queen Catherine approached, so did the sense of excitement at Court. A new queen meant a new start for all. And for some, perhaps an end.

This was what many foretold for Barbara, Countess of Castlemaine. 'She might be carrying the King's bastard,' Mall pointed out, 'but Barbara should remember his promise that he would never do what his cousin Louis did. Once he took a wife, he would not have the ill manners to insult her by keeping a mistress at the same time.'

'Aye,' added Lady Suffolk briskly, 'but that was before he found himself a bride.'

Would Catherine of Braganza, twenty-four, yet seeming almost a child, thanks to growing up in a convent and leading such a sheltered life, be alluring enough to make him keep his promise?

Mall was busily occupied distributing the vast amounts of objects that Catherine had sent ahead as her dowry—great vases of porcelain, cane furniture, cabinets of Eastern lacquer and painted calicoes for the wall, all more exotic than anything seen in England before. She also had the task of allotting rooms to the various Portuguese ladies who would be accompanying the Queen, and supervising servants with the airing of their beds, so that England might make a fine show of it.

Yet Mall, ever quick and alert to all around her, soon noticed that Frances was avoiding her, and confronted her.

'Tell me, Frances, what have I done to so

offend you that your eyes slip away every time they encounter mine, and you stay not five minutes in my company, as if I carried the typhus?'

Frances struggled with herself, unsure of whether to tell the truth or no. Yet one dishonesty was surely enough? 'I overheard you talking about me to His Grace of Buckingham.'

'I thought as much.' Surprisingly, Mall looked relieved. 'George always has some mad scheme to foist on me, and I play along to humour him. It means naught, I assure you. My brother's plans are harmless, for the most part.'

'Yet why should I be involved in such a thing?'

'It is a hare-brained scheme, no more. It could as well be Catherine Boynton or Cary Frazier he approaches. Worry not.'

Frances watched her warily. 'And why does he call you Butterfly?'

Mall laughed. 'When I was a child, King Charles—father of our present King—saw me up a tree and thought me a rare and lovely butterfly, and sent his men to catch me, that is all. And since then it pleases my brother and some at the Court to address me by the name of Butterfly.'

'And what of the poetry he said you write? Was that true? Do you indeed write verse?'

Brave and fierce Mall, cowed by no man, flushed the colour of a ripe tomato. 'I dabble a little. When the world angers me so much I can no longer speak it, but write it down.'

'May I read some?'

'It is not for the public eye.'

'I am not the public, Mall.'

'One day perhaps, in a moment of weakness, I will show you.'

Frances thanked her, and yet, she told herself, she would be warier of what she disclosed about herself to Mall in the future.

*　　*　　*

It was two weeks into May before Catherine of Braganza, escorted by Lord Sandwich, aboard the very ship that had brought the King back two years previously, the *Royal Charles*, finally arrived at Portsmouth, after a terrible voyage rocked by storms and buffeted by huge breakers.

Frances felt for her, coming as she herself had to a new country (even though her own was home) and having to understand the ways of its Court, so different from the stiff Spanish one.

Unlike Charles' first action on reaching England, which had been to kneel down and thank God for his safe arrival, they heard that Catherine's was to request a cup of tea. Sadly, though a chest of tea was stowed in the hold as part of her dowry, none was immediately available and she was offered English ale instead, which had the effect of sending her back to her cabin to lie down.

'Poor lady,' commented Jane La Garde, 'I hate ale myself. I only hope it was well watered-down.'

Eventually the Queen appeared to greet her husband-to-be, and was quickly spirited away for a secret Catholic marriage, before the official Protestant one soon after. The King, so the word came to Court, seemed happy enough with his bride, who was a sweet-faced, childish-looking woman.

The fact that she was accompanied by a fearsome entourage of Portuguese ladies all wearing enormous farthingales, the like of which had not been seen in England since Elizabeth's day, seemed only to amuse him. He even kept his good humour when they took particular delight in informing His Majesty that the Queen would not be able to perform her marital duty that night because the voyage had affected her monthly cycle.

'My dears,' Charles was overheard commenting to his Gentlemen of the Bedchamber, 'the Queen has got her flowers, so the King will have his cups. Bring me some good Bordeaux wine.' And when they poured it he commented ruefully, 'Mayhap it is as well. I am so tired by racing to be here that I could not uphold the honour of England in the bedchamber.'

While the Queen herself was modest and sweet, her entourage gave the King's courtiers great cause for mirth. Apart from the six frights of ladies-in-waiting, there were numerous confessors, her ancient nurse, a Jewish perfumer and, to the enormous amusement of the King, the Queen's own barber. A whisper came back to Court that the King wickedly asked his wife which part of herself she intended to shave. Fortunately his new wife did not understand the joke.

The Queen, for her part—content that Charles was both handsome and kind and not some cruel ogre—seemed very eager to fall in love with her new husband. And so they happily progressed to Hampton Court, where the Queen's ladies, with Frances among them, waited to make her acquaintance.

Here the little Queen wandered happily around Cardinal Wolsey's mellow red-brick palace, picked roses in the gardens, strolled through the water meadows laughing with the King, and went happily off to their bridal bed of crimson and silver, which, perhaps unfortunately, had been a gift from the Netherlands to his dead sister, Mary.

The King declared his intentions to be a good and faithful husband, and some people, including Frances, even believed him.

'Think you not,' she enquired of the other ladies, 'now that he has his Queen and they are so content in each other's company, that all will hence be different?'

Cary Frazier exchanged looks with Catherine Boynton. Lady Scroope shrugged her well-padded shoulders. Jane La Garde smiled supportively.

'Shall we tell her the truth?' enquired Catherine Boynton. 'Lady Castlemaine has this week given birth to a son and called him Charles.'

Frances gasped.

'The King has been visiting them every day. The Lady's husband has left her at last, and the King feels, since he has privately ruined her, he must now publicly support her.'

'Yet what about the Queen?' Frances asked indignantly. 'Does she know of this insult?'

All were struck silent at this thought.

'She will know soon enough.' Cary Frazier sighed. 'The King has kept his promise to make the other a Lady of the Bedchamber.'

'Yet he is a kind, good man!' Frances protested, remembering how concerned and angry the King had been, even over the trifle of her chilblains. 'How can he behave thus?'

Lady Scroope, older and wiser than the rest, simply shrugged. 'He is a man. And a king. He can do what he will.'

'It is those rogues and ne'er-do-wells he keeps company with, my lords Rochester and Dorset and their ilk, who think themselves poets and wits, who encourage him and tell him that a king should do as he wishes, and not listen to the pleas of a woman,' Cary Frazier pointed out gloomily. She had been the object of an obscene and anonymous poem, which all thought was penned by Lord Rochester, and had reason to feel resentful. 'Wits! If to talk of dildoes, and conies, which I am told is the woman's part, is wit, then they are wittier than all the actors at the King's playhouse.'

Frances, still new to Court convention, struggled between shock that gentlewomen could talk of such things and a strange rash pride that she had been included in so daring a conversation.

'They have been pouring venom into his ears,' suggested Catherine Boynton. 'That his grandfather King James chose whom he wanted to have in his bed, and so should he.'

Frances flushed furiously and glanced at Mall, remembering that it had been Mall's own father, the Duke of Buckingham, who had, according to the gossips, at one point been the object of King James' passion.

'They are telling him that unless he stands up to Queen Catherine, and bends her to his will, she will be as meddlesome as his mother, and it will be he who is the loser,' added Cary.

Remembering the many times she had seen Henrietta Maria cross swords with her son, this made at least some sense to Frances. Poor Catherine would be made to suffer because her mother-in-law so wished to dominate.

'And they point out that King Louis of France is

47

not constrained by notions of fidelity to his queen, but flaunts his mistresses where he will.'

'And the King of Spain also,' nodded Lady Scroope. 'Aye, these wits persuade the King that virtue is worthless and he must do as other kings do, or they will think the less of him.'

A silence fell as all contemplated the fate of lawfully wedded wives in the face of amoral, yet alluring mistresses.

Diversion from their gloomy thoughts came in the person of the Groom of the Presence Chamber, who informed them that a very large delivery had arrived and asked where it should be placed.

Lady Suffolk, as chief Lady of the Bedchamber, was consulted and the vast parcel was carried up the great stairs to the Queen's Apartments.

'But what is it?' enquired the little Queen, standing next to the package, which was as high as she was. She smiled shyly at her ladies. 'Shall we open it?'

Shouting with laughter, they fell upon the wrapping and tore away the waxed paper. Underneath was a layer of canvas tied securely with rope so thick that the small scissors Lady Suffolk carried tied to her waist were not strong enough to cut it. 'A knife! Go fetch a knife from the kitchen, Mistress Frazier,' she instructed.

Cary Frazier trailed unwillingly off, taking so long that by the time she returned they had almost undone the wrapping entirely, revealing a glorious gilded looking-glass, oval in shape and almost six feet tall, with borders of roses adorning each corner.

'But how beautiful it is!' exclaimed the Queen. 'And where does it come from?'

Yet no one knew.

'Perhaps it is a surprise gift from your husband the King, Majesty,' suggested Jane La Garde hopefully.

'I think that he would have told me,' the Queen replied, as her ladies amused themselves by propping the great mirror against the wall and laughing as they admired themselves in it, the younger ones taking it in turns to pose and primp.

'Come, we shall go and ask him.' The Queen, together with Jane and several pages, went off in search of him.

'Mirror, mirror on the wall,' laughed Cary Frazier, ever the most forward of their number. 'Who is the fairest of them all?'

'I am.'

The group swung round to find a violet-eyed lady with a bold, laughing expression surveying them all.

Her skin was a polished white to rival the statue of Isis in the gardens, her red lips pursed into a pouting rosebud of provocation. She wore a loose gown of amber silk, cut low on the shoulders revealing the frill of her chemise beneath, and suggesting a hint of alluring déshabillé as if she had only, at this late hour, just arisen from her bed.

'Barbara!' Mall whispered warningly. 'What do you here in the Queen's Apartments?'

'Since I am to be a Lady of the Bedchamber,' demanded the lady insolently, 'where else should I be?'

'In hell,' Mall answered in a furious whisper. 'Or dead on a dung heap, like Jane Shore, old King Edward's doxy, as you deserve.'

'It is as well you are my cousin, Mary Villiers, or it would be you who ended up on the dung heap,

49

mark my words.'

With an angry swish of silk, Barbara turned on her heel, pausing only to stop at the door for a moment.

'Ladies, I think you will discover that looking glass is meant for me. The King suggested I hang it next to the bed.' A mocking smile lit up her lovely features. 'I need not elaborate as to why.'

She closed the door, leaving behind a shocked and leaden silence.

'That,' Mall almost spat, 'was the Countess of Castlemaine. Seduced at sixteen and never looked backwards. They say she knows all the tricks of the whorehouse and practises each and every one of them to keep the King beneath her thumb.'

Frances knew better than to betray her ignorance and ask what these tricks might be. As a young woman coming to a Court famous for its licentiousness, her mother had indeed talked to her on the subject of gentlemen's baser inclinations. But these homilies had referred for the most part to *halting* unseemly behaviour on the part of any gentleman, while Lady Castlemaine's alleged skills and talents seemed, on the contrary, to be bent on encouraging them.

'Is my lady Castlemaine truly appointed to the Bedchamber?' Frances enquired in a low voice as they processed down to the Great Hall, where dinner was being laid out the next day. There had been rumblings amongst the ladies-in-waiting, not just at the rumour of Barbara joining their number, but also at the news that, in an attempt to economize, the food provided as part of their appointments was to be reduced at the maids of honour's table to a mere seven courses at dinner and supper. The scandal was that there would be no more than roast beef and mutton, goose or chicken, venison pie, rabbit or boiled mutton and a single tart washed down with Gascon wine!

To Frances, used to leaner times, it seemed like the most generous of banquets, but Cary Frazier and Catherine Boynton could be heard complaining loudly at the disgraceful lack of choice.

'You should have been with us in France,' Frances longed to shout at them. 'Then you would have known a hungry belly!'

Yet she knew there were other ways in which the royalist supporters had suffered. Her mother had painted the bleak picture to her. The young men had died in battle, but the young women had suffered, too. Without fathers, who were either dead or banished, and with no hope of a dowry, marriage was not possible for many of them. And without family protection, some fell into liaisons other than marriage—as Barbara Castlemaine had done at sixteen—and discovered that the path of pleasure was a dangerously seductive one.

The thought struck Frances that she herself was not in so very different a position. No nobleman would marry her unless she could bring property or land, neither of which she possessed. Would she, too, be tempted then to be mistress rather than wife?

The Queen had arrived and was processing, with the Countess of Suffolk in her wake, up to the High Table on its dais at the end of the Hall.

Frances had been shocked that even here at Hampton Court, which seemed like a private refuge, unlike the more official residence at Whitehall, the King's subjects often came to watch

51

the royal family at dinner, as if they were some new play to be commented on for public entertainment.

After the meal was done, the Queen announced that since it was a warm day she would like to go out to the water.

The King smiled. 'How I would love to join you. By the way, dear wife . . .' Silence fell as he handed her a sheet of paper. 'Here is the list of ladies for your Bedchamber. There is nothing you need do. The Chancellor has it all in hand.'

He had clearly expected the Queen to pass the list to one of her ladies, but Catherine scanned it then and there.

'A quill, please,' she requested, pulling herself up to her full height, which was not great. And yet, standing amongst that room full of strangers, all of whom understood the importance of the list she had been handed, she had a certain quiet dignity.

A Groom of the Great Chamber ran back, bearing the quill, puffing from his exertions.

'Thank you,' Catherine smiled, looking down the page until she found the Countess of Castlemaine's name. And, mustering all sense of her dues as a royal princess in her own right, she crossed it out with a flourish.

Frances gasped, secretly delighted that the Queen was making a stand against the insidious power of her rival. Rumour had it that Queen Catherine's mother had counselled her never to enter a room that contained Barbara, let alone accept her as an important member of her household.

'Poor child,' breathed Mall to Frances. 'She thinks she has won the battle. Yet she knows not her enemy. It is like throwing a lamb to a lion.'

Frances found the days that followed painful to witness. She was convinced the Queen had right on her side, yet as she watched the battle unfold she could see that, just as a sailor can find his way by the stars without chart or compass, Barbara understood every thought and weakness of the King's mind.

Barbara began to be seen walking about the palace with her two children—a rare sight indeed, since they were usually with their nurse.

'Have you noted the way she has cast herself as the wronged woman?' Frances whispered to Jane La Garde, impressed and outraged in equal measure. 'Ever since her husband left her—not before time, after what the poor man had to tolerate—she demands the King's loyalty. He says he has ruined her reputation, and now he must protect her! There is no thought of the Queen being sinned against.'

Frances, along with the rest of the Court, found the King's actions hard to fathom. He seemed so tolerant and humane—until he was forced into a corner and made to choose. Even his darling sister Minette had written that his behaviour was reprehensible.

Yet the King insisted that he was doing the honourable thing in championing Barbara against his wife.

'Only because it's what he *wants* to do,' murmured Catherine, and Frances could only agree.

The King continued to avoid the Queen and was sharp with his courtiers. Rumour had it he had written to his Chancellor, Edward Hyde, recently created the Earl of Clarendon, in the strongest possible terms, to insist that the Chancellor himself come to Hampton Court and force the Queen to back down.

The Chancellor did his best to explain to Catherine that kings had mistresses, and their wives accepted them. 'Indeed,' the Chancellor had confided, sympathetic and yet realistic, 'the King of Spain had four mistresses at once whom he flouted before his wife!'

Catherine remained unmoved.

The ladies-in-waiting tiptoed around, whispering about what would happen if the Queen refused to weaken. Would she truly return home, as she was insisting? And if she did, what would be their own fate?

The weeks dragged by, the sombre mood at Hampton Court belied by the glorious weather outside. Roses bloomed. Skylarks swooped. More and more courtiers abandoned Catherine, seeing that her power was so insignificant. The little Queen looked out of her window as some of her ladies played Blind Man's Buff among the rows of lime trees in the park. But not Frances. Indeed, she berated the others for abandoning their mistress.

Surely, she decided, the King must have a hard heart indeed to treat her thus? Yet, as his actions the next day demonstrated, Charles was no easy man to read. For he was also capable of great kindness.

A newborn baby girl was found hidden in the bushes in the Privy Garden and, thanks to its dark looks, accusing fingers were pointing at the Queen's Portuguese ladies, who could disguise a pregnancy beneath their vast farthingales.

Yet none would own the child.

'For once it is not mine,' quipped the King merrily. 'For I have had no acquaintance of the mother.'

'Unless my lady Castlemaine dropped it without noticing,' Mall whispered under her breath.

'Even she cannot have two in a week. It must be taken away at once,' announced the Countess of Suffolk. 'And given to some poor countrywoman who will bring it up to honest labour.'

The King looked anguished. 'When it is no doubt the by-blow of one of my courtiers. Nay, the child should have a better start than that.'

He delved in his pocket and pulled out a handful of coins. 'Tell them to bring her up a lady and to call her Lisbona. She can be the harbinger of our happy future.'

Even though there was no sign yet of that happy future, the King decided it was time he took his new bride and introduced her to London.

Indeed, they barely spoke. The capital's populace, not knowing the crisis that gripped the royal couple, and wishing to see their new queen for the first time, crowded onto every available vessel on the river. More than ten thousand craft, great and small, thronged the river until the water was invisible and the Thames resembled a wooden city made of boats.

Charles and Catherine, still at war, arrived at last, sailing on an ancient vessel, seated under a cupola of gold, surrounded by Corinthian pillars wreathed with garlands, which waved briskly in the sharp wind, while the great guns were fired as they landed at Whitehall Stairs and trumpets sounded a welcoming voluntary.

From the roof of the Banqueting House, Barbara Castlemaine, still in riding habit from her swift ride back to London, watched the arrivals triumphantly. The extravagant blue and yellow feathers on her Cavalier hat blew jauntily in the wind and a smile of victory lit up her lovely features.

And while Frances watched and waited, a strange occurrence took place.

Queen Catherine, missing the affection of her husband and conscious that this coldness between the King and herself was no way to get an heir, which would prove her best weapon against Barbara, suddenly decided to accept her rival publicly.

That night at supper, instead of the usual snub and averted face, the Queen approached Barbara directly and asked her how she did.

Covering up her great surprise, Barbara replied that she did very well.

A beat of silence followed before the Queen continued, 'I understand you are to be my Lady of the Bedchamber. My congratulations. A lady alone such as you should find protection any way she can.'

The King, seeing the two in conversation, came delightedly up. 'See how easy it is for you both to agree. The rift between you was naught but woman's contrariness.'

'Indeed, Your Majesty,' Catherine held his eye for a moment, then glanced at Barbara. 'And woman's contrariness is a subject you are much familiar with, I think.'

'Zounds!' whispered Mall to Frances. 'She has more spirit than I gave her credit for.'

From that day on, Frances had to admit, their

life was greatly eased, yet there was a small part of her that missed the Queen's brief rebellion.

Queen Henrietta Maria returned from Paris to take up occupation in Somerset House, bringing Frances' mother Sophia with her.

'I hear I come at a propitious time,' Sophia Stuart remarked, with a stiff kiss for her daughter. 'Peace is restored to the Court at last.'

'I would have thought you would champion the wife over the mistress at whatever cost,' Frances commented tartly.

'Oh, worry not. Barbara Castlemaine will meet her match one of these days.' The look she gave her daughter was long and impenetrable.

The other excitement was their move from Somerset House to the Palace of Whitehall, which what it lost in elegance, it made up for by being at the very heart of the King's pomp and power. It was at Whitehall, in the long Stone Gallery, that much of the government of England took place. It was also conveniently at a distance from Frances' mother.

Now that his household was settling down, Charles devised a round of balls and masquerades to keep all happy. The most enjoyable of all was held in the King's Chamber to celebrate the wedding of another of his illegitimate children— the newly ennobled Duke of Monmouth, to Anne Scott, a great heiress. There was supper and dancing, and the youth of the participants gave the occasion a delightful lack of formality that was unusual at Court events.

'Have you seen The Lady?' hissed Mall, pointing at Barbara. 'So loaded down with jewels that a pirate might land her! No one could have told her it was a simple supper, but then Barbara doesn't know the meaning of simple.'

But Frances did not hear Mall's diatribe.

In the happy, celebrating crowd that drank and danced she had glimpsed an unexpected face— the Duke of Richmond—and, despite her better judgement, her heart had leapt in her breast like a startled deer.

She glanced around to see if his wife was with him, yet he seemed alone. She knew he was aware of her presence because he bowed stiffly when she caught his eye, and the ghost of a smile lit up his handsome face, as if recalling some happy memory.

She hesitated then, wondering if she should go and greet him. Instead she found that he came to her.

'Mistress Stuart, it seems a different era since last we met in Paris.'

'Indeed it is. And now we have food, and warmth, and a merry Court.'

'And you are waiting on the Queen, I hear?'

'I am indeed. Do you visit from the country?'

Mall had told her, with some resentment, that he had inherited the very manor house at Cobham that she herself had lived in with her husband—his uncle—in happier times.

'I am named a Gentleman of the Bedchamber and have lodgings near the Bowling Green.'

The news that he was at Court came as a shock, and she forced herself to utter the next words. 'And you are here with your wife, no doubt?'

A shadow crossed his face. 'She remains at Cobham with the babe. She has not yet recovered from her confinement.'

The news that he had a child cut her to the quick.

His wife Elizabeth, she had heard, was little older than herself, and yet she had a home and babe. And him.

He seemed to feel the strain that descended and changed the subject. 'So, all is better here than at the French Court?'

She took his lead and answered brightly. 'Yes, all is better. Except that I miss my little French filly. The horses at the King's Court are big and heavy, built for men to ride.'

He bowed again. 'I must take my leave betimes. I have fulfilled my duties and return to Cobham in the morning. The bride and groom will soon be bedded, I think.'

'But they are children!'

He smiled at her shocked reaction. 'Do not worry. They will drink the posset and fling the stocking, then go back to their own beds. Even the King would not approve so corrupt an act as that!'

She looked at him, surprised at the tones of disapproval in his voice.

'Does the King offend your sensibilities?'

A wary look came into his eyes, then he smiled, deciding he could trust her. 'I admire the King's qualities, but not all his actions. His cronies tell him he can have whatever he wants.' He paused, his gaze fixed on hers for an instant. 'Yet no man can have everything he wants.'

'Or woman, either,' she almost answered.

Across the room, as the shouts of merriment and laughter heightened, she found that the King himself watched them.

Frances curtseyed. 'I must see if I am needed.'

He bowed. 'Farewell, Mistress Stuart.'

After he had left the trumpets and drums

sounded and the whole company escorted the young couple upstairs to bed. Little Anne Scott took the whole occasion in her stride. When she was older she would clearly be in charge of the marriage. The Duke of Monmouth, though but fourteen years, dressed in his brocade and lace, with his flowing black locks, amused all by seeming like the King in miniature.

After the stocking was flung, they were brought downstairs once again and the party continued with redoubled celebration. As the candles danced and the fiddles played old English country dances, Frances forgot the formality of being a maid of honour to the Queen and joined in such childish games as Hop Frog and All Hide with the Queen's dwarves and the little blackamoor boy who had come to Somerset House in the Queen's train. Finally she found herself donning the blindfold and being giddily twirled about the room playing Blind Man's Buff.

Laughing, yet so exhausted that she longed to collapse, she placed her hands over the faces of various ladies and gentlemen, feeling their contours for a familiar nose or chin—but always in vain. She had not been at the Court enough time to recognize many of its members in this fashion.

Until the last.

Still blindfolded, she encountered a face with deep furrows at either side of the mouth beneath a narrow moustache, and a luxuriant head of hair, half-disguised by a large hat.

Frances gasped.

There was only one man permitted to wear a hat when the reigning monarch was in the room.

And that was the King himself.

60

Chapter 3

'Your Majesty!' Frances pulled off the blindfold and dropped a curtsey.

Charles simply laughed and raised her quickly up. 'I have had enough "Your Majestys" this night to turn the head of a prophet. And most of them from some rogue or other that wishes a favour.' He studied her more closely. 'Odds fish, are you not the girl who pretended to be my sister at my mother's house in Colombes? Minette wrote to me that you were coming, but I have been somewhat distracted of late over this business of the bedchamber.'

Frances flushed in mortification at the memory of how she had tricked him.

Seeing her discomfiture, he came quickly to her rescue. 'Mall's doing, as I remember. She was ever a wild piece. All think I was in greatest danger for my life at the battle of Worcester, and afterwards up the oak tree. Yet they knew not the adventures that mad Mall led me into as a child. She had me climb the highest roof above the Matted Gallery when I was but eight years old, and tie my muckinder there as a flag to mark a pirate capture. My father loved her well and thought marriage to young Herbert might calm her down, but the poor lad died of the smallpox. A quieter fate than marriage to Mall.' He laughed affectionately. 'He married her then to my cousin James, the duke of Richmond, a true loyal soldier to my father, with whom she spent many happy years.' And then to Frances' surprise he added, 'Though many think it was to my cousin Prince Rupert that she truly gave her heart.'

Seeing Frances' reaction, he bowed deeply. 'But maybe I give a game away that is best forgotten. I remember you well now. You were the maid with the chilblains! Are they better, now you are home in England?'

'Indeed, they are gone altogether!'

He sighed. 'If only all our problems were so easily dealt with.' His natural gaiety returned. 'Since they are better, will you join me in a country dance? I would like to dance with a lady who for once does not have to talk into my shoulder.'

Before she had a chance to reply the King had swept her into the melee of couples who raced rambunctiously across the floor, to the accompaniment of much stamping and calling from the other guests. 'Tell me not that you prefer the pace of the Coranto or the Bransle?' shouted Charles. 'My cousin Louis prefers to be formal and stately and show off the fineness of his calf. My taste is for something livelier.' He raced Frances across the floor at a lightning pace. 'To me, these dances are the best of England! Know you this ditty? They call it "Cuckolds all awry".'

Before she could comment on the singular appropriateness of the choice, Frances caught an angry eye fixed upon her from the corner of the candlelit room. It belonged to the Countess of Castlemaine.

Frances put her chin up. 'Does not my lady Castlemaine like to dance?'

The King laughed. 'Not to such a tune as this. She cares naught about making her husband a cuckold, yet would never deign to dance to its tune.'

Frances glanced up at him. His tone held so strange a mixture of emotions for his mistress.

62

Grudging affection; resentment at her power over him; pride perhaps at the lady's disdain of all that was said of her.

'Besides,' he laughed at the irony of what he was about to divulge, 'the lady is breeding again.'

Hearing his words, Frances wished she could loosen herself from his hold and run away. Barbara had barely given birth to the last! It was so unkind that his poor wife could not conceive while his mistress seemed as fertile as a farrowing sow. 'Excuse me, Majesty,' she curtseyed as the feverish dancing finally stopped. 'I am afraid the music has given me a headache and I must seek my chamber.'

Charles bowed deeply, a twinkle in his dark eyes betraying a surprising shrewdness in guessing her true thought. 'I thought we Stuarts were made of sterner stuff. Yet, thank you, I have enjoyed the dance.'

In the general whooping and hallooing, Frances moved towards the door. Yet if she had hoped to slip away without attracting further attention, she was mistaken. A number of curious glances followed her, all appraising the time she had spent in the arms of the King and wondering how it might be exploited to the advantage of the various parties present.

*   *   *

'Mistress Stuart, what think you of my *confidantes*?' Cary Frazier, the most fashionable of all the Queen's ladies, twirled the small curls by her ears. 'It has taken my dresser one whole hour to perfect them so!'

Frances studied Cary's elaborate hairstyle with

its two thin strands elaborately arranged from her centre parting, leaving but one tiny curl in the centre of her forehead. They all sat in the Queen's Withdrawing Room waiting for Her Majesty to request their services. 'I like them very much indeed. It is just as the ladies wear their hair in France—the lovelock in the centre just as yours is.'

'What of my earrings, Mistress Stuart,' Catherine Boynton peered into a looking glass set on a stand on the dressing table. 'Would you favour the gold or the pearls with my ivory gown?'

Frances smiled to herself. Since her encounter with the King, all seemed eager to seek her opinion on the smallest trifle. Her style of dress, but one week since, the object of comment for being too French, was now envied and indeed copied by the other ladies. She had always preferred the softness of a chemise worn under her gown and pulled up to form a fluid frill above her neckline. The hint of chemise gave modesty, a quality not every lady here wished to emulate, and yet had a subtle allure that marked the wearer out as stylishly Parisian.

'What is your opinion of patches, Mistress Stuart?'

Frances was more than a mite surprised to find herself so suddenly cast as the arbiter of good taste, yet if her opinion was to be sought so eagerly, she might as well enjoy it. 'I have never favoured them. Despoiling your face with suns and moons, lucky horseshoes and the like seems to me a strange practice indeed.' She smiled impishly at the group. 'Yet when I am older I intend to have a coach-and-six on one cheek and a map of Orion on the other to disguise my wrinkles!'

Jane La Garde had been listening quietly, as

64

was her way. 'Lady Castlemaine is fond of wearing patches.'

'Indeed,' snapped Lady Scroope. 'Yet she lacks the freshness of Mistress Stuart's complexion, even if she is famed for her beauty . . .' She stopped abruptly.

The Countess of Castlemaine had entered the room, as quiet as a cat, and stood in the doorway listening.

She wore a loose satin garment that revealed a great deal of her creamy shoulders, tied up at either side with bows and flounces of Brussels lace.

'What I lack in freshness,' Barbara's voice purred with suppressed aggression, 'I more than compensate with experience.' She arranged her features into something resembling a smile. 'Yet you are right, Lady Scroope, Mistress Stuart has a quite unusual freshness. Like an apple in a dew-soaked orchard that is just too high to be plucked.'

Frances looked away in confusion.

'There is of course a drawback to such mouth-watering fruit.'

The other ladies studied her with varying degrees of resentment, yet none spoke.

'It can sometimes rot on the branch.' And with that, Barbara swept imperiously from the room.

Cary Frazier was the first amongst them to gather her wits together. 'You would think she was some Greek goddess visiting us poor mortals from Mount Olympus! And what was that garment she was wearing that hardly covered her nakedness? I am glad the Queen was not here to witness it.'

Frances smiled at a sudden memory. 'Mall says my lady Castlemaine dresses thus not because she is a Grecian goddess, but to cover the shape she has lost from continual childbearing!'

They all laughed, feeling a little of their power restored after Barbara's dazzling presence.

In the coming days Frances understood a little more of the problems that the King found harder to cure than her chilblains. There was to be a great feast given by Henrietta Maria, at Somerset House, where all the ladies were needed to wait on Queen Catherine. Indeed, so many of them that they did not fit on the royal barge. Frances, one of the most junior, elected to travel by wherry with Jane La Garde. They had hardly tucked in their gowns, holding them over one arm for fear of soaking the velvet and taffeta, when their red-faced wherryman began addressing his fellow oarsman. 'Heard you the grumbling in the alehouse last night over this blessed tax of the King's?' he demanded.

'Wherrymen like to give us the benefit of their opinion,' whispered Jane to Frances, 'whether you desire it or no.'

'The King's honeymoon is over, and that's for sure,' replied his fellow. 'Londoners may have put up the maypoles for him, but soon they'll want to tear them down. All he cares about is his mistresses, and he don't get *them* to pay hearth tax, I'll be bound.'

'Ne'er a truer word, John, ne'er a truer word.'

'And now the old Queen's returned, Popery'll be in by the back door, you wait and see. That traitor Monck, who brought the King home, I'd like to see him starve in a cage hanging above St Paul's.'

Then, as if he had talked of naught but the weather, or if the tide went in or out, the wherryman turned to Frances, all smiles. 'Where

66

was it you said you wanted, my ladies? How about a trip to the Exchange? Do a bit of shopping?'

'We are going to Somerset House,' Frances said firmly. 'To wait on the Queen.'

To her amazement the man was nothing daunted. Whether this were a good thing, for it meant he knew the King to be tolerant and could speak his mind, or a bad one because he could spout sedition without fearing the consequence, she knew not.

Smiling cheerily, the wherryman handed Frances up the great stone stairs from the river.

'Tell the King from me to stop taxing the poor and get his mistresses to earn an honest living, so they won't distract him from *his* work of restoring good government!'

'Take care, wherryman,' Frances replied with spirit, 'that your great mouth land you not in greater trouble!'

''Tis a free country, mistress. Or would you have us back to Old Noll's time, when brother informed on brother?'

Frances shrugged. She did not envy the King his task of restoring good government to a country where all men spoke their minds—and heartily disagreed with each other—about how that government should be restored.

The banquet laid out for them at Somerset House was to mark the Queen Mother's return.

'Yet some have noted it is also the Feast of the Assumption of the Blessed Virgin into heaven,' whispered Jane. 'Not the most tactful cause for celebration in a Protestant country.' Frances saw that the wherrymen had some grounds for their fears after all.

If the King was angry at his mother's flaunting

of her religion, he did not show it. Frances glanced at him across the room, standing amongst his busy courtiers in the Great Hall. One of them, whom Frances recognized as Mall's brother, the Duke of Buckingham, strode towards them. 'Mistress Stuart,' he greeted her enthusiastically, 'my sister said you were following by water.'

'Indeed we did, and an interesting time we had of it. We fancied ourselves having a simple ride to Somerset House, yet were treated to a guide on how the wind blows here amongst the populace.'

'Not troubled by one of these seditious watermen, I trust?' The Duke smiled, yet his smile was that of a lizard about to unroll his sticky tongue and catch an insect. 'I would have them all strung up from London Bridge as a lesson. Frenchmen marvel that we let our wherrymen talk to us as if they were our equals, and must listen to their opinions on the state of the nation when they but row us across the river. It is a world turned upside down.'

'Come, George.' The King had joined them with his minister Lord Arlington in tow, famous for the black plaster on his nose, received in battle and worn with pride. 'A man should be able to have his say, just as tender consciences must be respected, or the late troubles taught us nothing.'

'You are too generous, Majesty.'

'It is a fault I would rather have than pride. Come, Mistress Stuart, the musicians are beginning to play.' He gestured to the gallery above them, where ten or twelve players were tuning up. 'Will you take to the floor with me?'

Frances hesitated, reluctant to draw attention to herself so soon after they had last stood up

68

together.

'No false modesty, Coz,' chided the King. 'All said what a fine dancer Mistress Stuart was, when we tripped to those country airs.'

Frances raised her chin indignantly. 'I loathe false modesty, Majesty. I wondered simply if it might occasion talk.'

Charles shrugged. 'Let them talk! My wife knows you are the most innocent of flowers, and my Lady Castlemaine is indisposed.' He leaned in closer. 'Some say she is with Henry Jermyn, my lord St Albans' nephew, a very pleasing gentleman.' She saw the ghost of a mocking smile in his black eyes. 'By all accounts, he has far more address than I do.'

'How can you speak thus about a lady you profess to love, and who is mother to your two children!' Frances spoke before she thought. 'I am sorry, sire. I should not be so bold.'

'Please, do not stop.' Charles' smile widened. 'So few people speak the truth to a king, it is like drinking cold spring water on a burning day. We have an understanding, my lady Castlemaine and I, yet I would not call it love. We are earth and air, fire and water, opposite and yet complementary. Love, I am told, is a gentler thing.'

'You do not know for yourself, sire?'

'Indeed, Mistress Stuart, I do not.' He laughed almost bitterly. 'Is that not a fine thing in a man of whom it was said he had seventeen mistresses in his years of exile? They say love makes you care more for the beloved than for yourself, and this, I am sad to say, is not a thing I recognize. Except perhaps towards my sister Minette.' His eyes glittered like rain on sea-coal. 'Yet perhaps a man can change.'

Frances felt her skin flush an ugly red and longed

to pick up her skirts and run. Yet she knew every eye was upon them. 'Goodnight, Majesty. I see the Duke of Buckingham is signalling for your attention.'

She walked with swift, yet measured steps, her mind a swirl of painful confusion, cleaving her way through the curious crowd until she reached the dark of a passageway. Leaning back against the warmth of the wood, she let out a deep sigh.

'A touching scene, sweet Mistress Stuart.' The rustle of silk and a breath of heady perfume in the still air announced that Barbara Castlemaine had recovered from her indisposition and graced the feast with her vivid presence after all. 'The King is a practised wooer. Enjoy his favour. You may gain great things from it. But do not talk to yourself of love.'

Before Frances had time even to reply, Mall's brother, the Duke of Buckingham, appeared at her side. 'Do not listen to our dear cousin Barbara, who has something of a vested interest in these matters. Mall tells me you enjoy card tricks, and I would like to show you one I have learned in Italy. I think you will enjoy it.'

With a malicious smile at Barbara, he tucked Frances' hand into his arm and led her away.

Frances kept her thoughts to herself, but she trusted the Duke of Buckingham no more than the Countess of Castlemaine.

All at Court thought her a sweet simpleton, whose head could be turned by a smile from the King, or a childish card trick. Let them think it. She would bide her time and see which road she wished to travel. For now she was not sure herself. Yet she knew one thing for certain. She did not intend to be either plaything for one or decoy for the ambitions of another.

The strength of her determination was to be proved sooner than she expected.

*   *   *

Not two days later, as Frances was performing her morning toilette, Jane La Garde burst suddenly into her chamber, hardly even pausing to knock. 'Mistress Stuart!' she blurted, out of breath from running up the stairs. 'The King's messenger is below. He asks whether you have seen what a glorious day it is abroad and, since he hears you are a keen rider, whether you would deign to share it with him?' After this lengthy invitation she almost doubled up, gasping for breath.

Frances thought quickly. She could not refuse such an invitation without very good reason. 'Tell his messenger how honoured I am, but that it would take me so long to ready myself that the day will be spoiled, and I would not wish to deprive him of it.'

'Frances!' Jane gaped. 'Are you turning down the King?'

Frances fiddled with the lace of her chemise. 'Of course not. It is but eight of the clock and I am barely risen from my bed. It would take me an hour at least to ready myself.'

Jane looked at her askance, knowing how speedily Frances could ready herself when she desired. 'As well he did not ask Cary Frazier. She would not be ready till the next morn at least.'

Frances ignored the mocking tone in her voice. 'Is there bread baked yet to break our fast?'

'I will find a groom and ask. You had best

begin your ablutions since they take you so long to complete.'

But Frances had hardly taken off her chemise when there was a loud rap on her chamber door. Jane stood there, trying not to laugh. 'The King's messenger has returned. The King instructs you to dispense of your lengthy toilette. Your beauty shines brightly enough without added artifice, it seems.'

'Oh dear.' This time Frances laughed with her. 'In that case I had better summon a tire-woman to ready my riding habit.'

Fifteen minutes later Frances descended the stairs from the Privy Gallery into the Pebble Court of Whitehall Palace. Her riding habit, hastily shaken out by the tire-woman, was not made in Paris, as were many of her gowns, or even French-influenced. Even the haughty French, when it came to riding clothes, knew there was nothing so fine and correct as an English riding habit.

As was the fashion, Frances' habit was cut along masculine lines in amber brocade, edged with golden stitching, embellished with a turquoise bow at neck and sleeve and finished with a lace jabot. The more daring ladies favoured rhinegraves, a wide-legged pantaloon, but Frances preferred the elegance of a dove-grey satin skirt and riding gauntlets edged with rosettes of the softest grey leather. To complete the ensemble her bicorne hat sported three jaunty ostrich feathers in amber, gold and grey.

The groom smiled as he helped her onto the riding block. She waited for her usual horse to be led out, a placid bay, famous for being able to find his way home from any distance.

72

After a moment or two the stable boy emerged from the mews leading a high-stepping black mare, with red ribbons knotted into her shiny mane.

'A gentleman delivered it yesterday.'

'But I could never accept such a generous gift,' Frances protested, her heart racing.

'The gentleman said you would say that,' the stable boy grinned. 'And I am to assure you it is only a loan. The mare belongs to his sister, yet is too lively for her. He begs you will train her to be a suitable horse for a lady, and his sister will be eternally grateful to you.'

'Will she indeed?' Frances shook her head, still not sure whether to accept.

'If you do not take her,' the boy was grinning fit to split his face now, 'he said to tell you, the horse must be sold to a city merchant for use by his fat daughter.'

Frances pealed with laughter. 'Well, we cannot have that, can we?' She climbed into the side-saddle, sensing the horse's high-strung temperament. 'They would not get along at all.'

'His Majesty will catch up with you in Hyde Park,' announced the groom. 'I am to lead you there.'

The man mounted his own horse and led the way through the Pebble Court, past the Banqueting House and a troupe of soldiers exercising on the parade ground, and thence along Birdcage Walk, where the cassowaries and parrots chirped away in their cages.

Hyde Park was busy on so lovely a day, opened again to all-comers by the King at his restoration, just as his grandfather James I had first opened it. They passed the Ring, where all the highest society of London loved to come and display themselves and their fine equipages, for the envy of their friends and neighbours, but it was too early for so august a crowd. The ladies no doubt lay languishing in their chambers or closets with a cup of chocolate, while the menfolk nursed their heads and tried not to think of what they had lost the night before at Basset or at dice.

'Is it not a morning straight from Eden, Mistress Stuart?' Frances turned to find the King riding towards her, the plumes of his hat blowing in the sharp breeze. 'On such a day would not even God look at the world he had wrought and think it good?'

'He would indeed. And be consoled on all the days when it is not so good.'

'There have been plenty of those in recent years. Naturally I would think God is a royalist.' He threw back his head and laughed.

He was abreast of her now. She glanced at a group of courtiers who had remained at a decent distance, no doubt on the King's orders. The news that he had ridden out with her this morning would be round the Court like a forest fire even before they returned.

'Are you enjoying life in Whitehall, or do you pine still for the joys of Paris?'

'I enjoy it greatly. Yet I miss my sister and brother. And my father as well. My mother at least is here with me.'

'I miss my sister also. Minette is more precious to me than any other person on God's earth.' He winked. 'Of course I have another sister now, the Duchess of York, my brother's new wife, but it is not a fair bargain.'

74

Frances remembered all the scandal over his brother James' marriage. How James had secretly married Anne Hyde, the Chancellor's daughter, and got her with child, then ungraciously tried to repudiate the marriage on his friends' advice. There had been but one voice in the poor woman's favour, so it was said, and that the King's. He had even made a point of visiting her during her confinement, to stop the gossiping mouths. 'I had heard you were kind to the lady.'

'Aye. Of all men I do not like a hypocrite. I had to remind my brother that he must drink what he had brewed.'

Frances burst out laughing.

'Am I so humorous? If so, it is unintentional.' He smiled ruefully. 'I had thought to show you my best side!'

'And so you did. Yet it reminded me of my old nurse, who had a proverb for every occasion. "The company makes the feast." "Please your eye and plague your heart." "As you make your bed, so you must lie upon it." "Once a whore . . . "'

Frances stuttered to a stop, realizing how unfortunate was this pithy phrase of Nurse's. Yet the King seemed to laugh the more. 'I would like to meet this fierce moralist. I am sure we would have much in common.'

The idea of Nurse and a monarch of Charles' reputation sharing common ground was such an unlikely idea that Frances giggled. 'I do not think so, sire. My nurse is somewhat given to narrow-mindedness.'

'Then I could help her broaden it, and she could bring me back to the primrose path of virtue.'

'Are you not too far strayed for that, sire?'

75

Charles shook his head. 'I can see you have formed a pretty picture of me, living in my mother's house.'

By now they could see the orchard at the far end of the park.

'That is a fine mare,' the King admired.

Frances blushed. 'I am breaking her in for a friend.'

'How like you to ride at speed?' enquired the King, spurring his horse into a gallop.

Frances followed him. 'It is the best feeling on earth.'

'Not quite the best, but good enough!'

As the sun blazed in the morning sky they thundered across the green fields bordering the park, scattering deer and scaring a pheasant into sudden squawking flight.

'And your wife, sire,' she hit back deliberately, as soon as her breath was restored. 'How is she enjoying her new life here?'

'Well enough, I think, now that all those Portuguese frights have returned to their homeland. Come,' he took hold of her reins and turned their horses round, understanding why she had asked the sudden question. Frances was surprised how obedient the mare was to his touch. 'My wife is a good and kind lady, I take your heed and will not deliberately hurt her. Yet for now my belly cries cupboard, so let us go back. I know a place where the game pie is heaven-sent.'

And so it was that Frances Stuart, sixteen years old, had her first taste not just of supping in a London tavern, but of doing so in the company of a king.

Sharing the inn with a dozen astonished

cloth-workers, they sat in the saloon of the Leg and Bell hard by the aptly named King Street, and ate a dinner of raised venison pie, boiled mutton and Essex oysters, while the royal retinue sat next door and kept a discreet and respectful distance.

As they rode back to Whitehall Palace, Frances knew not what to make of it. Did the King simply want a joshing friendship with her? Perhaps, having met her in the company of his sister Minette, he saw her in something of the same light. A much younger sister, to talk to and escape with occasionally from the cares of kingship? Despite the King's reputation there had been no hint of the lover about his behaviour.

The King bade her farewell and rode off with his retinue, eager to play tennis before the affairs of state enveloped him. Frances smiled, feeling a sympathy for Chancellor Clarendon, who had the job of tying the King down to business.

As she jumped down from her mare, the thought of Mall came to her. Mall knew the King and was wise in the ways of courtly behaviour.

Yet before she had time to seek out Mall, her mother arrived from Somerset House to visit her, a rare enough occasion, since her mother was not given to displays of affection. She was, unusually, in the company of a man.

Frances was in the act of dismounting when they walked towards her. Frances recognized the red hair and formal bearing of Ludovic Stuart.

'You remember the Seigneur d'Aubigny?' her mother asked. 'He has come from Paris with the Queen Mother to act as her almoner.'

'A pretty mare, Mistress Stuart.' She could see he was eyeing the horse with more than usual interest. 'Indeed, my niece Katherine has one very like it.'

Frances wondered if she should admit the truth and decided against it. There must be black mares aplenty in London.

Her mother glanced at the horse and at Frances in her riding clothes. 'You have been abroad?'

'To Hyde Park,' Frances answered carefully.

'To the Ring? 'Tis early to be going there. Did the Queen wish to take the air?'

'I did not go with the Queen.' Frances hesitated. 'I went with the King.'

'Indeed?' Sophia Stuart, veteran of two Courts—that of Charles I and Louis XIV—paused to assess this interesting information.

Ludovic Stuart's translucent pale-blue eyes narrowed infinitesimally.

'I must leave you ladies. I have business of the Queen Mother's to attend to.'

'Did I do wrong?' Frances asked when he had left them. 'I tried to refuse, but he overruled my objection.' Her eyes darted to her mother's face, eager for some motherly guidance.

Sophia Stuart's face was curiously blank.

Perhaps her own mother, Frances registered with shock, was like all the rest and sought to work out what advantage could be gleaned from the King's interest.

'He did not . . . ?' Her mother's voice trailed off.

Frances turned away angrily. 'I would allow no impropriety. You must understand that. Besides, he treated me as I think he would his sister. Indeed, I wondered if it were really she that he wished to see, and I but brought her to mind.'

Mrs Stuart nodded. 'It is well. Yet be careful. We

78

must consider what this means. My advice would be avoid him when you can, and play the modest maiden in his company.'

'I need no advice where my own conduct is concerned, thank you,' she fired back. 'From all we hear, it is the King's deportment that is more worthy of concern than mine. I shall never succumb to entreaties that might bring shame upon myself and family.'

'No, indeed.' Sophia Stuart reached out and stroked her hair in a gesture of physical affection so rare that it made her daughter start. 'Yet it is harder to refuse when princes are doing the importuning.' She paused. 'I wish you had not admitted it in the presence of the Seigneur. There is something of the Puritan about Ludovic Stuart. He is too thin. And his eyes are like an eagle's. Watch out for him, as well as the King.'

*   *   *

And yet in the days that followed Frances found nothing but affability on the part of the King. He sought her out, but only to join in with her and the other maids of honour in childish games. Understanding that Frances, deprived of a normal childhood during her exile in France, loved nothing more than making castles of cards, playing All Hide and listening to jokes and stories, he told her stories aplenty.

'Yawn, yawn, yawn,' commented the gossip-loving Comte de Grammont to Lady Castlemaine one night in her glamorous apartments, as they all listened to the King tell the tale they had heard so often they knew it by heart, of his escape after the battle of Worcester. 'Is our new *divertissement* to be children's stories? Bring me back the dissipation of the old days.'

Barbara laughed. 'Ah, Count, you are angered because we are not losing to you at the card table.'

The Comte de Grammont made his living from fleecing the rich at all manner of card games—none of which involved using them to build castles.

He leaned in to whisper in Barbara's ear. 'And what is His Majesty's true intention behind all this childish amusement? That must be a question that interests you of all people, my lady.'

Barbara smiled dismissively. 'Ah, Count, I do not think I have much to fear from such a child as that. Shy virgins are not his style. If he laid a finger on her, she would cry rape and run screaming to the Queen or, worse, the Queen Mother. I think I am safe enough.'

The Count pursed his thin lips and cocked his head like an inquisitive cockatoo. 'And were you not a shy virgin once?'

'Not by the time I met His Majesty. His taste runs to riper fruit than she.'

'And yet, with a firm young apple, is there not a delicious joy in having the first bite?'

Barbara's violet eyes narrowed. 'What exactly are you suggesting, Count?'

'That you make a friend of this childish young lady. If the King truly wants first bite, perhaps it should be you who offers him the fruit. Gratitude can be as powerful as love. And longer-lasting. Goodnight, my lady.' The Comte de Grammont bowed deeply.

Barbara watched him gossip to different groups

80

of courtiers as he took his leave, and pondered on the wisdom of his words.

Chapter 4

Through all that chilly springtime Frances stayed in London, getting to know each nook and cranny of the Palace of Whitehall, as well as becoming familiar with her duties as maid of honour to the Queen.

Lady Suffolk, irritated that Cary Frazier's mind did not always seem to be on her job, called them together to remind them what these duties were. 'You will help the Queen to dress, ensure that her clothes are assembled for the next day's needs; you will arrange her hair, making sure she has all the necessities, such as pomade and curling tongs and other such small necessaries. Sometimes you will be expected to attend Her Majesty in public, on walks or to chapel, though this is truly the right of the more senior ladies.' She looked directly at Cary. 'It is for these services, you may recall, that you are granted *bouge* of Court, all your board, bread, beer, wine, candles and firewood, and your remuneration of sixty pounds. Are there any questions?'

'Do we not have a sum towards our clothing?' enquired Cary, who seemed happily unaware that the lecture was directed at her.

'Mistress Frazier, you do not. Yet if you are giving your custom to a mercer or silk merchant, the fact that you are an attendant to the Queen will guarantee you favourable rates.' She looked over Cary's robe of cerise silk, sewn with tiny seed pearls.

81

'Though it seems to me you do passing well already in that regard. Indeed, the Queen is hardly better attired than you.'

Cary flushed and closed her mouth, not wanting to find herself on the wrong side of the sumptuary laws. She was a simple 'Mistress' and only those of far higher rank than she were truly permitted to wear clothes as rich as hers.

Frances soon learned that Whitehall was more like a village than a palace, and was home not only to the King and his ministers of state, but also to countless courtiers, chaplains, ladies and gentlemen, and the thousands of servants who waited on them.

The government of Britain was decided in the Council Chamber and the Stone Gallery, which under Cromwell had been stripped of all its fine pictures. Some of these the King had found and placed back on the walls. It was here that a great crowd of hopeful plaintiffs waited eternally, each person yearning to catch the ear of the King.

Whenever the velvet curtains from the Bed or Council Chambers were thrown back, they fell to their knees and waited hopefully as the King progressed briskly past. Few received an answer to their plea, especially if it touched on money, since the King's Exchequer was as empty as a pauper's pocket, yet many were given a sincere 'God Bless You! God Bless You!'

Unlike his cousin King Louis, the Sun King, whose every waking moment was surrounded by elaborate ritual, some said Charles' Court was almost shockingly informal. The monarch also valued some time to himself, even if this meant rising at dawn for his 'morning physick' of a game of tennis or a stolen hour or two to play Pell Mell; or, once his business (or enough of it to get away with) was done, he would even go with his brother, the Duke of York, to Battersea or Putney or Barn Elms to swim in the Thames at sun-down.

And after this he would sup either with his wife, Queen Catherine, or just as often with Barbara Castlemaine in her apartments next to the Bowling Green. These were lavish affairs where, lit by a hundred candles in sconces and chandeliers, the most attractive of all the courtiers would dine at the Countess' excellent table, before the company was treated to gaming, music and dancing.

It was after one such occasion, when the King had again laughed and joked with Frances, that Barbara came and sat down beside her.

Frances stiffened, expecting a frosty warning of the type she had already received, yet for some reason Barbara simply smiled as she took a seat next to her.

'I have watched you with His Majesty,' Barbara began in a low, confiding voice. 'None but you bring out the softness in him. It is a blessing to him, and to us all. He has many burdens and wishes to make all happy, though he knows he must fail. No king can satisfy the demands of all those who took up arms to defend him, and accommodate the talented men who opposed him as well. And the King wishes to achieve a degree of religious toleration! Of course he will not listen to those who tell him this will be seen as bowing to the Papists. He will not talk to me of his pain, yet the marks about his mouth deepen with his troubles. Only with you does he laugh and seem to have not a care.'

Frances stared at her, frankly amazed.

Not once since she had arrived in London had anyone talked to her like this, as a person of understanding. Her mother seemed to see her simply as a chess piece for her own ambitions. Mall was possessed of so much certainty on every topic that she preferred to think for both of them. Yet the King's mistress seemed genuinely interested in her. All the same, Frances was canny enough to treat Barbara's approach with healthy scepticism.

'I am glad you think so, my lady. The King carries much within him, I think.'

'They underestimate you, the King's courtiers who think themselves so clever and astute,' Barbara replied. 'Even my cousin, the Duke of Buckingham, who is usually shrewd enough.' She glanced around at the gilded gathering, the women in their silks and taffeta, the men in velvet and lace neckcloths. 'They say La Belle Stuart likes only childish things. Castles of cards and Blind Man's Buff. That no lady has more beauty and less wit than she.'

Frances gasped at the outrageousness of the accusation, and at Barbara's gall in stating it.

Barbara simply laughed, yet it was a bubbling throaty laugh, a laugh of complicity and genuine humour. 'Be not offended. They are stupid men and jealous women, for the most part. Think yourself fortunate compared to what they say of me.' She leaned forward and lowered her voice. 'I am greedy, extravagant and wilful. I browbeat the King with my bullying and tantrums. I use the lowest whore's tricks to bend him to my wishes. I have brought consensus even between the Chancellor and Mr Evelyn: both think me the curse of the nation!'

'And are you not angered at such implications?'

'My dear Mistress Stuart, for the most part they

are true!' Her laughter rang out again, attracting not a few fascinated glances. 'Yet what of the benefits I bring, and gain no credit for? The King has an appetite that one lady could never satisfy, especially one who is convent-bred and sheltered from childhood, as his wife is. The King is like his leash of spaniels. He needs exercising or he will fall into a fit of melancholy.' The famous violet eyes lit up with humour. 'Indeed, it had not occurred to me before. I am no corrupting whore, but a national benefactress!'

Frances surveyed the King's celebrated mistress. She had expected to find Barbara cold and calculating, yet she was both witty and intelligent. Even her dress had an individuality that was all her own. The fashion at Court was for richly coloured gowns worn over a linen chemise that was softly pulled through sleeve and neckline. Barbara Castlemaine had chosen a gown of cinnamon satin, embellished by a draped and festooned foulard of golden brown, held in place by loops of bronze-coloured pearls. And this foulard was a signature that she always wore, in varying shades of silk, with every gown—a touch that was all Barbara's own.

Yet to talk of her appearance was to miss the point. It was not her clothes that drew men to her like craneflies to a candle-flame. Not even the celebrated beauty of those sleepy slanting eyes, or the sensuous appeal of that small full mouth, though those played their part. It was her daring that drew them—the sense she cared not a jot for the opinion of others, and would do exactly as she pleased.

Barbara Castlemaine behaved as men do: grasped what she wanted and let the Devil take the hindmost.

Frances Stuart, with a great deal more wit than she was credited for, knew that she had every reason to be wary of the King's mistress and intended to be. And yet, to her surprise, she found herself more drawn to Barbara than she had expected. She began to understand a new aspect of the King's attraction to her. Barbara was good company.

'By my troth.' The King had spied them sitting together and was bearing delightedly down upon them. 'The two loveliest women of my Court—in each other's company? Should you not be firing darts of venom, or at the very least offering icy stares to freeze the other over? The tongues will be wagging at this unholy alliance.'

'Then let them, sire, for tongues will always find a cause to wag,' smiled Barbara. 'For we intend to spend more time in each other's company, do we not, Mistress Stuart?'

'Then I would fain spend it with you,' offered the King eagerly.

'Ah, but we women need some time without men, or even kings, to share our secrets.' She fixed Frances with a mock-sardonic look, knowing her words were outrageous. 'I need to know Mistress Stuart's secret. How she can snare a king and keep her innocence.'

Even the King looked abashed at this. 'It is certainly not a trick that you could use, my lady.'

Barbara registered not the slightest offence, but turned her heavy-lidded gaze in his direction. 'Yet what a game it would make if I played the innocent and she the painted lady!'

Visibly stirred, the King allowed himself to be

led off by his retinue.

'How can you talk so to him, even though you jest?' Frances demanded, scandalized despite herself.

Barbara smiled her catlike smile. 'The reason is we are old friends, he and I, and understand each other better than any others. There are those who believe they have the measure of him, yet they do not. We are both creatures of opposites. The difference between us lies in that I *say* what I want, and he but thinks it. Come, visit me tomorrow and we will get to know each other better.'

Frances found her wrap of taffeta gauze and made her way through the curious crowd, looking out for one of the other maids of honour, to return together to their quarters. Yet it was Mall who stood in her path.

'Well, well, Mistress Stuart. I see you make friends in unlikely places. I am surprised to see the duckling so willingly visiting the fox.'

Fond though she was of the older woman, the implication annoyed her. 'Perhaps I am less the duckling and she the fox than you would brand us. She has an understanding of the King that none other shares.'

Mall smirked. 'Indeed she does. Especially the privy parts. And you envy this understanding and wish to share her wisdom. And where would that lead you, pray?'

'I like the King, that is all. He is a kind and charming man.'

'Indeed he is, as I know better than most, having been his playfellow. Yet where women are concerned, friendship is not his common intention.'

'Perhaps, then, I am not a common woman.'

'Perhaps you are not. I would not have you injured, Frances. The King is no cruel tyrant and will never take what you would not willingly give. Yet have a care of Castlemaine. She weaves a web, and you may find yourself caught within its silken trap.'

'And what if I intend to do some weaving of my own?'

Mall regarded her evenly, an unusual distance in her demeanour.

'Then I wish you good luck and will watch you spin with interest.'

*   *   *

The same gusto that Barbara put into her many love affairs she now put into winning Frances' friendship.

Frances, for her part, had enough sense to see exactly what the Countess was about. And yet, to her surprise, since Barbara's reputation was so shocking, she found that the lady they called 'the curse of the nation' could be a highly amusing companion.

Barbara had a gift for party-giving, always providing the very best food and wine, the sweetest singers, and was forever discovering French pastry chefs who produced mouth-watering delights to tempt even the most jaded courtier. She liked to have music playing always, from her morning levee to the moment she lay down on her great bed with its cloth-of-gold cover and golden tassels. Her taste in furnishings was exquisite and her eye for art unmatched. She seemed to have the supernatural gift of finding out exactly where magnificent works of art, stolen during the interregnum, had been taken and buying them back for a fraction of their value.

'Is that a painting by Master Rembrandt?' Frances marvelled, when a vast picture suddenly appeared and was being hung in Barbara's withdrawing room.

Barbara laughed her throaty laugh, which brought to mind ruby port and ripe cheese. 'Indeed it is. The High Constable of Norfolk found it in some yeoman's barn and thought it would look better here in my apartment—as long as he could deliver it himself. He did so late last night and left this morning, well satisfied with his bargain.'

She fixed her laughing eyes on Frances. 'Be not so shocked, Mistress Stuart. I have shared my bed for lesser reasons than that, I assure you!'

'Yet what about the King?'

'Since I am with child again, the King begins to worry that he may dislodge the infant with his yard.' She laughed uproariously, while Frances bit her lip at so explicit a reference to the royal member. 'Men, even kings, are so ignorant. Any midwife could tell him that it is not so, but I do not disabuse him. Besides,' she surveyed Frances with her head on one side, 'his interest starts to lie elsewhere, I fancy.'

Frances, understanding her meaning perfectly, raised her chin. 'If that is so, I know the lady well and think his chances of assailing her virtue are small.'

'Perhaps the lady knows not just how persuasive His Majesty can be.'

And certainly the King's campaign to win over Frances Stuart was charming and subtle indeed.

Every day there would be another amusement devised for her entertainment and delight. Masques, card games, dancing, outings to see the mechanical fountain in the Spring Garden, across the road from Whitehall Palace, and to the playhouse. Small gifts would arrive. Not the sort of expensive jewel, or bolt of silk, that a lover might send to his mistress, but kind, thoughtful things. A perch for her parrot, fashioned of wood with ornate knobs, which he took to at once; a calf-bound book of poetry; new packs of cards for Frances to build into castles; a hawk from Muscovy for her to train; a pretty glass box that played a tune.

As the weeks came and went, the weather remained cold, yet Barbara and Frances were warm and happy in a velvet-lined coach as they circled the Ring in Hyde Park.

'See, there is another equipage that has stopped to greet us,' Barbara pointed out, a frown wrinkling her brow. 'Mayhap you should go and see what they want.'

Frances looked at her askance, since it was cold outside and cosy in the coach. Yet Barbara insisted.

For a moment Frances wondered if it was some trick, and she would find the King inside and be carried off to who knew where. Her fears increased as she approached it, for all the leather blinds were pulled down, obscuring the occupants within. Frances was on the point of turning back when one blind rolled up and out from the window leaned her sister Sophia.

'Sophy!' she shrieked, all her apprehension having melted away. The other blinds were undone, revealing her father and her younger brother Walter. 'How can this be? I had no word or warning that you were coming to London!'

'Frances, we have come to stay,' Sophia gushed. 'We are to live at Somerset House and I am to wait upon the Queen Mother! Father will attend her as physician. It has all been settled by the King.'

Frances glanced back at Lady Castlemaine, who smiled and nodded like an indulgent aunt as Sophia jumped down from the coach. Clearly she had known of the surprise in store, even if Frances had not.

'Sophy, you are so changed.' She held her sister at arm's length and studied her. 'You were but a child when I left Paris, and now you are a lady! What is this hair arrangement you sport?'

Sophia's hair was the picture of Parisian elegance, brushed into far looser curls than was the fashion at the English Court.

'It is called a hurluberlu!' Sophy shook her curls out for Frances to admire.

She studied Sophy's gown with its nipped-in waist and rows of ribbon bows and asked her sister to show off the length of cloth that trailed behind her. 'Now I am to be a lady-in-waiting, I am allowed a train—at the French Court at least, I know not if it is the same here.'

'But you are so tall!'

Sophia laughed and raised her gown an inch to show off her brocade shoes with their red Louis heels. 'Not so tall as you, even with a little help from these!'

'Hey-hey, young ladies, is the talk to be of naught but fashion, when Walter and I sit ignored in this cold coach?'

Her father opened the door and jumped down.

'Oh, I am so glad to see you all,' Frances said

91

joyously. 'I am just accustoming myself to the ways of the English Court, yet I have missed you all sorely!'

Her father raised a wry eyebrow towards the coach and Barbara. 'It seems you have made some powerful friends. King Louis was not best pleased to lose Sophy after you left, and he values my poor skills also, yet King Charles insisted. You are the diamond that flashes most brightly at his Court, it seems.'

She reached up and kissed him. Unlike the unbridled ambition shown by her mother, she could sense his loving concern.

Frances glanced behind her, torn by mixed emotions. She was flattered, of course, by the thoughtfulness of the gesture, and delighted that her family were now to be in London, yet also somewhat disturbed. She liked the King and valued his friendship, yet was it true—as Mall intimated—that friendship was not truly what he offered?

Her father, seeming to understand something of her thinking, held out his arms. 'We are here now, sweeting, and will see how the land lies. Fret not. How could ill come from aught that brings so much pleasure to us all? The Queen Mother loves us, and now we will be seeing you. Indeed,' he laughed at Sophia, who was looking around at all the fine people in their carriages with envy and awe, 'it is your sister we will be having to watch. London, I fear, may go to her head faster than a dram of strong drink. Did Sophia tell you, we have Nurse with us? She will keep your feet upon the ground, king or no king. Can you not hear her now?' Her father put on the creaky voice of an old crone. '"*Gold can be bought too dear.*"'

Frances' laughter rang out, clear and sweet, into the cold air. 'Oh, Father, how delightful it is to have you all here.'

But when Barbara asked her the cause of all her mirth, she just shook her head and pleaded a family joke.

'I am glad to see you happy.' Barbara reached down a hand and helped her back into the coach. 'I have decided we need an entertainment to brighten these dull, cold days and I have devised a little play.'

'Indeed.' Frances loved ballets and masques. 'And what is the subject?'

'You will see. 'Tis an old mummers' masque. We are to have a mock-wedding, and I will play the groom and you the bride. It will be greatly comic, wait and see.'

All at Court were used to such diversions, and enjoyed them as much as watching professionals acting at the playhouse. Rather to Frances' surprise, she had discovered that it was equally popular, and accepted, for men to dress as women and women to dress as men on occasions such as these. Only one thing puzzled her.

'Yet I am taller than you. It should be I, surely, who plays the groom and you the bride!'

Barbara leaned back against the red plush of the coach and smiled mysteriously. 'No, no. It is you who has the blush of innocent youth. If I played a bride, there would be catcalls and cries to my bridegroom of "Alas, poor Cuckold!"'

Frances could see that this was so. 'I will be the bride then. And when do we perform this entertainment? Now that my sister and father are in London, I would like to bid them come and watch.'

At this Barbara became strangely silent.

'Will it be held at Whitehall Palace?' Frances persisted.

'Indeed it will. But for a private, not a public, audience.'

Frances began to feel a little uneasy. 'How private an audience?'

Barbara became of a sudden brisk and businesslike. 'You must wait and see. It will be a great game. You have my word on it. Tomorrow we will find ourselves the costumes.'

That night, after they had supped, Frances returned to her chamber and stood looking out at the dark and swirling river. The night had grown wild and the winds wailed over Westminster.

Next to her window the parrot sat forlornly upon his perch, plucking at his feathers. Thinking the weather had upset him, Frances reached out a hand to comfort him. The parrot nipped her finger.

'Ow!' Frances cried, licking the runnel of blood that ran from her fingertip.

'Clever bird,' replied the parrot balefully. 'Remember Charlie Stuart!'

'Aye.' Frances almost stamped her foot. 'And where is your precious Charlie Stuart? Wed to Mistress Elizabeth Rogers and living happily in Cobham Hall, while I face who knows what dangers here at Court!'

The parrot's yellow eye regarded her beadily. 'Virtue is its own reward,' it commented pompously.

'Except at this Court, Bird. Here, Bird, virtue is a worthless commodity indeed.'

*   *   *

94

'Come, Frances, for you it must be primrose satin with a chemise of purest white—the perfect combination for your fair colouring.'

Frances stood in front of a long looking-glass in Barbara's closet while a tire-woman adjusted the folds of her lovely gown.

'And what of you, my lady husband, what are you planning to wear?'

Barbara laughed. 'I will be a Court gallant, as vain as any feathered fop, I promise you.' She bowed deeply and doffed an imaginary hat. 'Good evening, my bride-to-be!'

Music struck up from the adjoining chamber, viols and lutes, playing the kind of old-fashioned merry tune favoured at weddings, and a sweet angelic voice began to sing a madrigal.

'Take Mistress Stuart next door while I change my clothing,' Barbara ordered the servant, 'and give her a glass of mead. Mead is the drink for weddings. It will allay your nerves. Go!'

Alone in the adjoining chamber, sipping the mead, Frances considered her situation. Something was afoot, she knew it. She must keep her wits about her and remember Mall's words that the King would never take what was not willingly given.

For extra courage she drank down the last of the mead, its lemon-and-honey sweetness steeling her resolve. She was not the pretty ninny people thought her. She loved to dance and sing, and if this was an entertainment she would enjoy it, while keeping her eyes open.

She strode into the withdrawing room to find a scene that took her breath away. Just as if they were on stage in Drury Lane, Barbara had gone to extraordinary lengths to make what awaited her as elaborate as any playhouse could produce. The room was decked with candles and flowers. In the gallery musicians strummed and sang. A venerable old man dressed as a minister stood holding a bible. Next to him three courtiers waited, one holding a band of gold. A page bearing a golden tray with two goblets knelt nearby, and a third, a tiny blackamoor looking nervous in a gilded headdress, clutched a stocking.

In the midst of it all stood Barbara Castlemaine, magnificent in richly embellished doublet and breeches, silk stockings and shoes adorned with red and white roses, her chestnut hair hidden beneath a flowing black wig.

Frances gasped. With a narrow pencil-thin moustache above her lip, she was the King to very life.

'Minister,' Barbara commanded in a low and rolling voice, 'let the marriage ceremony begin!'

The desire to turn and run took hold of Frances. This was no ordinary masque, like the countless home-made plays she had taken part in when she was in Paris.

The so-called minister stepped forward. 'Who gives away this lady?'

'That is my pleasure.' One of the courtiers bowed, took Frances by the hand and led her up to the minister.

'And where are the witnesses?'

Two men bowed and joined them.

'Dearly beloved,' began the mock-minister, as if for the world it was a real wedding ceremony. 'We are gathered here in the sight of God to join this woman to this man.' He nodded towards Frances and Barbara.

It was then, amidst the many curiosities of that curious event, that a further one struck Frances.

The King was nowhere present, which should perhaps have been a relief, yet made the elaborate performance even stranger since it did not seem to have an audience.

A moment later Barbara slipped a band of gold onto Frances' finger and all present in the room clapped.

'Come,' Barbara bowed low and kissed her hand, 'as tradition decrees, we must drink our sack posset.'

The page stepped forward with the two goblets, while all in the room cheered and stamped their feet in appreciation.

'And now—play us sweet airs, musicians—we go next door for the bedding!'

In true weddings this ritual was naught but a ceremonial, followed only for the families' amusement. Besides, Frances told herself, not much could happen in front of a room full of people. Yet still she felt uneasy as, her head high and one eye on an escape route if she needed one, she followed Barbara into the bedchamber.

'We must have the stocking thrown,' commanded Barbara.

The tiny blackamoor ran into the room and flung the stocking over his head, as was the custom at every marriage.

A lower, mellower laugh added to the general merriment and Frances turned to find that the King had suddenly appeared, attired in all his regal finery.

'My dearest Frances,' he smiled, his eyes fixed hungrily upon her creamy shoulders, 'I have come to take the place of my lady Castlemaine in this charming entertainment.'

The pages ran forward and began to undo the hooks of his brocade doublet.

'Thank you, Your Majesty.' Frances decided the proceedings had gone far enough. 'Yet I think it is time to end the entertainment now.'

'For what reason, pray?'

'An excellent good one, sire.' Frances kept her voice calm and humorous. 'That Your Majesty already has a wife. And I think Queen Catherine would not be grateful if I tried to take her place.'

A gasp ran through the room like ice cracking on a winter pond, threatening to pull all down into its freezing depths.

To the general amazement, especially of Barbara Castlemaine, the King began to laugh, softly at first and then in great rollicking waves.

'Odds fish,' he pronounced at last. 'Mistress Stuart speaks the truth. Good people, it is time to get to your beds.' He laughed one last time, as if remembering her words again. 'And better make those your own!'

Frances wasted no time in taking his advice. The evening had been odd in the extreme, and yet the King had accepted her withdrawal with his usual humour. Surely she could draw comfort from that?

Chapter 5

Everywhere she went about her duties in Whitehall Palace the next morning—in the Queen's Apartments, and the Matted Gallery, crossing the

98

Privy Garden and even when she accompanied the Queen to Chapel—a rustle of whispers followed in her wake.

She wondered at first if she imagined it until, outside the chapel, she encountered Sophia, who pulled her by the sleeve into the corridor that led to the Great Hall. 'Sister, tell me all! What truly befell between you and the King last night?'

'Naught.' Frances suddenly saw what all the whispering might entail. 'There was a silly charade of Lady Castlemaine's devising and I put a stop to it, that was all. It was no great matter, and I hope you will say so to any who ask you.'

'I have no need. It is all round Whitehall that Mistress Stuart turned down the King.' She giggled in the way she had done since the schoolroom. 'And after he had begun to undo his buttons betimes!'

Frances blenched and wished herself anywhere but here, in this great furnace of rumour, where every titbit of gossip made the flames burn brighter.

Walking back in Queen Catherine's train after Chapel, she looked only ahead. And then one more strange thing occurred. As she curtseyed and took her leave, Queen Catherine stretched out a hand and raised her up. Their eyes hardly met and yet Frances knew instantly that not just her ladies, but the Queen herself, had heard the latest rumour.

Frances thanked her and, as soon as she was able, slipped back into the Privy Garden, hoping for some moments alone before she should face the throng of dinner, and the knowing glances from the others on the maids of honour's table.

Light footsteps followed her and she turned to find Mall a few steps behind her.

'Well, Mistress Machiavell! I knew not you

99

were such a strategist.' Mall's voice was low and heavy with irony. 'Like all the rest at Court, I must congratulate you. Your words are repeated everywhere. All had thought you a pretty, childish thing. Now they sing a different tune. "From the sweetest wine, the tartest vinegar" is the new word on Mistress Frances Stuart.'

Frances turned angrily to face her mentor. 'How dare you think such a thing of me? I am no more to be congratulated for my clever strategy than for my vaunted simplicity, for neither comes near the truth. I was as much at fault as the King for letting myself become involved in so silly a charade. I thought at first it would amuse me to act the bride to Barbara's bridegroom, yet when I saw her change places with His Majesty, I had to stop the business there. I did not mean to have all laughing at the King, and heartily wish they would not do so.'

'Whether you intended it or not, you will be treated with a new respect. I have heard of no lady who has ever publicly spurned the King's advances.' Mall smiled wryly. 'Virtue will be a new experience for him.'

'Stop, Mall.' Frances was in true earnest now, eager that at least Mall should understand her. 'I did not refuse the King out of virtue. I refused because the life of a king's mistress is not what I desire! I know some yearn for it, but not I.' Mall had rarely heard such passion in Frances' voice. 'I wish for a home of my own, a husband, fireside, babes. And if I bed the King, any husband I find would be a cuckold like poor Roger Palmer, laughed at and pitied. I like the King, and value his company. He is kind and just and, though many find fault with him, I believe he truly tries his best

100

for his people.' Standing up to her full height, Frances had an authority Mall had never seen before. 'I did not use my innocence to trap him, as honey traps a fly. The facts were simple. I wished not to be the King's mistress, but his friend.'

Mall took a deep breath and whistled. 'I see you mean what you say. Yet one could not forgive the King for thinking otherwise when you came to the bedchamber, drank the sack posset and had the stocking flung, so that bedding you would be the natural consequence. Why in God's name did you get yourself into that farrago?'

Frances' shoulders sank. 'It was my vanity. I like to act or dance and be the centre of attention. I realized too late how this charade would end.'

Mall held out her arms. 'Frances Stuart, you have much to learn.'

Though closer to her mother in years, Mall had always been half-advisor, half-friend, worldly wise and yet young at heart, as a much older sister might be. ''Tis true, I do. You will have to guide me. And yet, when the King laughed, I thought all was well. I did not consider that the story would be repeated to every Dick and Harry.'

'Who now think you deep and devious. Ah well, 'tis worse in this Court to be thought virtuous than devious, so perhaps it is not so ill after all.' Mall squeezed her affectionately. 'Come, it is not so terrible. All will pass by tomorrow sun-up. Memories at the Court are short. Some lady will cuckold her husband, or a new play-actress catch the King's eye. Frances Stuart will be yesterday's rumour.'

Frances sighed. 'I wish there was somewhere I could go, a place where naught mattered and I could forget the Court and all its doings.'

'Such is not for you and me.' Mall laughed with a shade of bitterness. 'I have lived at Court most of my life. I was even born here.'

'Yet what of Cobham Hall? Did you not live there once, with your husband James and your babes together?'

Pain clouded Mall's eyes at the memory of what she had lost, and she looked sharply away. 'That was long in the past. But, yes, I was content there. Those old red-brick walls protect you well from the cruel world outside.' She shook herself. 'Yet it was but a passing dream. Not as solid as it felt. And now, your Charles Stuart, the parrot-giver, lives there and is Duke of Richmond, too. Aye, it's a strange world. Come, let us go. Dinner will be served and there will be more talk if we are missed.'

Like the tongue that seeks out the sore tooth, Frances found her thoughts winging to that world behind Cobham's comforting walls. It was a curious thought that so many longed to be here at Court, and saw it as the beating heart of their universe, while she longed for the calm and peace of a happy life in the country.

Banishing the painful thoughts from her mind, Frances followed in the wake of Mall's retreating back through the noisy throng gathered in the Hall. Silence fell as they progressed, and lasted all the way until they reached the maids of honour's table, where Cary Frazier and Elizabeth Hamilton moved swiftly aside to make them a place.

After a few minutes the hub returned to its usual buzz of gossip, intrigue and scandal—but hopefully not all about her.

Their meal over, they were about to stand and

102

return to the Queen's quarters when Mall's brother, the celebrated Duke of Buckingham, strode up, distinctive as ever with his swagger of self-importance and extravagant fair wig. He dropped suddenly to one knee and kissed Frances' hand.

'Fair mistress, virtue has never been celebrated before in this amoral place. Perhaps your goodness will set an example to us all.'

Frances smiled, ignoring the sting that lay hidden in his comment. The Duke was one of the chief proponents of the Court's celebrated immorality. 'And what of your behaviour, sir?' she enquired, in a voice as sweet as honey. 'You have so much more to atone for than I, it would give all the better example if you reformed your character.'

At that a booming laugh was heard from behind them. 'She's right, George. If you of all people discover virtue, everyone here will follow suit.'

'Aye, Majesty,' George Buckingham shook his head, 'yet some things are not worth the candle, even if it be a holy candle.'

Charles laughed again. 'I am sorry, Mistress Stuart, you may reform me, but my lord of Buckingham is a harder nut to crack.'

The King's amiable manner was a great relief. After humiliating him in public, she might have expected banishment. Or worse. Yet it seemed life could go on.

As if reflecting her reprieve from the royal displeasure, the weather warmed up and at last there were fine days when it was hard to stay inside the gloomier rooms of the ancient palace.

'Tomorrow we will go by water to my uncle's house at Richmond,' Barbara announced. 'The King will lend us his barge.'

'I will need to ensure the Queen can spare me.' Frances hesitated. She had intended to keep a safer distance from Barbara after the mock-bridal, yet The Lady—force of nature that she was—brooked no resistance. The Queen, for her part, was happy to spare Frances.

'You have been a friend to me, Mistress Stuart,' she murmured, to Frances' great embarrassment. 'And I will not forget it. I have plenty of maids to wait on me. Go and enjoy the clement weather, God knows if it will last.'

The Queen might have been less generous had she known whom Frances' companion was and that their excursion was in the royal barge, lent for the occasion by the King.

The sun shone on the river, malodorous as a rotting snake in London's midst, yet the air became clearer with every yard they rowed westwards, away from the metropolis.

The Royal Bargemaster, a cheerful man, seemed delighted to be going upstream, in the opposite direction from the blackened air and the countless wherries crowded with passengers that wove their way through the smacks, lighters and tall ships disgorging their cargoes beyond London Bridge.

To their right they passed the Neat House gardens on the north bank near to Pimlico, where many of London's vegetables were grown. Cabbages, cauliflower, artichokes and carrots all flourished there in abundance. 'And soon the food of the gods—asparagus—from the Neat House garden, boiled and dipped in seething butter.' Barbara closed her eyes and licked her lips at the thought. 'My God, I have a sudden fancy for them.'

'Mind you wash 'em first, in your condition,

104

my lady,' the Bargemaster advised. 'Since they be grown with ordure from London's laystalls. *No turd, no garden,* as the saying goes.'

'Thank you, Bargemaster.' Barbara grinned, catching Frances' eye. 'I will mind your advice.'

On the left side was the famous Fox Hall, a sixpenny boat ride across the Thames, with its recently laid-out walks and arbours for the delight of Londoners to sup and chase each other for a stolen kiss.

'That is, if you want to kiss some old whore in a vizard,' Barbara commented, 'and end up with more than you bargained for.' She laughed at her own humour. 'They do say the husband of the Duke of York's latest mistress deliberately got himself the pox and gave it to her, so she might pass it on to the Duke with his compliments.' She laughed uproariously at this prospect.

With Fox Hall behind them, they passed Barn Elms, with its ancient manor, where the King liked to come and swim with his brother, and which also doubled as a popular duelling ground.

'His Majesty hates duels,' Barbara confided. 'Yet he can never stop his courtiers' habits of killing each other. He says he cannot blame them, since some of them are the veriest rogues, and yet, he rails, have we not had our fill of senseless slaughter without adding to it?'

Frances smiled. She could almost hear the King's witty, yet world-weary tones in Barbara's words. Despite what was said of him—that he cared only for pleasure and neglected the business of guiding the country—Charles was a humane man.

At length they reached Richmond, where Barbara's uncle lived in an elegant manor by the riverside, with rolling gardens down to wooden steps where they pulled in and moored.

'Come, my uncle will have foods laid out in his Banqueting House.'

Frances followed Barbara down a path of flagstones bordered by sweet lavender, in which the bees buzzed, happy to see the sun after so long and cold a spring. The first pink roses, draped from a wooden trellis, hung in swags of scented beauty all around them. The flowerbeds bragged with colour. And everywhere birdsong filled the air.

'It is perfect, my lady. How fortunate your uncle is to have this place.'

'Hah! I would be bored here in a senn'ight. Come and eat. My uncle lays a good table.' She turned and smiled mysteriously. 'And after you have had your fill of pies and sweetmeats, I have a better surprise in store.'

Frances stiffened, all the wariness that she had formerly felt returning.

'Come, mistress, no more charades with lustful monarchs. As he told you, you have cured him of ignoble thoughts. He is all but sainted now, more's the pity.'

Frances laughed despite herself, at the unlikely vision of the King transformed into holiness.

The Banqueting House was a little gem, built of mellow brick with arched windows and elegant towers, reminding Frances of the doll's house she had owned in childhood and loved so deeply. It hung almost suspended over the river at the end of a meadow full of wild flowers. Barbara threw open a lattice window. 'Look, you can fish without moving from the table!'

Inside the house there was room only for a

table and ten chairs, each cushioned in a different jewelled colour. Ruby, amethyst, emerald, sapphire, amber, aquamarine, moonstone, opal. The heady scent of blossom filled the air from the curtains of tiny white flowers that all but covered one side of the Banqueting House. Candles burned even though it was bright day, adding to the sense of a place almost out of time.

The food laid out for their midday meal was equally appealing. Roasted squab, eel pie with oysters, capon with orange and lemon sauce, and an exotic-looking salad of French beans, raisins of the sun, samphire, pickled cowcumbers and blanched almonds. 'Hush!' whispered Barbara with mock-drama. 'My uncle's cook stole the receipt from Mistress Elizabeth Cromwell, the Protector's wife.'

'Was she so good a cook then?'

'Aye, the Protector ate like the King, as well as envying his crown. She counsels an accompaniment of shrimp and sturgeon. We have but roasted fowl.'

After they had eaten they returned to the river bank.

'Come,' Barbara turned, her eyes alight with one of her sudden enthusiasms, 'the weather is warm as summer. Let us swim!'

Swimming had been a popular pastime at the Chateau of Colombes in her years living with Henrietta Maria, and the water held no fear for Frances.

'Yet what if someone sees us?'

'There is none here but you and me! The bargeman is indoors being fed like a dog by my uncle's fat cook and will sleep after. My uncle is out hunting the deer.' She had already stripped off to her chemise and was heading for the steps down to the waterside.

Frances bit her lip and yet, tempted too by the cool water, so clear here next to that of the city, she soon followed Barbara, until both splashed about with shrieks and shouts of pleasure.

Finally, feeling chilled as the sun disappeared behind a cloud, Frances was heading back for the shore when, not six inches away from her, a huge black bird with a fish in its beak reared out from the water below, like some ancient and malevolent creature.

She cried out as if it were the Devil himself risen up from the depths of hell on Judgement Day.

A shout of masculine laughter greeted her as she clambered ashore and looked up into the laughing eyes of the King. 'Fear not, 'tis but my pet cormorant.' He held out a hand and pulled her out. 'My grandfather King James always fished thus, and had his own Keeper of the King's Cormorants. But you are wet . . .' His eyes rested a moment on the transparent silk of her chemise, which outlined her sweet young breasts. Tearing his gaze deliberately away, he began to undo his coat. And started to laugh again at the memory of the other night. 'Fear not. My intentions are much reformed since you taught me my lesson. This time I take my coat off only to offer it to you for warmth.'

Barbara too had emerged from the water, as brazen and beautiful as Aphrodite rising from the foam.

'I will summon a servant to bring us warm clothing. I keep many clothes here.' With a complicit glance at Charles she strode off.

Charles, in his concern for Frances, hardly

noticed.

'Remove your chemise. I will close my eyes. And cover yourself with my coat. There.'

Rather than stand dripping in her transparent chemise, Frances quickly changed under cover of his proffered coat, despairing that no matter how hard she might try to evade his attention, they were locked together by her way of life here.

Charles opened his eyes and began to dry her skin tenderly, as if she were a child in danger of catching cold.

'Strange,' he mused, 'I have many offspring, though sadly not with my queen, and yet never have I had the chance to bathe or dry them, such as I do you now. The price of kingship perhaps.' He stopped rubbing and smiled slowly, a strange sadness reflecting in his dark eyes. 'Do you wish for children, Mistress Stuart?'

'Indeed I do, one day . . .' she faltered.

'You are almost a child yourself. Come, let us pursue childish sports and get my cormorant to catch more fish.'

Frances agreed with relief. Once again she knew not what to make of the King. At times he seemed genuinely to be her friend and treated her with extraordinary tenderness. At others it seemed as if friendship was not what he sought from her, or was willing to accept. Was it his conscience, then, that prompted him to stand back when he sensed her fear or uncertainty? Or did he tell himself that he must treat her gently simply to win what he wanted? Perhaps, it struck her with wonder, he did not know himself.

Above all, when she was alone with him she felt the rift of power between them. He was older and

109

she very young. He the King, and she his subject.

Finding no answer, she sat at his side and watched him fish, wishing she could be more certain what the future between them held.

When Barbara returned bearing dry clothes she paused a moment, considering the King and Frances as they sat together on the river bank. There was a tenderness in him she had not seen before. Although she thought herself armoured against such things, this new protectiveness, so different from what passed between Charles and herself, caught at Barbara's heart and filled her with fear, as if she had suddenly foreseen her own death.

'Stop this, foolish woman,' she told herself. 'The tender suitor is a new role for him, that is all. Like the fisherman, he sees the need for patience and concentration. As he knows, one slip and the fish comes off the hook and is lost.'

Beyond them the black shape of the bird took off once more and swooped into the water.

As Barbara watched them, the parallel between herself and the bird struck her forcibly. Whatever the King pretended for the moment, he desired Frances and would rely on Barbara to help him get her, just as he used that bird to catch the fish.

She turned away silently, to leave them to their sport, consoling herself that she knew the secrets of his mind above all people, and that when he got that which he desired, he would certainly cease to want it and come back to her. Innocence, to a man like him, might seem alluring for a day, yet it would never eclipse the appeal of a skilful woman who knew how to give pleasure better than any other he had ever known.

As Whitsuntide approached, a panoply of pleasures was laid out before the ladies of the Court, bright and enticing as a pedlar's gaudy wares to a kitchen maid in Cheapside. Visits beckoned to see *The Humorous Lieutenant* at the new playhouse that had just opened its doors to eager Londoners; the fun of mastering the steps of the newest French dances awaited, as well as riding in the Ring at Hyde Park at the hour when fashionable people waved from one coach to another.

For once the King was too busy with affairs of state to join in, dealing with warring ministers, countless council meetings, interviews with ambassadors and with suitors of every kind. The Earl of Clarendon's gout played him up and made him testier than ever, and he offended the French ambassadors by refusing to speak any language save English. Yet he was grateful for the King's attention, remarking to Frances what a good head for business the King had, and that nothing ever got done save when he was present.

'I wish he worked not so hard,' murmured the Queen one sunny day when she had organized a hawking party and hoped in vain that her husband might join them. 'Which hawk will you have, Mistress Stuart?' Queen Catherine asked.

'The Book of St Albans lays it all down, ma'am.' Catherine Boynton recited from the famous old rhyme:

> *'An Eagle for an Emperor,*
> *A Gyrfalcon for a King,*
> *A Peregrine for a Prince,*

111

A Saker for a Knight,
A Merlin for a Lady,
A Goshawk for a Yeoman,
A Sparrowhawk for a Priest,
A Musket for a Holy-Water Clerk,
A Kestrel for a Knave.'

Catherine laughed. 'Nothing for a Queen? Then I will have a Merlin for a Lady. Yet what is that bird yonder?' She pointed at a glorious white-feathered creature with distinctive dark-grey markings, its head covered by a hood with a plume of feathers on top, its feet tied by two jesses, leather straps that could be pulled tight to keep it on the leather glove the keeper wore. Each leg had a brass bell that tinkled as it hopped about.

'It belongs to the King, Majesty. It was presented to him by the Ambassador from Muscovy. He asked me to bring it down and give it to . . .' The man faltered, overcome by sudden discomfiture.

The Queen straightened her narrow back. 'And give it to Mistress Stuart?'

The man bowed, took off the hood and delivered the falcon to an embarrassed Frances.

'Oh, poor thing, its eyes are all sewn up!' Frances exclaimed.

'It is always so, mistress,' explained the keeper. 'We sew up the eyes for the better training of it.'

'Yet is that truly necessary?' Frances asked.

The Queen turned her horse's head towards the field ahead. 'You are too soft-hearted, mistress,' she commented wryly. 'The law of the field is like that of the Court: no mercy given or asked. That is something I have had to learn and you will have to also, if you mean to survive here.' She rode off, leaving the other ladies smirking as they trotted off in her wake.

'She has claws then, the little Queen,' commented a rich and fruity voice.

Frances turned to find Barbara behind her. 'Do you not ride out with a hawk, my lady?'

Barbara laughed and patted her brocaded stomacher. 'Since I am carrying the King's child, I would not wish to risk the future of England.'

'Hardly that,' Frances flashed, 'since your babe would be born out of wedlock.'

Barbara smiled, refusing to take umbrage at Frances' slur. 'Better the wrong side of the blanket than not at all. They say the Queen intends to go and take the waters, in the hope of conceiving with the King.'

Frances felt a sudden pang for the Queen having to witness Barbara's constant fertility in the face of her own barrenness. 'Let us hope the waters are successful and she provides an heir.'

Barbara simply smiled, confident in her own overflowing fecundity.

How strange it was, thought Frances, watching the Queen's merlin swoop for the kill, that a whole nation could be so affected by a woman's capacity to conceive. If Queen Catherine produced no heir, the King's brother, the Duke of York, would one day be King, and he a suspected Catholic. So the whole dreaded matter of religion that had brought so much death and suffering might loom over them all again.

'There! Clever bird. She has killed her prey.' The Queen glanced at Barbara in triumph.

Suddenly from nowhere a violent wind whipped up, black clouds scudded across the sky, and day became night. A vicious rainstorm began, the rain coming down like the bars of a jail. Even the birds' feathers dropped and water hung off their dripping beaks.

'Quickly!' Barbara shouted to Frances. 'You are a good horsewoman. Let us go back to Whitehall across the fields. It will be quicker than by road.'

The ride back was exhilarating. Unhindered by crowded roads, they galloped across open country, broken only by stone walls and the occasional farmstead until they came at last to a toll-gate.

'It seems a shame to slow down after so exciting a ride and, if we do, the rain may catch us. Come!' Barbara spurred her mare on and sailed over the toll-gate.

Frances, balancing her weight forward on her side-saddle, laughed and followed suit, pausing only for a moment to look back at the astonished gatekeeper and fling him a handful of coin, more than enough to pay for their passage. If a pregnant Barbara could do it, so could she.

'Frances Stuart,' Barbara asked as they dismounted outside the stables in the Whitehall mews. 'Why did you pay? Will I never turn you into a reckless pleasure-seeker who breaks the rules with abandon?'

Frances shook her head. 'It is the Scots in me. We are a practical nation.'

She patted her horse, smiling as the mare nuzzled into her neck, thinking of he who had sent her the horse. Behind her she glimpsed Barbara speaking softly to Mr Chiffinch, Keeper of the King's Closet, Page of His Majesty's Bedchamber and Keeper of His Majesty's Backstairs, in other words the King's most private advisor. No one, and especially no lady, got access to the King's private apartments except through Mr Thomas Chiffinch.

Barbara and he were clearly hatching some plot together.

Barbara shook out her wet train, soaking Frances' feet as she did so. 'Forgive me, my dear. I am clumsy now that I am with child—everywhere except in bed!'

Frances caught the eye of Cary Frazier, who waited outside Barbara's closet with a message for her from Lady Suffolk.

'Look not so disapproving, Mistress Frazier.' Barbara rounded on her. 'I have heard from my Lord Rochester that when a man cannot satisfy you, you turn for your pleasure to a dildo!'

Cary Frazier flushed brighter than the brocade that lined Barbara's great bed. 'That is a calumny! You know Lord Rochester has a wicked tongue . . .'

'And has used it well on your cunny, from what I hear.'

Cary Frazier looked as if she might spit in Barbara's face.

'As all recognize, my Lord Rochester has a disgusting imagination about such things.'

'Which is why he makes such an excellent bedfellow, or so I am told.'

'Besides,' muttered Cary under her breath 'to fill a hole such as yours, with all the use it's had, he would need three dildoes.'

'What was that?' Barbara demanded.

'Naught of importance, my lady. I came because the Countess of Suffolk requires Mistress Stuart's presence and I must conduct her there at once.'

'Go, then. I wish not to look any longer on your face—'tis sour enough to make the milk in my breasts turn and poison the babe when it is born.'

Cary curtseyed and turned, signalling Frances to follow.

'And none would mourn the bastard,' she murmured as soon as they were out of hearing. 'For she has given the King enough of them already—if they are the King's, that is. For folk do say more gentlemen visit her than Madam Cresswell's bawdyhouse.'

'How keeps she, then, the King's devotion, if she is as loose a woman as you say?'

Cary Frazier laughed, a low gurgling sound like a dirty drain emptying. 'It is *because* she is a loose woman, so says the gossip. When she is with child, the King fears for its safety, so she takes him in her mouth instead.'

Frances' eyes widened.

'Some men find more pleasure thus. The Flemish whores are sought after for the skills they have in that regard. Mayhap The Lady has been in their classroom.' She dropped her voice to a whisper, glancing round to make sure they were not overheard. ''Tis also said she has called the barber to her privy parts, and they are as bald as the Spanish Ambassador's head!'

They had arrived outside the royal apartments.

'Sssh, we must speak no more of this in front of the Queen.'

Queen Catherine sat surrounded by her ladies, stitching an altar cloth with infinite patience. Although she had learned that toleration of her rival Lady Castlemaine was a more effective course of survival than confrontation, the two women were as different as saint and sinner could be. While Barbara mocked the tender feelings of true

116

believers by posing for Master Lely robed as the Madonna with her bastard son as the Christ child, Catherine was a pious young woman who enjoyed nothing more than collecting relics and adding another votive prayer to her vast collection.

Yet the King seemed to need and cherish both these ladies. Clearly he desperately required an heir and only Catherine could give him that. Fecundity might overflow from Barbara's breasts like some ancient Roman goddess of plenty, yet none of her offspring could solve the royal succession. Beyond that, it struck Frances that the King liked and respected his wife—provided she allowed him a long leash of freedom.

That night after supper large crowds of courtiers gathered in both the Queen's and Lady Castlemaine's apartments, as they often did for music, gaming and gossip. The activities in both salons were similar, but in Barbara's the crowd was racier and the stakes they gambled with higher. The King would often divide his time between both, laughing and dancing, yet when it came to bedtime, he was more often at Barbara's side than Catherine's.

The atmosphere in Barbara's apartments was feverishly gay until, with a flash of her famous violet eyes, Barbara would dismiss all, to be alone with the King.

Tonight he had stayed into the early hours and Frances, her eyes beginning to flutter, readied herself to leave. And yet, to her surprise, it was the King who announced his departure.

'Let us have some adventure planned for tomorrow,' he announced, 'when I have completed my business, so that I may look forward to it during my discussions of the Dutch incursions into our trade, with the Chancellor reminding me of the dire state of our Exchequer's finances!' He smiled in the easy, charming way that won him friends both high and low.

'He will be up at six playing tennis,' Barbara whispered. 'And his courtiers will have to catch him before they make him do any business.'

The King, shaking hands as he took his leave, came back to them one last time. 'Goodnight, ladies, and farewell until the rosy finger of dawn comes to stroke you softly into wakefulness.'

Barbara looked at him meaningfully. 'It will be midday before that, sire. Goodnight.' She hooked her arm into Frances'. 'Come,' she said in a low voice, 'stay with me. The dawn he speaks of is not far off and I hate to sleep alone.'

Frances regarded her warily, at the same time conscious of how dropping tired she was. Maids of honour had to stay up as long as the Queen, and of late Queen Catherine had started staying up almost till morning.

Frances yawned.

'Come, it will be like sharing with your sister. Here is a nightgown.' She held out a white garment of the crispest, finest linen.

The great bed was already turned back and a silken robe lay draped across it. At the foot a sleepy blackamoor of no more than five or six sat upon a velvet stool waiting to do his mistress' bidding.

'Be off, child, I need nothing more tonight.' Barbara patted his head, showing a surprising gentleness. Yet she was not so considerate, it struck Frances, to let him go to his bed earlier.

'I will take off my gown here.' Frances pointed

118

to the gap between the great tapestry that lined the wall and the wall itself.

'Such modesty!' Barbara laughed. 'As you will.'

When she returned in her nightgown, Barbara was standing at her toilette in front of her looking-glass, in the act of unstoppering a glass jar. 'Breathe in that,' she commanded.

Frances inhaled deeply and closed her eyes. The scent of jessamine was so strong that it was as if she were again in the gardens of the Palais Royal in deepest summer, where there was a small summerhouse enrobed in the tiny white flowers.

'Here, let me rub it into your temples—you will find you sleep as never before.'

She sat Frances upon a stool and tied her hair back from her face with a narrow band. Very gently she began to anoint Frances' forehead with the scented oil. It was a pleasant experience indeed.

'So,' Barbara enquired, as she kept up the slow, sensuous movement, 'how did you come by such a dull name as Frances? It is the name of an honest Scottish burgher's wife, fat and waddling, always on her knees.'

Frances, almost asleep with exhaustion and the pleasurable sensations, laughed all the same. ''Tis true! I was named for the wife of old Duke Ludovic Stuart.'

'Since they call you La Belle Stuart, I shall call you Belle.' Barbara replaced the stopper in the bottle. 'Come, to bed, before you drop to the floor.'

There was a kindness in Barbara's voice that confused Frances still further. She slipped into the great bed and felt the alluring delights of fresh linen, scented delicately with lavender.

'I change my linen every day,' laughed Barbara.

119

'A monstrous extravagance, and it means I am forever having sheets hung in the Privy Garden— but wonderful, think you not?'

'Indeed,' replied Frances sleepily, her fair hair fanning out behind her on the pillow like a ripple of corn-coloured silk.

'Sharing a bed brings back such memories.' Barbara's usual reckless gaiety was quietened for once. 'I used to share a bed often with Mall Villiers.'

Frances woke momentarily and stared at her in surprise. Mall had never mentioned such intimacy.

'We are cousins, remember, and saw much of each other as maids. Then came the troubles and all changed. The old King married her at thirteen to his kinsman. Then the boy died. Poor Mall, a widow before she was truly a bride. And then she married my cousin James, not for love, though she grew to care for him. My own parents died and I was left without a dowry, living off my wits. And the monster Cromwell put the King himself to death. Terrible times.' She closed her eyes as if to blot out so much death and loss. 'And in the midst of that, I fell in love! Clever girl that I was, so full of spirit and rebellion.' Frances heard the bitterness ring down all the years. 'I fell for one who wanted me not. He bedded me happily enough, but since I had no dowry offered no marriage contract. His Lordship needed a rich wife.'

Frances turned away, thinking suddenly of the new Duke of Richmond, with his halo of russet hair and laughing grey eyes. He had also needed his heiress. 'It angers me so, that we are ever at the mercy of money,' she railed with sudden fiery spirit. 'I hate it that we have no freedom of our own to

120

choose!'

'It is the way of the world. Now I have a king.'

Frances did not add, 'Aye, but he is not truly yours.'

'Sleep, or that dawn His Majesty talked of, will be upon us.' Barbara blew out the candle.

Frances rolled over to face the windows that looked towards the Privy Garden. Somewhere far below she heard the bellman call out, as he did his rounds, that it was two of the clock and a fine moonshine night. Next to her the greatest courtesan of the Restoration Court snored gently.

With a smile on her lips Frances fell asleep and had the strangest and most vivid dream.

She was not Frances Teresa Stuart, daughter of a humble Scottish lord, even if they were distantly related to the royal Stuarts; but by some strange and wondrous circumstance, she wore a crown and sat upon a throne of state. Frances Teresa Stuart was Queen of England!

She sat up, startled and shaking, to find that the reality was even stranger.

The bedclothes had been drawn back and the silken strings of her chemise undone so that her breasts were openly revealed.

Next to the bed stood the King—not in a dream, but in sure and certain reality, clad in nightshirt and an elaborate brocade dressing coat, watching her in an oddly abstract pose, almost as if he were not flesh and blood, but an effigy. By his side stood Barbara Castlemaine, with a look of proud possessiveness upon her face as if to say, 'See, here she is laid out before you, but in my bed, not yours.'

Seeing her awake, the King reached out his hand to touch her warm and living breast.

Despite the strangeness of the situation, and her anger at being so displayed, Frances' nipple stiffened at his touch. No man had ever treated her so before and, as his fingers brushed her flesh, she was filled with an exquisite and delirious sensation.

Shocked and mortified, for it reminded her of how she had felt when the Duke had looked at her so hungrily, she closed her eyes. Was she wicked beyond imagining, that she could feel so easily transported?

The King, intensely moved by the effect his approach had on her, cupped her chin in his hand and made her look at him, a smile of melting tenderness lighting up his harsh features.

The moment was so electric that, standing beside the King, Barbara's proud superiority gave way to a different emotion. She had thought the King would tire of Frances' girlish innocence, and had begun to wonder herself if it might hide a nature that was either cold or prudish. Yet the intensity of the young girl's response belied that suspicion. Frances was clearly capable of sexual passion. And the King believed he had been the first man to show her. Such a heady excitement would be powerful indeed—more powerful, perhaps, than any she could muster.

Frances, though shocked at her body's response, thought quickly. The only way out of this situation was not to play the outraged virgin, but to use humour.

She pulled the strings of her chemise together and sat up. 'Your Majesty!' she enquired matter-of-factly, as if finding the King standing six inches from her naked breast were the most natural thing in the world. 'Are you not cold in your night attire?

122

I could summon Mr Chiffinch to bring warmer clothes from your apartments, or is this a famous midnight ramble? I have heard so much of Your Majesty's boundless energy.'

A beat of silence followed, chillier than the wind that blew in the great windows.

In teasing the King she had gone too far. She would be sent from Court in disgrace, and maybe her family also.

Instead Charles cracked with laughter. 'My energy is indeed boundless, is it not? The sun comes up soon, and I shall go and divert that boundless energy into a tiring game of tennis. Goodnight, Mistress Stuart.'

After he had left Frances held Barbara's unflinching gaze. She had been betrayed by the King's sudden appearance, and both of them knew it. Any further trust or friendship between them was impossible. Without saying a further word, Frances slipped from the bed and gathered up her gown from the oaken chair. At the door she stopped and turned. 'I will not come again to these apartments,' she announced.

'And I will not invite you!' Barbara pulled her robe around her, all outraged imperiousness. 'Beware, Mistress Stuart, innocence is a hand that can only be played once, before it loses all its currency.'

'Unlike that of royal pimp and bawd? For it seems that hand can be played many times over, no matter how debauched the player.'

Barbara considered Frances' departing back. Had she underestimated the wit of a rival whom she had thought naive and childlike, yet who seemed to be showing remarkable resilience and ingenuity?

Frances made her way swiftly back to her chamber, her feet padding on the cold stone floors, avoiding the curious looks from the pages who played dice in the chilly corridors to keep themselves awake as they waited, yearning for their beds, for their lords to emerge, while outside the dawn beckoned.

Once she had gained her chamber, she sat down on the window seat and stared out at the light-streaked river. Her anger at Barbara had given way to confusion and even to shame. There could be no denying that what she had felt was pleasure. And the King had marked it in her.

The first of the sun's rays broke suddenly through the cover of cloud and lit up the room brightly, but they did not bring an answer to her problems. What tools did she possess, apart from honour and determination, to help her through the whirling torrents that surrounded her. Did she make her bed harder than it needed to be? Should she succumb and become the latest in a long line of royal mistresses?

'Yet it is not what I want!' She spoke the words aloud. *'And yet I cannot have what I want, for another woman possesses it already!'*

On the table next to her the parrot eyed her beadily as if it had witnessed the follies of many before her.

Yet counsel had it none.

Chapter 6

The Court of King Charles II was scandalized.

It had heard the rumour of the many mistresses His Majesty had enjoyed during his exile; it had seen him woo Barbara Castlemaine and raise her from commoner's wife to Countess; it acknowledged that Mr Chiffinch, Page of the Backstairs, sent hundreds of women up to the King's bedchamber; it had even accepted that the King and his brother frequented harlots in London's brothels, posing as ordinary gentlemen.

Yet it had never before witnessed anything like this: the King had lost his heart. And to a decent, honest and unmarried young woman of gentle birth.

Rumour was rife through the whole Court of how Frances Stuart had brought about this miracle. Not through the usual black arts of promiscuity and seduction, for it seemed the lady was virtuous. The King, sick with love, languished.

'He has even written *poetry*!' whispered Lord Rochester, chief among the wits, no more than twenty, yet he had been debauched, so it was said, at fourteen and lost no time since. He had gathered a group of gallants around him in the Devil Tavern in Fleet Street to listen to the King's verse.

Lord Rochester jumped onto the tavern table beneath the statue of Ben Jonson and began to recite:

'I pass all my hours in a shady old Grove . . .'

'. . . so that's what he's calling Castlemaine these days . . .'

'But I live not the day when I see not my love;
I survey every walk now my Phillis . . .
[for Phillis, read Frances, lads] *is gone,*
And sigh when I think we were there all alone;
O then, 'tis O then, that I think there's no hell
Like loving, like loving too well.'

'There's more, lads, there's more!'

'While alone to myself I repeat all her charms,
She I love may be locked in another man's arms,
She may laugh at my cares and so false she may
  be
To say all the kind things she before said to me;
O then, 'tis O then, that I think there's no hell
Like loving, like loving too well.

'But when I consider the truth of her heart
Such an innocent passion . . .
[aye, that's the problem, Charlie]
So kind without art . . .
[but more art than you expected, laddie!]
I fear I have wronged her; and hope she may be
So full of true love to be jealous of me;
And then 'tis, I think, that no joys be above
The pleasures of love.'

Lord Rochester shook his head. 'Well, esteemed monarch, she may have made you into a full-blown fool, but she has certainly made you no poet!' He banged his tankard on the table. 'Once I wrote

126

about our King that he never said a foolish thing—well, now he has made up for it. A toast to Mistress Frances Stuart. The lady whose stubborn virtue has turned our sovereign into a lovesick halfwit!'

*   *   *

When she awoke Frances had that strange feeling of knowing something momentous had happened, but not being sure exactly what. The King! She had woken up in Lady Castlemaine's bed, with her breasts uncovered and the King staring at her like a starving man at a beefsteak. And she had responded to his touch.

She sat up, watching the motes of dust drift down in the sunlit air, and shivered. In all the time since she had come here, she had never felt so alone. She must talk to someone, ask for their help and advice on what she should do now. But who? Her mother, she suspected, would have little sympathy, and might even feel that her surrender would be in the family's interest, and Sophia was too young and impulsive. Yet now her father was here. He was, she knew, greatly under her mother's dominating influence. And yet he was a kind man. She scribbled a message and summoned a page to deliver it to Somerset House, where her father was now part of the Queen Mother's household.

Walter Stuart wasted no time in arriving not two hours later.

She ran into his open embrace. 'It is this business of the King, Father. I know not what to make of him, or indeed how to conduct myself with regard to him. His interest in me is as a woman, I know that. He pursues me and, when he sees my

127

resistance is serious, he retreats again—but only to return to the fray once more. I have tried to avoid him, yet he seeks me out and I know not truly how to conduct myself.'

Her father, tall and fair-haired as she was herself, sighed. 'I wish I were a man of wealth or property with a great house that you could go to and hide away in.' He considered a moment. 'I am sure, if you wished it, you could stay with our kinsmen the Blantyres.'

Frances sighed, imagining her life hidden away in the wilds of Scotland, a poor relation, almost an unpaid skivvy. And she whose life had not yet even begun!

'Tell me though, sweeting, are you not a whit dazzled by the King's attention, being so talked of and envied?'

Her eyes danced with frank laughter. 'I admit at first I enjoyed being singled out. The King is a charming man, after all. Yet now I am overwhelmed by it and know not what to do.'

Walter Stuart sat down beside her. 'It is said that, wonder of wonders, the King truly loves you . . .'

'Yet, Father, there is the Queen! So all he can offer is to be my paramour, and that I share him with a dozen other ladies. It is not what I desire!'

Her father studied her. 'Have you given your heart elsewhere? Is there some other you already love?'

She looked away, knowing the hopelessness of her position.

'One only, and he not long married to a woman of property.'

'Unlike you . . . Dearest girl, I am so sorry we have not been able to help you in that regard. But

128

you are now waiting on the Queen and she will give you a dowry. That was why we wished this position for you. If you stay in her service, it will be your means to a marriage of your own.'

'If anyone will take me,' Frances murmured bitterly. 'Or anyone of honour, when the King lays his claim to me.'

'We will have to hope these new fine sentiments that he feels for you offer some protection. That, or that he tires of waiting and seeks a lady who is willing!'

'If only he would.' She smiled at the strangeness of her position. 'The quandary is, it is my very resistance that makes him pursue me more.'

Her father sighed, staring out at the river below, and Frances saw that he could not help her. His life had been spent in the service of the King, and he was no more sure of how she should behave than she was.

Mall was the only one of her acquaintance who truly understood the Court, yet there had been distance between them of late.

Perhaps it was time to reconcile. After her disappointing interview with her father, Frances went to seek out Mall, still abed even at this late hour, with little Mary next to her.

Mall started guiltily as Frances sat down on the edge of the bed. As befitted a daughter of the great house of Buckingham, and a maid of honour to boot, Mall had her own apartments at Whitehall, looking onto the Pebble Court.

'Good morning, my lady.' Frances experienced a pang of guilt. Ever since she had become closer to Barbara, Mall had kept a disapproving distance.

'So, how is the Great Whore of Whitehall

treating you?' Mall glanced at Mary, but she was used to her mother's outspokenness.

'I wish I may never see her face again!'

'Aha.' Mall pulled herself up against her pillows. 'Like that, is it? How has Barbara transgressed? Let her silken veil slip, and shown she is truly a bawd touting the cream of wenches fresh from the country—and you the creamiest of them all?'

Frances choked back a sob. 'She brought the King to look at me as I slept.'

Mall laughed, not unkindly, and patted her. 'If he only looked, you are different from a thousand other ladies, great and low.'

Frances felt a strong desire to confide her own reaction to the touch as well as her response to it, but could not, owing to Mary's presence.

'Come, let us get up and leave Mary to her nurse. Truth to tell, I am fascinated. If he has not bedded you yet, the King must be breaking his habits of a lifetime. I wonder, what is your secret?'

As Mall threw open the coverings, a letter fell to the floor. Frances reached down to pick it up, but before she could Mall snatched it and hid it in her breast.

'Ah,' smiled Frances, 'so I am not the only one with secrets. Is it from a gentleman?'

Mall helped Mary down from the bed. 'Go, sweeting. Find Nurse in the next chamber.'

Mary nodded and walked off, holding carefully in her arms the book she had been looking at.

'She has a greater look of you each day.'

'Aye, yet she has my husband's hair! It blazes like a new penny.' A sudden look of sadness came into Mall's eyes. 'My husband James had it, and his three brothers. They were such fine young men,

130

so full of laughter and of bravery. Cut down, all of them, before they reached manhood. George, not yet twenty-four, the bravest of soldiers at Edgehill, and young John at Cheriton. Bernard, who fought with Prince Rupert, was killed before the King's own eyes at Rowton Heath.' She shook her head. 'So much waste. That was why my James became the Duke of Richmond, through his brothers' deaths. And now it is your Charles.' She looked suddenly at Frances. 'And yet, have you not heard the news? I think perhaps the name of Richmond can never bring with it lasting happiness.'

Frances looked back at her, bemused.

But Mall seemed not to wish to talk of it further and made a show of changing the subject.

Instead Frances asked her about the letter she was attempting to hide in her bodice. 'So, Butterfly, from whom is this secret letter?'

Mall held her arms protectively round her chest and looked away, as shy as a bride at first bedding. 'From one I should know better than to be courting. He could charm the birds from the trees, yet this old bird should be wiser than to let him.'

'Not such an old bird. Besides, you have no father or mother to say nay to your choice. Or would your brother, the Duke, do so?'

'I would pay no mind to him.'

'What matters then?'

Mall looked in the glass and twirled a curl around her finger. 'He is a young man.'

'How young? Mall, you do not snatch out of the cradle, pray? And you eight-and-thirty years!'

'Sshh, no more now. Let us go abroad where we can talk the better.' She quickly dressed and, shouting to Mary's nurse that she would be back

131

betimes, they slipped out together.

'Come,' Mall reminded her, 'since it is the Lord's Day I have ordered my coach to take us to the Queen Mother's chapel at Somerset House.'

'Why so? Why do we not make our devotions here?'

'The worshippers are more plentiful at Somerset House.'

'Why should that be of concern to us?'

'Because we desire the biggest audience to witness you taking the Sacrament.'

Frances climbed into the coach, bewildered. 'Yet why should anyone care about that?'

'My dearest child, the Comte de Grammont, who makes his living through such things, has already laid odds that His Majesty bedded you last night. If you do not take the Sacrament, all London will take it as a sign that he is right. But if you do take it— and publicly at that—they may at least cease their chatter.'

Frances shook her head in amazement. She was sure Mall had to be making far more of this than was needful.

The chapel was as full as on Christmas Day, and Frances thought they would have no chance of a pew until she spied her mother beckoning them forward to the rows reserved for the Queen Mother's ladies, which happened, to Frances' mortification, to be in the fullest possible view of the whole chapel.

She knelt and bowed her head, amazed at how many people were crowded in, since this was a Catholic church. Before the late trouble there had been masses held here from six in the morning, with the confessionals continually thronged, followed by Vespers sung by the Capuchin monks.

Cromwell's men, she knew, had put a stop to that. The Capuchins were silenced and imprisoned and the chapel desecrated, despite being owned by the Queen. Now, so many years later, its restoration was only just completed.

Frances found the familiarity of the mass comforting. Growing up in France she had been lulled by its rhythms since early childhood. Its invocations and responses were ingrained in her as deeply as a lullaby, the sound of the *Kyrie* and the *Gloria* as familiar as nursery rhymes. Even the smell of the incense and the puttering of the candles had a reassuring sense of recognition.

She almost forgot her surroundings and the strange and dangerous world in which she now found herself. And yet, was it not far better than in France? She was no longer a grudging guest, but an honoured member of the Court. She would find a way of dealing with the King's attentions. It was not so great a matter as she had made it.

The priest had made his way into the gilded pulpit and had begun the reading.

Lost in her thoughts, Frances was conscious of heads turning towards her, one gentleman even smiling strangely in her direction. And then she realized why.

The gospel reading was from Proverbs 31. 'Who can find a virtuous woman? For her price is far above rubies.'

She kept her eyes fixed doggedly on her Bible and ignored all around her.

Mall's elbow jogged her into consciousness. The Queen had already left her pew and knelt at the altar taking communion. Now it was their turn.

Frances straightened her back and walked down

the aisle in the Queen's wake until she too knelt at the altar. Those that had insisted on her virtue smiled at her fondly. And the broadest smile of all, tinged—it seemed to Frances—with a great dose of relief, belonged to her own mother.

And yet, she asked herself as she sat back in her pew, *am I truly so innocent as these people think me?*

The memory of the King's touch came back into her mind and she had to bow her head to hide the sudden rush of colour it brought to her cheeks.

And yet, surely a woman did not have to be either virgin or whore? Was there not some other way to find peace and happiness than this?

She bent her head to take the wafer. *Help me, Lord, through the perils of my situation, and as Moses opened the sea for the chosen people, show me also how I may cross these swirling flood waters to the sunlit bank beyond.*

And yet she heard no answer from the Lord and, when she turned and walked back down the aisle, she found a gaze fastened on her that was so unexpected she almost stumbled.

At the end of the third pew stood Charles, Duke of Richmond.

The sunlight filtered through the stained glass and burnished his bright hair, giving him the air of a Renaissance angel. Yet he seemed not to see her, and indeed to be oddly detached and in a world of his own, not acknowledging her presence in any way.

The thought cut through her that perhaps this was deliberate, that he also believed she had surrendered to the King, as so many others seemed to do.

Yet she must not think of him. He had a wife of his own, and a daughter too, safely stowed in

134

Cobham.

She had arrived back at the Queen's pew and fell gratefully to her knees, hiding her face in her hands so that he would not see the disappointed hopefulness that shone from her eyes. The rest of the service sped past and, by the time it was over, Charles had disappeared.

'Come,' Mall took her elbow. 'Let us find your mother.'

As they followed the congregation towards the church porch, the crowds suddenly stopped and a hush fell.

Barbara Castlemaine, gorgeously attired in midnight-blue silk, her bare shoulders clearly visible beneath an ermine wrap, strode into the chapel and made for the confessional box.

'Not before time,' murmured one courtier to another.

'I hope the priest has the morning free, for the list of *her* sins.'

In Barbara's regal wake followed a nurse and two small children.

Frances had seen both children on previous occasions, but rarely together as they were today, a small boy and a girl, holding hands. And what struck her as never before was that from their black curls to their flashing Medici eyes, they were the exact image of their father, King Charles II.

Mall followed her gaze. 'Aye,' she whispered boldly, following Frances' thoughts, ''tis true of all the King's bastards. They are their father to the living, breathing life.'

Barbara swept past them without so much as an acknowledgement.

'Good riddance,' shrugged Mall. 'Let us get

outside into the fresh air.'

Frances' heart quickened. Would he be among the throng, hoping to catch sight of her? Many had gathered to gossip and exchange greetings in the gardens outside the chapel. Some made for the stairs to catch wherries or barges up- or downriver. Frances scanned the crowd, but saw no sign of the Duke anywhere.

Her mother suddenly emerged from the crowd and, without a word of explanation, embraced Frances tightly. This was so unusual it took her aback. The look on her mother's face was all quiet congratulation, and not a little relief. Frances raised an eyebrow at Mall. Her mother had discerned, like the rest of the congregation, that the prize was still intact.

To keep her temper, Frances broke away. They would be going to the Great Hall to break their fast, since none could eat before taking the Sacrament.

Although she felt almost faint with hunger, Frances could bear no more of her mother's glowing looks. 'I wish for a little air. I will follow after.'

Her mother shivered. 'But it is cold and you must be famished, Child.'

'I have had spiritual sustenance enough,' Frances replied, avoiding the ironic look Mall was casting at her, and knowing she would smile if she looked in her direction.

Yet when they had left, Frances did not turn her steps southwards towards the fountained gardens, but northwards, across a courtyard and beneath a brick-covered walkway that led through the gatehouse onto the busy and bustling Strand.

A row of shops stretched westwards and eastwards here, all owned by the Queen Mother as part of the dowry she had brought to King Charles I.

Frances gazed towards the Maypole, but found not what she sought. On the far side of the Strand a maze of narrow courts and alleys unfolded. Avoiding the hackney coaches waiting at the stand there, she dodged through the horses and stood for a moment, holding up her dress.

Why was she doing this, when her gown would be mired and her favourite shoes, with their red silken roses, ruined also?

And then she caught sight of him and halted.

He had just given a shilling to a beggar girl, who was cradling a baby in her arms.

'Thank you, master,' said the girl, her pinched and dirty face lit by a sudden grin. She seemed little more than a child herself. 'I can eat now, sir, and the baby 'n' all.' The girl weighed him up for a moment. 'Here, sir, would you hold her while I put this shillin' in me shoe?' She smiled engagingly. 'Only you can't trust nobody these days, can you, my lord?'

Frances almost laughed at how he would react. Gentlemen did not hold babies, especially those belonging to beggar girls.

To her astonishment, he took the baby and held it tightly, placing a hand under the child's small head and smiling tenderly at it.

'How old is she?'

'Six months, sir.'

'Six months,' he repeated, sighing. Then, on a whim, he reached into his pocket again. 'Here, take a golden angel for her.'

'An angel, sir?' The girl looked at the golden

coin as if it might be red-hot and burn her small and dirty hand. She reached up suddenly and kissed his cheek. 'The Lord love you, sir.' She tucked the coin into her other shoe. 'Shall I take her now, sir?' she asked, shy now and yet eager to make off with her good fortune before the gentleman changed his mind, or the great hand of authority came down on her shoulder and announced that it was all a mistake.

Charles looked up and saw Frances. To her astonishment she saw tears were coursing down his handsome face.

He quickly handed the baby back.

'She liked you, sir. Thank you and good luck to you.' The beggar girl scurried off down a narrow alley and was soon gone from sight.

For a beat of time they stood across the busy roadway from each other, eyes locked, saying nothing.

'Master Stuart,' Frances produced finally. 'I mean Your Grace. How do you?'

'Call me not Your Grace. I never expected the honour and find it mighty strange. I am well enough, I suppose.'

She saw now that his somewhat boyish looks were haggard, as if he had weathered some great storm and feared that he would not see the shore again.

'Are you, sir? Forgive me, yet you seem a little changed since last we met.'

'Aye. Is it so marked upon my features then?' He looked away. 'My wife Elizabeth died of the childbed fever a month past, and our sweet daughter followed her.'

Frances gasped. This must be what Mall had meant when she talked of the curse of the name of Richmond!

138

She reached out a hand in quick sympathy. 'I did not know. I am sorry indeed to hear of your misfortune.'

Charles Stuart, so gay and teasing when they had last met, shrugged weary shoulders. 'Yes. Despite my great good luck in becoming the Duke of Richmond, I did not think God had smiled upon me. Indeed, I fell into some desperation.'

'As well you might, at such a cruel blow—your wife and child torn so cruelly from you.' She moved closer, and as she did caught a pungent aroma of brandy.

Without meaning to, she wrinkled her nose in surprise.

'Aye,' he nodded, his voice hard and bitter, 'I found my consolation in strong waters. Are you shocked? Do you see me beyond the pale of redemption?' Before she could answer, he continued. 'Yet you are raised high indeed.' The hurt and bitterness rang out like a chisel on cold stone. 'At Court everyone talks of La Belle Stuart and how the King loves her as he has never loved another woman, and this time with his heart as well as his—' He broke off.

'Indeed, sir,' Frances replied, hurt at his savage tone, 'you should not listen to Court gossip. Today it says the King loves me, and tomorrow it will tell you he loves another lady.'

'Yet I even witnessed Lord Rochester, who knows His Majesty as a close friend, announce that he had never seen the King so in love as he is with Mistress Stuart. My lord Rochester proclaimed that he had not thought the King knew what love was, until he met the fair Frances.'

'You forget. The King has a wife, sir. And I have

139

no thought of being a mistress.'

'Then I can find it in my heart to feel sorry for the King.' Charles produced a slow and painful smile. 'For I have also known what it is to love with no hope of winning the beloved.'

The expression in his eyes cut through to her soul so that she had to look away.

'Mistress Stuart! Frances! There you are.' Any questions she might ask herself about his meaning were cut short by the arrival of Cary Frazier, as usual the very picture of fashion, despite having to walk across the muddy cobbles of the Strand to seek her out. 'I have hunted all over the Court, your chamber, the Queen's Apartments—aye, even the gardens and stables,' she said breathlessly, the chill air bringing colour to the pale make-up of her cheeks. And then, as if bestowing an award: 'The King requests your presence in his Closet.'

The Duke's eyes locked on hers in bleak acknowledgement of their discussion. 'You see the problem, Mistress Stuart.'

'Come, Frances, you cannot keep the King waiting.' Cary took her arm. 'It is a rare honour. Few indeed are bidden to his Closet.'

'King Charles is no tyrant. As I understand it, he does not command his subjects' presence on pain of death or being confined to the Tower. I may refuse, I think.'

Cary looked at Frances in astonishment, as if she had taken leave of her senses. 'He wants you to come because he has some great surprise to show you, which he thought would give you pleasure.'

'Mistress Stuart,' the Duke bowed, his grey eyes mocking, 'go to your monarch. Do not deprive him of the pleasure he promises, on my account.' He

140

turned abruptly away and the last she saw of him was as he pushed open the door of the Crown and Anchor tavern.

'What a churlish young man!' whispered Cary under her breath. 'And did you not think he smelled of the alehouse already?'

'And so might you, if you had lost your bride and your babe also,' Frances shouted over her shoulder as she walked back fast through the carriages of the busy Strand. 'In our gilded cage we are kept from such things, yet believe me, they exist. A dram or two of brandy might at least be a small consolation.'

Cary Frazier's eyebrows looked as if they might ascend from her face like spiders up their web, at this strange reaction from the usually calm Frances. She glanced after the Duke, wondering if there was some mystery here.

A carriage stood hard by to take them back to Whitehall Palace. Away from the bustle of the busy Strand, open fields unfolded to the north and they passed the green spaces of Horse Guards Parade and in front of it the newly dug canal in St James' Park in which cattle grazed, ankle-deep, drinking their fill, as if it were some deep rural scene.

'So, Cary, know you what manner of surprise awaits me in His Majesty's Closet?' Cary shook her head. 'I have never been there. I know they call it his Cabinet-Closet and it is where he keeps all his curious collections and scientific instruments. It is strictly private, and very few are allowed in, so you are mightily honoured.'

As they passed through the Holbein Gate with its four octagonal towers Frances stared out at the busts, roses, portcullises and coats of arms set into the walls, together with great life-sized medallions of Henry VII and Henry VIII that gazed down upon her, and felt increasingly nervous.

The famous Mr Chiffinch stood at the back stairs and handed her down from the coach.

'His Majesty is waiting for you, mistress. Be good enough to follow me.'

The whole Court knew about Mr Chiffinch and his wife, and how they selected women from high and low who might catch the King's fancy, if only for a night. Barbara had once castigated their taste for the obvious and the common. 'If she is chosen by Chiffinch, she will be either hoyden or harlot. They know nothing of wit or charm.'

He was also known for his prodigious drinking. It was rumoured that he acted as Charles' spymaster, inviting courtiers to his lodgings and plying them with strong waters—occasionally spiked with the celebrated King's Drops—which loosened their tongues so that they gave away all their secrets, and those of their neighbours also.

Chiffinch bowed low, his narrow eyes scanning Frances as if she needed to face some secret test of his own devising.

Sensing his scrutiny, she stood upright and looked him in the eye.

'You are passing tall, mistress,' was all he commented.

She almost confessed that her sister called her the Giantess of Bermondsey, but stopped herself in time. Such ineptitude would confirm those who called her naive and childish.

Instead she replied coolly, 'And proud of it. I find it makes me the less taken advantage of.'

'Indeed?' he replied and she thought she detected the ghost of a smile.

On the way to the Cabinet-Closet they passed up the back stairs and down several passageways until they came into the King's Bedchamber.

Frances gazed around her at the marble flooring and vast chimneypiece in black and white marble, at the beautiful furniture in solid oak and gleaming walnut decorated with elaborate designs of fruit and flowers; at the day-bed supported by Grecian figures; and everywhere the ticking of clocks. She could count seven at least all chiming the hour, yet none at the same instant.

Although she tried to fix her attention on the clocks and other objects of interest she found her gaze irresistibly drawn to the railed-off alcove where the King's great bed lay, with two flying boys holding back the heavy curtains that separated it from the rest of the chamber and above it, at the very top, two great gilded eagles.

Mr Chiffinch followed her gaze. 'His Majesty modelled it after King Henri IV's bed in the Louvre Palace.' He smiled to himself. 'Though they do say ours gets the greater use.'

Frances ignored the implication of his words and kept her eyes on the painted ceiling panel above it, depicting Providence rescuing the King from the famous oak tree after the battle of Worcester.

'His Majesty awaits you in here.' He pointed to a further closed door with so knowing a smile that Frances imagined the King behind it, wearing naught but his brocade dressing gown and laid upon a couch waiting for her. And after her own response to his touch, how could she stand by her claims of innocence?

She took a deep breath and pushed open the door.

143

Chapter 7

The scene that awaited her could not have been further from that of her imagination.

Far from lying déshabillé on a day-bed, the King was dressed in his usual fine clothes of black velvet laced with gold and silver, and over these he wore a canvas apron like that of a carpenter or some other artisan, and on his left hand was perched a bird.

He laughed at her expression, shrewdly guessing some of the thoughts that had been going through her mind. 'Poor Belle, for that is what I hear my lady Castlemaine has taken to calling you. Did you expect the Beast waiting to defile your innocence?' He laughed, yet there was tenderness in it. 'My dear, I am neither Beast nor Bluebeard. Come in.' He turned to a man standing next to him, of middle years, who sported a grey periwig. 'Progers, give the bird to Mistress Stuart to hold.'

Still astonished, Frances held out her arm.

Instead of hopping onto the hand Mr Progers had offered, the bird flew straight to Frances.

'See what taste he has, Progers!'

Progers smiled gently, instantly understanding the role he was being cast to play, defusing some hidden tension between Frances and the King.

'Indeed he has, Majesty.'

'Mr Progers is my Groom of the Bedchamber, Belle. And also assistant in divers of my experiments.'

She glanced round at the piles of papers covered in numbers, the diagrams pinned to the wall, an oil painting of the dissection of a dog, plus countless

144

instruments, which she assumed had some scientific purpose. His Majesty's passion for the sciences was common knowledge.

'Yet this bird beats all. I have only had him a day and he has learned to whistle better than Progers here.' Mr Progers smiled gently, content to be the butt of the King's jokes. 'Listen, he can already imitate the ticking of a clock.'

The bird obligingly ticked.

'And he can strike the hour also!'

Head cocked to one side, the bird struck ten o'clock.

'He can imitate the bellman . . .'

The sound of a handbell rang out through the room and after it the bellman's voice, as if he had been standing there next to them: 'Twelve of the clock, masters, and a fine cold moonshine night.'

'Is that not the Eighth Wonder of the World, Belle?' asked the King delightedly, as if nothing— not the gift of princes, nor a hoard of gold—could give him greater pleasure. 'Best of all, he has learned a song I have taught him to sing to you.' He took the bird onto his own hand. 'Come now, Bird, do your best for Belle.'

The bird fixed Frances with his beady yellow eye, as if he well understood his role in courting and entertaining her, and began to sing.

'Early one morning,
Just as the sun was rising,
I heard a maiden singing,
In the valley below.

Oh, don't deceive me,
Oh, never leave me,

145

How could you use
A poor maiden so?'

Frances clapped her hands and laughed. 'He truly is a divine minstrel. And yet, why is it, Your Majesty, that in songs maidens must always be deceived and forsaken?'

The King looked at her intently.

'Sometimes it can be the man who is deceived and forsaken.'

Frances looked quickly away.

'Shall I take the bird again, sire?' asked Mr Progers.

'Give him seeds. He has earned his reward.'

Eager to divert the King, Frances turned to the equipment laid out on a table. 'What experiments are you conducting at the moment, Majesty?'

Charles smiled sadly. 'How to keep a broken heart beating.'

He reached out and took her by the wrist, while Progers disappeared discreetly with the bird.

'It is an experiment you could help me with, fair Frances.'

She felt the warmth of his breath on her neck as he leaned downwards, and then his mouth was on hers.

After a moment he looked down at her, his black eyes scanning hers. 'Are you truly as cold as you wish to appear? I know I felt the tremble of true passion awake in you the other night.'

Frances looked him in the eye. She did not understand what had governed her response, yet she knew one thing: at the Duke of Richmond's hungry look, she had felt an answering stirring. With the King her response had been without

146

emotion, as when you shiver at the cold. But how could she tell him that? She broke away in genuine confusion. 'Majesty, I must go. I have many duties to perform.'

'To my wife the Queen? Whose presence you so often like to remind me of? Go, then.'

After she had left, the King summoned Progers.

'Ask Mall—the Lady Mary—to come to me, if you would. I will await her presence here.'

He turned back to his experiments. But Progers could see that his heart was not in them.

*   *   *

Mall had been readying herself to go hawking with the Queen when Progers discovered her, and the peremptory summons to the King's presence raised curious eyebrows among the other ladies.

'I wonder what His Majesty wants with Mall so urgently?' commented Catherine Boynton in a low voice.

'As if we did not know,' smirked Cary Frazier, pulling the stiff damask of her gown a little lower to expose another inch of bosom. 'The chaste Diana still eludes the hunter's arrow. Let us hope he soon bores of the pursuit.'

Mall followed Progers' upright back, her mind racing.

She also guessed the object of her summons, yet was unsure how to answer it.

'My dearest Butterfly!' Charles greeted her with a ready smile. 'How does your little Mary?' Charles loved children and always remembered their names.

'Well, Majesty. She grows apace and looks more

147

like her brother Esme every day.'

His face clouded in sympathy. 'Aye, that was a terrible loss. The smallpox, of all the distempers, is the cruellest. I still recall the grace and laughter of my brother Henry, and sister Mary also. They say her son William has never recovered from the loss of his mother.' He took Mall's hands in his. 'Yet we must have our gladnesses also in this vale of tears. Mall—Butterfly—I am distraught. I am indeed like a butterfly caught in a net that bats its wings ever wilder and wilder until it is released or dies.'

Mall bit her lip. 'And what can I do to help release you, Majesty?'

'Help me to win her. Mall, I must have her.'

Mall had never heard such ardour in his voice since he was an eager young man, on whom life had not yet written either suffering or disillusion.

'She is the sun in spring, the breeze that ripens corn—only she can renew me and lift me from the melancholy that settles upon me like a freezing fog.'

'She is just a young maid, not this goddess you believe her to be.' Mall sighed. Despite his protestations of love, Mall knew Charles well enough. It was indeed Frances' resistance that fanned the fire. When he came to know the real girl, and understand her determined practical nature and her dislike of Court life, he would soon tire. And at what cost to her?

Besides, Mall mused, she loved Frances herself as much as if she were her daughter or sister. She had seen the hurt Frances felt at being used, and the rift it had almost caused between them, and knew she could not do it.

'If it were any other you asked me to win for

148

you, I would gladly help. Yet I would surrender my most precious pearls or diamonds, or even my good name or position at Court, rather than betray Frances.'

'Is being worshipped by a king so great a betrayal then?' Anger sharpened into bitterness in his voice. 'Some might call it an honour.'

'It is not what she desires,' flashed Mall, knowing how great a risk she ran in trying to be honest. 'She is not like Lady Castlemaine, sire. Wealth and advancement are of no great import to her.'

'Then what is it she yearns for?'

'A home of her own. A husband, fireside, babes . . .'

Charles cracked with bitter laughter. 'And she cannot lead so blameless a life with such as I.'

'You are the King, sire. And there is the question of the Queen.'

'Indeed.' He turned from her and began angrily to wind one of his clocks.

'And who does she see sitting across the fireside, in this dream of domesticity?'

Mall hesitated. She thought she could read Frances' heart.

'Who? Tell me!'

'It seems to me she has conceived a tenderness for the Duke of Richmond, sire.'

'My cousin Charles Stuart? That sot! How could she prefer him to me? He only has his title through your misfortune and the noble acts of his brothers. Besides,' it struck the King forcibly, 'has he not a wife also?'

'I believe she died in childbed, sire. His babe followed.'

'And this touches the tender heart of Mistress

Stuart! Aye, and blinds her to his faults of being a drinker and a wastrel.' He seemed to come to a decision. 'Summon her back here. Now!'

With great misgivings Mall instructed the Page of the Backstairs to discover Mistress Stuart and bring her to them.

After a short time Frances arrived, a pale look on her lovely face, her grey eyes full of questioning.

'I forbid you,' almost shouted the King, whirling round. 'I forbid you to lower yourself to the level of my cousin the Duke of Richmond!'

Frances' eyes flashed in anger and fixed accusingly on Mall.

'Whether you accept my suit or not, you will undertake to see my cousin Charles Stuart no more. He is not worthy of you, and never could be.'

Frances turned her head away. 'Is that all you require of me, Majesty?'

'You know it is not!' He caught her wrist and held it until it hurt. 'I desire your love. I desire that your eyes light up with tenderness when I walk into a chamber. That you run towards me and embrace me so that a sliver of gold leaf could not be pressed between us.'

Frances turned away. His definition of love moved her—it was one she could almost have drawn up herself. The agony was that she could not feel it for him. 'I left the Queen playing Basset, Majesty, and promised I would return to finish the hand.'

'Blast Basset to hellfire! Go, then.' His voice was grey and thick like some decaying, dead thing.

Frances walked slow and proud from the chamber. She wanted to reach out a hand to him, but knew it would only confuse all things further.

Once outside the King's Bedchamber, she ran past the surprised Chiffinches, their mouths 'O's of astonishment, like the two little birds their name conjured up.

Yet she did not find the Queen, to play at Basset as she had promised. Despite the King's prohibition, she ran instead to the set of apartments next to the Bowling Green that belonged to the Duke of Richmond. Being careful that none of the King's cronies were playing bowls, she slipped through the Orangery and knocked on the front door. The young servant woman who admitted her said that the Duke was in his closet reading. She was a girl about the same age as Frances herself, with a lively eye and cheeks like russet apples.

'I shouldn't say this to you, but you're the only one that's come near him. I hope you can cheer him up, mistress. First his lady wife and then, in the wink of an eye, the babe also. He doted upon that babe. I've never seen a man who loved his child so. I said to Cook at Cobham a dozen times, "If ever I find a husband, may he love our child the way the Duke loves his little daughter." To think they've both gone to their Maker.' The girl shook her head sadly. 'We tried to get his sister to come and lift his spirits, but she has troubles of her own, it seems. And the Devil's been leading him by the hand to find consolation where he shouldn't, if you get my meaning.'

The Duke was sitting in a high-backed oak chair, with a volume of poetry in his hand and a tumbler of brandy at his side.

He looked at Frances as if she might be some figment of his imagination.

Frances exchanged a telling look with the servant

151

girl.

'Mistress Stuart!' He got clumsily to his feet, dropping the poetry book, which she saw was a calf-bound volume of Shakespeare's sonnets. 'I did not expect you here.'

'I hoped you might offer something warming. It is cold enough outside to delight the Ambassador of Muscovy. Some tea perhaps? The Queen has made the brew quite fashionable.' Without a word she picked up the brandy glass and handed it to the servant girl, who briskly removed it.

'I'll bring it directly, mistress.' The girl looked relieved that Frances had said nothing of her disclosure.

'I wished simply to convey my sorrow and sympathy at your recent loss.'

She was startled to hear a sob escape him.

'She was just eighteen, my poor Elizabeth. The gentlest girl, quiet as a little mouse, yet with the kindest nature. Strange, I did not wish for the match.' He glanced at her with swift intensity. 'Indeed, I had my reasons for opposing it. Yet my Uncle Ludovic arranged all, and laid it down as my bounden duty to my family. Yet I would never have wished such a thing as this. And little Isabella so soon after.' He looked away, his face haggard. 'They said it was the putrid fever. Five days!' She heard the catch in his voice and wished she could comfort him. 'From the first shivering fit to being laid in her coffin, it was but five days.'

'I am truly sorry for your loss.' She laid a hand on his arm for the shortest of moments and his anguished eyes locked on hers.

'I should not have sent the horse to you.'

'It was an act of kindness, surely?'

152

'Not kindness, no. I have asked myself,' his voice dropped so that she could barely hear it, 'if I was being punished for that one rash act, and it was Elizabeth and Isabella who paid the price.'

Frances shook her head. 'I am sure God acts not in such vengeful ways. Besides, you overstate the greatness of the sin.'

'How can you know how great the sin truly was?'

'If it were so, then I too played a part in it.'

They stood silently regarding each other, and it seemed to Frances as if time stopped—the clocks no longer ticking, the sounds of the busy Court unheard. She knew not if it was guilt or anger that made her wish to cry out against the world they both inhabited, where life was marked out by family and duty, and they could neither of them speak of what they truly felt.

They hardly heard the knock on the door, and it was only when the maid, anxious now, bustled in leading a tall, thin man with short grey hair and pale eyes that nailed you to the spot, that they took in their surroundings.

'Uncle Ludovic!' The Duke shook his head as if dream was turning into nightmare. 'I did not expect your presence.'

'Clearly not.' His hawklike gaze switched from one to the other as if they were wicked children, instead of a young man of twenty and a girl who was old enough to command the love of a king. 'Yet it is as well I came, I think. With your wife hardly cold in her grave, it is hardly fitting to receive Mistress Stuart here alone. And do you forget we are bidden by Lord St Albans to dine with him tonight? I see you are not dressed and ready.'

The Duke bowed to Frances. 'Thank you for the

153

kindness of your sympathy, Mistress Stuart. I regret that I had forgotten this engagement.'

'I must leave also. I hope your grief will lessen as time passes. I will pray for you, and for your wife and babe also.'

The Duke thanked her and withdrew to change his apparel.

Frances was about to ask for the maid to be summoned so that she could leave, when she found the Seigneur d'Aubigny's uncomfortable gaze upon her again.

'Mistress Stuart, what was the meaning of this visit? To come here alone without even a chaperone is the behaviour of a loose woman, not one whose innocence is trumpeted throughout Whitehall!' His tone dropped to a threatening whisper. 'Perhaps reports of your innocence have been exaggerated?'

'I came to offer my condolences,' Frances replied frostily, refusing to be cowed.

'Yet do you not see, mistress, that you can only cause my nephew pain? After the scandal of his parents, Charles knows it falls to him to redeem the family honour. Do you not see that to give love, where family duty decrees another course, is not a possibility? It matters not if he has long admired you—he is in no position to court a young woman who has no wealth or property, and whose father is a mere Court physician. My nephew has a position, a title, a great house and a hundred servants to support. Do you think he can just please himself in his choice of wife?' He stepped closer to her, so that she could feel almost physically the waves of his disapproval.

'Seigneur d'Aubigny, you mistake me. I came

154

simply to offer my sympathy and condolences.'

'Indeed?' The question sizzled with suspicion. 'Do you think, mistress, that what my nephew needs now is sympathy, a mere month after the death of his young wife, from one who can offer him nothing, and who is the chief object of desire of the King and therefore in a position to do him actual harm by her concern for him?'

Frances longed to slap the man for his proud, cold disapproval, to shout that he had misunderstood her motives entirely.

Yet had he?

She straightened her back and looked at him, eye to eye.

'For his sake, I will leave then. He has my sympathy that, apart from his sister, you are his only relative.'

'And intend to remain so.'

She turned, furious that this bitter, narrow man was accusing her of damaging the Duke's interests, merely by visiting him.

Damn the man to hell! It might not be ladylike or Christian, yet it was precisely what she felt about Ludovic Stuart, 10th Lord Aubigny.

As she turned to leave she glanced above the fireplace, where two large portraits caught her eye. The first was of a beautiful young woman with russet hair, dressed in amber satin, holding a coronet of flowers and gazing out with a serene, optimistic air. Next to it was a young man in his early twenties with haunting, slightly mournful brown eyes.

Beneath the portrait was an inscription in Latin. For the first time Frances envied her brother Walter his long hours with his classical tutor.

'It means "Love Is Stronger than I Am",' Ludovic Stuart informed her. 'George Stuart and Katherine Howard paid a heavy price for their forbidden love, and I am not about to watch their son make the same stupid mistake.'

Frances took her leave, trying to hold on to the shreds of her dignity. She ought to go and find out if she had any duties with the Queen, yet she could no more prevent herself running to look for Mall than a fly can stay out of treacle.

Eventually she found her in the Queen's Closet, helping Lady Charlotte, Keeper of the Queen's Sweet Coffers, place rose petals amongst Catherine's fresh white linen, which had been drying in the kitchens on account of the cold weather.

As soon as Lady Charlotte left to seek more petals, Frances seized Mall's hands. 'Tell me, I must know. What was the scandal concerning the Duke of Richmond's parents?'

'It was a sad tale, as I recall. They fell in love and married against their parents' wishes, much to the anger of King Charles, who was his guardian. Then George Stuart died a hero at the battle of Edgehill, leaving his wife with two small children and not a penny to live on. Her family never forgave her and she had to eke out a life abroad.'

'How could her family do such a wicked thing?'

Mall regarded her evenly. 'Families can be cruel when it comes to issues of marriage and succession. They were supposed to marry other people and they refused to, out of love. It was considered a great sin and all condemned them.'

'So that is why the inscription says "Love Is Stronger than I Am".'

156

'Frances,' Mall interrogated finally, 'why do you wish to know this? If you still have a tenderness for the Duke, after what the King has said, I advise you to let it go. For both your sakes.' She took hold of Frances' hand. 'See, it will soon be Yuletide, and the Court plans many wonderful delights. There will be much to distract you, believe me.'

Mall's words turned out to be no less than the truth. There were Christmas masques and mummers' plays, entertainments in Lincoln's Inn, stilt-walkers in the Strand, and wassailing in the King's orchards to encourage a bumper crop of next year's apples.

*   *   *

In January the weather was suddenly hot enough for June.

It was so strange and unexpected that the parliament ordered people to keep a fast-day and pray for a return of seasonable weather, lest it meant a plague would come, or at the least a sick summer.

Valentine's Day came and went.

'Thank God for a clear frosty day at last,' Mall breathed, when at last the heat abated, bringing with it the start of Lent.

She bought Frances a small box wrought in pewter, called a poor box, and abjured her every time she thought about the Duke to put in a forfeit for the indigent and needy.

On Ash Wednesday Frances had to smile in the chapel at Whitehall when the famous Scots preacher Dr Creeton decreed, to the astonishment and outrage of all, that it was incontinent during

157

Lent even to sleep with your wife. She couldn't help glancing at the King and wondering if this meant that he should also abjure the bed of his mistress. But the King was paying so little attention that he was fast asleep and snoring.

The end of Lent was in sight at last and Frances, realizing there were now far fewer forfeits in her poor box, thought she might be recovering at last, when Sophia burst into her chamber, big with news, their father a few steps behind her.

'Frances,' she exclaimed with the casual cruelty that only sisters are capable of, 'I have just heard the news. The Duke of Richmond is to marry again. To one Margaret Banaster of Boarstall, who brings him five thousand pounds a year—and a stepdaughter almost as old as you are! They are to be married at Cobham, now that Lent is over. I heard our mother say it was a good thing too, and she hoped the lady would keep him on a short leash, far away from the Palace of Whitehall. Do you think that is because of you?'

Frances bit her lip, hoping to draw blood, so that at least there might be some outward release of her inner turmoil. The Duke of Richmond would be doing exactly what his uncle demanded of him. Yet she could not help but hate him for it. She turned to find her father's eyes upon her, soft with sympathy.

As soon as they left her alone, the parrot, which had been silent of late, echoing her own mood, looked up, his beady eye apparently bursting with avian wisdom.

'Shall I tell him of my feelings?' Frances demanded. 'That love is stronger than me, too? That I understand why his parents risked all, despite what their destiny decreed?'

The parrot considered her for long moment. 'Confess and be hanged!' it finally announced.

Frances smiled to herself. This was the saying the King had taught to his bride Catherine, before she knew any English, and had laughed merrily when she finally repeated it.

'Confess and be hanged it is!' She would go now and tell the Duke all.

She grabbed her cloak from its hook and changed quickly into her riding habit. She paused an instant, wondering if the King himself had had a hand in this proposed marriage. Whether he had or not, for Frances—alone and unescorted—to throw herself on the Duke's mercy, in frank challenge to the King's prohibition, was dangerous indeed. Thankfully, in her coffer she found the vizard she had borrowed from Cary Frazier on some jaunt together, which would hide her face from prying eyes.

She ran down to the Pebble Court and requested that the filly be brought from its stable.

She was about to climb into the saddle when it struck her that she did not precisely know in which direction Cobham lay. Trying to sound more confident than she felt, she enquired of the Master of the Stranger's Horse.

'Cobham, mistress?' He tugged his beard thoughtfully. 'That depends on whether you mean Cobham in the county of Surrey or Cobham in Kent.'

It had never occurred to Frances that there might be two Cobhams. She tried to think of any clue that Mall might have let drop. She seemed to remember some story of a river trip. 'I think perhaps you journey there by water,' she offered.

'That'll be Cobham in Kent, mistress.' He glanced at her mare dubiously. 'It's a long way for one young horse, though. You'd best be taking a wherry to the Bridge, then going by water to Gravesend and hailing a hackney for the last stage.'

Was he just making the journey sound more daunting than it was, out of disapproval? And yet riding alone to Cobham, when she hardly knew the way, seemed foolhardy in the extreme. 'Thank you for your help. I will do as you advise. Could you ask for my horse to be stabled again?'

'With pleasure, mistress.'

He watched her as she made her way towards the Whitehall Stairs. If he wasn't much mistaken, she was the King's latest lady friend.

He wondered where she was going, and in such a hurry, and whether he ought to mention it to anyone in the Palace.

Frances pulled her cloak tightly round her, taken aback at her own sense of daring. Not only was it highly unusual for a young woman to journey out alone, but she was engaged on a venture that had been expressly forbidden by the monarch himself.

As the wind whipped her hair into tendrils, she gazed out across the busy Thames. London Bridge was still the only crossing other than by water, and as usual it teemed with activity, crowded with hawkers and tradespeople of every type. Although she might have been tempted by the haberdashers, lace-sellers and milliners on another occasion, today she walked under the bridge, fascinated by the racing water that tumbled and churned beneath its arches with the tide, and boarded a tilt-boat bound for Gravesend and Tilbury.

This end of the river was even busier, especially

downriver from the Pool of London, where all the deep-water ships laid to and landed their cargoes, to pay their duties at the Customs House. Here was the beating heart of Britain's trade: sea-coal from Newcastle; spices and sugar from Guinea and the Indies; tobacco from the Colonies; furs from Muscovy. And, in exchange, fine British cloth, especially the famous soft new draperies that had overtaken the scratchy heavy wool, as well as dyes, linens, calicoes, timber and silks. Everywhere were the shouts of merchant seamen giving and getting orders, the slap of ropes in the wind and the clanging of ships' bells. Frances sniffed the air, which was heavy with pungent aromas. There was cumin and ginger, clove and cinnamon, strong enough almost to spice a sack posset.

The boatman pushed off from the bank and they began to slip downriver. The tide was with them and they quickly left behind the mayhem of the quays and the Customs House. Soon all was wide and green and silent, with only a few small cottages on either side and the occasional church spire, half-buried in verdant water meadows. Now and then a cow wandered to the edge and stared at them, as if they were visitors from a far-off land. Everywhere wild flowers were beginning to bloom, harebell and wood anemone, tiny scarlet pimpernel, early purple orchids, almost bridal in their extravagance.

In some strange way it seemed that the green landscape waited for her. She could breathe here, away from the heat and the intrigues, where each person wanted something and thought nothing of using each other to get it, and where the straightforward was seen as simple, to be mocked and laughed at.

Neither the waterman nor any of his customers disturbed her excited thoughts. Their honest faces seemed not to be looking at her and wondering what so fine a lady was doing, alone and unaccompanied. They nodded and smiled, and when the craft drew into Gravesend, the boatman helped her out and wished her well. From the quay she hailed a hackney coach and the driver nodded respectfully when she asked for Cobham Hall.

They trotted the last few miles between deep hedgerows full of songbirds.

'How far now?' she asked the coachman.

'Not long, mistress. Not long now.'

It was only when they turned off the turnpike and headed down the sweeping carriageway, with the house almost in sight, that she truly began to lose her confidence. What was she doing here, and what did she expect from Charles Stuart? Even if she was right and he had feelings for her, how could she expect him to fly in the face of all that was anticipated of him?

If she had been on horseback she would have turned home, and indeed was almost ready to ask the coachman to do so, when the house came into view. It stood, proud and clear, imprinted against the pale blue of the afternoon sky. Cobham Hall was built of tawny brick, mellowed by the years, with two turreted towers at the end of each wing, and a rambling manor house in the centre.

Yet it was not the imposing grandeur of the house, or its forest of tall Elizabethan chimneys, or the beauty of the scrolled stonework that adorned each doorway that caused Frances' heart to still in astonishment.

Cobham Hall, to the very last detail, was

the self-same house that she had drawn in her commonplace book, time after time, ever since she was a small child, in countless sketches and paintings. She had not known that such a house existed, and yet here it was in front of her.

If she had needed a sign that she was right to come today, surely this was it?

Already, seeing her approach, the great front door was opening and the young servant girl whom she had met in London, now dressed formally in black with a white canvas pinafore, awaited her arrival.

Summoning her dignity, Frances climbed down from the hackney coach.

'Good afternoon, my lady.' The girl dropped a polite curtsey.

'Good afternoon to you also. Is your master within? If so, can you inform him that Mistress Frances Stuart desires a word with him?'

The maidservant wrung her hands in some distress. 'He is not at home, mistress.' And then, seeing Frances' dejected response, she added, 'He may be back later, perhaps. He has gone to the carrier to make sure the new mistress' furniture has arrived safely from Boarstall.'

For an instant Frances' heart stalled. 'The new mistress. Is he married already then?' Frances felt her stomach lurch as if she had been kicked hard.

'Aye, my lady. They wed two days past. It would have been sooner, but marriages are banned in Lent and the lady had some business with the disentangling of her late husband's estate, which was as snarled up as my mother's wool when the cat's had it, it seems.' The girl noticed how pale Frances seemed, and that she leaned on the lintel for support as if she might sway or fall. 'Between you and me, mistress, all this is his uncle's doing. I heard them exchange such words three days past! It was like a fight for entry to the gates of heaven—or hell.'

She looked anxious. She was of an age with Frances, and had sensed at their last meeting some hint of romance and excitement about her visit, which strongly appealed to the girl. Now she was even surer of it.

'Sorry, my lady, can we offer you a cup of tea at least? His Grace has it sent special from London.'

Frances shook her head, her palms sweating, desperate now to make her escape, but remembering that she had stupidly sent the hackney coach away.

'Know you how I might command a horse or coach back to Gravesend with all speed?' she enquired.

''Tis not far. Let us see if there is one in the stables that you might have the use of. The groom can bring it back later.'

The girl led Frances round the side of the house, towards a neat block with six or seven half-doors, over which a row of horses gazed calmly back at them as if they possessed all the wisdom of the universe.

Yet before they had time to find a groom, they heard the sound of hoofbeats and, to Frances' great consternation, Charles Stuart, 3rd Duke of Richmond and 6th of Lennox, thundered into sight, the steam from his horse's flanks rising into the pure, clear Easter air.

An expression of immediate delight, followed by confusion, clouded his features. 'Frances! Mistress

164

Stuart! What do you here at Cobham?'

Frances shot a look at the maidservant, whose fascinated eyes strayed from one to the other, grateful that her master did not seem angry.

'Susan, you may return to your duties. Thank you for welcoming Mistress Stuart in my absence.'

The girl dropped a curtsey. 'And when will the new mistress be arriving, Your Grace?'

'Shortly—is all prepared?'

He turned again to Frances, who was wondering if she could invent some story to cover her embarrassment.

But before she had time to speak he took her hands in his, and she felt the powerful pressure of his touch on her skin. 'Frances, tell me truly, what brings you here today?'

'I heard you were to marry once more and wished to make sure it was what you truly wanted.'

He looked suddenly exhausted, as if at the end of a lengthy fight. 'Are we ever permitted on this earth to do what we truly want?'

Before she could stop herself, Frances blurted out, 'Your own mother and father did, did they not follow their hearts' desire?'

'And lived hidden away from their families until my father died at Edgehill, aged twenty-four, and left my mother to bring up my sister and myself in the direst poverty.'

'There are worse things than poverty.'

'Hunger? Cold? Wondering where the next meal is coming from, and whether your own family will ever acknowledge you again?'

'And with your new wife, you will suffer none of these indignities?'

His grey eyes clouded like a storm at sea. 'If

165

I could choose to do what I truly wish, it would not be to marry Mistress Margaret Banaster, but another altogether.' He held her gaze for a long moment, before looking away towards the fields and farms that surrounded the manor. 'And now,' the bitterness in his tone was sharp as a knife, 'I have a wife and stepchild who arrive this very afternoon.'

Frances saw with relief that a horse was being led from the stables and she climbed the mounting block. 'Goodbye, Your Grace. I wish you well in your new estate.'

She pulled the horse's bridle so that it turned away from Cobham Hall—the place she had recognized with her own inner eye, and had known at once for the home she longed for—and began to ride fast in the direction of Gravesend, while Charles Stuart, looking like a man who had seen his own death, watched her go.

In less than five minutes she had lost sight of Cobham.

Frances brushed a tear from her eye and rode hard until she reached the toll-gate, where she called to the gatekeeper, asking him to lift the barrier. While he ambled out of his cottage, a smart yellow coach approached. As it halted alongside her she saw with a shock that it was painted with the Duke of Richmond's crest on the side.

A sour-faced woman, beyond the first flush of youth, with an equally plain girl sitting behind her, pulled up the leather blind that kept out the elements and leaned out, demanding of the toll-gatekeeper how he dared to keep her waiting.

'Do you not know who I am?' she demanded, pointing to the coach's crest.

Even though he was a coroneted duke, Charles would never have commissioned so showy a coach himself; nor, from what he had told Frances, would he have been able to afford to. The lady had clearly wasted no time in announcing her new-found status to all and sundry.

Frances hoped he would not have reason to regret his new alliance. For it seemed he had married a harpy.

She was grateful that there were few people on the barge from Gravesend. At one end a group of men discussed taxes and the rumblings of war with the Dutch. At the other a huddle of old women cradled shopping baskets and bundles of washing on their knees. Frances sat down a few feet from them.

Lost in her thoughts, Frances did not hear their conversation until she realized they were talking of the Duke.

'I hear he has married up at the Hall,' announced a fat woman carrying an even fatter hen.

'About time too,' replied the goodwife with the laundry.

'Now, Prue, it is not so long since he lost his little wife and babe.'

'All the more reason to wed again. My Kate's husband John is his farrier. His steward, Mr Payne, says the Duke hasn't set his mind to anything since. He has five score depending on him, and all of them relieved he has wed again. Now all he needs is a fine bouncing heir.'

'Aye,' cackled the lady with the laundry. 'Yet I hear the widow he has married is old and ugly.'

The owner of the hen laughed raucously. 'Then he should snuff the candles, remember the old

167

adage "All Women Are Fair in the Dark" and get on with his business!'

Frances turned away. She had been stupid and naive to think that people could do what they wished in this life. Whatever their feelings might be for each other, she could have married the Duke only if she possessed a large dowry, and there was no chance of that.

As the barge stopped at London Bridge, dusk was beginning to fall. She looked out at the twinkling lights of a thousand wherries and came to a decision. If the happy home she longed for was to be denied her, then she would dance and flirt and go to plays and masques and balls, and make the most of being young and free and desired by a monarch.

Yet for now she needed to think up a story convincing enough to cover her absence.

Chapter 8

The first thing Frances did when she returned to her chamber was pull out the wooden chest she kept stored in her closet. It was here that she hid away all the precious keepsakes of her childhood: a thank-you note from Minette, a lock of her younger brother Walter's hair, a miniature of the spaniel dog she had owned as a child, and other small treasures. She rummaged through various childish poems and sketches until she found what she was looking for: a drawing of the house that so resembled Cobham Hall.

She stood contemplating it for an instant, lost in

silence. It was indeed uncannily similar to the house she had just visited.

No point dwelling on that. If it were fate or some deep, unknown desire that had produced the drawing, it was doubly cruel that it was the home of another woman. Standing stiffly, she tore the sketch into a dozen pieces and threw them onto the fire.

Realizing at last the lateness of the hour, she fetched the gown she would change into for supper when there was a rap on her chamber door.

Mall burst in, with little Mary in tow.

'I'faith, Frances, where have you been all day? The Queen called for you and I had to say that you were visiting the sick, which I am sure she did not believe, and indeed concluded you must be with Castlemaine or the King. She was not happy and wished me to remind you of your duties.'

'I was indisposed. I felt a chill coming on and took to my bed, that is all.' Frances turned away so that Mall could not see her face.

'Your eyes are bright enough, and your skin glows, for one who has been in her bed all the day.' She suddenly took Frances' hand. 'Be careful you do not play a dangerous game, sweeting.'

Frances turned, a determined smile on her face. 'Any game I played is finished and lost. And now I intend to enjoy what Court life offers. What entertainments are planned, think you? I wish to see a witty play, dance the latest dances, wear a vizard and visit Vauxhall Gardens, where the rogues and the shady women are found . . .'

'Do you indeed? What has happened to the girl who likes to build houses of cards and play at Blind Man's Buff?'

'She has grown up.'

169

'I hope we do not all miss her.' There was a sadness and intensity in Mall's voice that Frances had not heard before.

'Come, help me with these hooks. I am late and my tire-woman has been called to other tasks.'

Mall stood behind her young friend and they held each other's gaze in the looking glass, though Mall was so much smaller than Frances that she almost had to peep over her shoulder. 'Breathe in.'

Frances had put on a gown of pale-blue satin with a chemise of ivory silk. As the older woman watched, she tweaked the neckline so that half an inch more of her breasts was revealed.

Mall—twice married, and well aware of the ways of the world—was conscious of mixed emotions. The King would no doubt be delighted at Frances' new outlook. Yet Mall felt almost like a mother whose babe has set aside childish things.

Frances pinched her lips to give them colour and searched for her fan on her dressing table.

From its perch the parrot eyed her mournfully. 'Remember Charlie Stuart,' it instructed, though in surprisingly tentative tones, as if in some uncanny way it knew the suggestion would not be popular.

'Your Charlie Stuart has wed an old, ugly, rich woman, and I trust she makes him suffer for it! Her pretensions of grandeur will no doubt beggar him in less than a year, and it serves him right.'

Mall's lips twitched into a smile, which she quickly suppressed. So that was the way the wind blew. Well, mayhap it was for the best, despite the heartache. Even though the King was a generous man, God alone knew how he would react, had Frances truly preferred his younger cousin.

'Come, let us sup and plan your programme of

170

pleasures.' Mall picked up a shawl and placed it over the parrot's cage. She thought it might come up with one of its witty rejoinders, but it did not. The parrot knew when it was beaten.

*   *   *

The change that came over Frances after her visit to Cobham was remarkable, and indeed was noticed by all.

She seemed to shake off all her engaging openness and abandoned her love of games. The ready laugh that had echoed through the Queen's Apartments was replaced by a polished sophistication. The milk-and-honey of her complexion was discreetly assisted by paint; her neckline became more daring; and she even wore the patches she had despised, as the tools of old women and those who had suffered from the smallpox.

The King found her more alluring than ever, as the new Frances dallied with him shamelessly, flirting and hiding behind her fan, even allowing him the kisses she had hitherto forbidden. Why not, she concluded, enjoy his admiration to the utmost?

A stifling heat descended suddenly on London, filling the air with dust so that even the street vendors stopped crying 'Cherry ripe!' or 'New chairs for old!' and sheltered from the blazing sun down darkened alleys, fighting the rats for the little shade they could find.

The playhouses, always hot and overcrowded, were doubly so. Ladies tried to hide their sweat by drenching themselves in perfume, but still some fainted in the pits waiting for the plays to start at three of the afternoon, when the sun seemed hottest. Nothing daunted, Frances frequented plays almost every day at the Duke's House and the King's House, greatly enjoying *The Indian Queen, The Court Secret, The Slighted Maid* and smiling bitterly to herself at *The Rival Ladies.*

Despite the sun, she drove out in the Ring at Hyde Park, relishing the new fashion for coaches with glass windows, which allowed a greater chance to see and be seen. She gambled at Basset and Hazard, and spent all her maid of honour's allowance on new hats, gowns, gossamer wraps and painted fans made of chicken skin. And all the while she flirted with the fops, and matched verbal swords with Court wits like Lords Buckhurst and Rochester, who began to revise their opinions of her.

'Handsome is as handsome does,' reminded Nurse tartly, torn between pride at her charge's beauty and concern at the painted butterfly emerging from its modest shell.

'Frances Stuart,' marvelled her sister Sophia, 'you are like a different lady entirely. I thought I was the gadabout in the family.'

'Good.' Frances snapped her newest fan shut, refusing to think about what might have been, 'For I was a great slow-top before. Now I am lucky if I have five minutes to sit down together.'

Sophia Stuart was not the only person to notice the transformation in Mistress Frances Stuart.

Barbara Castlemaine smiled at it, for she reckoned it meant the gilding was beginning to peel off the innocent lily, and that what had drawn the King to her would soon be lost.

Mall watched it with a touch of sadness, knowing its source.

172

Mall's brother, the charming yet devious Duke of Buckingham, noted it and thought hard how best to use it to his advantage.

To this end he approached Mall after supper one night as she watched the King partnering Frances in some energetic country dancing. They were in the Queen's Apartments, though the Queen herself was sitting at the card tables. It was a fine sight, with the gentlemen all dressed in velvet and laces, and the ladies in their silks and taffetas, the pearls in their ears catching the light of dozens of candles.

'Well, Butterfly,' her brother whispered, leaning down so that the curls of his fair periwig tickled Mall's cheek. 'What think you? Has the fair Stuart succumbed? De Grammont thinks not, and he is the master of all gaming. The King, he says, would be less polite if she had. And if he is right, we must act fast, because this brazen new demi-virgin is teasing His Majesty to the point of madness. He neglects all his business in contemplation of her, so Arlington tells me.'

'And what do you plan to do?'

'We have a scheme. We have formed a committee for the getting of Mistress Stuart for the King.'

A laugh escaped Mall, which she could not contain. 'I thought committees were for regulating the Poor Laws and limiting the vapour from sea-coal.'

'You do not take this seriously enough. The King will be so grateful when we overcome her resistance that our influence with him will increase tenfold. Arlington is with me, and Ashley, Lord Bristol, and Sir Charles Berkeley.'

'Not Clarendon, I take it?'

'They hate Clarendon. He is a narrow-minded old man who treats the King as a schoolboy. He would only disapprove. He should stay away from the Council and mind his gout. It would be better for all.'

'Especially you,' murmured Mall. 'And how exactly are you gentlemen going to persuade Mistress Stuart, when she has so long resisted?'

'We are arranging it so that they are alone together where none can interrupt them.'

'A royal rape then? How charming! Do you employ Lord Rochester as your pimp? I hear he has wide experience of such things.'

'Mall, listen. The way Mistress Stuart conducts herself is not fair to the King. First all innocence and Blind Man's Buff, and now the kind of provocation Madam Cresswell no doubt teaches to her wenches so that she may sell their maidenhead a dozen times over! Any man would take leave of his senses.'

Mall followed her brother's eyes as they rested lustfully on Frances, happily dancing with the King.

'Including you, I take it. Stay, George, I will listen to no more of this. Mistress Stuart is something of a weathervane, true enough, because she knows not her own heart; and what she truly wants, she cannot have. Yet she is honest and I will have no part of this "committee". Indeed, I strongly advise you—and the rest—to give up such thoughts at once and leave the King to his own devices.'

Mall heard no more of her brother's scheming because the Queen decided, with no further ado, to take the waters in Tunbridge Wells.

Her sad and secret agenda was known to all: the waters were noted for their health-giving properties. Among countless other distempers that they were famed for helping, one was that of procuring pregnancies in childless ladies. By now the whole Court had come to believe that the Queen was barren, and to blame Lord Clarendon for it, since he might benefit from this, given that his daughter Anne Hyde was married to the King's brother, the Duke of York, and her children would be next in line to the throne if the King had no legitimate children of his own.

Speculation was rife as to which of her maids of honour the Queen would take with her. Frances, still eager for any diversion that would take her mind off Cobham, was delighted to be included in the favoured few.

*　　　*　　　*

Frances had to admit that Tunbridge Wells was a delightful place to visit after the dust and mud of London, especially in summer, and they were all grateful to go there, as indeed was the King.

Here, the greatest mixed with the less great, all renting small houses that stood, cheek by jowl, along the mile-long road that ran to the Wells. The atmosphere was more village than town, yet with all the amenities of shopping and socializing so beloved of the Court.

There was a long walk, shaded by spreading chestnut trees, under which the company assembled each morning and strolled, gossiping, while drinking the waters. On one side of the walk was a long row of shops selling toys, lace, gloves, stockings and all the other little necessaries so essential to the fashionable personage. On the other side was a market where fresh-faced country girls, in neat straw hats, sold game, fish and flesh, vegetables, flowers and fruit. For here the entertainment was that each household catered for itself, with the lady of the house enjoying the novelty of doing her own marketing!

As soon as evening came everyone left their little palace to meet at the Bowling Green, where under the stars they could dance in the open air on a lawn softer and smoother than any carpet in the world. There was gaming too, and plenty of intrigues to keep the gossip-mongers busy.

The King, of course, did not stay in a rented house, but at the lovely seat of Summer Hill, owned by Lord Muskerry and his lady, who was very near to giving birth—a fact that did not stop her engaging in all the delights that Tunbridge Wells offered: the balls and entertainments, the hunting and hawking and even greyhound coursing.

To her considerable embarrassment, of all the Court beauties, only Mistress Stuart had the honour of being invited to Summer Hill.

This so infuriated Barbara Castlemaine that she arrived in high dudgeon and outraged even the most morally lax courtiers by parading her royal bastards—so like the King, with their black hair and flashing dark eyes, that they could have been minted from the same coin—up and down the chestnut walk.

One morning Frances was riding in the Queen's coach when they drove past Barbara and her babes, deep in conversation with the heavily pregnant Lady Muskerry.

The Queen looked swiftly away, yet Frances saw the glint of a tear in her eyes at so vivid an image of fecundity.

176

As Lady Muskerry bid Barbara goodbye, they passed Lords Rochester and Buckhurst strolling in the opposite direction.

'At least there's one brat who won't come out looking like His Majesty,' announced Rochester, in a loud whisper.

'Then he'll be the only one,' replied Charles Buckhurst and they both folded up with laughter.

Frances waited until these merry gentlemen had passed, then asked the Queen if she might get down and buy some lace.

'Of course. I will look for you later at the Bowling Green,' Queen Catherine smiled her sweet smile.

Frances waited until Her Majesty's coach was out of sight and walked swiftly towards Barbara.

'How delightful, Lady Castlemaine,' she commented, 'that you take so sudden an interest in your progeny. Is it the sun that has gone to your head? Or is it your deliberate intention to cause the Queen pain?'

Barbara's famous violet eyes narrowed, giving her the look of a maenad eager to tear apart the flesh of her rival. 'Indeed, Mistress Stuart, dare you ask me that? When your very existence, and the knowledge of her husband's lustful longings for you, must cause her far greater grief than any I engender?'

'I think you may find, my lady, that unlike yourself,' and she glanced meaningfully at the babies, 'I may at least be given credit for resisting.'

'And you think yourself so noble for it, so shiningly innocent! Yet I saw how you responded when the King touched you. There is a word for such as you, Mistress Stuart.' She dropped her voice to a dangerous hiss. 'A prick-tease.'

'And there is another for you, my lady Castlemaine,' Frances flashed back, itching to strike that spoilt, rapacious face. 'A whore. Yet whores have the excuse of poverty, while you are the daughter of a viscount. So not only are you a whore, but a willing whore—and, as my nurse is fond of saying, once a whore, always a whore. Now you are young and lovely, but one day you will be old and none will have you.'

The sound of applause broke into her consciousness and she turned to find Lords Buckhurst and Rochester clapping wildly. 'My dear Mistress Stuart,' congratulated Lord Rochester, with a malicious glance at Barbara, 'it is said of you that you are simple and childish, yet it strikes me that you have wit enough to hold your head up in any company. Admit it, Barbara my love, you are the past and Mistress Stuart is the future.'

And yet her scalding encounter with Barbara brought her to her senses. There was truth enough in the accusation. She had, since her disappointment with the Duke, led the King on with false expectations. All had noticed it, even the corrupt Rochester. For now she would enjoy the simple pleasures of Tunbridge Wells and try to think of some way out of her dilemma. Exchanging her favourite silk slippers with their white shoeroses for stout shoes she headed for a walk in the fields to think.

She was rewarded by the beauty of the day. The sky was the palest blue with high, scudding clouds and a wraith of mist, as delicate as one of her organdie wraps, that still hung across the treetops, giving the scene a dreamlike quality, which suited

178

her mood as she contemplated her future.

The problem as she saw it was this: to secure a husband she needed a dowry, and she had none. This left the option of finding a gentleman who cared naught for such things, and yet they, she suspected, were as thin on the ground as rose petals in January.

She turned her steps, ready to walk back, when the sound of a twig snapping behind her made her suddenly jump.

A young man was following her, watching. He was tall and dark-haired with a silky beard and glowing eyes. Though richly dressed, he seemed somewhat uncomfortable in his body. Indeed, he brought to mind the heron that had sometimes perched on the edge of Minette's pond at the Palais Royal—watching, immobile, on long spindly legs.

'May I help you, sir?' she asked kindly, not wishing to frighten the heron away.

He hesitated. 'Are you not Mistress Stuart?'

'I am indeed. And who are you?'

'Geo . . .' He stumbled. 'George Worthington.'

He fell into step with her. As they walked along, Frances kept up an easy chatter, commenting on the blue of the sky and the beauty of the day, until he seemed to gain in confidence.

'Are you not taking the waters?' he enquired.

'I am afraid I suffer from the rudest of health.'

He laughed delightedly. 'Not even a few little symptoms, such as all Court ladies have? Ennui? A headache from the late hours you keep?'

Frances laughed. 'I try to be abed before the dawn.'

'And do you not like to gamble all night at cards or dice, like the other ladies?'

'Sir, I do not have the funds.'

'Even from the King?'

'I do not wish for the King's funds.' She stopped and looked at him, eye to eye, emboldened by his engaging manner. 'Indeed, you may advise me on a question I have been turning over in my mind.'

He bowed, looking suddenly older than his years, grave as an owl. 'I will do my best.'

'What should I do? I have been wandering here this last half-hour wondering. Become the King's mistress or run away from Court? There seems no other choice for such as I, whom no honest man will wed because I possess no dowry to extend his lands or restore his fortune.'

He looked at her, his eyes afire. 'Surely there must be gentlemen aplenty who would marry you, dowered or otherwise. Are not beauty and wit enough to satisfy a man of discrimination?'

She smiled at him, teasing gently. 'I have not found such a man.'

He took her hand and cradled it against his chest. 'Then you have not searched in the right places.'

Without noticing they had come again to the chestnut walk, now thick with courtiers, who watched their approach curiously.

Frances put away her smile of easy familiarity and took her leave with a formal little curtsey. 'Goodbye, Mr Worthington. I hope your advice is correct as well as generous.'

She looked around the crowd of interested onlookers, hoping to see a friendly face.

But the face she encountered was an unwelcome one.

Barbara Castlemaine, swathed in an

inappropriate gown of bronze satin, which revealed more of her voluptuous curves than was seemly at this or any hour, regarded Frances with a smug smile of satisfaction, which, Frances remarked, gave her a noticeable double chin.

Without exchanging a word, Frances gathered her robe over one arm and tripped towards the busy market where the stall-holders eagerly cried their wares.

She refused to be cowed by Barbara.

As she passed, her eye alighted on a particularly pretty fan, depicting a Grecian goddess leaning on a pretty handmaiden, who had a definite air of Mall's daughter Mary. She stopped to buy it, leaning on the wooden post that supported the great canopy, which threw its welcome shade over the entire stall. The trifle would give Mall great pleasure.

She smiled to herself, remembering her encounter with the young man and how pleasant and unaffected he had been, and wondering if he would be attending the greyhound coursing that the Queen had requested this afternoon, that she might watch her own dog chase the hare.

As she watched the shopkeeper wrap her fan in a silken cloth, she caught the sound of a familiar voice and, through some instinct, stepped back into the shady area at the side of the stalls.

George Worthington was walking through the market with a polished older man, whom Frances instantly recognized as the Comte de Grammont, one of the wittiest and most scurrilous courtiers in Whitehall.

'My dearest George,' de Grammont purred, 'of course you are in love with her, who would not be? She is lovely as the day is long. Just as I

181

was utterly besotted with Mademoiselle La Motte Houdaucourt, maid of honour to the Queen Dowager in France. And when I found that King Louis also desired her, I refused to stand back, even though it was an unwritten rule that once the King spoke to a lady more than once, all her other lovers withdrew. Instead of withdrawing, as a sensible man would, I sent her perfumed gloves and apricot paste. I left elegant boxes on her doorstep. And did I win the fair mademoiselle's hand with my foolish bravery?' He paused, suffering again at the painful memory. 'No, I was banished from the French Court forever and had to come here, to this barbaric country!'

'So you do not think I should pursue my acquaintance with Mistress Stuart?'

'My dear boy, are you mad? The King loves her to distraction! You would find yourself sent on an expedition to Guinea in the company of Prince Rupert, or some such life-threatening venture!'

'But I am not in the army,' protested the young man stubbornly.

'Then it would be a diplomatic mission to some distant part, which needed your particular skills. Believe me, George, you might as well seek out the smallpox or the plague as fall in love with La Belle Stuart—for all three will prove equally fatal!'

Frances, hidden in the shadows, felt her spirits plunge. So, this was the truth! No man of honour would dare to touch her. She was a leper, dressed in silk and jewels. She might as well go forth ringing a bell, warning all good men to keep away.

'Your fan, my lady,' the stallholder broke into her leaden thoughts.

She took the package, half-hoping that George

182

Worthington would resist the counsel of his worldly advisor and run back to find her. But he continued on his way, listening intently to the Comte de Grammont, while Frances felt hot tears slide down the face that was turning out to be not her fortune, but her undoing.

Chapter 9

A wave of fury overwhelmed her at the impossibility of her situation and she knew that, even with a mother and a sister to turn to, only Mall would truly understand her feelings. Her mother would simply shrug and Sophia would have succumbed to the King some time ago, counting her pearl necklaces as she did so.

Frances kicked a stone as hard as she could. Perhaps it would be better if she were more like her sister.

But she was not and never had been.

Mall was not lodged at Summer Hill, but in a house near the Wells, not far from where she stood. Like many of the houses rented by the gentry here, it was far below her status. And yet this gave them all the excuse to dispense with any but the most essential servants, and to play house, almost as if they were Gypsies camping in the wild. Frances loved it.

Given the lack of servants, it did not surprise her when she knocked on Mall's door to receive no answer, not even from a cook or kitchen maid, for they might be out marketing, and she thought she could see Mary playing beyond in the fields.

She was about to depart, deciding Mall must have joined the Queen's party, which had gone to watch the greyhound coursing, when she thought she heard a sound from the floor above.

Gingerly she climbed the narrow staircase.

A strange silence filled the house. It was so manifest that Frances stopped to listen to it, watching the dust motes catching the light of the afternoon sun.

She had just turned to leave when she noticed that the door to Mall's chamber stood open. A shaft of golden sun was lighting the wood of the floor, almost as if someone stood holding up a prism to bend the rays. Without thinking, Frances leaned forward to touch the warmth of the wood and gasped.

The room was barely furnished, apart from a coffer, a table by the window with carved legs and the great wooden bed, which took up most of the room. And on the bed, like Adam and Eve before the Fall, Mall lay sleeping, entwined in the arms of a beautiful young man.

Her head rested against his neck, and her white skin shone like the polished marble of a statue against the golden sheen of his shoulder. All around the floor their clothes were strewn as if discarded there in the height of their abandon.

Frances' first response was to withdraw as swiftly as a shadow, but the young man had opened his eyes. She saw they were golden like his skin, flecked with a deeper brown. He reached out a hand to greet her as if for all the world they were at some ball or rout in town. 'Tom Howard. Glad to meet you.'

He gently shook the sleeping figure beside him.

'My lady, Mary, time to wake and face the realities of the afternoon. I must away to London. Wake.'

It was so strange to hear Mall addressed neither as Mall nor as Butterfly, but by her given name of Mary.

She opened her eyes sleepily and smiled as they lit upon her golden lover. 'No, Tom,' she hid her face in his shoulder, breathing in his skin as if it were some sweet perfume. 'I never want to leave this bed again in all my life.'

He laughed. 'Nor I. And yet we must. See, here is an angel come to waken us.'

Mall looked at Frances, seeming to take in her presence for the first time.

'Is all well?' she sat up. 'There is naught the matter with little Mary?' She had ever been alarmed at Mary's safety since the sudden loss of Esme, her dear son.

Frances shook her head, guilty that she had come to burden Mall with her problems. 'No, I saw her run and jump in the meadow with her nurse.'

Mall leaned forward so that her hair fell in a curtain of chestnut across Tom's chest. 'How tempting a thought! Shall we too cavort in the meadows, sweeting?'

He laughed, catching her hair back in one hand and kissing her neck. 'Not we. We would affront the populace.'

The lightness left her eyes a moment. 'Because I am a crone of almost forty and you a gilded youth but half my years?'

'You know I meant not that.'

Frances was taken aback at his tender protectiveness. It was as if Mall were the wilful child and he the wise and judicious parent.

Tom took Mall gently by her shoulders and eased himself from the bed, wrapping the sheet around himself to cover his nakedness. 'Sadly, I must return to London for my turn of duty.' His tone was suddenly sad and serious. 'Excuse me, mistress,' he bowed to Frances, picking up his discarded clothes as if he had simply dropped his handkerchief and must retrieve it. 'I will dress next door, my lady, to save your blushes.' The ready smile had returned.

'And I should be gone to find if the Queen desires my services.' Frances turned towards the door, but Mall caught her hand and held it. 'No, stay. Tom goes and, when he leaves, the sun will go out for me. I will need your comfort.'

Frances sat down on the edge of the bed, stroking Mall's hand, in which the years revealed themselves more than in the glow of her chestnut hair, or the gleam of her hazel eyes. How strange that she had come to ask for comfort and would end by giving it. Perhaps they could give solace to each other.

Tom came into the room again, dressed in black velvet, laced with silver. He bowed and held out a rose.

'As a love token it is not much, but I plucked it fresh from the bower outside the window. Its vivid hue reminds me of you.' He raised it to his nose. 'And its sweet, irresistible perfume.'

'Then take it with you, give it not to me.' Mall tucked it inside his doublet.

'I will keep it close to my heart.'

Behind the playful words Frances could sense a bitter sorrow, and saw that her envy for Mall and her carefree young lover might be misplaced.

He leaned down and kissed her, his eyes

186

suddenly streaked with pain.

'Goodbye, my lady. I hope we will meet soon again.'

And he was gone.

Mall waited until she heard the last of his steps on the stairs, then let out a groan of anguish as if she were in the final throes of childbed.

Alarmed, Frances knelt beside her.

'He goes abroad,' Mall whispered hoarsely, as if each word choked her. 'He killed a man. My glorious, golden Tom. It was in a duel, but no matter. You know how the King hates duelling, and Tom is Lieutenant of his bodyguard. And now he has to flee abroad and hope for the King's forgiveness.'

'How did it happen, what was the cause of their duelling?'

At this, Mall looked doubly anguished. 'It was over Lady Shrewsbury. I know, I know, I should be angry with him and never see him more. Anna Maria Talbot is a whore to rival Cousin Barbara. Only three and twenty and yet she has had a string of lovers. Even my own brother languishes for her.' Mall pushed herself up on the pillows. 'It is a silly tale. Tom invited her to sup at Spring Garden and took a piper from his regiment to play a serenade. Then Henry Jermyn, that stupid pocket-sized Lothario, who fancies he can paddle in any lady's palm—and not just her palm either—decided to woo her and laughed at the piper. Young men's blood runs hotter than spiced ale when the poker makes it sizzle, and so Tom called Jermyn out. They fought the next day and Jermyn's second was run through and killed.'

'Can not Tom beg His Majesty's pardon and

offer to make amends?'

Mall shook her head. 'It is worse because he is of the King's bodyguard. If he stays he will be locked in the Tower and guarded by the very men he commands.'

Frances cradled Mall in her arms. 'How long must he stay away?'

'I know not. Until the King can be persuaded to forgive him.'

*   *   *

The Queen was merrier at Tunbridge Wells than any had ever seen her. She dispensed with much of the ritual and ceremony that ruled her life at Whitehall and threw card parties and suppers, and staged impromptu dancing on the lawn outside her apartments. This greatly simplified life for her maids of honour. Catherine Boynton enjoyed dallying with her Dick; Lady Suffolk napped in the afternoons and Cary Frazier succumbed to a cousin of Lord Buckhurst, who then disappeared leaving her broken-hearted, but not, fortuitously, with child, though she greatly feared so and danced an indecorous jig at the appearance of her monthly flowers.

The reason underlying the Queen's happiness was, however, sadly short-lived. Unlike Cary Frazier, she was desperate to find herself in the family way, but despite regular imbibing of the spa waters this showed no sign of occurring.

Frances came upon her one morning as she took an early stroll under the chestnut trees. There was the beginning of a chill in the air, and the Wells, the source of much enjoyment as well as the health-giving water, were beginning to seem a little mournful. The Queen sat by one of the fountains sipping from a glass. Her eyes were closed and Frances realized that she was uttering a prayer. She caught the words 'Santa Maria', though the rest was unintelligible to her, being in Portuguese.

Queen Catherine opened her eyes and, before she could register her usual politeness, Frances saw a swift look of pain cloud her childlike features. 'Mistress Stuart, good morrow.'

Frances dropped a curtsey.

'No, not here.' The Queen shook her head. 'This is no place for such formality. Here we are all friends.' She sighed. 'Tomorrow the King wishes to return to Whitehall.' It sounded like a punishment. To Tom Howard, who had killed a man, prison meant the Tower, but to the Queen of England it seemed prison meant the Palace of Whitehall.

'Can you not stay alone, Majesty?' asked Frances gently.

'My place is with my husband,' she insisted, her head suddenly high. 'Being married to a king, one must learn patience.' She looked Frances in the eye. 'I have had much opportunity to learn patience.'

The Queen put down her glass and walked away, leaving Frances in turmoil. She had not intended to cause grief to the Queen. And yet during those days she had encouraged the King's advances, was she not as guilty as The Lady of causing her hurt?

Her thoughts, like the dog that gnaws its own paw, returned again to Cobham. How was he faring with his sour-faced duchess and her plain daughter? And she longed to be anyone—a shepherdess or a serving girl—if she could be allowed to make her own choices.

189

Without Tom Howard, Mall was ready to return as soon as she could. Frances helped pack up all the Queen's belongings and then her own. Next morning she and Mall were waiting for the coach to take them back when a trumpet sounded and they looked out of their window.

It was the King himself, leaning out of his coach of state calling up to them. 'Come, ladies, I offer a ride to London. My lady Castlemaine is in high dudgeon because I refused to take her and her brats. I love my children, but not on uncomfortable journeys. My wife has gone ahead, since she wishes to drive very slow.' He winked at them gaily, his dark eyes alive with devilment. 'We tried the business of getting an heir last night and the physician has told her to lie flat. She has also prayed a great deal, like my cousin Louis' wife is apt to do in the same event. It worked for them, so I must live in hope. Come!'

Frances looked at Mall and shook her head at so personal a revelation. Yet the King was so prone to take one by surprise with his candour and high spirits that it was hard to judge him harshly. His faults might be many, yet there was nothing of the hypocrite in him. The story came to Frances' memory of Lord Rochester pinning a scurrilous verse on his bedchamber door announcing:

We have a pretty witty King
Whose word no man relies on
Who never said a foolish thing
Nor ever did a wise one.

And of how, instead of having Rochester clapped in jail, as he would have been entitled to, the

King had laughed and pointed out, "Tis very true, since my words are my own and my deeds are my ministers'.'

They were no sooner settled in the coach than the King turned to them. 'Well, ladies, heard you about mad Henry Jermyn?'

At the mention of the rival that her beloved Tom had duelled with, Mall turned white as whey. But this, as it turned out, was another matter. 'He bet De Grammont five hundred guineas that he could ride twenty miles on the same horse on the high road in less than an hour—and won!'

Since the usual speed on horseback was but eight miles an hour, the ladies had to be impressed.

The thought of how livid de Grammont must be at losing so great a sum made Frances smile. Even for a gambler, five hundred guineas was a king's ransom.

'Why look you so happy at the Count's misfortune, Belle?' the King demanded.

'I was just thinking what my nurse would say, Majesty. Many go out for wool and come back shorn.'

The King laughed uproariously. 'I must remember to remind him of that.'

But Mall did not join in the laughter. Her mind was on other things. 'Do you not think Jermyn a wild, ungovernable man?' she asked the King hopefully. 'The kind who might get into a fight without thinking of the consequence?'

'Aha,' replied the King. 'You are thinking of the duel with northern Tom Howard? Jermyn is wild indeed, but I am angrier by far with Howard. Tom is of my bodyguard. On his part it is a serious offence. And I must answer to young Rawlins' family, remember, whom he untimely killed.'

The rest of the journey passed with Mall in glum silence, and Frances attempting to divert the King before he guessed the reason for Mall's interest.

When they reached Whitehall, Frances alighted first, her chamber being nearer to the Holbein Gate.

As soon as Frances had disappeared inside her lodgings, Mall turned to the King and, shedding all thoughts of discretion, demanded, 'Majesty, what would it take for you to pardon Tom Howard and restore him into your good opinion?'

The King eyed her levelly, as understanding began to dawn.

'So that is the way the land lies. Is he not green fruit for your tastes, Butterfly?'

'I am not so old! Besides, your father married me off at twelve, only to be widowed within a year, and then at sixteen he wed me to his kinsman. I grew to love my James, yet it was a love borne of duty, not of choice.'

'And you have chosen Tom Howard? Penniless and a younger son? He has pride and passion beneath that calm exterior, 'tis true. Yet you are the daughter of one of the greatest families of all England. It will not do. I cannot pardon him— unless . . . ?'

'Unless?'

'I have already told you what I desire most in this life.' His dark, liquid eyes held hers. She thought she saw a flicker of shame beneath the laughter. 'I would surrender my immortal soul if she would give herself to me, may God forgive me. If you persuade her to listen to my entreaties, I will pardon Tom Howard.'

'I have told you I cannot.'

The King's expression hardened. 'That is your choice and you must live with it.'

*   *   *

Autumn approached, bringing with it a strong melancholy wind that stripped the trees of their golden leaves even before Londoners had time to admire them. Not that Londoners treasured nature as much as they appreciated the more civic delights: playhouses, street hawkers and the hum of trade. Soon the pleasures of the chestnut grove at Tunbridge Wells seemed a distant memory.

Barbara dropped her bastard with her usual ease and the Queen did not conceive, despite the King's night-time attentions and his prayers.

Without Tom Howard's youthful spirits, Mall felt as melancholy as the weather. She felt her leaves were falling like those from the trees. Soon she would be as bare and gnarled as they were.

The sight of her daughter Mary—who, in contrast to her mother's autumnal woes, was growing as fast as a new shoot in springtime—saddened her also. Soon Mary would be old enough to be betrothed, as Mall had been herself at eleven. She might even marry and leave home, and abandon Mall to her withering old age.

It was Frances who first noticed the change. Mall, playful and brisk, always ready with her sharp eye and sharp tongue to prick the pomposity and licentiousness of the Court, was strangely subdued.

Frances attributed it to the loss of Tom, and came up with schemes to distract her from her misery. 'Come with me to Covent Garden today,' she wheedled, finding Mall still abed past the dinner hour. 'I go to have my portrait made, by request of the Duchess of York. She is collecting all the Court beauties and I, it seems, am one! It will be just us two and the painter, Lely. You can make me laugh and the portrait will be spoiled, and I will not mourn it.'

Mall sat up, interested despite herself. 'What? Give up the chance to be a painted lady in the company of the loveliest whores in the land? I wager Barbara is there, and that strumpet Lady Shrewsbury who caused my Tom's downfall. And mayhap Diana Kirke, who despite her pedigree ought to charge by the night. Besides, I would welcome the chance to berate Master Lely. How durst he paint my cousin Barbara in the guise of the Madonna?' Even the unshockable Restoration Court had gasped at the sight of Lady Castlemaine sitting as the model for the Virgin Mary with her bastard child as Jesus. 'Know you the best part?' Mall reached for her wrap, warming to her theme. 'Barbara sent the picture to some nuns in France to serve as altarpiece—until they discovered which whore sat for the model of Mary, and then returned it!'

So it was that, in a surprisingly cheerful mood, Frances and Mall called for a coach to drive them to the Piazza in Covent Garden, and the studio of one Peter Lely, Principal Painter to the Court of King Charles II.

The coach let them off next to a narrow alley leading to the Piazza. They kept their distance from two fops who were jostling each other in their desire to keep to the wall and avoid slops from

194

the upstairs window. One of them already had his sword out and looked ready to murder the other, yet they stopped and bowed at the sight of Frances and Mall.

Nevertheless, it was with a sigh of relief that they emerged into the elegant beauty of the Piazza, once the site of the convent garden for Westminster Abbey before the dissolution of the monasteries, with its delightful terraces and colonnades so recently designed by Inigo Jones 'to attract Persons of the Greatest Distinction'. At which it had been very successful, since three earls were known to have bought houses there, though these noble gentlemen were already looking askance at the hawkers and traders, who were multiplying like flies in the hot August sunshine, with their cries of 'Ripe damsons!' 'Hot mutton pies!' and 'Buy my Kentish strawberries!'

Frances stopped to listen to a penny ballad singer who was rendering a funny, but very bawdy song about the King and one of his love affairs. She laughed and threw him a coin.

'Zounds, mistress,' Mall teased. 'Laugh not. It is probably about you!'

The studio of the Principal Painter was on the first floor of Numbers 10–11, facing north, which is the good light for painters.

Frances, expecting emptiness and light, or perhaps a lone fiddler to provide soothing music, was astonished to find the studio as full as a fairground on a feast day.

In one corner a tall young man was busy painting flowers and fruit on a large canvas; in another they came upon an artist busily engaged at filling in the outlines of hands, and colouring dramatic

195

background scenes of mountains and clouds.

In the next room a bearded gentleman rendered rich draperies, a great swathe of tawny silk lying in front of him so that he might faithfully capture its shimmering lustre.

'Master Lely is most prized for his draperies, yet I knew not that he employed another hand to paint them,' whispered Mall, not thinking they were overheard.

'What is good enough for Masters Rubens and Van Dyck is good enough for me,' boomed a jovial, plump man in a light brown periwig and whiskers to match, whom Frances guessed must be the painter himself. She smiled, thinking how he brought to mind a ginger tom they had owned in the Palais Royal, which had proved the best mouser in Paris. 'Like my own, the works of those giants proved so much in demand that they could not complete every last detail with their own hands. They had to turn to others for help, as I do myself.'

Frances glanced round, resisting the temptation to stroke him, and noting that rather more than just the final details seemed to be being painted by the hands of others.

'So, mistress . . .' He cocked his head on one side, more rooster now than cat, 'how shall we depict you for this portrait? As a shepherdess with crook and lamb? A Roman Flora? Ceres overflowing with plenty?'

Frances shook her head.

'Venus, then, with gauzy draperies, arising from the foam?'

Frances suddenly recalled her first meeting with the Duke of Richmond when he had likened her to Diana. 'Save that pose for my lady Castlemaine. I shall be a chaste Diana.'

To the astonishment of Peter Lely, La Belle Stuart delivered this revelation with a broad wink. Why, he wondered, did people call her naive, for she seemed to understand the undercurrents of Court symbolism only too well.

'You will be the virgin goddess of the hunt?'

'Indeed.' Frances nodded mischievously. 'I shall leave the amorous conquests to The Lady, and run chastely through the groves of Whitehall hunting down only those who are so pompous or hypocritical that they deserve to suffer, and smite them down with my arrows.'

'Mistress,' Lely smiled back, 'then there will be few who escape the wrath of your bow.'

While he talked, the painter was already setting to work, sketching the outline of Frances' face in chalk on paper.

When he had finished he showed her the likeness, and she nodded.

'You have caught my Roman nose to the life, and the way my lower lip is fatter than the upper. And yet the eyes? Think you not that you give me too much the sleepy look of Lady Castlemaine, whose eyes ever hint of the bedchamber, even when she is in the Chapel saying her prayers?'

Lely laughed. 'Some do say I give the same gaze to all my subjects. The fatal Barbara has bewitched me with her sleepy enchantments.'

Frances snapped her fingers and made him jump.

'Then wake! For I am a filly of a different colour.'

Master Lely looked back at his work and changed the eyes to make them wider, with a look both modest and yet sensuously alluring, which exactly captured Frances' particular charm.

'That is better, at least I am myself now!' Frances congratulated him.

He made her stand one more time, in front of the painted background of a cloud-lit forest, and put a bow into her hand.

'Hold it in your left hand—thus.' He arranged her outstretched arm so that she held the bow at waist level. 'And now, with your right hand, catch hold of the drapery of your gown and pull it back, as if you were about to step forward and pursue some pompous person with your bow. Exactly!'

Another stroke of chalk on paper and he had finished, pausing only to find the exact shade of her amber gown from the great pile of stuff he kept in silk and satin, taffeta and cloth-of-gold, linen and velvet, in every hue from violet to vermilion, so that he might work upon painting the drapery even when his subjects were not present.

'Goodbye, mistress,' Peter Lely bowed low. 'I flatter you not when I say it has truly been a pleasure, and bid you return as soon as you may, to continue the likeness.'

'I will, sir,' promised Frances.

And she proved as good as her word, sitting for him three times more at his request until he told her that, with hard work and good fortune, the next visit might be her last.

Yet when she returned as requested, she was surprised on two counts. The first was a pleasurable surprise. Master Lely had all but finished the painting and it was a likeness that delighted her.

The second was that the King was present.

He had brought his dogs and several of his more

198

rascally courtiers, Rochester and Sedley, and all stood studying her portrait critically.

Charles stared at the painting for several long moments, stroking the narrow line of his moustache—his dark eyes, which could damn or praise exuberantly, fixed upon the figure of Frances.

Time ticked away. And then at long last he turned to Peter Lely.

'Master Lely, I salute you. It is a masterpiece. You have caught the velvet of her skin, the eyes like a faun's drinking at a dewpond at dawn, the golden glint of her soft hair! You will make me a copy as soon as ever you may.'

Master Lely smiled in pleasure and relief as the King bowed and departed.

Yet as soon as he had gone, Mall distinctly heard the comment Lord Rochester made in a low voice to his friend Sedley.

'For God's sake, man. Will no one cure the King of this demeaning passion? He neglects his business and lets the country go to wrack and ruin. If his only recovery is in having her, then have her he must. Then he can return to Castlemaine and we can all get some peace.'

Mall's eyes flickered to Frances, yet mercifully she seemed to have missed his cruel words.

Outside in the Piazza the King awaited in the royal coach.

Frances held out a hand of farewell to Master Lely, before bestowing her sweetest smile upon Lord Rochester. 'Perhaps you should mind your words, my lord. If the King did indeed enjoy me, as you so kindly say he must, it might not diminish, but increase his passion.' Rochester froze as her eyes swept over his handsome, dissipated face. 'And I could prove a dangerous enemy. The faun too may grow into a stag.'

Chapter 10

The chill winds began to sweep down over the Thames and make all shiver and hope it would not be another winter when the river froze deep enough for bear-baiting and a frost fair to take place on its icy surface.

Yet there were many entertainments to divert them. The Queen had become quite a practised hand at cards and held regular parties in her apartments; there were new plays at the King's and Duke's Theatres; Cary Frazier brought tidings that the new French draperies had arrived at the silk merchant next to the Cock and Hen in Long Acre; there were games of Pell Mell, and each morning even at this time of year the King played an energetic game of tennis.

But the best thing of all was that Frances' brother, Walter, had finished his studies in Paris and had arrived in London to join the Inns of Court and begin his training as a lawyer.

He arrived to visit her at her apartments on the day the Queen had fortuitously given them the morning off, since she had a head-cold and wished to stay in her chamber to breathe in a comforting infusion of oil of eucalyptus. Frances and two of the other ladies had been debating what to do with their sudden free time.

'Walter! When did you come to London?'

She reached up and kissed the tall, gangling boy, amazed that he had grown so much since last she saw him. 'Look at you! You must be almost two yards high.'

He ducked out of her embrace, smiling shyly, so like her in appearance that anyone would know them at once for brother and sister.

'And handsome also.' She stroked the long fair curls, almost girlish in their profusion, though there was nothing feminine about her strapping brother.

'Frances!' He shied away, colouring up as the other ladies giggled.

Looking at her little brother, Frances felt overwhelmed by a tide of tenderness. He was sixteen, the age she herself had been when she arrived here two years ago, with all the shy uncertainty of his years. Anger spurted suddenly in her that so much had been heaped upon her at so young an age, coming to terms with the English Court and then finding herself the object of the King's desire, and with no help from her own mother in charting the reefs and whirlpools of her new life. She determined that she would do all she could to protect Walter from what could be a harsh as well as an enticing world.

'We have a morning to ourselves, so what would you like to see? The wonder of London Bridge? The New Exchange? A visit to the playhouse?'

'I hear that Jacob Hall, the rope dancer, displays his skills this morn in Lincoln's Inn Fields,' Cary announced.

'Why would he wish to see a rope dancer?' Catherine asked. 'Surely such a show is for those who frequent Bartholomew Fair?'

'Who are so far beneath you?' Cary placed a

finger beneath her nose to mock her friend. 'They say Jacob Hall is my lady Castlemaine's new lover. That she wished to know if his dexterity extends to the use of his other parts!'

Frances glanced at her brother to see if he was shocked, but he was laughing with the rest of them.

'And does it?' Frances laughed.

'She hath not told us.' She glanced at Frances quizzically. 'You were her great friend, not we. Sleeping in her chamber and all. All the rest of us were stark amazed. The Lady is as friendly to other women as a spider is to a fly. They do not live to tell the tale.'

'I would like to see the rope dancer,' Walter reassured her. 'I have seen them in France and would like to see how this man compares.'

'Let us see this Jacob Hall then. It will be a great diversion.'

'I will need my cloak, if we are to go by water.' Catherine shivered.

The wherryman was mightily impressed at having a cargo of three young and pretty ladies and a young gentleman, and when they told him of their destination he talked to them incessantly of the wonders he had seen at fairs. 'A giant seven feet tall and a pig which, I swear to you, had three heads, and, as I live and breathe, a goat that stood on its hind legs and quoted the Psalms.'

Frances and Walter burst out laughing, delighted to be in each other's company after so long. 'You are got so tall! A true young gentleman.' His looks were not entirely hers. Though they shared the same fair hair, he had their father's gentle brown eyes, and an air of touching optimism that she hoped London would not dent.

'I am sixteen,' he grinned. 'Old enough to start a career, or so Father tells me.'

'I had not known you wished to be a lawyer.'

'I do not! Who with a heart in his breast would wish such? I wish to go to sea, yet Father says such as we cannot afford to send me.' He looked at his sister, wondering if he could trust her. 'I had half a mind to go to some dockside alehouse and get myself press-ganged.'

'Say not so! You might end up on some ill-fated voyage to Guinea.'

Judging by Walter's gleaming eyes, this did not hold out the horrors to him of disease and even death that it did to her.

'Wait a while and you can go to sea soon enough,' offered Cary. 'My father says the talk of war with the Hollanders grows wilder every day. Last week a Dutch ship refused to lower its flag to ours in the high seas, as has always been the custom, and the Duke of York was all for sinking it.'

They alighted at the Temple Stairs, shaken at such a thought, and rode the last mile in a hackney coach.

The crowds that packed the Fields were so thick it was as if they had come to see not a rope dance but a coronation. And yet the populace, recognizing the quality of the young women and boy, made a path for them as if Moses had commanded the Red Sea to cleave in two, until they found themselves at the front, where they seated themselves on a wooden bench.

A young lad leapt to his feet and demanded eighteen pennies for the privilege of each seat.

'We could have seen a play for half a crown!'

protested Catherine Boynton crossly. 'Instead of some acrobat.'

'I will stand you your seats with pleasure, ladies.' They turned to find Lord Rochester sitting behind them, with Sir Charles Sedley and the Comte de Grammont. The last thing Frances wanted was a favour from him, after their encounter at Master Lely's studio when he had been so insulting and she so rude. Yet before she could stop him he had handed over the price of all four tickets. It was on the tip of her tongue to quip that she hoped the money was his own, since Lord Rochester was always famously in debt.

Trumpets blew, and to the beat of a tabor drum a man marched up through the crowd, bowing and flinging back his cloak as if he were the King himself.

To their surprise he was both young and handsome, with long brown hair and a ready smile.

As he approached he made a point of waving to every lady and bowing to the men.

When he reached the front row he stopped and, sighting three young ladies from the Court, bent down on his supple knees and kissed the hand of each.

With a flourish he produced a black ribbon and entreated Frances to tie back his long hair. Then, with a great show and more banging of the drum and sounding of the trumpet, he tested the hempen rope, pulled it tighter and leapt atop it. He began to walk up and down, smiling and undoing the strings of his chemise as he did so, until a swathe of handsome chest was exposed. The women in the audience clapped and catcalled.

'Why stop there, Jacob?' cackled a crone behind

them. 'Show us your yard!'

Jacob Hall bowed. 'My yard is not for such as you, Mother.'

The old lady elbowed Frances. 'Go on, you ask him. He'll do it for you, I'll be bound.'

Frances looked round to find the Comte de Grammont's sticky gaze fastened upon her.

The banter over, Jacob Hall began his display of skipping, balancing, tumbling and dancing, and all the while his gaze was fixed on Frances for so long and so intently that she was forced to look away.

'Zounds, mistress,' whispered Cary, quite put out. 'You already have the King at your feet; The Lady will never forgive you if you have the rope dancer also.'

Frances turned her head away to break his gaze and found de Grammont still watching her with a strange, assessing look in his eye as if he could not decide whether he hated or lusted after her.

High above them, Jacob Hall bowed and informed them he would now perform his most dangerous manoeuvre of a triple somersault and land upright upon the rope.

Walter leaned forward, enthralled. 'I bet you half an angel he cannot do it!'

Frances smiled, wondering where her brother thought he would get such a sum, when de Grammont leaned forward and said, 'A betting man, are you, Master Stuart? In that case I accept the wager.'

Walter had hardly had time to take in the transaction before Jacob had landed safely on his feet.

'Oh,' Walter began, flushing dangerously. 'I am truly sorry . . . I did not bring any money with me.'

'Do not worry, Walter.' Frances swept de Grammont with a steely look. 'I am sure the Count only jested about the wager.'

She wound her arm through her brother's and marched him off through the crowds, with Cary and Catherine twittering protestingly in her wake.

Rochester and de Grammont watched them depart.

'If I do not mistake it, that young man is ripe for the plucking,' commented Rochester with a lascivious wink. 'Know you what they say in the East? A woman for duty and a boy for pleasure . . .'

'Come now, John,' de Grammont, a great lover of women, said, tutting, 'do not lead Master Stuart down that path. Besides, I have mind to lead him down another. Mistress Stuart has a sharp tongue. She made some sally to the King on the subject of my losing the wager to Jermyn and rendered me a laughing stock.'

'Aye,' Lord Rochester assented. 'And she warned me at Master Lely's studio that I should not underestimate her.'

'Then she should not underestimate *us*. Let us take that fledgling brother in hand and show him a little of London.'

'The pleasure will be all mine.'

*   *   *

Frances delivered Walter to the stairs of Somerset House before continuing on to Whitehall.

'Farewell, Brother,' she waved. 'And be wary of strangers!'

They entered the palace through the Shield Gallery where it was usually quiet and empty, and

206

were surprised to find Mall and her daughter Mary there, walking up and down staring up at the shields and coats of arms that lined the gallery's panelled walls. 'She wanted to know what the family crest resembled,' Mall explained, 'so I brought her to besee it.' She dropped her voice. 'Now she is near to being betrothed she takes a sudden interest in her heritage. See, Mary, there is the Villiers crest!' She pointed at the crest. 'And there is our family motto: "The cross is the test of truth." So,' she raised an eyebrow at the three young women, 'what do you three do, looking so guilty?'

'We went to see Jacob Hall, the rope dancer,' confessed Cary, smiling. 'And he lost his heart to Frances.'

'And, Mall, the best news! Walter is come to London and we shall be seeing him often.'

Mall smiled, pleased for Frances, who had needed a diversion since the Duke of Richmond's marriage.

'Come,' Catherine chivvied. 'The Queen may be calling for us.'

Mall watched them skip off, young and free. It was said that Catherine Boynton hoped soon for the two-thousand-pound dowry that maids of honour were usually awarded by the Crown. Would Frances be given the same? And would any man of rank settle for so modest a sum? But then would any man be mad enough to offer for the woman the King loved so passionately?

Mall sighed, relieved at least that her brother had abandoned his ridiculous committee for the winning of Frances for the King.

Frances said goodbye to the others and ran to her chamber, tired after their expedition, to throw cold water upon her face from the ewer that the Groom of the Bedchamber provided every other day, before finding out what her duties might be. Yet she was surprised to find that something had been left on the great half-tester bed.

It was a large and extravagant basket of fruit. There were crisp apples, plums with the purple blush of autumn still upon them and, in the centre, a pineapple, so new to English shores that the builders of Covent Garden had adopted it as their fashionable symbol.

And yet there seemed to be no card or message from the giver. She would have to ask the Groom who delivered them. Shrugging, she helped herself to an apple and noticed that something was buried in the straw that lay beneath the fruit. She delved inside, feeling like a child with its hand in the fairground bran tub, hoping for a hidden treat.

Instead she gasped. The surprise buried in the straw was a pearl ring, and tied to it by a silken thread was a card inviting her to an entertainment to be given in the King's honour the next night, by the Duke of Buckingham at his mansion, Wallingford House. She stared at the ring, dumbfounded. If these were the invitations, how lavish would the party itself be?

As with any young woman who enjoyed balls and outings, her first thoughts were of what gown she would wear. She ran across to the press where her best clothes were stored and pulled out the apricot organdie dress than Minette had given her. It was too grand for many occasions, but not for this one. She shook it out and the folds shimmered like sunset reflected in water.

A knock on the door interrupted her reverie.

The Groom of the Bedchamber bowed. 'Her Grace of Buckingham, Mistress.'

Frances tried to hide her surprise at such an unusual occurrence. Visitors were usually received in the Great Hall or Withdrawing Room. A visit to her chamber, especially from a lady she hardly knew, was strange indeed.

The Duchess of Buckingham had once been plain Mary Fairfax, daughter of one of Cromwell's most trusted generals and betrothed to the Earl of Chesterfield, with the banns twice read, when the glamorous George Villiers burst into her life and carried her off instead. It had been a great to-do and Cromwell had not been happy at the Duke's nearness to the King, but somehow it had gone ahead.

Yet Mary had paid the price for her choice of husband. The Duke had led her a merry dance and still did. She seemed to love him all the same and always did his bidding, however great her misgivings.

'Good evening, Mistress Stuart. I see you have received the invitation to our little entertainment.'

'Indeed, yes, Your Grace.' Frances flushed with embarrassment that she had already spread her gown on the bed; it seemed so childish, like the guest who cannot wait for a party.

Mary smiled. She was not a beautiful lady, and indeed looked a little old and tired. Being married to the Duke must be taxing.

'We wished to say that the evening is in the nature of a surprise to the King, and very select. The Ambassador of Muscovy will come, and the highest members of the Council, but none of the usual flighty ladies of the Court. My husband sees you as a young woman of sense who can hold her own at such an occasion.'

Frances remembered the eyes of the Duke of Buckingham on her at the various occasions when they had met. It was not her good sense that he had seemed to be appreciating then. 'Thank you, Your Grace. Kindly tell your husband the Duke that certainly I can hold my own. Yet the Duke's own sister, Mall, will certainly be attending?'

The Duchess turned away and fingered the fruit in the basket. 'I do love pineapple, do not you, Mistress Stuart?'

'I have not had the pleasure of trying it.'

'Along with other things you have not tried, I hear.' A curious expression crossed her face, half-wistful, half-lascivious.

She was indeed a strange lady, Frances decided.

'Mr Rose, the King's own gardener,' continued the Duchess nervously, '. . . ha-ha, such a fitting name for a plantsman . . . has grown one in the royal glasshouses. You will be in honourable company tomorrow, by the way. Lord Arlington, Sir Charles Berkeley, the Ambassador of course . . .'

'Yet not Mall?'

'Mall dislikes such formal occasions and, frankly, she can be a little outspoken.' She fiddled with the fringe on her sash. 'You have heard of the pranks she played as a child, hiding up a tree pretending to be a butterfly. And she is suspected of writing quite scurrilous poetry lampooning the King.'

'Unlike my lord Rochester, who writes outrageously scurrilous verses and yet whom the King loves all the same?'

The Duchess ignored the interruption and hurried on. 'And now this ridiculous business with

210

Tom Howard. She is near twice his age and he has not a penny, besides having killed young Giles Rawlins over that whore Lady Shrewsbury.' Her face grew red and her voice rose in anger at the mention of Lady Shrewsbury, making Frances wonder if her husband the Duke might also be a victim of the fatal Anna Maria. 'Has she no shame? Nor care of her family name? All in all, we have decided it would better to keep the occasion from dearest Mall, so that she is not offended at the exclusion. You do understand? I may count on your discretion?' She fixed a smile on her homely face, which seemed as false as the silk flower in her hair. 'Now I must seek out the Queen. We look forward to seeing you tomorrow and will send a coach for you at quarter to the hour.'

Frances felt like insisting that if Mall did not come, neither would she. Yet she knew the storm that would ensue, and Mall would not thank her for it. She wanted no further scandal about her love for Tom. 'Until tomorrow then.'

And now she must keep the occasion hidden from Mall, which made her uncomfortable, especially as Mall was like a terrier seeking a rat, when it came to secrets and gossip. So Frances decided the best policy would be to avoid her until the occasion was past, when she could regale her friend with tales of how hideous the night had been, and how pompous the Duke and Duchess with their pineapples and their pretensions. Mall, she knew, would be a ready audience.

The best way to avoid Mall's company was to go out riding. Mall did not share her delight in daredevil jumps and harum-scarum gallops across muddy parkland.

Frances changed into her riding habit of brocade with the elaborate paisley edging, and her lace jabot tied with a blue silk bow at the neck. She thought about seeking out Walter for company, but it would take too long to send a message and wait for the reply.

She stood in front of the looking glass to fasten her hat with its red feather, then stood back a moment to survey herself. She looked at her own image, the soft fair hair, the delicate skin of youth, the eyes the King had said reminded him of a faun. And yet, she thought, raising her chin, there is my nose. It was a serious Roman nose, the nose of a substantial woman, not a silly young girl.

'Let them underestimate me if they will,' she murmured to her own reflection, and smiled. Yet it was not a gentle, tender smile, but one of cynicism and rebellion. There was something about tomorrow night that aroused her suspicions and she was determined to be on her guard.

'Up there and at 'em!' encouraged the parrot. 'Show 'em what you're made of.'

'Thank you, Bird,' she acknowledged and bowed so low to her avian friend that the red feather on her hat tickled the ground.

Frances rode out under the brick gatehouse past the bigger apartments into which Barbara had just moved—causing considerable disruption, and designed to prove that she still had power over the King—and out through the Yard into St James' Park. A battalion of soldiers practised formation on Horse Guards Parade, splendid in their buff coats. She stopped for a moment to watch them, thinking of Tom Howard, and of how they could somehow persuade the King to let him return.

She spurred on her horse and galloped with the wind in her hair, free as a bird, feeling her heart expand and her cares disappear like a morning mist when the sun appears. As the parrot had said, she should show them what she was made of.

*   *   *

She was fortunate the next day that Mall was not in evidence.

That being the night of the entertainment, Frances dressed with extra care. Cary Frazier insisted on helping and stood, primping and poking, pulling her gown from her shoulders and dusting them with a hare's foot of powder until she was finally pleased with her friend's appearance.

'That gown truly becomes you, yet what will you wear about your neck?'

Frances disgorged a mound of jewellery, none of it valuable, onto her dressing table while, on its perch, the parrot's eye lit up as if it spied some long-lost pirate treasure.

'We will let the bird choose,' laughed Frances. She held out her finger and the parrot hopped straight onto it, surveying the jewels. Squawking, it swooped down and picked up a necklet of yellow brilliants.

'Yellow with apricot?' grimaced Cary. 'Your parrot has poor taste.'

Yet when she clasped them around Frances' neck the shade of the stone perfectly enhanced the cool grey-blue of her laughing eyes.

There was a knock on the door to tell them the coach had arrived. The groom handed over a green velvet box. 'The coachman brought these for you, mistress.' His face was as blank as a brick wall. 'From the King. He begs you wear them tonight.'

Her heart beat wildly as she opened the case. A string of the largest pearls she had ever seen gleamed out at her, their nacreous depths beckoning and alluring. She could almost feel the warmth of their touch on her neck.

'They are greater even than Barbara Castlemaine's,' breathed Cary enviously.

Without meaning to, Cary's remark had put her on her mettle. 'Aye, and yet I prefer the parrot's choice.'

'You have to wear them. They are sent to you from the King! To wear your yellow baubles would be taken as the grossest insult.'

Frances slipped the pearls around her neck, wishing they did not have the feel of the hangman's noose.

'You are the strangest girl, Frances Stuart. You have a king at your feet and you treat it as an inconvenience.'

Frances grinned, her face lighting up with sudden mischief. 'Then may I have the wit to resist his grasp and yet not find myself imprisoned in the Tower!'

'Amen to that,' agreed the parrot as Frances picked up her wrap and set out.

The distance from Whitehall to the Duke of Buckingham's mansion was not great and, had a coach not been sent to collect her, Frances might have taken a sedan chair. Instead a large and lumbering carriage with the Buckingham crest on the side awaited her at the Great Gate.

'Good evening, mistress,' the coachman greeted her.

214

The Duke of Buckingham had moved from York House, where he and Mall had passed their early years, to Wallingford House, but a stone's throw from Whitehall, for greater convenience. He lived here during the summer in great state, leaving for his estates in the country during the winter months. It bordered on Spring Garden in one direction and Charing Cross in the other, and the Duke had filled it with magnificent paintings by Rubens, Vermeer and Van Dyck. During the Commonwealth all these works of art, and much of his grand furniture, had been looted or stolen, but George Villiers—like his cousin Lady Castlemaine—had managed to get most of it back, so that the house Frances visited was as impressive and ornate as ever.

The coach rumbled over the cobbled stones— passing the peg-legged chair-mender who sat with his bundle of willow repairing broken rush seats and a vendor of carpet beaters whose cry made Frances smile: 'Buy a pretty little stick to beat your wives or dust your rugs!'—and deposited her at the imposing entrance to Wallingford House.

She looked up at the vast windows, blazing with a thousand candles, and felt a shiver of apprehension.

'Nonsense!' she reminded herself sternly. 'Remember, you are a woman who can hold her own.'

The Duchess stood amongst a knot of people in the enormous black and white chequered hallway. Frances recognized the Earl of Bristol, who was currently high with the King, talking to Lord Arlington—always recognizable from the black plaster across the bridge of his nose, hiding the scar he had gained fighting in the civil war—and the Earl of Shaftesbury. Behind them stood Sir Charles

Berkeley.

All of them turned at her entrance and watched her curiously, as if they had been waiting for her arrival.

Beyond them a great bear of a man clad in white silk from head to toe, laced with frogging, and with a huge bushy beard, who had to be the Ambassador of Muscovy, was deep in conversation with a tall gentleman whose back was towards her.

'Have you met the Ambassador, Mistress Stuart?' enquired the Duchess.

At her words the unknown gentleman turned sharply and Frances almost dropped her fan. It was the Duke of Richmond.

For the briefest of moments their eyes locked.

She forgot where she was and that they stood in a room full of guests. She looked round to see if his sour-faced wife accompanied him, but there was no sign of her. Indeed, there were no other ladies present except the Duchess and herself, giving the gathering an air almost of a meeting of the Council instead of the entertainment that had been promised.

As if the same thought struck the Duchess, she signalled to a group of musicians above them on a balcony, who instantly struck up some lively air on viol and tabor.

'Come, gentlemen.' The Duchess seemed to remember her role as chatelaine. 'To dinner!'

They followed in the wake of a groom liveried in blue velvet with the badge of the Buckingham family upon his arm, up a wide stone staircase to a large dining chamber, the walls of which were lined with dark-green moiré silk, on which vast gilded mirrors caught the reflections of the many candles,

216

creating an effect akin to the stage at Drury Lane. Paintings lined the walls and Frances found herself staring up at the proud, melancholy face of King Charles I. The table was ornately decorated not just with the usual silver plate and Venetian glassware, but with a vast silver flagon, embossed with a wild boar on one side and a unicorn upon the other; in the centre of the table were huge pyramids of fruit and flowers, and even, not a foot away from her, an entire stuffed peacock, his glorious tail feathers nodding in the draught from an open window.

Frances found herself seated next to her host, who chattered on about the days when he used to build her houses of cards and make her laugh with his impersonations of some of the people present. Yet her glance kept straying across to where Charles Stuart sat, and when it did, she found his eyes equally fixed on her. Instead of a smile of polite recognition, they simply looked at each other silently, as if between them no words were called for or necessary.

'Now, mistress, try some of these excellent silver eels.'

The Duke of Buckingham piled her plate high with lobster, rare beef and tiny quails, all on a skewer, until she had to protest that she could eat no more. Her glass was filled continually as if from a fountain.

After they had supped they removed to a pretty banqueting house for their sweetmeats and desserts.

'Good evening, Your Grace,' Frances addressed the Duke of Richmond, when she could extricate herself from their host. 'Came you tonight from Cobham?'

Charles Stuart's gaze rested upon her with such tenderness that she had to look away.

'I am staying in London at present to fulfil my duties as Gentleman of the Bedchamber.'

'And yet the King is not here?' She looked around, realizing for the first time the strange absence at the heart of the proceedings.

A silence fell on the room at her words and Buckingham looked swiftly across at Arlington, as if it were a signal for some action to begin.

The Duke of Buckingham cleared his throat. 'You are most perceptive, mistress. And yet he is here. He is at present in the summerhouse, at the bottom of my garden, where he is so absorbed in one of his scientific experiments that he could not tear himself away, even for the company gathered here. Indeed, he most especially requested that you visit him, that he may show you the wonder of it.'

Her eyes darted to the Duke of Richmond's. 'Yet does he not conduct his experiments in his laboratory at Whitehall?' Her steady voice faltered.

'For the most part, yes,' blustered Buckingham. 'But this was something to do with the natural world and he wished to do it here. Will you go to him?'

The soft murmurings of conversation stopped, as if a fox had barked in the midnight wood and all had fallen silent and still.

Frances stood erect, her head high.

When she passed the Duke of Richmond she pretended to drop her fan and, as they both leaned down to retrieve it, she whispered, 'If I am not returned in fifteen minutes, pray find an excuse to come and seek me out.'

His hand touched hers. 'Upon my life, I will do so.'

And, with the silent gaze of the whole company fixed on her, she walked alone down the sweeping stone staircase towards the summerhouse.

It struck her, as she summoned up her courage and all of her wit, that the whole occasion had had a strange leaden deliberation, as though it were but the preamble rather than the main event. Which meant the true purpose of the evening lay ahead— and it was to throw her, like Daniel, into the Lion's Den. She remembered being read the story as a child of how Daniel prayed to God, and God sealed the mouths of the lions so that they could not devour him.

She straightened her back and made herself as tall as she could. With or without God's help, she did not intend to be devoured by the King.

Chapter 11

'Where is Mistress Stuart?' Mall enquired of Cary Frazier as both dined at the maids of honour's table in the Queen's Apartments.

Cary, bound to silence by Frances, tried to change the subject. 'Have you heard that the Queen is to give Catherine Boynton an extra five hundred pounds towards her dowry, that she may wed her Dick Talbot?'

It was on Mall's lips to quip that it would be better to give Dick Talbot the money *not* to marry Catherine, given his reputation. Yet who was she to criticize? Since the duel, many thought Tom

Howard a villain and a ne'er-do-well and yet she knew he was neither.

'Cary Frazier,' she looked Cary full in the eye, 'I did not ask of Catherine Boynton, or of Dick Talbot, of whose amours I care not one jot. I asked about Mistress Stuart.'

Cary sighed. Deception was not her strong point. People always told her they could read her like an open book. And it was unreasonable of Frances to expect her to lie blatantly.

'She had an invitation.' Cary helped herself to some mutton pie, roast venison and a few lampreys.

'From whom?'

Cary hesitated.

'From your brother, the Duke of Buckingham. To Wallingford House.'

'My brother?' repeated Mall, her suspicions sharpening.

'And his duchess, naturally.'

'To what occasion?'

'An entertainment of some sort for His Majesty.'

The blood rushed from Mall's head at this revelation.

'And who else was bidden to this entertainment?'

Cary looked at her as if she had lost her mind. 'Well, not you or I, clearly. And not the Queen, for she sits up there upon the dais.'

'Cary, tell me truly. Was I deliberately not to know of this evening's work?' She clutched Cary's arm.

'Oww . . . yes, I do not know . . . Yet I think perhaps they wanted you not to know of it.'

Mall jumped to her feet. Her brother had gone ahead with his plans for the royal rape.

Another thought struck Mall, no doubt sent

220

by the Devil to tempt her. The King had said he would pardon Tom Howard if Mall helped to get Frances into his bed. Tonight, at this very hour, the seduction might be happening. And if he succeeded, the King would be so overjoyed at achieving what he had so long yearned for that he might forgive Tom anyway. And if he heard that Mall had discovered the plan and yet not stopped it, he would be doubly grateful.

Mall shook her head to chase away the shameful thought. Was she losing all honour and kindness in the cause of her own selfish love?

There was one way she could stop this conspiracy, and only one.

While the other ladies watched her, gossiping behind their hands, Mall ran swiftly towards the door, pausing only when she saw the little blackamoor whom the Queen loved to pet.

Mall dropped down on her knees and whispered to the child, 'Tell the Queen there is a party at the Duke of Buckingham's house and that my lady Mary says it is a rare entertainment that she should not miss. Can you remember that?'

The boy nodded solemnly.

As soon as she saw him head for the dais at the top of the room, Mall half-ran down the stairs, through the Vane Room and the length of the Privy Gallery, until she reached a set of rooms she had hitherto avoided.

Taking a deep breath, she knocked on the door.

A servant answered, dressed in gold brocade, wearing golden stockings and gold and white shoes, far richer than any of the Queen's attendants.

Breathlessly Mall gave him the same message. 'My lady Castlemaine should come post-haste to the Duke of Buckingham's.'

Without awaiting an answer she rushed to her own apartment to find her cloak, and began to run across the Pebble Court towards the palace gate, praying to a God she too often ignored that they would be in time.

The darkness outside meant that she needed the help of a link boy to light her to Wallingford House. He, excited at having so great a lady to conduct down the Mall, whistled until a small crowd of his fellows appeared, all hoping for a generous vail, so that she arrived at her brother's doorstep in a blaze of torches.

* * *

Frances walked through the darkened gardens towards the summerhouse with her head high and her wits sharpened.

It was a wild October night with the clouds scudding past a crescent moon, leaving the skies one moment black, the next streaked with a pale, glimmering light, the kind of unsettling weather that made you hurry past graveyards, keep your head down and pull your cloak tight.

The path to the summerhouse was through a clump of trees and tangled ivy. Her heart contracted when she saw that it was in complete darkness, without even so much as a candle's glow illuminating it. Was she wrong about the King? Had he indeed persuaded himself that all deeds were acceptable in the dark?

Gingerly she opened the door. 'Your Majesty?' she asked tentatively.

'Over here, Frances,' came the reply.

The clouds shifted suddenly and a squib of light briefly lit the room.

The King stood at one end, peering up at the night sky through a strange wooden tube.

'Come and look,' he beckoned. She crossed the room, dark as a dungeon again, and stood next to him, the blood pounding in her ears. He placed his arms around hers, holding the tube steady so that she might look through it. 'Galileo's telescope. He showed how the earth is not the centre of our universe, but the sun, and earned himself the hatred of the Church and ignominy among his peers.' He sighed suddenly. 'How I hate it when ignorance and superstition win over knowledge and progress. What do you see?'

Frances began to recover from her surprise. 'Stars, sire.'

He laughed. 'Indeed you do. Do you know which stars?'

'My father showed me the North Star when I was a maid.'

'Did he tell you that of all the stars, only the North Star stays fixed in the night sky? That sailors from the oldest times saved themselves from shipwreck thanks to the North Star?'

He took the telescope out of her hands and turned her to face him. His dark eyes glowed with desire, darker even than the night around them.

'Frances, come to me. How long have I loved and desired you? Be my true North, the one fixed point in my universe.'

He pulled her close to his body and she felt the hardness of him against her, and gasped. Yet he had a wife. If she succumbed she would be his doxy, as the others were—the Castlemaines, the actresses, even the women in the stews of London he was known to frequent. Besides, there were other arms than his that she longed for to hold her.

'Sire,' she pulled away, 'I cannot.'

His face hardened, the deep lines around his mouth suddenly like fissures, his eyes narrow and angry. She wondered if she had misread his nature and shrank away. As she did so, he grabbed her necklace to pull her back to him, but the string broke, scattering the pearls all about them like a shower of gleaming hailstones.

Before he even had time to react Frances heard dogs barking and suddenly the Duke of Richmond appeared at the door, surrounded by a blaze of light, like the Archangel Michael wielding a sword of fire.

'Your Majesty,' he announced, and to Frances' astonishment she saw the blaze of light was the work of nine or ten link boys wielding torches. 'Be warned. We have some unexpected visitors.'

And then from out of the darkness, violet eyes blazing like a Fury loosed from hell, Barbara Castlemaine launched herself upon them. 'What goes on here?' Her gaze swept over Frances, taking in the broken necklace. A cruel smile spread across her lovely, spoilt face. 'I hope he has had you at last, mistress, for you are not worth a hundredth of the suffering you have caused him.'

Frances saw the Duke stiffen, and his hand stray to his sword arm. Did he think he could kill the King or the King's mistress?

'You misread the situation, my lady.' Frances made her voice as matter-of-fact as if she talked to a razor-grinder or ballad-seller. 'The King was simply showing me the alignment of the stars. My necklace became entangled in the telescope, that was all.'

''Tis true, my lady,' piped up the leader of the link boys helpfully, clearly hoping that some advantage would flow from the observation, 'they was just looking up at the sky, no hanky-panky nor nothing.'

Frances picked up the tube and offered it to her rival. 'Are you interested in seeing the North Star, Barbara?'

For answer Barbara grabbed the telescope and broke it in two, shattering the lovely polished wood with its gilded leather casing.

'The Queen is here also, sire.'

'How in God's heaven did she get wind of this night?' He turned to Barbara. 'Or you, my lady?'

Barbara snorted. 'Dearest Mall told us. She sent a message that it was an entertainment we must not miss.'

For a moment it seemed as if he would have Mall sent immediately to the Tower, yet with one of the sudden volte-faces that characterized the man, he clapped his hands, struck by the supreme ridiculousness of the situation. 'My wife has come for an entertainment, has she? Then she shall have one. Come, Richmond,' the King threaded his arm through the Duke's with apparent joviality. 'Let us find His Grace of Buckingham, that we may have music and dancing until the dawn sends us to our beds.'

After they had left, Frances bent down and began to pick up her pearls, hoping to still the beating of her heart.

'There has been mischief here tonight, and I intend to get to the bottom of it,' Barbara almost spat. 'How many lives have you now, Mistress Maidenhead?'

'I have but one life and mean to live it how I choose.'

'Then you will fail. I have done that all my life and it has earned me naught but notoriety.'

'Yet I wish it through finding a good man to love and escaping the life of the Court for fresher air.'

'And who will take you—dowerless, and desired by the King?'

Frances turned her face away and made a play of finding the scattered pearls, so that Barbara would not see the pain in her eyes.

Back in Wallingford House every candle had been lit, and the sound of jigs and Corantos filled the night air.

The King made a point of dancing every dance with his queen.

An uneasy silence fell on the room as Frances entered it. No doubt she had been the chief object of gossip and conjecture ever since she had left earlier, each man wondering whether their plan had succeeded and the King had had his way.

She briefly entertained the thought of facing them, hands on hips, as if she were an actress in Drury Lane and announcing, 'I am sorry, my lords, but your plan was foiled by the Duke of Richmond and a band of link boys! What think you of that?'

Gradually they began to tut and turn their backs, and it seemed she might become a social pariah not for succumbing to the King, but on the contrary, for resisting him. Seeing her plight, the Queen, a good six inches smaller than Frances, smiled and beckoned her across. 'Mistress Stuart, you are alone. Come and join in our set to dance a Bransle.'

Frances smiled gratefully, knowing the act was deliberate, to restore her credit. She put her hand to the set and looked downwards, concentrating on her steps and so avoiding the eye of the King. When the music finished she curtseyed and excused herself.

'Stay awhile,' a voice behind her said gently. 'Will you not join me on the floor, mistress?'

She found the Duke of Richmond at her back, holding himself in readiness for the dance.

And so, for the second time that night, Frances found herself in the arms of a Charles Stuart. Yet this one was young and eager, with a merry instead of a cynical eye. While the King had the height, and was spare from his energetic games of tennis, this Charles was more solidly built and she felt like thistledown in his arms.

Yet he also had a wife, she reminded herself bitterly.

'How fares your house at Cobham?' she asked, to break the silence that had fallen between them.

'Beauteous indeed in its autumn colours.' She heard the deep affection for the place in his voice. 'I hope to plant an avenue of lime trees.' His voice altered. 'Yet my wife says it is too great an extravagance, and she would prefer to spend the money on coming to London.'

Frances felt the cold blast of reality. What childish dream was she living in, which drew her to him? 'Your wife does not feel about the house as you do?'

'She says it is like a great hole in the ground that we pour our money into. Pardon, *her* money into.'

The next words that she forced herself to utter cut her like a knife into soft flesh. 'Perhaps she will grow to love the place as you do, when you have heirs to run around the parkland.'

A dark shadow crossed his handsome features, like a cloud presaging rain. 'I greatly doubt it. She has felt the fear and suffering of childbed once and informs me that she does not intend to repeat its pangs.'

'You cannot mean . . . ?'

Frances fell silent, aware that she of all people could not ask such a question.

And yet he answered it for her. 'Indeed. The usual consolations of matrimony are denied me.' A look of sudden disgust crossed his features. 'Not that I would wish them. The delights of country life are also lost on my wife. She pines for the drama of the city.'

'How strange.' Frances thought of the many drawings she had made of Cobham's mellow, comforting warmth. 'If it were mine, I would never leave it.'

His arms tightened around her for a brief second.

'The King did you no harm, I truly hope?'

'No.' Frances shook her head. 'Yet I was glad of your arrival.'

'With my avenging link-boy army.'

She smiled at the memory. 'I saw it in your face, you would have drawn your sword upon the King.'

'Aye. And shown myself a traitor.' His grey eyes held hers. 'And yet, by keeping it in its scabbard, I was a traitor to my heart.'

All around them the merry music seemed to stop. Frances broke away, her pulse racing. The duke bowed.

'Remember me to your parrot.'

228

'It is my parrot who never lets me forget your existence.'

Charles smiled and kissed her hand.

'Then I can only give him thanks. Farewell, Mistress Stuart.'

'Farewell, my lord Richmond.'

She turned to find Mall's eagle gaze upon her, yet Mall shook her head and said nothing.

'Thank you for summoning the Queen.' Frances saw at once how much it must have cost Mall to risk the King's disapproval.

Mall shrugged. 'Love can wring the heart and twist the guts. As I think you are perhaps discovering.'

*   *   *

Rather than ignoring her, the Queen paid Frances particular attention after Wallingford House. She invited her to chapel, to play cards at her apartments in the afternoons and even help her try some new hairstyles, since she declared that Mistress Stuart was always the most stylish lady in her Court. For this Frances called in the assistance of her sister Sophia, since she paid more attention to fashion in hairstyles than she did.

The other ladies, especially Cary Frazier, looked sullen at this, since Sophia was maid to the Queen Mother, yet Sophia herself was delighted. She arrived from Somerset House with a bag of pins, combs, metal tongs and a small charcoal brazier, which every lady in Paris, she declared, would no more leave behind than her gowns or satin shoes.

Of course, Frances remembered, the Queen had her own barber—the very one of whom the King had asked where it was he shaved her.

Her Portuguese duennas had simply looked on boot-faced and disapproving, no doubt deciding that the King was little better than the Englishmen they complained of, who were so unrefined that, right in the middle of London, they stood up against the walls to relieve themselves even when there were ladies present.

Sophia produced a small book with various woodcuts featuring different hairstyles, the merits of which she proceeded to explain to Her Majesty. 'I wear mine in this one—the hurluberlu,' and she pointed to a style that had a mass of curls issuing from the nape of the neck in riotous profusion. 'Frances favours this one—an arrangement "à la négligence" and Lady Castle—' She stopped abruptly, clapping her hand over her mouth like a child that has taken the Lord's name in vain during catechism practice.

'Lady Castlemaine favours which style?' the Queen asked calmly.

'She prefers wired locks at the moment.'

The Queen smiled suddenly. 'Then I shall also. What is good enough for Lady Castlemaine must surely be good enough for the Queen, think you not?'

Her ladies looked at her in surprise. Her meaning was quite clear and the comment showed more wit and spirit than was usually found in her manner. Perhaps the Queen was truly learning to hold her own.

Sophia began to search in her bag for a wire frame to attach to the Queen's hair that it might stand out from the sides of her head, then fall flatteringly in ringlets to her shoulders.

'Your Majesty's hair is wonderfully thick,' she admired.

The little Queen shone under the beam of her praise. Clearly she received little of it at other times.

'You will need no false curls or ringlets such as French ladies buy.'

'And, also, it is dark,' endorsed Cary Frazier, 'which is very much the fashion at the moment. Unlike some poor ladies.' She stole a glance at Frances' tawny-blonde locks. 'Heard you what befell my lady Lauderdale when she tried to change her hair from red to black?' She lowered her voice so that they knew some juicy scandal would follow. 'She soaked her hair with a posset of lime, ceruse and powder of gold sold her by an apothecary, and must leave the potion on all night to gain the full benefit by the morrow.'

'And did it work?' Frances enquired.

'Indeed it did. By morning all her hair was black as night.' Cary fell about laughing. 'It was also on the pillow next to her, every lock! She was bald as a coot and has worn a wig ever since. Even in bed with his lordship.'

'Cary Frazier, I believe not a word of that harum-scarum tale,' chided Lady Suffolk, the Queen's chief Lady of the Bedchamber and Groomess of the Stool, who had joined the group.

'I had it from the servant who dresses her hair,' insisted Cary, looking hurt. She collapsed in giggles again. 'And now Lord Lauderdale wears his wig in bed too, to keep her company!'

Sophia heated the tongs on the tiny brazier while she carefully divided the Queen's hair down the middle of her head.

She peered suddenly at the parting, noting an unwelcome visitor, which held fast to the root of the hair. 'Majesty, may I have your permission to remove a royal louse?' Sophia enquired.

'Mistress,' the Queen quipped gaily, 'is that a respectful way to describe my husband?'

This time all the ladies dissolved in laughter, even the pompous Lady Suffolk.

By the time Sophia had curled the Queen's hair onto the wires and divided the side sections into small tendrils draped over her forehead, finished with a tiny curl or *confidante* in the middle of her forehead, the whole morning had flown past. Yet a new hairstyle was not enough to satisfy the newly restless Queen.

Later in the day Frances was busy helping Charlotte, Lady Killigrew, Keeper of the Sweet Coffers, in her task of maintaining the Queen's gowns, hats, feathers, fans and perfumes. They had just placed bunches of lavender and dried rue amongst the Queen's clothes, folding them carefully between layers of lawn in the great press, when the Queen suddenly came to find them.

Frances stopped folding to stare at their mistress in open-mouthed astonishment. Catherine of Braganza, Queen Consort to Charles II of England, who had arrived on these shores wearing a farthingale so enormous and old-fashioned that all had laughed at her, was standing before them dressed as a man! She wore the wide pantaloons known as rhinegraves, fashionable with the racier sort of gentleman, a tailored riding coat with lace frothing out at the neck, and sported a Cavalier hat bearing an eagle's nest of feathers on top.

'Mistress Stuart. I am told you are the best

rider of all my ladies.' She signalled to the little blackamoor who always followed in her train. 'Give the clothes to Mistress Stuart, Guinea.'

Frances smiled at the tiny boy and held out her arms to receive the burden.

'Quick! Go and change in your chamber. We are going on an adventure. We ride out to Worsley End, where we mean to admire the countryside and shock a few of my people. Yet, do not worry, they will not recognize us in this attire!'

'Are you sure His Majesty will make no objections to such a scheme, Majesty? Gentlewomen out, alone and unaccompanied even by grooms or servants?' Frances asked, in alarm.

Catherine's black eyes glowed impishly. 'He is perfectly happy with the idea—mostly because he does not know of it! And I forbid any of you here to tell him.'

After she had left, Frances whispered to Lady Killigrew, 'What has come over the Queen? She has seemed a different lady of late.'

Lady Killigrew shrugged. 'Mayhap she is tired of being overlooked by her husband and wishes to cut a dash of her own.' She looked meaningfully at Frances. 'It must be hard to be surrounded by so many mistresses when you are naught but the wife.'

'It would certainly be one in the eye for my lady Castlemaine if the King began to notice he had one,' Frances conceded. 'Just to be safe,' she added in a whisper, 'if we are not back by fall of dusk, you had better inform him.'

*   *   *

Worsley End was a fine mansion in its own grounds

near the pretty village of Isleworth. They made the first leg of the journey by hackney coach—and even that was an object of delight to the Queen. To ride in a common coach!

'Do you think we will be stopped by highwaymen?' she asked and clapped her hands in anticipation. 'They would certainly be surprised to find three women dressed as gentlemen!'

Fortunately for any highwayman who inadvertently held up the Queen of England—for which treasonous act the punishment would be hanging, drawing and quartering—they arrived at their destination undetained.

Three fine horses waited for them in the stables, which the Queen had already bespoken. She had not, it became apparent from the chaffing and good-humoured banter from the grooms, vouchsafed her royal identity.

'Well, my fine sirs,' the head groom winked at his underling, 'may you have a good gallop. It's a grand enough day for it. If you head through the park and over yon hill, you only have three or four gates to jump.'

Cary Frazier blenched. 'Might we not pass by the road?'

'If you are willing to go back three miles, young sir.'

'Come, gentlemen.' The Queen rallied them. 'What is it you say in England? Tally-ho!'

Frances soon forgot her strange garb, or indeed the fact that instead of riding side-saddle, she was having the strange experience of riding as men do. Once she felt the wind freshen her cheeks and watched the clouds dart across the hills, leaving a pattern of light and shadow like the patchwork quilt

234

on her old nurse's bed, she felt truly happy.

Ahead of them, a gate loomed.

The fear struck Frances that here she was riding out alone, and the Queen of England was her sole responsibility. If Catherine fell from her horse and was injured, it would be she who would be fully accountable.

She jumped the first gate easily, and the Queen afterwards, but Cary shook her head, her face greyer than ash. 'I am sorry, Your Majesty. I am too much the woman after all. I will wait for you at the stables.'

They jumped two more gates and finally came to the brow of a hill where, laid beneath them like a rich Mortlake tapestry, the valley glowed in the afternoon sun.

'Let us sit awhile,' Catherine suggested.

Frances nodded, suddenly shy to be alone with the Queen, whom she waited on, yet hardly knew. And the thought struck her that perhaps today was a deliberate charade to get her alone and admonish her for her nearness to the King, or to warn her off.

Yet Catherine said nothing about Charles.

She laughed at Frances, so tall and striking in her men's clothing. 'What a height you are, and how dashing!' She elbowed Frances raucously. 'Indeed, you make so pretty a youth that at Whitehall or St James' you would have to walk with your back to the wall!'

Frances blinked. The Queen had certainly learned much since she had come here.

They came upon a fallen tree and tied their horses to it, seating themselves on its gnarled trunk, which felt as warm to the touch as any cushion.

'Tell me, Mistress Stuart,' Catherine asked

impetuously, her great dark eyes intent, 'you know the King as well as I. What does he desire from his queen?' Before Frances had time to form an answer, Catherine rushed on. 'His people wished for a Protestant princess, yet they took me because I brought them wealth and the chance to trade, which my husband says they care for more than any religion. Yet they hate Catholics. Though even that they would pardon me, if I could produce an heir to the throne.'

The haunting brown eyes looked suddenly away and fixed upon the distant hills.

'You know not what it is like . . . every month I look to my flowers, praying they will not come and hoping I am with child.' She bit her lip until it whitened. 'I hope, and pray, and light candles, and offer novenas to Our Lady, because she is a mother and must understand this longing, this eating pain . . . And then my flowers come and I know once again that I am not with child, and I weep.' She looked down at her hands. 'I know what they say of me, in the streets of London. "What is of less use: a worn-out shoe or a barren queen?"'

Though it was a great a breach of protocol, Frances reached out a hand and took hers. 'You have time yet, Majesty.'

'I am seven and twenty years old.' And indeed it seemed a shock that this childlike figure should be so much a grown woman. The thought lay between them, until Catherine could resist no longer. 'How old are you, Mistress Stuart?'

Frances rose to her feet. 'We should return, Your Highness. Cary Frazier will begin to fret.'

'Tell me, Frances. I truly wish to know.'

'I will soon be nineteen, Majesty.'

236

'Nineteen!' repeated Catherine as if the word somehow pierced her soul. 'Is a wife's only purpose to bear her husband children?' she demanded, suddenly passionate. 'Does not affection, or love, or cherishing of all his hopes and schemes count for aught then?'

'It ought to, Majesty, and I am sure, indeed it does.' She thought of that other Charles Stuart, tied to a wife who did not care for or cherish him, and wondered if sometimes the cruelty of the marriage lottery cut both ways. 'The King values you greatly and would not listen to such idle comment from his subjects.'

'Aye, but for how many years more? And if I can never produce the longed-for heir, and must watch my lady Castlemaine increase her litter every year? In place of the lawful son he longs for, my husband's throne will pass to his brother James!'

They stood, frozen, contemplating this tragic future. If the Duke of York became King, another war might engulf the country. And all because Catherine could not produce an heir.

She began to untie her horse. 'Come, we must go. If we do not find her, Mistress Frazier will begin to fret indeed.'

They saw Cary Frazier waiting for them, anxiously scanning the lane. 'Oh, thank God Almighty. It is two of the clock and they will raise the alarm if we are not back before long.'

As they turned their horses towards Isleworth village they saw more people now, old women with faggots of wood on their backs, weary ploughmen heading home, children skipping, and goodwives passing the time of day with each other as they drew water from the well. In the centre of the village they became conscious of someone pointing, and a ripple of excitement, as young girls of six or seven ran across the green to take messages, so that more inhabitants began to crowd their cottage doorways. Frances could swear she heard the word 'Queen' and realized, with mounting panic, that they had been recognized. Suddenly a crowd of villagers was running towards them.

To Frances' horror she saw that it was an angry mob coming not to welcome their consort, but to abuse her for her Catholicism and her barrenness.

'Go home to Porchugal!' shouted one.

'You're no more use than an empty gourd to shake at children to scare them at night!' accused a wizened old crone, leaning out of her cottage casement to shove her whiskered face up close to the Queen's.

'Listen to me,' demanded Frances of the people who had gathered, gesturing to Cary to ride on with the Queen to safety.

Frances was no mean horsewoman and, as she spoke, she climbed onto her horse's back, a trick she had learned as a child.

The crowd gasped.

'She did not ask to be your Queen, but was sent here.' Frances knew only too well how it felt to be allowed little say in your own destiny. 'She can no more choose to conceive a child than you,' she pointed to the old crone, 'can choose to sprout a sheaf of whiskers from your chin!'

The crowd laughed as though it were an impromptu Punch and Judy show.

'And you, sir,' she pointed to a cross-eyed man in the front row, 'did you choose to see the world at sixes and sevens as you do?'

She was grateful to God for sending her a young woman who had lost her entire set of front teeth. 'And you, mistress, would you not prefer to chew on a fine beefsteak instead of sippets of bread soaked in milk, as an infant does?'

'I would, young master, and that's the truth, but I couldn't stop 'em falling out thick and fast as acorns off an oak tree!'

By now she had the crowd in the palm of her hand. 'I tell you, friends, the Queen has no more choice in these things than you do. And mayhap we should chide the King a little in this matter.'

'But the King has a quiverful of bastards!' countered a young man.

'Yes, but if he kept his arrows for his queen, they might the more often hit their target.'

The laughter was so universal that Frances chose this moment to jump down onto the horse's back with a wave of her hat.

'Farewell, good people. To the King and Queen of England!'

To her great relief the crowd threw back an echo, with even a gentle hurrah, as she rode off to join Cary and Queen Catherine.

'Frances Stuart,' Cary Frazier murmured as she caught up with them half a mile away. 'You are as full of surprises as a basket of snakes.'

Frances smiled, relief flooding through her, for indeed she had been both shocked and frightened at the violence of the crowd's response.

Queen Catherine was also visibly shaken, and the rest of the journey was taken up with trying to calm and reassure her that she was not universally hated.

'We had better not talk of this day's work,' she murmured to Cary after they had returned

239

safely. 'The Queen will not suggest we go abroad unaccompanied again, and mayhap we should have been more careful.'

'How could we know those yokels would recognize the Queen and turn on her?' Cary asked angrily.

'It was a mad prank.'

'Which was why she wanted to do it. To show she had spirit, and it is not Castlemaine who sucks all the pleasure from life.'

'Let us be discreet all the same.'

Yet if the Queen was cast down by the encounter, she hid it well in the days that followed, filling her time with masques and fishing trips and, greatly to the disapproval of her devout Protestant subjects, holding card games in her apartments even on a Sunday.

One night they were all bidden to a great gathering in the Banqueting Hall to honour the Ambassador from Muscovy, and to their great delight the Queen declared they must come in Russian garb.

Frances, recalling the fateful night at Wallingford House, would rather have not encountered that great bear of a man again, yet soon she allowed the excitement of the other ladies to infect her with their laughter and anticipation.

'What shall you wear, Frances?' demanded her sister Sophia, jealous that she had not been bidden to the event.

'Oh, I have better things to do than worry over such a matter as that,' was Frances' stern reply. Yet she could not stop the smile that followed. 'Sophy, Sophy, shall I go dressed all in white, to remind him of the snowy steppes of Russia?'

Sophia clapped her hands. 'That would indeed be perfect. By the way,' she added, 'have you seen aught of Walter? He seems to be forever out. I asked Nurse where he goes, and she says two fine gentlemen come to call for him almost every day. She scolds him over it, she says, because they keep him out till the birds are singing in the trees. Do you know who that would be?'

'No,' replied Frances thoughtfully. 'Yet I shall make it my business to find out.'

'Come with me to buy all you need for your costume,' wheedled Cary who had been listening to their conversation. 'I go to the Royal Exchange to buy silks for my own gown, and after to the fur merchant in Thames Street, at the sign of the White Bear.'

Frances smiled in agreement. Cary always knew where the newest goods were to be found, before any other lady of the Court.

'What think you of this silver lutestring?' her friend asked as, later that day, the two stood in front of the looking glass in the silk mercer's. In the end, after trying his patience with endless bolts of cloth, Cary had the man beaming at her order of peach moiré, laced with *point de Venise*, which she intended to complete, in honour of the occasion, with a rakish beaver hat.

For her part, Frances chose a length of white velvet.

'Is it not too unadorned?' Cary cocked her head to one side.

And yet, at their next port of call, the fur merchant's, when she surveyed Frances draped in white velvet, the skin of an arctic fox about her shoulders, she nodded in agreement.

241

'You call to mind a snow queen,' she breathed in admiration.

'Not an evil one, I hope, who brings winter to freeze the summer lands. Perhaps I shall cast a spell on my lady Castlemaine!'

'And turn her into an evil witch?'

'No, no, to turn her into a good woman.'

'You would need powerful magic indeed for that!'

When he saw how lovely his young customer looked in his fur, and heard of where she intended to wear it, the merchant generously reduced the cost of the pelt by three angels.

'See,' whispered Cary, 'the magic is working already!'

As they returned with their packages, laughing and chattering about the banquet, Frances decided she would pay a visit to Somerset House soon, to elicit from Nurse her description of the gentlemen who had taken Walter in hand. London, like all great cities, had its fair share of cardsharps and fraudsters, and numerous other unsavoury people who would take advantage of an innocent young man, and she did not intend Walter to fall into their clutches.

*   *   *

The Banqueting House, despite its name, was rarely used for banqueting or feasting, but for receptions, masques and the entertaining of ambassadors. Frances had rarely set foot inside it and could not fail to be struck by its impressive proportions. It took a master such as Inigo Jones, the King's Surveyor General, to design such a masterpiece.

242

Before she joined the throng downstairs, she stood in the first-floor gallery amongst the crowd of Londoners who had come to watch the spectacle, admiring its fluted Corinthian pilasters and the great squares of its parquet flooring. She looked up at the most famous thing of all: its ceiling painted by Rubens depicting the late King James I seated next to Minerva, holding a shield and thunderbolt to drive the errant figure of Rebellion towards the flaming depths of hell.

As she watched, trumpets sounded down below as the King entered, processing with a train of courtiers across the red-carpeted dais to sit upon a gilded throne. As she followed his familiar figure, taller by a head than all his courtiers, she wondered if the memory of his father—who stepped from this very gallery, with head held high, out to meet his execution—had troubled his mind.

A few steps behind the King, Queen Catherine followed, clad in pale-blue satin, solemn now, with no sign of the laughing roisterer of the other day's escapade.

Frances hurried down to join them, hoping the Queen had not missed her or needed some small service.

She need not have been concerned, for tonight the Ambassador had joined them, arrayed in a doublet of purple silk, with purple roses on his shoes of the latest fashion, as if he hailed from Paris, not snow-bound Muscovy. He bowed deeply to the King as a string of attendants arrived, staggering beneath armloads of furs: pelts of marten and beaver, otter and Siberian wolf, arctic fox and the fur of the stoat called ermine; and, the most highly prized of all, sable from Irkutsk. For a moment it seemed as if every animal from the Russian Empire was laid before them here in the Banqueting House. Then came carpets from Persia, glowing in amber and midnight and dusty pink in the candlelight, the finest work Frances had ever seen.

'And now a little curiosity, much sought after in our country.' The Ambassador produced a small jewelled case, which he opened before the fascinated eyes of the Court, 'Sea horses' teeth!'

'I thank you, sir, for your great generosity,' said the King.

Just as he signalled to the Groom of the Great Chamber to remove the gifts to an anteroom, a crash made all in the vast Banqueting House turn round and stare, as a small figure in blue satin, pale as death, slid suddenly to the floor.

Chapter 12

A momentary hush filled the room before the King cried out.

'The Queen! Send for one of my physicians to attend the Queen.'

A crowd gathered as the King took hold of one of the furs he had just been given and wrapped it around his wife's small body. 'Has she fainted?' he demanded, his eyes alight with concern.

One of the first to come forward was Walter Stuart, Frances' father, who was in the company of the Queen Mother. He felt Catherine's forehead and tried to open her eyes, yet she remained insensible. 'I think it is more serious than that, sire.'

'Grooms!' shouted the King. 'Carry the Queen to her apartments. Gently now! And find more physicians. I have twelve, for pity's sake. Summon them!'

The Groom of the Great Chamber picked up the frail bundle, still wrapped in fur, looking almost like a child who had been found half-dead in the forest.

As he turned, a path appeared through the crowd of silent and shocked onlookers.

The King followed immediately, with various of his Gentlemen of the Bedchamber close behind. As they progressed through the crowd a whisper of speculation began, at first almost like the rustle of dry leaves, then growing into a wall of sound as four hundred courtiers, advisors, mistresses and servants speculated as to what was the matter and what it might mean for themselves, the monarchy and the country if the Queen were seriously unwell.

As Frances Stuart, concerned both for the King and for Catherine, for whom she had sympathy and affection, made her way in the royal wake with the other ladies, she became a aware of a strange and uncomfortable occurrence: throughout the huge crowd people were nudging each other and subtly pointing in her direction.

She glanced behind her to see if some other person were the object of their speculation, yet there was none.

She shook her head, telling herself that she was becoming as fanciful as an old crone, and that if people were interested in her it was probably to wonder if she was as sad as she ought to be at the Queen's sudden illness.

As darkness deepened, all the Queen's ladies gathered outside her apartments to see if there was any task they might perform for her.

While they waited, quiet for what was usually a noisy flock of birds, Alexander Frazier, Cary's father and one of the King's leading physicians, arrived and was among the first to be admitted into the Queen's Bedchamber.

'Much good he'll do,' whispered Mall to Frances, hiding her mouth with her hand so that Cary might not hear. 'Old soak that he is. Good enough for delivering Castlemaine's bastards and curing Rochester of the clap, but I wouldn't trust my life with him any more than I'd sit in a pigsty in a white smock. He'll probably give her the King's Drops and that'll be an end to it.'

'Are the King's Drops not famed as a great restorative?'

'From too much Rhenish wine perhaps, or a bad oyster. Yet if you were truly ill, would you like hartshorn and dried viper in oil, soaked with the skull of a hanged man?'

'Is that truly what they contain?' Frances held onto a chair at the thought.

'So it is said. Yet His Majesty greatly believes in their efficacy. Mayhap because of the five thousand pounds he paid Dr Goddard for the formula.'

'Do you truly think her life may be in danger?' Frances asked.

Mall shrugged. 'She looked half-dead to me already, poor lady.'

At that moment Alexander Frazier poked his head out of the room and beckoned to Cary and Frances. 'Come. We need you to find clean linens for the Queen. They are being perfumed by Mr Chase the apothecary, her women tell me.'

From behind him a great wailing started up.

'Tis her Portuguese women. She has begged the King to be given into their care and now it is halfway 'twixt Babel and Bedlam in her apartments. Go! Run fetch the linens.'

When they returned, burdened down with piles of fresh shifts, sheets and chemises, they found that it was indeed a sad and extraordinary sight inside the Queen's apartments.

The room, though large, seemed half its usual size, crowded as it was with physicians, courtiers, Portuguese attendants, black-robed monks and the Queen's perfumer, who pushed his way through the throng swinging a censer, as the priest did with incense during mass.

The dimness of the light and the intense heat emanating from a vast fire, being fed constantly with logs by two blackamoor pages, added to the strangeness of the scene. The red glow of the flames cast a freakish light over the proceedings, it seemed to Frances, like a vision from hell imagined by some medieval painter.

At one end the Queen's barber—he whom the King had teased her about in happier days—was now taking his razor to her hair, the one truly beauteous feature that she possessed, beyond her lustrous dark eyes. Next to the great bed her duenna sat waiting with a strange-looking cap, made out of what seemed to be the kind of rags that a leper would discard.

Alexander Frazier sighed and whispered to them. 'It is a cap of relics, thought to be miraculous by her Capuchin friars. Poppycock, of course, but she seems to wish it.'

It was on the tip of Frances' tongue to ask if it were any more strange to give essence of viper or oil from a hanged man's skull, but for the Queen's sake she kept her peace.

The Queen, in the midst all this activity, resembled naught so much as a lifeless doll, white and still in the middle of the vast bed.

The King, meanwhile, paced up and down with his long strides, anxiously questioning his physicians.

'What is your diagnosis, gentlemen. Come, tell me quick!'

Frazier hung back, but not so George Bate, who had attended on the smallpox of both the King's brother and sister. 'We think it is the spotted fever, Majesty. Her women say she complained of a severe headache yesternight, and of a stupor that made her hard to wake this morn. Yet she wanted greatly to come to your Majesty's banquet and got up later in the day.'

'She is too good. And what other symptoms do you find?'

'A red rash, sire. And her forehead burns like a beacon.'

The King looked across at her. 'Poor lady. What fear you next?'

'That a humour should go to the head. We are preparing a julep of black cherry and some oil of nightshade. I will ask one of her ladies to bathe her forehead constantly. Beyond that, we keep the fire banked up and pray.'

Charles sighed. 'Her monks and priests do that apace.'

'You should sleep, sire. There will be many to watch.'

Charles nodded, his face white with worry and exhaustion. 'Do you mean to bleed Her Majesty?'

Into the beat of silence that followed Frances plunged, remembering how years ago Minette, the King's beloved sister, had refused to be bled, having seen how it weakened her sister Mary, and ascribed her own survival from the smallpox to holding out against the practice.

'She looks so weak, Majesty. Could a decision not wait until she is stronger?'

The King nodded. 'Thank you for your concern.'

Back in her own chamber, Frances dropped to her knees to pray for the Queen's survival, and so tired was she that she fell asleep still kneeling at the bed.

She awoke to find bright October sunshine dazzling through the window and the palace abuzz. The Council had already met and discussed the crisis. When she went down to the hall to break her fast, she spied Mall and her brother the Duke of Buckingham deep in conversation.

'Of course if she were on the throne,' Mall was confiding in a low, excited voice, 'she could persuade the King to forgive my Tom.'

'Forget your paramour,' her brother replied, his voice barely audible. 'If she were Queen, we would have more important matters to address than Tom Howard.'

They fell guiltily apart as Frances approached.

'Have we fresh news yet of Her Majesty?' Frances enquired.

Mall shook her head and began to pour some ale into a goblet and hand it to Frances. 'The bread is good, fresh from the bakehouse, and I have a message from your mother. She comes to visit you this morning. Perhaps she will know more, from her nearness to the Queen Mother.'

Frances ate her bread thoughtfully. In all her time at Whitehall her mother had hardly ever visited her. Her sister Sophia did so regularly, yet whenever she wished to see her mother, Frances had to visit her at Somerset House. It must be some matter of great import to bring her here.

It was two of the clock and dinner was over before her mother made an appearance, and when she did Frances could hardly believe her eyes. For her mother was not alone. She came in the company of a much older lady, dressed in black with a black vizard covering the top half of her face, reminding Frances of an ancient crow, and also with the Queen Mother herself!

Curious eyes followed them as Henrietta Maria commanded that they all retire to Frances' own chamber.

Once inside, her mother began to pull the curtains to block out the day and prying eyes. 'Frances, this is the Duchesse de Grise, a venerable relative of the Queen Mother's. She wishes to make sure you are in the best of health.'

'I?' Frances asked, startled. 'I flourish. It is the Queen who has the distemper.'

'Indeed,' Henrietta Maria looked grave. 'Mistress Stuart, her women have requested that she be given the Last Sacrament this very afternoon.'

'Oh, the poor lady. Her life has not been an easy one.'

'No. And we all pray for her. Might you lie down upon the bed?'

Frances turned to her mother. 'What is this business? Is there some contagion you fear I may have taken?'

250

'Listen to your elders and betters, Daughter,' Sophia Stuart said sternly.

Frances lay down, yet not obediently. There was a look of distinct rebellion in her eyes as she reluctantly complied.

'Now, young lady.' The black crow was lifting up her gown. Frances tried to protest, but was held by her mother in a surprisingly strong grip. 'I will not detain you long. This is a simple procedure, common among the prospective brides of kings.'

Frances hardly listened, so startled was she that the old woman had parted her thighs and had breached her undergarments as expertly as any determined lover, and had then placed two fingers inside her very privy parts.

'How dare you, you filthy crow!' Frances kicked so hard that the old woman staggered back.

'Ungrateful little hussy,' snapped the Duchesse.

'Frances, cease! This is important. Have you granted His Majesty the last favour? Be truthful now, for your answer carries much weight.'

'No!' Frances tried to sit up, pulling her clothes around her. 'Though I know not what business it is of yours.'

Henrietta Maria turned to the crow. 'Does she speak the truth?'

'Yes. *Oui*. Though from her conduct I would rather deny it. Hoyden miss!'

Now Henrietta Maria was wreathed in smiles. 'That is excellent news.'

'Yet why should it matter to any but myself, if I had granted the favour or no?' Frances demanded.

'Silly child,' her mother tried to stroke the fair curls that had fallen loose from her coiffure while she had kicked out. 'If you are to have a chance of being Queen, your innocence is paramount. You are to be greatly congratulated on protecting it.'

'Indeed,' Henrietta Maria commented tartly, 'it is little short of a miracle, knowing my son and the morals of his Court.' She turned to the old woman. 'And there is no reason you can find why she should not bear children?'

The Duchesse de Grise shook her head. 'The womb seems as it should be.'

'From now on you must be doubly diligent in the protection of your honour,' counselled her mother, eyes lighting up at the prospect of the glory ahead.

Although her blood sang in her veins with anger at her mother and Henrietta Maria behaving like two madams measuring virgin flesh, Frances kept her temper level.

'May I remind Your Majesty and my esteemed mother of several things you may wish to consider?'

The older women eyed her warily, as if the goods they had purchased might not be of as high quality as they had thought.

'The Queen is not yet dead.'

The two women shrugged at this minor difficulty.

'And if she were, I have no desire whatsoever on God's earth to become Queen of England.'

Three sets of eyes regarded her in blank amazement.

Her mother was the first to react. 'And what if England needed you, and you might do her much good? You are the perfect age for childbearing. You could have a dozen children and give the King an heir. If he has no legitimate heir, his brother James will succeed him with the children of Anne Hyde. There may once again be anarchy in this land. What think you on that?'

252

Frances curtseyed, her head erect and answered levelly, 'I think I will pray for the swift recovery of Queen Catherine.'

When they had gone Frances was left alone with her thoughts. Anger and disgust filled her at this unholy alliance between Henrietta Maria and her own mother. Worse than that, there was fury that her mother could subject her to so demeaning a practice—and through trickery, without her consent.

And, indeed, the entire incident confirmed a thought she had only dimly formed, but which now became clear as bright day. The role of a queen was hardly to be envied. Her primary function was not to decorate a Court, to bring it music or learning or beauty, or even to make the King a good wife. It was to produce an heir. The truth was that Catherine had been watched almost from the day of her wedding for signs of being with child. Indeed, Frances had seen how Lady Suffolk, chief Lady of the Bedchamber, took the management of the royal bed sheets entirely upon herself. Until now, Frances had thought this simply to do with cleanliness, but now she understood its import. It was to see if Catherine's monthly flowers were present or not.

Did she desire such scrutiny? What if she too were barren like the Queen, forced to travel as the Queen did so often to Bath and Tunbridge Wells to take the waters, in the hope that they would make her fertile, doomed to an endless sense of despair each month, knowing that she too had failed.

And what was it to be Queen of England, when your husband—kind and sympathetic though he might be—flaunted Barbara Castlemaine in your

253

face and endlessly pursued ladies like Frances herself? She had no illusions that if she ever married him, the King would soon look elsewhere. It was in his nature.

And yet, if she did not wish to be Queen of England or the King's mistress, what did she want?

Looking quickly over her shoulder to see that none was near, Frances delved beneath the mattress of her bed and pulled out a well-used leather book. Perched on the end of her great bed, she turned the pages carefully so that they would not fall out of their fragile bindings. And then she remembered, she had torn up the one image which, all her life, had spoken to her of home, hearth and happiness.

She put the book away in its hiding place and turned to her parrot, her only link with the life she desired. 'Am I so deluded, Bird, that I might turn down a king, for a man who already has a wife?'

Yet for once the parrot, usually so full of words and wisdom, had no answer for her. And then, just as she was leaving her chamber, it finally spoke. 'Love's not Time's fool . . .'

'That, my feathered friend, is something that to my cost I am learning. So the Duke of Richmond taught you Shakespeare, did he? Then he knows the lines that follow:

Love alters not with his brief hours and weeks;
But bears it out even to the edge of doom.'

In the days that followed, a curious lull descended on the Queen's ladies. They waited around the palace, hoping either for news or to feel useful again.

254

'If the Queen does not recover, will we lose our board and positions?' Catherine Boynton asked, to a general look of disapproval.

'Shush, Cate,' replied Cary Frazier. 'You will get to the bed of your beloved the sooner.'

'I wish you were right,' she collapsed gloomily. 'Yet I might not get there at all if the Queen dies before I get my dowry.'

Frances could listen no longer and walked out into the cold air of the Whitehall gardens. Here she was surprised to find Lord Clarendon, the Chancellor, approaching on gouty knees, leaning upon his stick, and steeled herself for yet another appeal.

Yet there was none. Instead he took her hand and pressed it gratefully. 'I wished to thank you, Mistress Stuart, for dealing honourably with the King and for considering his wife. Of course all will say I have a vested interest. That I wish for a barren queen so that the children of my daughter Anne may ascend the throne. Yet I have long witnessed your kindness, and if there is ever aught that I may do for you, while I have the power, do not hesitate to ask it.'

Frances' mind flew at once to the Duke of Richmond and his sad, mistaken marriage. Yet no Chancellor could remedy that, only God Almighty.

'I am happy too,' he continued, a mischievous smile lighting up his well-fed features, 'in that you make The Lady *un*happy. She has never had a rival such as you—beauteous and also gently bred. She must be worried indeed. If you were Queen, her reign would truly be over.'

Frances laughed gaily, bringing a look of query to the Chancellor's shrewd eyes. 'My lord, she will

255

surely outlast either you or me, because she wishes it more than we two.'

He smiled back. 'Yet it will never make her content.' He slipped his arm through hers. 'I am on my way to find the King and ask how the Queen fares. It will be a pleasure if you will accompany me.'

Frances noted with amusement that he took the deliberate route past Barbara's windows, that she might see them together and add to her concerns.

They heard the King before they saw him.

He was shouting at the Queen's Portuguese doctors and attendants, who had long since decided she was dying and were insisting, in the manner of her country, that each and every servant and family member take their leave of her in turn, until she was exhausted as well as ill. They were also requiring Catherine to make her will, profess her faith out loud and receive the Last Rites of the Catholic faith.

At the same time her personal physician had ordered that she be treated with the pigeons. Although it was not unusual for a pair of pigeons to be slaughtered and placed upon the feet of a sufferer, in the belief that dying people cannot take their leave of life if they are touching pigeons, it created yet further chaos.

'Charlatans!' the King bellowed, his patience at an end. 'Quacksalvers! Leave my wife alone this minute.'

The Queen looked up at him and smiled weakly. 'Let the priest stay. I must make my peace with God.'

Charles nodded, his face softening. 'As you will.'

Frances and Lord Clarendon stood back to let

the priest enter. 'Young woman,' he addressed Frances curtly, 'be kind enough to lay these out on that table.'

Frances, head bowed, placed a crucifix, a bowl of holy water, a sprig of rue and a lighted candle on the table next to the Queen's great bed.

'First you must make your confession,' he told the Queen.

'What hath my sweet wife to confess?' muttered the King impatiently. 'She has spent her whole life in prayer and pilgrimage.'

'Hush, please.'

King or no King, the priest shot him a look of reproach. He took the sprig of rue and sprinkled holy water over Catherine, then held the crucifix to her lips to kiss and began to intone the Latin words of the rite of Extreme Unction.

'*In nomine Patris et Filii et Spiritus Sancti, extinguatur in te omnis virtus diaboli per impositionem manuum nostrarum* . . . In the name of the Father, and of the Son, and of the Holy Ghost, may all the Devil's power over you be brought to nothing by the laying-on of our hands.'

'My wife is not in the Devil's power,' interrupted Charles impatiently.

'Majesty, respect your wife's wishes.' Lord Clarendon hobbled over and led the King away from the bed.

The priest began to anoint her eyelids with oil.

'May the Lord forgive you for whatever evil you have done through the power of sight . . .'

Afterwards, in the same manner, he anointed her ears, nostrils, lips, hands and feet, forgiving any evil that she may have done through their agency.

Catherine made a confession of her sins,

professed her belief in God and was at last given 'the viaticum', the sacred Host that would be food for her eternal journey.

Her faithful duenna slipped to her knees at the bedside and began to weep.

Catherine, until this moment calm and contented, began to toss and turn and mumble strangely.

'I would be alone with my wife,' the King announced abruptly.

The priest shrugged and tutted, blessed her one last time and left. Her ladies and attendants, Frances and the Earl included, started to follow.

Her physician hesitated.

'The fever is rising, sire. She becomes delirious.'

At that, Catherine sat up in her bed.

'Where is my son?' she demanded in a high, clear voice, believing in her delirium that she had finally produced the longed-for heir. 'For I know I was delivered of a very ugly boy.'

Everyone in the room stood stock still, save the King, who answered his wife tenderly. 'He is here. And a very pretty boy, too.'

'If he be like you,' Catherine replied, her glittering eyes fixing on his, 'then it is a fine boy indeed, and I would be very pleased with it.'

'Poor lady,' whispered Lady Suffolk to Frances, 'she thinks she has given birth to the King's son at last.'

Catherine quietened and lay back and then, just as suddenly, sat up once more. 'How do the children?' she demanded.

'Well, well,' replied the King, his voice catching. 'Yet they have want of a mother. And I of a wife.'

'Nay, nay.' She seemed all of a sudden to return

to clarity. 'When I die you will find a better wife than I. One who can give you what I cannot. A child.' She saw the tears glitter unshed in the corner of his eyes. 'Weep not. I would willingly leave the world, but for you.'

The King possessed himself of her hand. 'Then stay in it and live, for my sake.'

All in the room crept out, moved to silence by his devotion, which was certainly genuine, however temporary they feared it might be.

Chapter 13

For weeks Queen Catherine hung between life and death, and outside her sickroom Court and country continued to speculate over her successor.

One October night there was a storm so terrible that Frances woke up. Beneath her window, at the mooring next to the Privy Stairs, the boats banged together and the waves were as high and angry as any she had seen in the Channel. She looked out, terrified, and saw the strangest sight of her life. An owl sat on the windowsill and, as she watched, the bird turned its head so that its great eyes faced backwards from its body and stared at her.

Frances gasped. All knew that owls were an omen of death. She was so sure that the Queen had died that she fell to her knees and begged God to carry her soul to heaven.

'Please, Heavenly Father,' she prayed, knowing the weight of expectation that would fall upon her own shoulders from the Queen Mother, from her mother and from the King himself if the Queen had truly died, 'as you are my witness, I do not wish to be Queen of England.'

As if in answer to her prayer, and contrary to all expectation, the Queen began to rally.

Her vertigo subsided, and the great tumult and perturbation of her brain diminished until, after three weeks of fever, she sat up and asked Lady Suffolk, in Portuguese, for *mamelada do quince*, which, to the delight of the King, her duenna translated as quince jam. He sent at once to his chief gardener to procure some without delay, despite the fact that it was almost the month of November.

'It is a miracle!' cried her duenna. 'The cap of relics has saved the Queen.'

Yet Catherine would have none of it.

'It is not to the cap of relics that I owe my delivery,' she corrected tartly, 'but to the prayers of my husband.'

Outside the sickroom her ladies sighed with relief.

'Have you heard what the naughty Comte de Grammont is saying?' Mall whispered to Frances as they came from chapel, where they had been to thank God for the Queen's return to health. 'That one should never follow one's noble impulses. When he thought she was dying, the King told the Queen that she must live for his sake. And now she has. So, thanks to his generous and selfless actions, she has recovered and he will not get a new wife.' She looked at Frances meaningfully.

'The Comte de Grammont should find some better uses for his wit,' Frances replied, 'besides poking fun at people better than he is.'

Nevertheless she wondered at the strange

260

complexity of the King's nature, generous and yet selfish in equal parts, and considered whether he too was thanking God.

Barbara Castlemaine, ripe and luscious in a gown that spoke more of the bawdy house than the house of God, stood suddenly in their path.

'So, mistress, I hear the game is over and our beloved Queen recovers.'

Frances, head up, held her ground. 'If so, then I am greatly relieved.'

'Indeed? Even though all cast you as her successor? Not that I believed it. You are not the only one to whom the King looks, after all.'

'Ah,' Mall fluttered the pages of her prayer book, 'yet she is the only one sufficiently stainless, related by blood to the King and,' she paused and added, as sweet as sugared almonds, 'who has not bedded half of London.'

Barbara reached out to strike her, but Mall ducked the blow.

'Besides,' Mall added maliciously, 'since my brother's committee for the getting of Mistress Stuart as the King's mistress has failed, he has another.'

Barbara pretended not to be interested and started to walk away, then halted.

Mall smiled, waiting to reel in her reluctant catch.

'And what is that?' Barbara finally enquired.

'A campaign for the King to divorce the Queen and pave the way for the getting of a new wife.'

For a brief moment Barbara looked shocked. 'He will never do that. He has just rescued his wife from the brink of death.'

'Not yet. But when he tires of fidelity and

261

remembers he has no heir, he might,' Mall speculated.

From her own reading of the King, Frances thought this unlikely indeed. She was grateful that now life might return to normality. Everyone about the Court had stared at her and whispered behind their hands for weeks. Now they would stop.

Mall accompanied her back to her chamber and it was she who saw the missive first. A folded parchment with a red wax seal sat upon her dressing table next to the parrot.

'I know not who has taught that bird poetry,' Frances laughed, 'yet he can quote the verses of William Shakespeare.'

Mall fell upon the missive and inspected it. 'The crest of the Dukes of Richmond! I should know, since it is mine also.' Holding it away from Frances, who struggled to stop her, she proceeded to open it and read out loud:

'Dear Mistress Stuart,
I encountered the poet Edmund Waller, who was writing the enclosed verses on the theme of the Queen's recovery. I send them to you because I also celebrate the Queen's recovery, yet for a greatly different reason, which I think it will not be too hard for you to divine.'

Mall began to read the verses, in a mock-deep voice that would not have shamed the London stage.

'He that was never known to mourn
So many kingdoms from him torn,
His tears reserved, for you, more dear,

262

More prized, than all those kingdoms were!
For when no healing art prevail'd,
When cordials and elixirs fail'd,
On your pale cheek he dropp'd the shower
Revived you like a dying flower!'

'How touching!' Mall grinned. 'That man Waller should be shot for his execrable rhyming. He wrote a better panegyric praising Cromwell than the one he did of the King, remember. Yet how surprising my nephew the Duke, whom many here brand a gambler and drinker, and dull-witted to boot, is at heart so much the romantic.'

'He is not dull-witted!' Frances took the letter and tore it in two, 'Though what it should matter to him that the Queen recovers and I am not to replace her, when he already has a wife of his own, I know not.'

'Silly Charlie,' endorsed the parrot.

'Enough from you,' Frances scolded and placed a cover over the protesting bird. 'It is time I forgot both you and your master!'

*　　　*　　　*

Walter Stuart, unaware of the intense speculation that had surrounded his sister, looked forward to a visit to the Bear Garden on Bankside with his two new friends. He did not quite know why they seemed eager to show him the sights of London, and to stand him drinks and food at half the alehouses and ordinaries of Drury Lane, but he was willing enough to believe what they told him.

'When you love a city, she is like a woman to you,' Lord Rochester had boasted. 'You want your friends to enjoy her as much as you do!'

Walter had not yet enjoyed a woman at all, but much admired this racy talk. He had heard that the Earl, though so young, was a famous wit, and was ready to laugh at anything he said, even if it were only to hail a hackney coach.

Indeed, Rochester was getting rather fond of the lad and had to be reminded by the Count that their intention had been to spite his pious sister, not to sign him up amongst their cronies.

'Today we will get him to wager on how long the bear may last, and end by picking a quarrel with him. I think, if we show some wit about it, we may persuade him to call one of us out.'

Rochester shrugged. 'I am no hand with a sword—it will have to be you then.'

They made their way across the river to the wilder side of the Thames where bear- and bull-baiting took place. Today the famed Brown Bear of Breedon, which had seen off every dog thrown in the pit to maul it, was on display.

Walter, who had never been to a bear-baiting and had a tender heart, tried not to feel moved by the great angry creature with its fierce red eyes, shackled by its leg to a post, as specially trained snarling mastiffs were thrown into the pit and began to attack it from all sides. Without meaning to, he even raised a cheer when the bear picked up a dog in its powerful jaws and flung it four-square into one of the other boxes.

'I wager ten guineas he lasts no more than fifteen minutes,' announced de Grammont.

'Twenty,' offered Rochester.

'I do not think he will be defeated at all,' countered Walter, who was struggling with the

264

pleasure that he was taking in the spectacle, while acknowledging that it evoked the cruellest of emotions in him and in all who watched.

'And how many guineas will you lay on it?'

His honour as a young blade in the company of these two polished courtiers demanded that he lay at least some bet, even though he had but a few groats of his own. He would just have to hope he was right about the bear. 'Five,' he offered cautiously.

Walter became conscious that a middle-aged woman, dressed in a gaudy green and purple striped gown, who had been urging the dogs on at the top of her voice, was now staring at him from the next box. 'Do you not think,' the woman commented to the gentleman with her, 'that downy-faced youth is too young to be in that roguish company?'

A tall man with russet hair, which he wore curling down to his shoulders instead of a more fashionable periwig, stared at Walter with sudden interest.

'Look! Look!' cried de Grammont. 'The mastiff has the bear by the throat.'

With a terrifying roar, the bear tried to shake off the huge dog, but the animal held fast.

'I hear they are trained by hanging them from a tree by their jaws,' Rochester laughed.

The great bear, bleeding from five or six open gashes inflicted by the pack of dogs, seemed to stagger like a drunken man from a tippling house and, growling with a desperate angry defeat, fell to the floor.

Walter, forgetting his bet out of pity for the fallen creature, cried out, 'Oh, he is dead, poor animal.'

'Indeed he is, and that means you owe me five guineas!' crowed de Grammont.

Walter blenched. 'I do not have it precisely to hand.'

'Then you will have to find it soon, will he not, Rochester, or no man will go in company with you again.'

Walter tried to stop himself shaking, knowing how foolish he had been, and that he had no way of acquiring the money he had lost. He could not appeal to his father, who had always opposed gambling. He could imagine the response he would get if he even asked. 'A fool and his money are soon parted, and you are even more of a fool for losing money you do not have!'

The maid who carried tankards of ale to the guests suddenly appeared in their box and handed a purse to Walter. 'The gentleman over there sends you a message. He has need of a young tutor for his wife's daughter and hopes you might take the commission. He sends five guineas to mark the arrangement, if you will agree to it.'

Walter looked thankfully across at the occupant of the adjacent box as if he were Moses opening the Red Sea.

His two dissipated companions stared at each other stormily.

'A generous act by the Duke of Richmond,' sneered Rochester.

'Aye,' seconded de Grammont loudly so that the Duke would hear. ''Tis a pity it's his wife's money.'

The Duke's hand crept to his scabbard as he eyed Rochester with dislike. 'At least I have a wife,' he replied evenly. 'I hear even the King cannot persuade Mistress Mallet to take the noble Earl as

266

her husband.'

Rochester stiffened. He had been unsuccessfully courting Elizabeth Mallet, known as 'the fortune of the North'.

'Mayhap she does not care to catch the pox,' the Duke suggested silkily.

'Better risk the pox than dull-witted boredom,' countered Rochester.

'I will gladly accept the commission and the five guineas,' interrupted Walter, out of his depth, but relieved all the same. 'And would thank you for the offer.' He bid them swiftly goodbye.

'Straight-laced as his sister,' murmured the Count under his breath as Walter departed.

'His sister is worth a dozen of you,' countered the Duke with a dangerous glint in his eye. 'Though honour is a concept I would not expect you to understand.'

'Is there anything worse, Richmond, than being a priggish bore?' asked Rochester.

'Oh yes, my lord,' smiled the Duke, his sleepy grey eyes widening. 'Being you.'

*   *   *

To her surprise Mall awaited Frances in her chamber. Not this time to read her private letters or abjure her about the hopeless case of caring for the Duke of Richmond, but because she had some tidings of her own.

One glance at her shining eyes told Frances all. There was good news of Tom Howard.

'He is pardoned! Some of his officers from the guard petitioned the King for his return. And even His Majesty agrees that the King's Staircase is a duller place without Tom Howard, with his great brawny beauty . . .'

'Mall,' interrupted Frances, 'the King did not speak of such!'

'No,' laughed Mall, ''tis my own memories that come back to me.' The smile left her face as swiftly as thunder clouds hide the sun. 'Oh, Frances, so help me God, to think I even considered helping the King into your bed in exchange for his pardon! He begged and beseeched me to persuade you, yet I could not do so. I told him I would do aught he asked of me but that. And remember it was I who told the Queen and The Lady of my brother's plans so that they might come to his house and thwart them.'

Frances softened. 'Indeed you did, had not the Duke of Richmond done so first. What world is it we live in, Mall?'

'A strange one. Yet we have the love of each other.'

'And let us never lose that.'

'One thing, Frances, I do not wish my brother to know at once of his pardon. My brother Buckingham will sabotage it, else.'

'Yet there are those who know of it already. You petitioned the King, remember, and keeping a secret at Whitehall is like catching raindrops in a net.'

'Frances . . .' Mall looked suddenly like a young girl when the sun shines on a May morning. 'We plan to wed.'

Frances gasped, then tried to cover up her astonishment. The idea of Mall marrying a man half her age did indeed seem scandalous. 'I wish you happy.'

'Aye.' Mall shot her a merry look, reading her thoughts. All at once she was the hoyden who had climbed the tree and earned the name of Butterfly. 'And he is a Papist to boot, and has only what he earns from the King. Besides which, he has a mother he dotes upon, who may not thank the heavens for such a daughter-in-law as I.'

'Think you that is why—?' Frances stopped short.

'He loves an old woman like me? Because I bring to mind his mother?' Mall snorted. 'Then I hope he does not do to his mother what he does to me!' And she winked broadly.

Frances hid her face in her hands. 'Mary Villiers, you are a bad woman!'

'I am,' agreed Mall, still smiling, 'and yet I love my Northern Tom.'

'You make him sound like a cat!'

'Yes, and shall have his cream,' Mall all but purred.

'Why is he called Northern Tom?'

'There is another Tom Howard, though old and wrinkled, not like mine.'

'And when will he be home, your Northern Tom?'

'He has already set out from France.' She looked suddenly anxious. 'Oh, Frances, I hope he still loves me, for we have my brother and his mama to contend with, and neither will want this match, you can be sure.'

And yet it was another match altogether that Mall's brother came to complain of the next day.

Mall was in her apartments reading love poetry with Frances and her daughter Mary, soon to be betrothed also, when George Villiers, 2nd Duke of

269

Buckingham, inveterate schemer and confidant of the King, stormed in, his blond periwig askew and his nose red from either choler or too much ale for his morning draught.

'Sister!' he bellowed at Mall. 'I come from that self-righteous old prig Ormonde, who tells me his son is betrothed to your daughter. How can this be, when Ormonde is my sworn enemy and does all he can to defeat my schemes for advancement in Ireland.'

'Yet it is not your interests I seek to promote, but Mary's,' Mall replied, as calm as he was angry. 'Richard Arran is a steady young man, and she will be a countess to boot.'

'So it is true then! You will send her to live in the bogs of Ireland, among savages, with no culture but dancing jigs in hovels for entertainment.'

Thirteen-year-old Mary looked nervously from one to the other. 'Surely it is not so, Mother?'

'Your uncle exaggerates because it is not in his interest.'

'*In my interest*?' shouted the Duke. Frances thought his fiery red nose might explode in his fury. 'Ormonde dares to send me a note suggesting that since, after seven years, my own marriage "hath not brought forth any children", all the Villiers estates be settled on your daughter Mary. You must send him and his son packing!'

The Duke should have known his sister better. 'May I remind you, Brother, that I was widowed twice and have had to forge my own way ever since? I desire that Mary has a settled life and, if it is across the sea and three hundred miles away from Court, all the better!'

The Duke of Buckingham's mouth snapped shut

270

like an angry fish as he left them.

'Zounds!' Mall shook her head. 'I did not know Ormonde had written such a letter. It was not the wisest course of action with my brother.' A naughty smile crept into her eyes. 'And to remind him that he and the Duchess have no offspring . . . ! He probably goes hotfoot now to my lady's bedroom and tries at once for an heir.'

'Mother,' Mary interrupted unhappily. 'Is what my uncle says true? Will Ireland be such an uncivilized place? And so far from here. I had not thought of these things.'

'And neither will you now,' Mall replied briskly. 'There is much to be recommended in Ireland. The countryside is very green, I hear, and they have a great love of hunting and horseracing . . .' She stopped, unable to think of other delights and not noticing, as Frances did, how downcast her daughter seemed to be.

'Mall,' Frances asked, when Mary had been despatched sorrowfully on some errand, 'does not your brother have a point? She is so young, and Ireland is so far. She has had but you since Esme died.'

'And now she will have a husband. And soon babes.'

'Were you happy when first you married?'

Mall shrugged. 'I was widowed at thirteen. At sixteen the King wed me to his kinsman James and I became a duchess.'

'And now you have Tom Howard.'

'And if I have,' Mall said boldly, 'have I not earned him? I have done my duty, been a good wife and bred my children. Then my Esme died at eleven years old, my darling golden Esme, and

271

broke my heart. And now I am finding a proper husband for Mary. And a kind one too, who is young and handsome and will make her a countess. She could do much worse. And I think I am entitled to my happiness.'

Frances nodded, hoping that others would see it as she did—above all, the mother whom Tom Howard adored.

Queen Catherine's recovery drew on apace, as Frances deduced from the difference in behaviour from the Court towards her. When it was thought Frances might be Queen, many had sought advancement by trying to become her new friend, sending her perfumed gloves, satin slippers embroidered with gemstones, and sweet bags. Now, realizing she was not to be the new Queen, they retreated. A few cast her pitying glances, and from her rivals she noticed looks of triumph.

Yet none save Mall understood her relief, or its secret reason in Cobham Hall.

In a surprisingly short time, having taken the waters once again in Tunbridge Wells to aid her convalescence, the Queen desired entertainment and sent for her ladies.

She still looked pale and wan, as milk does when the cream has been scooped from it, and yet there was a feverish gaiety about her that Frances had never seen before. She darted instead of walking; played with her gloves, pulling them on and off, and laughed at everything that was said, funny or not.

'Poor lady,' confided Cary Frazier, 'mayhap she came so close to death that she cherishes life all the more and wishes to enjoy it.'

As if in endorsement of this, the Queen clapped her hands. 'Let us go to a playhouse this afternoon.

I would see a comedy to lift all our spirits.'

She chose *Love in a Tub* by the fashionable Sir George Etherege, playing in Lincoln's Inn Fields, and they all drove there together in the royal coach.

It was a silly play, in which the French servant lost his trousers and was put in a tub as revenge by the rival servants of a widow-lady, yet it made them laugh, and from the safety of their box they enjoyed the atmosphere of the playhouse with its bawdy banter, the orange peel thrown onstage, the fops and the wits, the ladies in their black vizards and patches, the jostling and crowding, all lit by blazing candles in a hundred sconces and chandeliers.

After the clapping ceased, Sir William Davenant, the theatre's manager, paid a visit to their box, flapping with excitement at his royal visitor. 'Your Majesty,' he bowed so low that the ladies feared his periwig might fall off, 'what a delight to see you restored to your loving people. And to grace my poor show! Though some say it is as lightweight as a fowl's feather, it has brought one thousand pounds to the house in the course of the month.'

'Indeed, sir,' Frances teased, 'perhaps you should get all your players to remove their trousers?'

Amidst the laughter he enquired if the King would be coming.

'I am afraid he is much taken up with this Dutch business,' replied the Queen. All London was discussing the worsening relations with Holland, and how the Hollanders were besting them on the high seas, and beating their ships to the best trade routes, and that it was time the English fleet taught them a lesson.

'Will it be war then, Majesty?' William Davenant, his pockets full of gold from his new hit, did not like the thought of war. As with the spread of plague and spotted fever, it emptied the playhouses faster than Frenchmen caught the pox.

'I know not,' replied the Queen. 'The King tells me parliament is all for it, and the Duke of Buckingham has asked to command a ship . . .'

The giggles from her ladies at the thought of the Duke, with his red nose and blond periwig blowing off in the wind, made the Queen look quellingly at them, until she laughed too.

'Indeed,' she confided as they left the box and headed out through the crowds, who parted respectfully for them, 'my husband says there is scarce an Englishman besides himself who does not passionately desire war.' The groom held open the door of the coach. 'He speaks of men, of course. Women do not want war—they see there is too much to lose.'

'Not all women, Your Majesty.' The ladies turned to find Barbara Castlemaine, in amber silk, with a blue satin wrap, and on her head a great Cavalier hat nodding with blue feathers, emerging through the crowd. 'War is noble,' she insisted. 'We should send in the fleet and gain a quick victory.'

The Queen eyed her levelly, a hint of faint disdain in her manner. 'My husband the King says if there was ever such a thing in war as a quick victory, he has never seen it. Yet why do you wish for war so keenly, my lady Castlemaine? Have you a lover you wish to dispose of?'

The groom slammed the coach door shut, to the sound of merry laughter from her ladies, who had never heard the Queen speak so boldly, as Barbara fumed and swore revenge, standing alone on the cobbled walkway.

Frances was still smiling at the expression on Barbara's face when she opened the door of her chamber and stopped, rooted in shock.

Across her great canopied bed with its red damask hangings were spread two sleeping figures. Tom Howard, golden and glorious as any young god, his tawny hair ruffled by sleep, lay face down, entirely naked, while Mall, still in her gown, her laces undone so that her breasts spilled out over the stiff brocade, slept next to him.

It should have been as base as any scene in a bawdyhouse or brothel and yet it was strangely stirring. Perhaps it was the arm he had thrown out across her chest to defend her from all invaders— save himself—or the sight of the naked flesh next to the clothed, but Frances felt a sudden rush of heat to her cheeks.

And she knew then what it was she longed for.

She wanted this abandon, this spilling out of body and soul to another—yet not with the King, who desired her and yet would soon tire of her, but with one who offered himself to her forever. Behind her she saw the parrot stretching as it prepared to speak, and raised a finger to her lips. It turned its head and fastened her with its beady eye, as if they two alone shared some ancient secret. And as she tiptoed silently towards the door, it tucked its head beneath its green-grey wing and slept.

Later Mall came to explain and to apologize at the use of Frances' chamber. Frances did indeed feel somewhat aggrieved to be implicated in Mall's affair, without her permission even being sought. Yet her friend's shining eyes and air of singing contentment undid all criticism. Mall seemed a girl again.

275

'Frances, he is divine! Can skin be soft when the body is hard? Can there be such tenderness in one who is a rough soldier? And the skill . . . something has happened to gentlemen since the days of my other husbands. My first was but a boy, and my dear James, though I loved him deeply, was all for frontal assault and never tarried to ease the entry by such delicious devices—'

'Mall, cease!' Frances felt the blood rising to her cheeks once again. 'You begin to sound like my lady Castlemaine!'

Mall stretched luxuriously. 'Yet she practises them to gain her power over men, while Tom has no thought but that of pleasing.'

'I am very happy for you.'

Mall sighed. 'Then you will be alone in your contentment. My brother will try to stop it, Lady Suffolk my aunt will declare it disgraceful and undignified, my daughter will find it disgusting, and I shall ignore them all.'

Frances embraced her. 'And God speed you, for I am beginning to learn how fragile the search for happiness can be.'

'Thank you, sweeting, though I am not sure it is God that I may look to, to prosper my friendship with Tom Howard.'

'Or his mother,' Frances pointed out, before Mall returned her sally with a pinch.

'I will deal with his mother when the time comes. Thanks be that she resides in Naworth Castle in the county of Cumberland, and hopefully that is where she will stay.'

*   *   *

All the Queen's ladies were glad to see the back of that doleful year, when their mistress had so nearly died, for they had affection for her and a new respect that one who had much to contend with in her childlessness, the disappointment and muttering of the people at having no heir, and the King's wandering attentions, had found a path through Court life with a new zest. She marked that Yuletide with masques and feasts, and brought in jugglers and fire-eaters, such as would not shame Bartholomew Fair. But still she hoped for that longed-for babe, and cried bitterly when twice it seemed she was with child, to find that all was a false alarm.

Spring came, and afterwards a wondrous summer such as few could recall. The whole Court took to the river, and rowed back and forth to Hampton Court and Greenwich, taking many of their pleasures upon the cooling water.

Yet beneath the heady delights of a fine English summer the talk of war loomed ever greater.

'Come,' the King commanded Frances one summer morning as the royal barge rowed towards Greenwich for a picnic by the river's edge there. 'I have a wish to show you my dockyard at Deptford. There will be time for frolicking by the river after.'

The thought of visiting a shipyard instead of a picnic at Greenwich was not enticing, and she was still wary of being alone with him, yet she saw that he was entirely focused on his navy in the face of the trouble ahead.

'This was the way the pilgrims left for Canterbury.' Charles pointed to a small village on the shoreline. 'Read you your Chaucer? They knew how to live then. No time for manners and refined behaviour—it was in and out up against a wall.' He slapped her on the rump and made all the rowers laugh, then bowed to her in apology. 'I am sorry, Belle, I am a crude fellow for a king.'

Before she could reply he turned her round to look at the scene unfolding before them. The King's Yard covered thirty acres with two wet docks, three slips for men-of-war, a mast basin and ponds, a great smith's shop, forges for anchors, sheds for timber, great sails and rigging lofts, and inside the storehouse the finest machinery in the world for spinning hemp and making ropes and cable.

'My dockyards are a grand sight, are they not? Great Queen Bess knighted Sir Francis Drake on this very spot.' His face clouded momentarily. 'We ruled the seas in her day. Now the Dutch best us. Their ships are smaller and swifter than ours, aye, and cheaper to make also. And they refuse to salute our flag at sea, as has always been the custom, in recognition of our superiority. And now there is a desire for war, and yet I lack the brutal appetite that induces rulers to break the peace.' He looked out to sea. 'I have seen enough of killing in my lifetime. What think you of that? A king who does not wish to go to war.'

Frances, touched that he should care for her opinion, replied gently. 'I am sure you have your reasons, Majesty.'

He laughed. 'I do. And one of them is that we are not ready, according to the diligent Mr Pepys, my Clerk of the Acts, whom I have always found to be both honest and wise. I shall put them off and we shall talk of happier things. See, there is the great garden of Mr Evelyn.' He pointed to a fine house surrounded by parterres and holly hedges, woody walks and a magnificent oval garden. 'I visited him last year and he showed me his designs, all planted when the moon was new and the wind westerly, as he holds is most propitious. He plans to write a book laying all down, for others to follow.'

The vision of Cobham Hall came in her mind and how it, too, could have a garden like this one. 'I would love such a garden above all things,' she declared with a sudden passion. 'Aye, and a house with brick chimneys, and towers at each end, surrounded by its own park.'

He looked at her strangely, almost as if seeing her through new eyes. 'Then we must find you a husband.'

'I have no great dowry, sire,' she panicked. 'Save that which I will gain from waiting on the Queen. Besides, I am in no hurry to wed.'

'The royal purse might furnish one.' He took her hand in his. 'What kind of husband do you desire?' He spoke as if she were choosing new perfumed gloves. 'He would have to be a generous one, who shares his possessions willingly.'

It was as if a sudden wind blew from the river, biting and chill. She could not understand how one moment he might be kind and generous, full of enthusiasm for his ships and people, and then so cynical and calculating. The kind of husband he would want for her would be as my lady Castlemaine's once was—a willing cuckold. Though even poor Roger Palmer had had his price and had torn off the mask of complaisance at last.

'And yet, as God is my maker, I would never desire a husband who would be prepared to do so.'

'Then may you long rejoice in your unwed state, mistress.' A harsh tone came into his voice, which she had not heard before. 'Until the day arrives when mayhap you will be old and willing.'

Chapter 14

'Come with me to St James' Park,' Mall pounced on Frances. 'I cannot go alone, and I must be outside in this glorious sun or I shall wilt like a flower that has no water!'

'Why cannot you go with Mary?'

'I am in disgrace with Mary. She compares her betrothal to that boy Richard Arran to the manly glory of my Tom. I have told her there is naught between us, but she suspects otherwise.'

'And that surprises you?' snorted Frances. 'When you look upon Tom Howard as if it were Yuletide and he a tasty marchpane?'

Mall pouted. 'She could hardly be betrothed to a penniless yeoman of the guard as I am, could she?'

'Yet it is permissible for you, one of the greatest ladies of the Court, to be so?'

'Hah! The stupidest thing is that none would care if I wished merely to bed him. They might laugh at me, but would soon forget about it, yet if I wish to *wed him*, that truly shocks all in this immoral place.' She looked out of the window and sighed. 'Come, Frances! See the day we have been given. The sky is the blue of heaven. We can dip our feet in the new canal, and eat mulberry tarts in the gardens.'

'Let us take Walter, then. I doubt he has yet sampled the joys of walking by the canal.'

They sent a messenger and, by good fortune, Walter was available and returned in the

280

messenger's company.

Frances surveyed her tall, gentle brother. He seemed more haggard, less the fresh-faced youth than when they had last met. 'You are not burning the candle at both ends, I hope?' Frances asked, concerned.

'Indeed, I am hardly lighting it at all,' Walter bowed. 'I am the very model of a well-behaved young man.'

*   *   *

It was indeed a glorious day. They walked across Horse Guards Parade, and into the park by the canal where small boys fished, listening to the birds singing as if it were the first morning of creation. 'I did not know that London held such peaceful spots as this,' Walter marvelled.

'It is not all fleshpots and gambling dens,' teased Mall.

Walter flushed as if he took the jibe personally.

Frances looked around quickly to see if anyone was passing by and, confident they were alone, removed her stocking and slid one toe into the cool water.

'Did I not tell you that Mr Storey, who keeps the King's birds, told me there are two crocodiles loose in the park?' Mall enquired, laughing. 'They were the gift of a chief from Guinea. Just like the pelicans from the Ambassador of Muscovy.'

'I am sure there are neither pelicans nor crocodiles in this canal.'

Frances dried her foot and they strolled towards the Mulberry Gardens, which was little more than an orchard, overgrown and full of hidden places.

'You know what wicked Lord Rochester has written of this place?'

At the mention of Lord Rochester, Walter coloured and looked away.

'If Lord Rochester has written something, it will certainly be scurrilous, though I concede possibly also witty,' Frances replied.

Mall began to recite.

> *'And nightly now beneath the shade*
> *Are buggeries, rapes and incests made.'*

'Well, he would know about those,' commented Frances tartly, 'since he is responsible for most of them. I do wonder the King tolerates his behaviour.'

'Because he is entertaining. No matter how wise and honest the King can be when he exerts himself, he likes more than anything to be entertained. He even laughed when my brother Buckingham called him "Father of his people" and added, "Well, a good many of them." Rochester maintains that all London, high and low—from rag-pickers to fine ladies, footmen to fops—come here for assignations.'

'And all encounter my Lord Rochester in the bushes,' added Frances.

Walter had fallen silent, and looked like a boy caught stealing apples from a neighbour's orchard, yet he said nothing.

Mall found a bench and they sat down beneath a huge mulberry tree. 'I see no rag-pickers or fine ladies here now,' Frances pointed out.

They had not been sitting together five minutes when Mall jumped up, cursing. 'God's blood! That bird has shat upon my favourite gown!' She rubbed at the red stain that was spreading in her lap.

Frances forbore to mention Nurse's dictum that the mulberry was, of all fruits, the most stubborn to clean. 'Mall, who is the young woman staring at us from that bench?'

'No doubt one of my Lord Rochester's heiresses or chambermaids,' Mall continued, rubbing at her stain.

'We will soon discover which, since she is walking towards us.'

Mall looked up, and as she did so she forgot the mark and her whole body stiffened. 'It is my lady Shrewsbury, and no greater strumpet graced the name of nobility. It was she who insulted Tom and caused the trouble between him and Giles Rawlins! She has no doubt spotted Walter and looks for another conquest, no matter how downy-cheeked. Look at her, so youthful and already she runs to fat. They say she eats sweetmeats and bonbons even in her bed. How stupid gentlemen are to fall for such a butterball. She will be gross before she is five and twenty. Well met, my lady,' Mall challenged rudely before Frances could stop her, 'have any more good men died for you of late?'

Frances studied the young woman who came towards them. There was something of Lady Castlemaine about her face, as if she had got all she desired and it had not satisfied her. She possessed the same white skin, full pouting mouth, with the hint of indulgence in the fleshy line of her cheek. And Mall was right—she did eat too many sweetmeats.

She smiled at Walter, who stared back as if his nose were pressed up against the baker's window contemplating a frangipani tart.

'I see you have spoiled your gown with that red stain,' Lady Shrewsbury remarked. She seemed unruffled by Mall's insult. 'It cannot be your flowers, for you are too aged for that—or else they have been stopped by Tom Howard's bastard.'

Walter looked from one to the other, shocked. Ladies did not behave like this in his experience, and certainly never used such language.

Before Frances knew what had happened, Mall had taken out her handkerchief and flicked it hard across her rival's cheek. 'For such an insult as that, I challenge you to a duel! Unless you are too lily-livered and will allow men to die for you, yet never defend yourself.'

'What empty brag is this?' Anna Maria Shrewsbury demanded. 'We are women. We cannot fight a duel!'

A smile of triumph lit up Mall's hazel eyes. 'You wrong me, my lady. I was taught to use a sword by the best in the land, Prince Rupert of the Rhine. The day after tomorrow: dawn, at Barn Elms? Mistress Stuart here will be my second. We should dress in men's clothing to less attract the attention of busybodies trying to stop us.' Mall turned to her companions. 'Mistress Stuart, Walter, shall we take our leave?'

To their surprise the fleshly Anna Maria did not look cowed.

She eyed her adversary malevolently. 'You should know, Mall Villiers, that I have fenced with swords all my life.'

'Excellent, then it should be a more equal fight.'

'Mall,' Frances tried to laugh off the encounter as a joke, 'you are not serious about this mad

284

scheme?'

'Never more so in my life. She can get that whore Barbara to be her second.'

'Yet, Mall, consider. The King hates duelling among men. What punishment would he give for discovering the practice amongst his *ladies*?'

'No doubt he would laugh and find it excellent sport, yet worry not. I would wager you a bag of guineas that Madam will not turn up. Her kind gets men to do the dying. They do not risk their beauty with a duelling scar. Mayhap after today she will be more careful at whom she directs her insults.'

'Oh, Mall, Mall, is it true about Prince Rupert?' Frances had heard a whisper of Mall's early love for the Prince, but that her marriage had prevented it from blossoming.

Mall was silent a moment and a ghost of a wistful smile lit up her face.

'Indeed it is. He was a brave adventurer and gave me lessons in many things. Swordsmanship was but one of them.' The look she shot at Frances told her all she needed to know about the nature of their love. They saw that Walter was silent and pale. 'I think . . .' he began hesitatingly, 'that I should offer to do the fighting for you?'

Mall blew him a kiss. 'A man cannot fight a woman,' she said gently, not wishing to point out that he was too young and inexperienced.

Seeing the worried expression on Frances' face, Mall slapped her on the back, already the swaggering gallant, as if in anticipation of the encounter. 'Do not concern yourself so. I do not intend to make her husband a widower, just to scare her into tightening her stays a little in the company of gentlemen. By the way, I meant it about dressing

285

in male attire. It will attract less attention. Another thing, not a word to Tom about this business. He would be shocked by my hoydenish behaviour.'

'And perhaps concerned for your safety,' Frances added.

'Oh, pish. My lady Shrewsbury would never dream of taking risks with her precious person.'

There was something about this statement that rang a warning bell with Frances. Lady Shrewsbury was thought by many to be a ruthless woman who used others. Since she could not get a man to actually take her place, she might stoop to some other low or dangerous game. A footpad to attack Mall in an alley, or some other way of disabling her rival.

Yet surely this farrago would end in naught? The scandal would be so great it would ruin them both. Had Mall not considered that if she carried this venture through, then her Tom, a captain in the King's own guard, might feel he must sever their connection? But Frances also knew Mall through and through. The leopard changed its spots sooner than Mall did. To climb down was not in her nature. Knowing that further persuasion would be fruitless, Frances went to her chamber to think.

If she were Lady Shrewsbury, she would pay some rogue to do her dirty business, whom none could associate with her. Anna Maria, she decided, would do the same.

The only way she might find out was to see who visited Lady Shrewsbury and perhaps even follow them. Yet how could she, a lady of the Court, do such a thing? It had been dangerous enough to go roistering with the Queen, yet for this she must be alone. She could not even ask Walter to accompany her, for he was too young and innocent of the ways of the world. And yet, if it were discovered, and she were unmasked for spying on Anna Maria, it would be she who lost her reputation and caused the scandal. She had better not be discovered.

Frances had always despised the use of vizards—so popular with ladies to cover up their faces when they went on illicit assignations, or simply to protect their skin from the sooty London air—but today she praised the Lord for the fashion. To be doubly certain of hiding her identity she pulled out from her press the buff soldier's outfit she had worn when posing for a painting.

With her fair hair brushed loose, a great tricorne hat and the vizard hiding her face, she looked strange, like a mummer or a street actor escaped from Bartholomew Fair, and some might stare at her, yet even if they did they would never guess that it was Mistress Stuart, the King's great desire, disguised beneath. In this useful get-up she walked swiftly, head down, out of Whitehall and up towards the Strand.

Protected as she was by living within the Palace precincts, it was easy to forget life out on the streets, with its brutish, noisy energy. All around her vendors cried, dray horses thundered across the cobbles, people swerved out of their way, soaking themselves in the filth of the channels that ran down the centre of the street.

A flower-seller in a bonnet entwined with all the flowers of the garden stopped her hopefully. 'Buy a flower for your lady, sir? Only a penny a bunch!'

Frances hid her smile and almost fell over a poor man lying in the road next to an open sewer choked with urine and ordure from the latrines. And yet this was the better end of town, where the gentry lived and carried on their business. Whitechapel and the outlying parishes were a hundred times poorer and more overcrowded than this.

In the Strand near the Maypole she hailed a sedan chair to carry her to Chelsea, where she knew the Earl of Shrewsbury and his countess lived.

From the comfortable cloth-lined interior she surveyed London as she passed. On the corner of the street going down to the river an old man was squatting down to excrete in plain view of all, as unashamed as a newborn babe. Ragged children buzzed everywhere like flies on a dung heap. Not that their betters set them any lessons. Drunken gallants weaved out of alehouses, grabbing at any pretty maidservant out on an errand. At least the air today was clearer than in winter, when the constant burning of sea-coal left the entire city in a blur of soot, with smudges of black landing on the faces of all, high and low.

At last they arrived at a house in distant Cheyne Walk that was both large and beautiful, built of red Tudor brick, with a long gallery on its southern side overlooking the river. Anna Maria had done well for herself. Not that it seemed to satisfy her.

After paying the chair-men she stared up at the vast building.

'They do say,' one of the chair-men, a wheezy old gent whom she was surprised could manage so active an employment, called back to her, 'that it has fifty hearths.'

'Aye,' echoed the other, young and thin with a face like a weasel's. 'And their servants don't get to warm their backsides at any of them! Good day, young sir.'

Frances paused, wondering what she had thought she might achieve by coming here. She walked round to the southern side of the house and, as she did so, passed a tavern bearing the sign of the Magpie and Stump. At least in here she might pick up some gossip about the grand lady who lived next door.

The landlord eyed her with enthusiasm as a good customer for a slow afternoon. 'So, young gallant, what will your pleasure be on this fine day? A flagon of good English ale or, by the looks of you, perhaps a little fine Bordeaux wine? The barrel only just opened, and only twelvepence a quart. As drunk by His Majesty himself!'

Despite her nerves Frances made a mental note to recount this exchange to the King, since it would certainly make him laugh, then saw that she would never be able to do so. Even the King would consider a venture such as this beyond the pale.

Frances opted for the ale and settled in a quiet corner opposite the door, where she could see who came in while surveying the rest of the tavern's customers.

In the next booth sat a Jewish gentleman with long black hair and a curly beard, whom she deduced was an old clothes-seller from the curious fact that he sported a pair of boots slung around his neck and wore no fewer than three hats piled on his head, putting her in mind of the tower of an ancient church.

Next to him two old women, one of them with a live goose in a basket on her lap, shared a glass of porter and debated with all the fiery fluency of members of the Privy Council which made noisier guards, the goose or the guinea fowl.

On her other side a lively argument was unfolding as to whether the law prohibiting beating your wife at night was to prevent domestic cruelty or because it made too much noise and woke the neighbours.

'It is the God-given right of every Englishman to beat 'is missis,' insisted an unappealing-looking type in a greasy waistcoat. 'Old Noll knew that. In fact I 'fink it might even be one of the Ten Commandments.'

'What?' disputed his neighbour. 'Thou Shalt Take a Broom Handle to Your Lawfully Wedded if she gets on your Wick? I don't think so, Bill.'

Frances was just beginning to ask herself what she could possibly discover here when she noticed a worried-looking man next to the bar, who kept glancing towards the side entrance as if waiting for someone to arrive. He was less shabbily dressed than the rest of the customers, his suit being of black stuff, edged in lace. On his lap he lovingly nursed a small package wrapped in some kind of cloth, as if it were as precious as any firstborn son.

After a further five minutes of nervous glances he began to get up from his chair.

'Good day, Master Apothecary,' grunted the tavern-keeper. 'I must come and see 'ee soon for some more of that white vitriol for my little problem.'

The man nodded. Frances would have loved to know what the tavern-keeper's problem was, but instead she waited a moment before paying for her shot and discreetly following him.

The man ducked, looking frequently over his shoulder, away from the river down a small street she saw was called Cook's Grounds, which wound its way between high Tudor walls, until emerging in a mews. Frances, hardly able to believe her bravery in following him, flattened herself against the brickwork and decided this must be the stable-block for Shrewsbury House.

The apothecary waited until, finally seeming to lose patience, he disappeared inside the long, low building to emerge a few moments later with a frightened-looking boy of about twelve or thirteen. The boy was now in possession of the precious package. The boy then ran, clutching it to him, through a wide arched gateway in the direction of the house and garden. With one final furtive glance, the apothecary headed back towards the river, while Frances, her pulse racing, hid and pondered what it meant.

What if Lady Shrewsbury intended to go ahead with the duel and had purchased poison to dip on the end of her sword tip, as Frances had read they did in Italy. And even if this had too much the whiff of Webster's tragedies, she was sure the furtiveness of the man's bearing and this secret delivery did not bode well.

Mall, she knew, would scoff and call her alarmist, and maybe she was right. But then there was the other matter of the scandal that the duel would cause, whether it were fatal or not.

Something Mall had said about Lady Shrewsbury's taste for sweetmeats echoed in her head. Inspiration came to Frances. The way to put an end to the duel, she concluded, was not through tragedy, but farce.

She glanced up at the back windows of Shrewsbury House and gasped, certain that someone stood there looking down at her. Before anyone could raise a hue and cry she ran as fast as she could, glad to be in hose instead of skirts, back towards the embankment, where this time she caught a wherry downriver to the Whitehall Stairs. From there she could slip in the side entrance past the Bowling Green and in through the Privy Garden with its famous sundial, where the King set his watch every morning after his daily game of tennis.

Yet what if someone recognized her and asked her business? She kept her head down and walked fast until at last she gained her chamber.

Not half an hour later, hair curled and wearing the latest fashion, Mistress Frances Stuart, Court beauty, was able to emerge once more.

She meant to seek out Mall and tell her what she had discovered, yet before that she desired some advice from her old nurse, who had knowledge of medicines and potions as deep as any apothecary's.

By the time she had done so, it was already suppertime.

'Where were you today?' Jane La Garde whispered. 'The Queen called for you and you were nowhere to be found. She is grown pettish of late. She wishes for a clean shift four times a day and none of us can help her change it. She almost stamped her foot that you were not there to put on her lavender gloves, and she shouted at the page of the back stairs when he pinched her shoe as he put it on her.'

They looked at each other as the possible significance dawned.

'Could she be with child, think you?'

'The King would be the happiest man in the land if she were.'

'And The Lady the angriest woman.'

They smiled at each other. 'Let us hope she is.'

They had just begun supper when Mall slipped in next to them at the maids of honour's table, looking unusually flustered.

'Let me hazard a guess,' Frances whispered as she passed her a dish of silver eels. 'The King has discovered this mad duel and demands your presence.'

'Worse!' Mall shuddered at the sight of the eels and passed them on. 'Tom's mother pays a visit to inspect me. And which day has she chosen? That of the meeting with my lady Shrewsbury.'

'Excellent,' Frances beamed. 'In that case you are going to have to call it off. And without loss of honour to either.'

'It is because of honour that I cannot call it off.' Mall's voice rose in her anger and contempt for Anna Maria. The ladies and gentlemen around them had begun to turn and listen. 'Lady Shrewsbury is the kind of woman who allows men to die for her and laughs about it later. I wish her to know what it feels like to stand alone against an opponent with a sword in their hand and to fear your own death.'

Frances lowered her voice. 'And what if the death turns out to be your own? Or you injure her and the scandal is so great you are both ruined? What will Tom and his mother think of you then?'

Mall laughed. 'The ever-sensible Frances. You would never make a Cavalier!'

'It is the Scottish blood,' Frances conceded. 'I am destined to be practical.' She touched Mall's sleeve. 'The lady is not worth the risk.'

'Too late now. Only God can stop us.'

But the sensible Scottish blood did not run in Frances' veins for nothing. And she did not intend to leave the matter in the unpredictable hands of the Almighty.

The rest of the company went to the Queen's Apartment after supper to play cards and listen to some new musicians from France. Yet Frances felt too tired, and besides she had other things to think about.

On the way to her bedchamber she passed a couple embracing in an alcove next to the Matted Gallery. She hesitated, not wishing to disturb them, when the man stepped out of the gloom and stood for a moment illuminated in the light of the torch in its sconce. He was young and handsome and laughing, with russet hair, and all at once her heart contracted, for though he was a stranger he had an air of one whom she had tried with all her heart to forget.

And failed.

At her return the parrot squawked a greeting.

She eyed it warily, for it seemed at times as if it knew every thought that passed through her mind. 'Say naught, Bird. Indeed, mayhap I should find another home for you, for daily your presence reminds me of him I cannot have.'

She moved towards its cage. The parrot watched her warily. And then, like an ostrich that hides its head in the sand and believes itself invisible, the bird placed its head beneath its wing and was silent.

Early next morning, after mass was over in the Queen's chapel, Frances journeyed by water to the shop of one Widow Wyatt, in St Mary le Bow, an old acquaintance of her nurse, and one in whom that venerable lady placed far greater trust than in

294

any male apothecary.

The widow, Nurse explained, had taken over the shop when her husband died, and ran it with more wisdom and knowledge than any male counterpart, much to the disgust of the Guild of Apothecaries, who held that though a woman might understand herbs and potions, she could never grasp the exact numerical proportions required in the true calling of the apothecary.

Frances would know the shop, Nurse explained, by the sign of the unicorn outside it.

She looked up at the signs. There was a cupid and torch designating a glazier's; a Jack-in-the-Green denoting a distiller's; and next to it a cradle, the sign of a basket-maker—but no unicorn.

At last she found it, at the far end of the street. The shop was small, but unlike its neighbours, which were mere lean-tos with open frontages, the widow's shop was enclosed. The back walls were lined with large jars printed with Latin names, and there was a strong yet not unpleasant smell of aloes and herbs within. Glass jars of powders lined the counter, labelled with such terms as 'Hartshorn', 'Unicorn horn', 'Pearls' and 'Ivory'. In one corner an apprentice was grinding tutty.

When Frances explained her order to the Widow Wyatt, the old woman laughed. 'Is this intended for a rival in love?' she asked and laughed loudly. 'If so, it will put an end to any amorous inclinations, I'll be bound!'

They shook hands. It was agreed that the widow's apprentice would deliver her order to the Countess of Shrewsbury this very evening at Shrewsbury House.

Frances was about to leave when she

remembered one last detail. 'Mark the gift from a lovelorn admirer. That should pique the lady's vanity.' She grinned at the widow. 'Not that it needs great prompting.'

All her life Frances had been accustomed to seeing Mall as part-mother, part-sister, part-example. Mall the fearless. Mall the writer of wicked poetry; Mall the Butterfly brought to King Charles I; Mall the great Court lady, so grand she could behave like a hoyden and get away with it.

Yet she had never before seen Mall the spineless.

Faced with the prospect of meeting Tom Howard's beloved mother, this was the woeful condition in which Frances found her. 'He talks of her as if she were more friend than mother, and a treasured one at that,' Mall wailed. 'He paints her as a paragon, educated, the perfect mistress of the castle, managing the land, disciplining the servants, and whose conversation is famed throughout the county.'

'Come,' Frances reassured, 'no woman is without fault this side of paradise.'

'And know you the worst of it?' her friend asked gloomily. 'Her name is Mall! Before she married she was Mall Eure, and has never been a Mary. Will you come and stand beside me in this ordeal?'

Frances agreed, wishing to do all she could to help her friend and champion, and intrigued on her own part to meet this shining pattern of womanhood.

Mall dressed carefully in her third-finest clothes, wishing at once to give the impression of being a great lady, albeit a modest and chaste one.

Together they hailed a hackney coach to St Martin's Field, where the Howards kept their

296

London home.

'Is Tom not coming with us?'

'He is there betimes,' said Mall, taking a deep breath as they drew up outside a fair house sitting in its own large gardens.

If the two women were expecting a neat, housewifely matron, they were doomed to a surprise. Lady Mary Howard was dressed, from slipper to shawl, in claret-red of a surprisingly fashionable cut. Her dark hair was streaked with grey at the temples, and tied back in a more severe style than was usual amongst Court ladies. She was almost as tall as Frances, with fine blue eyes and an intelligent brow. The only thing that marked her out from the London lady was the glowing clarity of her complexion, untouched by soot or smallpox, and free from the touch of the hare's foot or the patch.

Her son Tom stood next to her, a hesitant look on his handsome face as if unsure what volcanic eruption might ensue from the meeting.

All at once he saw what a tricky question of precedence presented itself. Mall Villiers had been permitted by the King to keep her title after her husband's death, and was still styled Duchess of Richmond and was therefore of greater standing than a mere baronet's wife.

Ignoring such matters, Mall immediately curtseyed. 'I have heard so much good of your ladyship from your son.'

'Have you now?' replied Tom's mother robustly. 'And I have always sympathized with your poor mother. Bad enough to lose your husband to another woman. But to be the King's favourite!'

'Mother . . .' interrupted Tom. 'Remember the

297

Duke of Buckingham was murdered!'

'Aye, and much rejoicing there was for it in the North of England. I am sorry, I should not speak so of your father. It was all a long time ago. And things not much better now under the present King, though at least he confines himself to women.' She turned to Tom. 'Tell me, how many women does the King have?'

Before he could answer or deflect his outspoken parent from this unfortunate speech, she continued unabated.

'I'd have him gelded if he were a stallion in my possession, but I suppose we'd all be lost, since we need his heirs. Not that he seems very able in that department. Only gets bastards, as far as I can see.'

Even Mall was struck dumb by this discourse.

Not so Frances, who was finding Lady Howard entirely delightful. 'Ah, my lady, but you would not talk of gelding if you knew the King. He has a charm that is all his own.'

Lady Howard put her head on one side, all at once reminding Frances of her indiscreet parrot. 'And who are you, pray?'

'I told you, Mother, this is Mistress Frances Stuart,' supplied Tom, looking shaken.

Mall Howard looked at Frances with sudden interest. 'The famous Mistress Stuart? The only woman in the kingdom to resist the King's advances? The lady whom he might have married, if the Queen perished? Tell me, I am fascinated, how have you held so long onto your honour?'

'Mother, please . . .' cautioned Tom.

But Frances laughed. 'I like the King, and he likes me also. And he knows that, unlike some, I want nothing from him, so he cannot bribe me.'

She grinned at the older woman. 'That and a little cunning and subterfuge!'

'I wish the other ladies had your skills, my dear. Believe me, I'm no Puritan, but there'll be a judgement on the Court before long for its licentiousness. Not that I'll care. I'll be safe in Naworth, thank the Lord. Yet I worry for Tom here. He always was my favourite of the litter, unlike his pompous brother, the Earl.' At last she turned to Mall. 'And now I hear that he has lost his heart to you, and that if you marry it will cause a great scandal.'

Mall looked suddenly vulnerable. 'I love him more than my very soul, my lady.'

'Love! Pah! Can you not just bed each other, like all the rest here? Yet I suppose you have done that already? He is a grown man able to make his own mistakes, and a younger son to boot. What business is it of mine?'

Tom took her hand. The bond between them was startling. 'I want you to accept my choice, so that I do not have to hide my feelings from the mother I love.'

'I can accept your choice, sure enough. Yet, dearest Tom, that is not to approve it.'

He nodded sadly. 'Then acceptance will have to be enough.'

As they left the Howard house and walked through St Martin's Field, Mall whispered, 'Now I have to hope tomorrow's business does not spoil even her acceptance of me.'

'Then withdraw!'

'Frances, I cannot.'

Frances sighed and hoped that her other plan would then come to fruition.

The next day dawned, raw and chill, even though it was summer. Duels were traditionally held at first light to evade the authorities, and Frances had agreed to rouse Mall from her chamber, which she did with a heavy heart.

She found her up and dressed, sitting on the edge of her daughter's bed. 'Go to, Mama,' Mary demanded, half-asleep. 'Why are you dressed in gentlemen's get-up?'

'It is a whim of the Queen's. She likes us to go out among the populace so that none know her.'

Mary seemed to accept this odd behaviour without further questioning.

'Goodbye, my Mary. Remember that I love you.'

Mary looked at her curiously. 'What a strange thing to say. One would think you were going on a journey.'

This seemed so prophetic that Frances could not bear to catch Mall's eye.

As they hailed a wherry for Barn Elms both fell silent. There were few craft going upriver and they soon arrived at their destination, feeling tense and serious. They walked swiftly to the duelling ground, but no one waited for them.

'When the second arrives,' Mall instructed, 'we will agree that we only duel to first blood. There is no need for more. That will be enough to teach her a lesson.'

Yet still no one came.

After another fifteen minutes Mall began to whistle. 'I do not think they are going to show.'

'And thank God for it.'

Just as they were about to leave, they heard the sounds of a boat arriving. Frances' heart sank like a stone. Yet it was not Lady Shrewsbury, but a page wearing her dark-blue livery.

The boy bowed. 'The Countess of Shrewsbury sends you her regrets, but she cannot meet her obligation today. I am afraid she is indisposed.'

Frances bit her lip. 'In what way is my lady indisposed?

The boy looked wooden-faced. 'I could not say, Mistress. I am but a page of the back stairs.'

Frances produced a small purse of coin and clinked it enticingly. She shook the purse so that two coins fell out, which she held out to him. 'Are you so sure you know nothing of my lady's indisposition?'

The boy grinned and took them. 'Very little, mistress. Except that it followed hard on eating a box of marchpanes. And afterwards my lady was confined all night to her close-stool.' He winked at them both broadly. 'It was the cook's opinion that some jealous wife may have laced the sweetmeats with jalap.'

Mall looked swiftly at Frances before throwing back her head and laughing, all her anxiety dissipating with the mist that hung on the trees. 'Well, Mistress Stuart, I suppose there is more than one way of learning a lesson, as the Countess of Shrewsbury is at this moment discovering. And this was naught to do with you, I assume.'

'What do I know of roots and herbs that make a body evacuate so violently that it is tied all night to the close-stool?'

'What indeed?'

'Mall, for the love of your Tom, I think we should keep this quiet.' Frances was deadly serious now, wanting to protect Mall from her own dangerous impulsiveness. 'The truth is, we have had the luck of the Devil this day. If she had come and you had fought, even to first blood, the scandal might have ended any chance of your union. And, Mall, believe me, when you have found a man you love and there is even the smallest chance of having him, do not squander it!'

'Aye, you are right. I have been unwise.' Mall caught her solemnity. 'So you still hanker after the Duke, and he a married man—and to a termagant who makes his life a living hell, from what I hear? How strange is fate? To be the one woman the King desires, when all you long for is a man whose wife does not even value him. There is strange planning in Nature, to be sure!'

'Why cannot I accept that he is married and look elsewhere?'

Mall slipped an arm around her, making an odd sight. Two young gallants comforting each other. 'He has not aided you in that. Besides, love does not let us women off the hook easily. Why else am I standing here upon a duelling ground in gentlemen's clothing, with a sword in my hand?'

Frances laughed. 'With you, who knows? You were ever a mad piece!'

'Shall we return to Whitehall?'

The mist was lifting from the trees in the clearing where they stood, revealing a bright day, which promised to be warm. The birds sang joyfully. The air was as clear as fresh running water. Even the river had a translucent beauty they had not noticed on the way out. They both felt almost a reluctance

302

to return to the choking stink of London, with its dirty, soot-filled air and filthy streets full of the ragged poor. Yet London was the centre of their world, and the King and Court its highest pinnacle.

'Come,' Mall grinned. 'If we go now, we will be in Whitehall before the Court has even risen. The King will be at tennis, his ministers waiting by the side to try and interest him in the day's business, and he giving more heed to his spaniel dogs! None will even know that we were here.'

Yet in that they were wrong.

In London the story of the failed duel was already being whispered about behind elaborate painted fans, and gentlemen in long curled periwigs were laughing at it.

Lady Shrewsbury, it seemed, was no kinder to her servants than to her discarded lovers, so they took great pleasure in spreading the true cause of her indisposition.

Mall, meanwhile, had listened well and seen that, to achieve her ends, she must cease to be the madcap Butterfly, lurching from unsuitable scrape to scandalous encounter, but must instead be virtuous and modest—a hard task for a member of the wild Villiers clan.

To this end, as dinnertime approached, she changed into her most discreet gown, of pale-primrose sarsenet, whose lining of stiffened cotton more than protected her modesty. She eyed herself in the looking glass, satisfied.

'Zounds, I would almost make a nun!' she murmured and headed off in search of Tom and his mother, who were dining with all the Court in the great dining hall.

Mall stood at the entrance to the hall, amongst

the bustling grooms of the kitchen and ewery, trying to pick out Tom in the crowded room. Courtiers packed three great tables, leading towards the dais where the King and Queen sat with the highest nobles of the land. Above, in the gallery, subjects of His Majesty gathered simply to watch the royal couple dine.

At length she found him. Precedence decreed that she herself must sit at the maids of honour's table, yet she wished to exchange at least a word and greeting with Tom.

And then a curious thing happened. A whisper went round the hall like the buzzing of a great swarm of bees released suddenly from the hive. And then someone at the top table began to clap, and Mall, to her amazement, saw that the applause was intended for her, and she had no choice but to acknowledge it with a queenly nod of the head.

All the same, she approached Tom and his mother with trepidation, knowing that she could expect a cold show of disapproval.

'So,' Lady Howard enquired stiffly, 'what is this undignified tale we hear of ladies duelling? And to defend Tom's honour. Can he not defend his own, that a woman must do it for him?'

'My lady—' began Mall apologetically.

'Quiet!' commanded the formidable matron, getting to her feet. 'I never liked that Talbot woman, nor her mother, either. And know you what I said to Tom? "Who else do you know who would pull such a hoyden's trick as this?" And what did you reply, Tom?'

'That there was but one other lady I could call to mind who would behave with such outrageous impropriety.' Tom Howard, his eyes as clear and

304

blue as a summer sky, began to smile. 'And that is you, Mother.'

*   *   *

Now that she had been accepted by the forthright Lady Howard, Mall proceeded to win over her beloved's mother further with drives round Hyde Park, shopping in the new arcades, buying perfumes from the best apothecaries and a trip to the playhouse. At Frances' request, they brought Walter with them. They decided upon *The Indian Queen*, 'a tragedy in heroic verse' at Mr Killigrew's theatre in Vere Street.

Mall's taste ran more to the comedies of Mr Etherege than to tragedy, yet she was still enthralled by the magnificent scenic devices, the battles and the sacrifices onstage, with spirits singing in the air, which the play offered. Beck Marshall, splendid as Queen Zempoalla, wore an Indian dress made of real feathers. They bought small, sweet china oranges from the orange girls, and Mall pointed out all the disreputable characters, from Orange Moll to Lady Castlemaine. Barbara sat in a box to their right, only just dressed, cooling herself with a fan fashioned from painted chickenskin and bright-blue feathers.

To Frances' horror, she started to make sheep's eyes at Walter.

'Has she no shame?' demanded Frances. 'He is barely sixteen. She must be ten years older than he!' Even as she said it, she recalled that Mall was far more than ten years older than Tom. Yet Mall had not taken exception.

'They said she took the Duke of Monmouth to

305

her bed, and he the King's by-blow, when he was only fifteen,' Mall whispered low so that Walter could not eavesdrop.

Frances bit her lip, torn between shocked laughter and the desire to protect her brother. Fortunately Walter did not seem to have heard.

Three rows below them the louche Lord Rochester lolled in his box. 'He lusts after Frances' friend Lizzy Mallett,' confided Mall to Lady Howard, who was greatly enjoying the Court gossip.

'And even more after her fortune,' Frances pointed out tartly, thinking of the irony of having money or not. 'Poor Lizzy! She is the most beautiful girl, and yet is forever known only for her fortune.'

They became aware that Lord Rochester was waving at them, or more particularly at Walter, who had set his face in the other direction as if his life depended upon it.

'Walter,' Frances enquired, puzzled, 'why is that unpleasant man trying to attract your attention?'

Walter was deeply relieved when Mr Dryden, the celebrated dramatist, wearing a very comic wig with two great points like Devil's horns, stopped to exchange a few words with them. 'And who is this handsome young man?' he asked of Walter. 'So fine-looking he must make all the ladies' hearts beat faster.' He turned to Mall and Frances. 'That is, if they had hearts. Have you ever thought of the stage, young man? We could do with handsome heroes like you. My lead actor is forty-two and still plays lads of sixteen.'

'I am studying at the Inns of Court,' blurted Walter, shy beneath the lazy, penetrating gaze of Lord Rochester, who was still watching, 'yet more than anything I wish to go to s-sea.'

306

'The sea, eh? What did you think of the sea-battles onstage?'

'M-magnificent!'

When they had congratulated him for his part in writing the play, Mr Dryden nodded his head like a pompous turkey. 'Yes, but I am better at the tragic. Comedy is not my strength. I lack that gaiety of humour that is required by those who do it well.'

'Pity he writes so many comedies then,' whispered Mall to his departing back.

But the greatest delight for Tom's mother was when the King, sitting in the royal box and catching sight of Frances, actually stood and bowed to them.

'To be bowed to by a monarch . . .' enthused Lady Mary, losing all her hard-bitten northern good sense in the face of royalty.

'Indeed, he would lie beneath Frances' feet if he got the chance,' Mall replied, forgetting whose company she was in. 'If only my lady Castlemaine could have learned our Mistress Stuart's skill. No need for all her bawdy bedroom tricks—so tiring, after all. The answer to win the King's undying love was simply to say "No". It has proved greater than all the love potions the quacksalvers could distil.'

Frances laughed and shook her head, then stopped, stock-still, like a hart at the sound of the huntsman's sudden horn.

Not five feet away, the only gentleman present not to emulate the King's habit of wearing a periwig, his russet hair about his shoulders, his gaze fixed intently upon her, stood the Duke of Richmond. And next to him were the plain young girl and the shrill and unpleasant woman whom she had seen that day arguing with the toll-gatekeeper so close to Cobham Hall.

307

Chapter 15

Frances could still remember those forbidding features, the long haughty Roman nose, the thinning hair the colour of mouse, the pale skin that was more whey than ivory. Above all she recalled the sneer of assumed superiority. Margaret Lewis, née Banaster, now Duchess of Richmond, seemed greatly older than surely she must be, unless of course she had lied about her age to her prospective husband.

Frances stole a look at the gun-metal silk of her gown, cut low over the bodice revealing almost as much décolletage as Lady Castlemaine. Yet where Barbara's flesh gleamed and invited, Margaret's was pale and withered like the leather book bindings in some dusty library. The new Duchess of Richmond had the distinction of achieving a style that both revealed and repulsed in equal measure.

Reluctantly the Duke brought them over.

'I have been asking myself,' Margaret announced to the assembled company, 'if I might have my picture painted, and wondered who are the most sought-after painters of the moment? I have heard talk of Mr Lely, and yet others speak of a Master Wright. After all, if you must outlay such an outrageous sum as I have heard they require, you do not want to mistake their talent.'

'That depends,' Mall replied carefully, 'on what effect Your Grace desires to achieve. Master Wright tends towards the real and natural. Master Lely takes Court beauties and dresses them as shepherdesses, in drapes that seem as if they might fall off at any moment.'

'Oh,' breathed Margaret, not realizing she was being teased. 'Then it is Mr Lely for me! Perhaps not a shepherdess, but in the pose of some goddess or other?'

'I am sure Mr Lely would be overwhelmed at the honour.'

'One other thing,' Margaret continued unabashed. 'It is a matter to which I have given some thought. Why do you also carry the title Duchess of Richmond, without even the addition of "Dowager"? And of the two of us, I assume it is I who takes precedence, as my husband is the present Duke?'

The box stilled. It was almost as if down in the pits the fops and the orange-sellers, the apprentices and the ladies of dubious repute stood still, waiting for Mall's answer.

'Mama,' her daughter Mary tried to interrupt. 'I do not think . . .'

'Hush, girl,' her mother silenced her. 'What do you know of such things?'

Mall Villiers, daughter of the great Duke of Buckingham, widow first of Charles Herbert, heir to the Earl of Pembroke, and then to James Stuart, Duke of Richmond and royalist hero, who had offered himself in place of the King on the scaffold, turned to consider the new Duchess.

'I remain the Duchess of Richmond because the King himself desired me to do so,' she replied evenly. 'Indeed, madam, your husband only has his title because my son Esme, the loveliest boy that ever was, died of smallpox at the tender age of eleven. And I think you will find it is I who takes precedence, despite your husband's lucky inheritance.'

A look of intense annoyance settled on the face of the new Duchess.

'Though for myself,' Mall continued, 'I find the matter of little interest.'

Frances had to hide her smile, knowing that Mall did care very greatly for precedence when it suited her. 'It is the person who earns the respect of others, not their position or title, that matters. Do you not think so, Your Grace?'

Margaret did not answer. Instead, announcing that she had glimpsed an acquaintance, she swept grandly out, taking her plain and shy daughter Mary with her.

An awkward silence fell upon those remaining, and then wicked Mall began to laugh. 'I am sorry, my lord,' she turned to the Duke, who stood pale with embarrassment. 'I hope I have not offended your wife.'

The Duke sighed and shook his head. 'She did not seem thus when I paid her my respects.'

'Women never do. And no doubt, as with all gentlemen, you were blinded to her faults by the size of her portion. What do they say? "Marry in haste, repent at leisure?" Mind you, she certainly seems mature in years.' Mall winked. 'Mayhap she will not last too long.'

'She is hardy as an ox,' the Duke replied with a self-deprecating smile. 'She will permit me and the servants no fires, even in the harshest of winters.'

'Then stand up to her!' Frances flashed, suddenly impatient with him for ascribing all this to Fate. 'And if we are to trade proverbs, I know which one my nurse would offer: "You have made your bed, now you must lie in it."'

310

'You are right. I shall make a stand. I have already refused her desire that we instal ourselves in London.' He glanced at Frances, yet she kept her eyes fixed ahead. 'For a start, she would ruin me.' Charles smiled, a look of genuine amusement lighting up his grey eyes. 'You may be surprised to learn it, but it takes a considerable outlay to dress as my lady does. And I could not bear to see what the Court made of her. Yet I feel for her daughter. She is a kind girl, and beneath the homely exterior has a fine mind and good intentions.'

Frances knew not why she spoke, but found herself making an offer that made Mall look at her sharply. 'She might come and stay with us for a while. A maid of honour's post is too much to hope for, since half the land desires them, but there is always work for helpful hands.'

Charles looked at her as if she were an angel of goodness. 'Could she indeed? I think she would flourish in a different climate. Away from her mother.'

'I am sure she would.'

'I will make the arrangements then.' He raised her hand briefly to his lips. A fire spread through her like a spark to a trail of gunpowder.

When he had left she found Mall's cynical gaze fixed upon her.

'Look not at me so. I do it because I understand the girl's desire to escape. I was a plain child once, overgrown and overlooked.'

'Nothing to do with the Duke, then? You do recall the arrangement, I suppose? Board at Whitehall comes to us but through our duties.'

'Pish to that. We are entitled to seven dishes apiece at the maids of honour's table, and Mary can share my dole.' She grinned at Mall. 'And she can have your eels, since you hate them so.'

'And bed?'

'There will always be a groom's or page's pallet. She will not mind. She wishes to escape, remember.'

'Frances,' Mall put a gentle hand on her friend's arm. 'Ask your heart why you do this. Is it truly because you were moved by her plight—though heaven knows anyone would pity a girl with that harridan as her mother? Or is it not more through her connection that you make her this offer?'

She held out her arms and Frances ran into them. 'You know me too well.'

'Aye, and worry for you.'

*   *   *

Despite Mall's reservations Mary Lewis, plain and unloved, came to live in the Palace of Whitehall, much to her mother's great and continuing annoyance, and was deeply grateful for the thirty miles that divided them.

She proved a popular addition, winning over the jealous ladies who saw her at first as an interloper, fetching and carrying, spotting who might need a wrap and who gloves, ever smiling, nothing too much trouble.

The glorious summer finally transformed itself into a long and golden autumn. It had been a year of exceptional delight with long days upon the water, masques in the gardens, balls and card parties, riding out to hawk and hunt, and comedies to entertain. Yet there were also moans and complaints among the ordinary folk, the chair-men and the wherrymen, the tailors and the tallow-makers, that things had not changed so much under the King as they had hoped. And the distant rumblings of a war with the Dutch were growing louder, so that even the ladies of the Court began to hear them.

To stir up the people further some strange omens had beset the City of London. As the winter chill settled on it, and Yuletide beckoned, a strange, bright star called a comet arrived in the sky, trailing a tail of light behind it and bringing with it fear and trepidation.

'Do you recall the star that arose in the noonday sky, almost rivalling the sun, on the day the King was born?' Lady Suffolk asked, trying to calm the jangling nerves of the maids of honour and persuade them there was nothing strange about this arrival in the sky. 'We all thought surely it heralded a king who would bring prosperity, peace and stability, did we not?'

But this new star stayed in the sky for days— bigger than all the other stars, reddish in colour, with a tail fanning out behind, which people likened to a birch besom.

'Even the King and Queen have been sitting on the roof of the palace marvelling at it,' Jane La Garde admitted.

'Yet the people are not marvelling.' Mall shook her head, a line of worry furrowing her brow. 'Tom says they speak of it with foreboding, saying that comets foretell the Apocalypse.' All the Queen's ladies were listening now. 'And there is a man, one Solomon Eagle, a Quaker minister, who has taken to running through the streets each night, naked as Christ on the cross and wearing naught but a loincloth, with a dish of burning coals upon his head, warning all that a terrible scourge will soon come down upon them to punish them for their sins—and we at the Court above all, for the great licentiousness of our ways!'

Even Cary Frazier, the most brazen of all the ladies, looked pale at this nightmarish vision.

'Tom says in the taverns and tippling houses people talk of little else. And there is worse.' The ladies crowded round, silent as the grave. 'Though it is not the season for it, two Frenchmen are said to have died of the plague in Drury Lane, and now no one dares go there.'

'But it is not the time of year for the plague,' objected Jane. 'Plague is a summer distemper.'

'Aye,' seconded Lady Suffolk, 'a green Yule makes a fat churchyard, or so they say, but this will be a white Yule, and cold as the tomb betimes.'

They all fell silent, wondering what it might mean.

But the strange uncertainty of that time, when people began to look at their neighbours suspiciously and cross themselves, and pray to God for his mercy even though they had not done so for many years, had at least one happy outcome.

When Mall announced that she and Tom Howard were to wed, it did not cause the scandal she had expected; indeed, hardly a ripple registered on the frozen millpond of Court society.

'It is to be as quiet as can be imaginable,' Mall told Frances, hardly able to contain her joy. 'We are to wed in St James' in Duke Place. And you and your little protégée are to be bridesmaids.'

'But what of your own daughter Mary?'

'Mary has set her face against our union,' Mall

314

admitted sadly.

'And the rest of your families?' They both knew she was referring to Tom's mother.

'We thought it best not to bid them come. It will be easier for them to accept the deed when it is done.'

'I am beyond happy for you!' Frances congratulated her. 'Yet why do you not marry in the Queen's Chapel?'

'At St James' we need no banns to be read and need not broadcast our union to all and sundry— above all to my brother Buckingham, who will thunder along to the King spouting about the great name of Villiers being dragged through the mud by this disgraceful union.'

She took Frances' hands in hers. 'Tom says when he gives up soldiering he will become a vicar at St James'. They conduct two thousand marriages a year in a parish of but a hundred and sixty households. Imagine the profit in that! Though most are because the bride is underage and has no permission.'

Frances forbore to say that this would not be their problem.

*   *   *

The day dawned grey and overcast. It was almost the shortest of the year and the sun seemed not to want to raise his head, even to celebrate Mall and Tom's nuptials.

The small party, joking to fight off their subdued mood, made their way to Aldgate in two separate carriages. The church was a large brick building, nothing hole-in-the-corner about it, with three great windows and a fine tower with a weathervane

315

on top.

A young woman drawing water from a nearby pump bid them good luck, which cheered Mall, who felt she needed it.

Once inside the wedding did not start well.

The minister mistook Mary Lewis for the bride, and looked a trifle shaken when Mall stepped up to the altar instead.

And, just as the vows were to be exchanged, there was a great commotion at the back of the church. All turned to find Lady Mary Howard, in mud-splattered red riding habit, demanding from the verger to be admitted.

'She cannot prevent us now?' asked brave Mall, all of a sudden losing her nerve.

Tom held tight to her hand. 'I would not let her!'

'Have you come to object to this union, madam?' demanded the vicar hopefully. Clearly he felt it went against God and Nature.

Lady Mary Howard launched her considerable bulk towards the altar. 'To object to it?' she repeated. 'I have just ridden almost three hundred miles to offer my blessing!'

Frances, Mary and the bride-men cheered and it was a happy party that emerged from the church, to find a large crowd of the ragged poor waiting outside, summoned by the young woman of the pump.

'Be watchful, my lady,' counselled the vicar. ''Tis their custom to follow the bridal couple home and create a rumpus outside their bedchamber while the bedding takes place, until they are paid to leave.' He paused, surveying the unlikely couple once more, suspicion returning at the oddness of the pairing. 'There will *be* a bedding, I take it?

316

It is needful, you know, for the marriage to be consummated.'

'Do not concern yourself on that score, Reverend,' Lady Mary Howard replied in robust tones that could be heard halfway across London. 'For I rather think the bedding has taken place already.'

Tom threw a handful of coins into the crowd and the wedding party made off while the going was good, to avoid any undignified altercations outside their bedchamber.

Afterwards they repaired to the Three Nuns Tavern in Aldgate Street, famed for the rare quality of its punch, where the bride and groom were toasted to a long and loving life together.

As the coach carried Frances and Mary back to Whitehall later that night, she tried not to imagine the bedchamber over the tavern where Mall and Tom were to spend their nuptial night. And though she willed it not so, the image of Tom, young and strong and handsome, approaching his lady and unlacing her gown, gently at first and then with wilder passion, kissing her shoulders and slipping his hand inside the silk of her chemise, brought a race to her pulse.

She was brought back to earth by Mary nudging her to say that the coachman had spoken.

'I won't go near Drury Lane, mistress, on account of the distemper there.'

Frances nodded, recalling that she had heard something of this.

As they passed instead through the parish of St Giles in the Fields they saw that two houses were being boarded and padlocked, while a bailiff nailed a piece of paper up and painted a great red cross on

317

the door with the dread words 'Lord Have Mercy Upon Us'.

As the coach passed by, they heard the beseeching cries of the householders within, muffled and desperate, as if on a ship that was sinking to the bottom of the ocean.

It was almost a relief to find the Court was taken up with its usual frippery concerns. When they joined the rest to sup, Cary Frazier and Catherine Boynton were bickering over which one should join the Queen in her apartments for evening prayers.

'Neither wishes to go,' whispered Mary Lewis, who had come to understand the ways of Whitehall quicker than any gundog learning to retrieve its partridge. 'Mistress Frazier because she hates how long the Queen spends telling her rosary, and Mistress Boynton because she hopes to see her lover.'

It was a marvel how much Mary picked up. When Frances asked how she knew so much of Court ways, the girl smiled and said, 'Since I am small and plain, it is as if I am a piece of furniture. They pay no more mind to my being there than if I were a gate-legged table or an oaken chair.'

'When in fact,' Frances pointed out, 'you are sharp as a pin, with as fine a wit as any young lady I have encountered.'

Mary smiled with such pleasure that it touched Frances' heart. Clearly her mother was as sparing with loving words as a miser with his coin.

Suddenly aware of how hungry she was, Frances surveyed the meal laid out before them and set to with a will. There was a tempting array of roast beef and goose, baked mutton, lamprey pie and a tart of spinach, with creamy syllabubs and sweetmeats to finish.

'With the fear of this contagion about, when I go to the Queen's apartments,' complained Cary Frazier, 'she will badger me to seek preventatives for her, since she knows my father is one of the Court physicians. Indeed, she is quite hysterical about it. They had an outbreak in her country when she was a child, which carried off her favourite uncle, and now she wishes to protect the King. The King!' Cary laughed, 'Who has eight physicians besides my father.'

'She does not trust the English physicians,' Mary murmured. 'I heard her ask her Portuguese ladies if they knew of any remedies from their own country.'

'Well, really . . . And if she wishes to protect the King, she should stop him and the Duke of York roistering on the town with known harlots.'

'You should not refer to my lady Castlemaine so,' chipped in Jane La Garde, and they all began to giggle.

'So the Queen fears this distemper truly is the plague?' Catherine Boynton asked, suddenly anxious.

'The King's Council sent two physicians to the house in Drury Lane to see if it were indeed such,' offered Mary. 'It was they who ordered the household be shut up.'

They all stared at her. 'How know you this?'

'The Queen's blackamoor told me. The one that is her page. He was very afeared because they have much plague in his homeland. He said the Queen prays about it each night and lights candles also, to intercede for forgiveness for the ungodliness of the Court.'

'My father is not persuaded it is the plague,' Cary

319

shrugged. 'Yet if it be, then we shall all leave. The only preparation for the plague, he says, is for all to run away from it to the country.'

The cries of the people from behind the door with its red-painted cross in St Giles came back to Frances.

'*All?*' Frances asked, angry at such advice. 'You mean all the poor and ragged people also?'

They all stared at her. 'Well, no . . .' Cary replied, piqued. 'I meant the Court.'

'I do not think Mistress Frazier meant to be unfeeling,' interposed Jane La Garde, ever the peacemaker, 'just that we should not panic and lose our faith in God, for the King and the authorities will act, if it is needful.'

And, for the sake of good manners, they left it at that.

The weather at least came to Londoners' aid. A cold so brutal that none wished to venture out swept down on the city, and with it severe frost and sharp winds. The Bills of Mortality showed no further deaths from plague, and the city breathed a sigh of relief and went about its normal business of buying, selling and making goods, and filling the alehouses with good cheer.

The winter progressed to Yuletide, yet the twelve days of feasting were muted this year. January passed, and hard February snapping at its heels. At Court, the talk was once again of the hated Dutch and whether there would be war and, amongst the maids of honour, of Valentines.

All the ladies enjoyed the tradition of drawing a gentleman's name from a hat and waiting for him to shower her with gifts and love tokens. It was the one day of the year when a lady might accept a gift from any gentleman without the slur of impropriety being laid upon it.

Catherine Boynton received a dozen pairs of gloves, and Jane three pairs of silken stockings.

'Lucky Jane,' Cary Frazier peeped jealously over her shoulder. 'Silk stockings are fifteen shillings a pair in the Royal Exchange! And he has given you a garter for them into the bargain.' She made a face, clearly thinking that she would have been the better recipient for such a lavish gift than plain Jane La Garde.

'And what has your Valentine given you, pray, Mistress Frazier?' Jane enquired sweetly.

'I drew the Queen's apothecary,' complained Cary. 'And did he give me some rare and valuable gift? Some oil of foxes? Or a vial of virgin's wax?' She shrugged dismissively. 'Only this piffling bag of flower pollen, which he says French ladies much prize for their complexions. Pah! I could have gathered it myself in summertime.' She looked slyly at Frances. 'And what of you, Mistress Stuart. Who is your Valentine?'

The Countess of Suffolk, the most senior Lady of the Bedchamber, looked at her sternly. 'Did you not know, mistress?' There was a certain satisfaction in her tone. 'The King has chosen to be Mistress Stuart's Valentine.'

Before Cary could react, the sound of trumpets was heard and they all stood up straight and moved back, unconsciously forming two parallel lines that led straight to Frances.

'Mistress Stuart,' the King bowed low to Frances' curtsey. 'I wish you the day's happiness and beg to present this little trifle.'

He handed her a bag made of purple velvet.

321

Frances took it and held it by her side.

'Come now, open it up.' His Majesty was all excitement, like a young boy who has bought some trifle for his beloved and longs to see her pleasure and approval.

Frances untied the strings and withdrew a pair of pendants made of the largest, most gleaming pearls she had ever seen.

'Your Majesty,' she began, holding them out towards him, 'I could not accept a gift of so great a price.'

'Of course you could,' Charles pushed her hand away, laughing. 'Beauty deserves fitting adornment. Besides, the parliament believes they vote me money and I fritter it on my mistresses. Yet all know that you at least—to my great chagrin—are not my mistress, so at least they cannot accuse me of it this time!'

He seemed very amused by his own joke as he bowed again and disappeared with his courtiers, telling Frances that he would desire her company later at Lady Castlemaine's apartments.

'There is to be dancing and pretty boys singing French love songs. Barbara may be faithless and extravagant, but she knows how to entertain!'

After he had left the ladies crowded round to inspect the pendants.

'I have never seen lovelier pearls,' breathed Catherine, 'not even on my lady Castlemaine or the Queen.'

'Nor I,' breathed Jane La Garde. 'They must have cost a thousand pounds at least!'

'More like eighteen hundred,' pronounced Cary Frazier.

'Is there anything you do not know the value of?'

demanded Lady Suffolk.

'There is one thing,' Catherine Boynton gestured at Cary's privy parts.

'Oh, Cary knows the value of that all right. A baronetcy at the very least, and mayhap a viscountcy or an earldom!'

Frances left them all to ready herself for her duties with the Queen. Today she was glad to leave the gossipy atmosphere of the maids' quarters for the more serious and pious company of Her Majesty.

Yet the mood in the Queen's Privy Chamber was not pious, but verging on hysteria. Her little blackamoor page, whom she delighted in calling 'Guinea', for that was the land whence he came, had brought news that had thrown them all into great fear.

'There has been a riot in the parish of St Giles,' whispered Lady Suffolk. 'More houses were shut up against the plague and a cross and paper fixed, authorizing the procedure, and the populace came and tore down the paper and opened up the house. The matter is to be addressed at the Privy Council this very morning. This boy overheard the Lord Chancellor discussing it and ran to the Queen, so now all are at their wits' end, praying and lighting candles!'

'Mistress Stuart,' the Queen turned to Frances beseechingly. 'Know you if Cary Frazier discovered aught to protect against the plague from her father the doctor? My poor Guinea is truly afeared of catching the distemper.' She sat with the little boy on her lap, in a lapse of precedence that would have shocked her courtiers. Yet Frances saw how great her concern was, less for herself than for the

323

frightened child, and was touched. Perhaps it was because, with no longed-for babe of her own, this engaging little scamp had won the place in the Queen's affections that her own child might have had.

'I will ask her.'

'I do it secretly because my husband the King thinks I make too much of it, and that it is our job as monarchs to calm the people, not inflame them with our private fears.'

Frances thought of the pompous Dr Frazier, more skilled at flattering the great by listening to their paltry symptoms and treating courtiers with the French pox or helping Court ladies slip their by-blows, and being well paid for it, than at treating real diseases. Faced with a hint of the plague, he would be the first to take a coach for the country. She thought at once of Widow Wyatt, whose calm good sense had so impressed her. Would she know any remedies against the plague that the Queen could use?

Frances resolved to pay her a visit and discover.

*   *   *

When she hailed a wherry the next morning Frances could already sense a change in the air since the day of Mall's marriage two short months ago. Today, when the wherryman took her money, he placed it in a jar of vinegar 'to cleanse it against the distemper', a practice she had never known before.

As they rowed towards the City she caught sight of more houses with red crosses bearing that fatal message 'Lord Have Mercy Upon Us'.

'Are many houses shut up?'

'The City is so far spared, within the walls at least. But beyond in the outer parishes, where the people are so close-packed, the contagion spreads apace.' The wherryman looked sombre. 'Now the parishes hire their own people as searchers and watchmen, and who knows if neighbour gets revenge on neighbour by saying they have it when they do not.'

She alighted at Three Cranes Stairs and walked northwards, crossing Watling Street towards St Mary le Bow hard by Cheapside. Even here, in the bustling heart of the City, the narrow streets were emptier than before and passers-by eyed each other warily, sometimes crossing over to the other side. Now and then the passing bell tolled its mournful message, denoting a burial: nine strokes for a man, seven for a woman and three for a child.

Frances was grateful to reach the aromatic warmth of the widow's shop.

'What brings you to my door?' smiled the widow, with a twinkle that caused deep crevasses in her leathery skin. 'More rivals to send to their close-stools?'

Frances laughed. 'No, thank you. But by your good offices I was able to prevent a duel.'

'Indeed? I am glad to hear it. If more men had to stay in the privy, mayhap we could put an end to quarrels and wars! And what may I do for your ladyship today? A strange time to come calling, with the contagion spreading. If it were not for the Dutch besting us at sea, the King would be finding a reason to leave London and take the Court with him, I fancy.'

'Perhaps he might. Yet it is about the contagion that I come. Know you of any true preventatives

325

against it?'

Widow Wyatt shrugged and turned to the rows of jars behind her. 'Some say sponges soaked in vinegar held in the mouth.' Frances nodded, thinking of the wherryman and her coins. 'Others valerian and rue. Myrrh or powdered viper. The quacksalvers hawk verbena, claiming the Devil revealed it as a secret and divine medicine.' She laughed at the stupidity of the populace in believing them.

'And you yourself?'

'I observe others. The rich leave and are rarely stricken. The merchants who have ships move their families aboard and anchor in the river. Amongst those who must stay, those who keep themselves apart fare best.'

'And if they do succumb?'

'There are treatments. Sweating is the best, to bring the infection to the surface. I have a doctor friend who survived and gave me guidance. Tell your friend to burn incense and rosin, light fires, use sulphur or brimstone.' The smile reappeared in her cracked face. 'It may not keep the plague at bay, yet it will reassure and at least not harm, as many other remedies might.'

Outside in the street they heard a sudden wailing and looked out to find a house being shut up on the far side of the road, its occupants, a young woman and a girl, crying piteously from a window on the first floor. 'It is but one young servant girl who ails,' the woman shouted across to them. 'And we do not know for certain if she truly has the contagion. Now we are all to be locked up to perish!'

'So.' The widow shook her head sadly. 'The distemper comes even to the City now.'

'What think you of this shutting up?'

'I do not value it. It sets neighbour against neighbour. The rich pay the watchman to turn the other way, that they may run. Others bribe the physician to say it is spotted fever, not the plague, and are let out. Better to take the one who ails to a pesthouse and let the others free.'

Frances waited as the widow measured out the incense and sulphur, then broke a fragment of amber-yellow rosin from a sheet, wrapped it in paper and tied it up with string.

'Good luck, mistress. I hope all goes well with you and yours.'

The Queen was grateful for the remedies and began to burn them at once, until a satisfying fug of aromatic air fought with the foul-smelling stench of burning sulphur.

'See, Guinea,' she told the little boy. 'That will stop the infection coming here. It cannot see through the smoke.'

Amazingly, the boy lost his fearful look and smiled up at her, full of trust, while in the background her priests and Portuguese ladies tolled their rosaries and mumbled their endless prayers of intercession.

Mary Lewis also awaited Frances, full of news. 'My mother and the Duke come to London tomorrow, to Master Lely's studio. She is to have her painting taken there.'

'Indeed?' Frances repressed a smile. 'As a Grecian goddess?'

'No. She has hit upon a more dignified pose, as she calls it.'

'And what is that?'

'As St Catherine.' Mary was near to laughter

now. 'She is to copy the same pose as the Queen herself. She invites us to go and watch her.'

Frances knew it would be better not to risk seeing the Duke, even with his wife present, for her own peace of mind, and yet here they were with the shadow of death all around them and the drums of war beginning to sound. How did she know there would be a sound and safe tomorrow?

She would go and risk it.

Master Lely's studio in the Covent Garden piazza was always a place of buzz and busyness since he had so many commissions on his hands, even in these dread times. As well as Master Lely and his assistants, there would be crammed in the sitters, their entourages, even down to their yapping dogs, and often some musicians to provide entertainment. If the sitter were a woman of less-than-perfect repute, her protector, who was no doubt paying for the painting, would often be present also. As Master Lely occasionally exploded, the place was closer to Bedlam than a home for the Muse.

When the Duchess discovered she was not to have Master Lely paint her entirety, she harangued him with such vehemence that he almost refused to paint even her face.

As the undignified squabble continued, Frances found the Duke at her side.

'I wished to thank you for your care of Mary,' he said in a low voice 'She is so changed I would not have taken her for the same person.'

'The pleasure has been mine. She has the quickest of wits and a rare understanding of her fellow-beings.'

'And yet none noticed these capacities before you did.'

She looked away, yet felt her spirit soar at the warmth of his appreciation.

'And how fare you in these troubled times, Your Grace?' She forced herself to move the talk away from herself and her good qualities.

'I have naval duties in Dorset since I am Lord Lieutenant there, and will have more, if this war against the Dutch proceeds.'

'And do you think it will?'

'I fear so. Out of London, all are hot against the Hollanders. They call them butterboxes and fat cheese-eaters, and see them as paltry enemies.'

'And are they so?'

Before he had the chance to answer her, one of Master Lely's assistants interrupted them, and with great ceremony handed the Duke a small package wrapped in cloth, tied loosely with string.

Very coolly the Duke reached out to take the package, as if it were of no more importance to him than his tailor's account, and began to slip it into his pocket. Something about the coolness of his manner caught her interest.

With a teasing air she made a sudden grab for the parcel and it slipped to the floor.

And as it did so, the cloth became undone and the contents revealed.

It was a picture in miniature, a tiny copy of one of Master Lely's masterpieces, the kind of token sent by lovers and prospective brides and bridegrooms to their beloved, small enough to be carried in a pocket next to the heart.

But the sitter was not Margaret, the Duke's new wife. It was Frances herself, holding a bow, in the pose of Diana the huntress.

Frances stooped, quick as a flash, and picked it

up. Before he could stop her, she slipped it behind her, serious now. 'How did you come by this picture?'

Charles stood straight, unrepentant now that all was discovered. 'I had it copied by Dwarf Gibson from Master Lely's painting. It is quite a common practice.'

'And is it common to have paintings of ladies other than your wife?' She could not keep a teasing tone from her voice.

'Entirely usual, I assure you.'

Frances knew she should stop, but something impelled her onwards. 'And why would you have a painting made in little of myself as Diana?'

The Duke stood straight and tall, his grey eyes no longer sleepy, but almost angry now. 'You know why. Do not ask further. It is beneath you to taunt. May I have the picture returned to me?'

He reached behind her back, and as he did so their lips almost touched. She could almost feel their breaths mingle and she closed her eyes.

'Well, well, what a fair tableau this is, to be sure!'

The familiar voice, usually humorous and sardonic, was harsh and accusing.

Guiltily, Frances and the Duke turned to face the jealous fury of His Sacred Majesty King Charles II.

Chapter 16

Frances held her ground, yet she had never seen the King so angry as he stood before them, dressed from head to toe in midnight velvet, a froth of lace at his neck and a murderous gleam in his eye.

The King had learned many things during his long exile when he had been dependent on the help and self-sacrifice of others: patience, tolerance, a generous heart, the desire to squeeze the last drop of pleasure from life. He had also developed the instinct to survive and to hide his true feelings when it suited his own or England's interests.

Yet he did not hide them now. His black eyes burned with resentment and his tall frame bristled with anger. He had the air of restrained violence that a pugilist might possess.

Frances dropped a curtsey. 'Your Majesty.'

The King snatched the miniature from behind her back and studied it. 'A pretty thing. Yet perhaps your depiction as Diana, the chaste huntress, rings a little false, mistress?'

Frances raised her chin defiantly. 'It is as honest as ever it was.'

'I am glad to hear it. I would not like to see another granted the favour that I have so long sought from you.'

He turned to the Duke. 'And you, sir. You neglect your duties as Gentleman of the Bedchamber and, worse, as Lord Lieutenant of Dorsetshire. Know you not that we are near to war with the Dutch? Your duties call you to patrol the coast against infringement, not to dally in London with my wife's maids of honour.' He moved closer to the Duke. They were almost of a height, yet while the King's face was lean and harsh, the Duke's still held the bloom of youth about it. 'I suggest you go there now.'

For an instant the Duke stood still, and then, knowing that resistance was futile, he bowed.

Yet before he could retire the Duchess sailed

into the room with assumed grandeur as if she had been born to the role. 'My lord husband,' she breathed, not noticing at first to whom he talked, 'the dead colour is all laid down and the outline drawn. I am to come back tomorrow for the face to be painted.'

The King turned. 'Then you will do so without the pleasure of your husband's company.'

'Your Majesty!' Margaret gasped.

'And may I suggest you make sure the Duke minds his duties in Dorset, instead of making a nuisance of himself in London.' With a click to one of his gentlemen who was holding back his boisterous spaniels, the King took hold of the leash and departed, with his dogs yapping at his side.

'My lord!' Margaret flashed at him angrily. 'What have you done to so offend His Majesty? And just when we wanted to claim your place at Court and move to town.'

'You could hardly come now, with the plague taking hold, Mother,' Mary pointed out. 'It is rumoured the Court itself will move, if the contagion spreads.'

'Silence!' She turned on Mary venomously. 'Who would want the opinion of a plain and stupid child.'

'Mary is neither plain nor stupid.' Frances took a step towards the girl.

'And who asked you, pray? What relation do you stand to my daughter, that you interfere when her mother honestly chides her?'

Frances knew she was on shaky ground, but continued all the same. She had come to love Mary, and the girl was also her one link to the Duke. 'As one who has got to know her in the last few weeks and found her full of both wit and spirit.'

332

'Hah! She is useless as the cracked millstone at Cobham! No suitors consider a face like hers, since there is no great portion to persuade them, even though I have told them they need not look in the fireplace when they poke the fire, but to no avail.'

Mary flinched at her mother's crudity.

'Let her stay on at Court then,' Frances suggested, controlling her temper for Mary's sake.

'She has her uses. I have had to take on an extra maidservant since she has been in London.'

Frances caught Mary's eye warningly. They both knew that was all she was—or ever would be—to her mother. 'She will have a better chance of finding a husband here at Court than in Cobham.'

Margaret surveyed her nastily. 'It has not worked for you, though, mistress, has it? Or will no one sweep up the King's leavings?'

Frances' palm itched to strike the odious woman.

But she did not need to. Her husband took her roughly by the arm and hustled her out, almost bumping into one of the painter's startled assistants. 'Tell Master Lely we are cancelling our commission. I will pay the charges incurred so far.'

'How dare you . . . ?' began the Duchess.

'You can resume your portrait when you learn some manners. And you may start by bidding farewell to your only child. You would not wish Mistress Stuart to poison the Court with tales of your cruelty, I take it?'

'Goodbye, Daughter,' Margaret blurted reluctantly.

'Goodbye, Mother.' Mary dropped a deep curtsey, which she instantly converted into a hop, skip and jump when her mother left the room.

They had not long to celebrate their freedom from the Duchess' sharp tongue.

'Have you heard the news?' demanded Cary Frazier, so excited she had even forgotten to colour her cheeks with Spanish paper. 'The King has declared war on the Dutch!'

Bad-tempered sniping over trade in Africa, as well as clashes between Dutch and English ships in the Channel, had been growing for months, yet the King had resisted war, despite pressure on him from every side. Now it seemed he had finally cracked.

At first nothing seemed to change, apart from the bonfires that were lit all over London in celebration. Then, a week or so later, as Frances was returning with the other ladies from the King's Playhouse where they had enjoyed *The Indian Emperor* with a new actress, Nell Gwynn, in the role of Cydaria, their coach was halted on the corner of Bow Street and the Strand. A great crowd had gathered there, listening to another wild prophet akin to the famed Solomon Eagle. This man, though not half-naked, proclaimed himself an astrologer. He had raised himself onto a makeshift tower like a pulpit, from where he harangued the people below.

'Think back, good people, to the blazing star or comet we all beheld in the Yuletide sky. Did we not predict that it would foretell death and disaster?' Many in the crowd nodded their heads and nudged their neighbours in agreement. 'Did we not tell you that unless you all repented . . .' he noticed Frances' coach halted in the roadway and pointed at it, 'aye, and the Court give up its rank lasciviousness and stinking corruption, what would follow?'

He fixed them with a baleful stare. 'Pestilence, my friends!' As if to underline the terrible word a funeral procession, with its knot of mourners dressed in black, wove its way out of St Paul's Church in Covent Garden and crossed the road nearby, the passing bell sounding seven times denoting a woman's death.

The crowd murmured in agitation and one or two crossed themselves in the Papist manner. 'And after Pestilence, what would follow . . . ? War!' He banged a saucepan lid in a martial manner, which made all jump and the children start to cry and whimper. 'And next Fire! And after Fire, Famine! And all this unless you repent of your sins.'

One or two amongst the crowd fell down upon their knees and began to confess out loud that they had lied or stolen or were evil adulterers, and that the Lord should indeed have mercy and deliver them from the first part of this prophecy.

Frances and the other ladies sat in silence as the coachman drove on.

'Come, come,' Frances turned to the rest. 'This is superstitious nonsense. Comets are simply stars that move slowly across the sky—they are not harbingers of doom and disaster. Men like this so-called astrologer simply use omens and signs to sow panic and gain power over the ignorant.'

'And are succeeding, more's the pity.' Catherine Boynton pulled her cloak tight around her shoulders, as if she could shut out the fear she had seen in people's eyes. 'I wonder if the King knows such things are going on in his streets.'

As well as the impending war, and the threat

of plague, Frances grew more and more worried about Walter. She tried to find him several times in his lodgings near Lincoln's Inn, where his fellow-students reported hardly catching sight of him for days.

'Leading the high life with those rich friends of his,' nodded one sagely.

Frances listened, troubled, remembering her brother's strange behaviour. Had Walter been stupid enough to keep company again with Lord Rochester and his ilk, courting God knew what ruin?

She was pondering whether she ought to go to Somerset House and tell her parents, when Mary came running to find her, her wavy hair flying about her madly and her face white with worry. So agitated was she that she approached Frances in full company of the other ladies, including the Countess of Castlemaine.

'Hush, Mary,' Frances attempted to calm her down, thinking the panic outside had finally got to her also, 'what is it that disturbs you so?'

'It is the Duke of Richmond! My mother sends a message. A warrant arrived yesternight from the Serjeant-at-Arms to convey him to the Tower.'

Frances listened in disbelief. 'On what grounds?'

'For neglecting his duties as Lord Lieutenant of Dorsetshire when the country is at war with the Dutch.'

Frances felt as if her heart had been ripped from her body. Visions of racks and dungeons filled her mind and she had to take hold of a chair-back to stop herself falling down.

'What shall I tell my mother?' Mary asked anxiously.

336

'I will try and discover what it means. Is she allowed to visit him?'

Mary shook her head. 'I know not.'

'Go to her, she may need your comfort and support.'

After Mary had left, Frances stared out of the window at the Thames running sluggishly below, trying to work out what she could do. She did not notice Barbara cross the room to stand beside her.

'Do not play the innocent with me, Mistress Stuart.' Barbara leaned closer to her ear, and as she did so the laces of her silken dress fell open, revealing the white mounds of her breasts, greater than usual since she was again with child, though all doubted it was the King's. 'You and all the Court know why the Duke finds himself in the Tower, and it is as much to do with neglecting his duties as if the sun rose because it was night-time.' She took hold of Frances' wrist and held it so tight it pained her. 'Innocent women do not lead on their king till he is half-mad, and then toy with the heart of another woman's husband.'

Frances longed to slap that lovely taunting face. And yet Barbara spoke a truth. She had not been innocent in this matter.

'I will listen to a lecture from you, my lady, on the day you repent of your own indiscretions.' And, summoning as much dignity as she could muster, she left the room, while the other ladies whispered behind their hands, reckoning who had won that encounter.

She would seek out Mall. Mall knew the King's mind as well as any woman, even the Queen or Castlemaine.

As officer of the Yeoman of the Guard, Tom

Howard was entitled to a small billet near the King's Back Staircase and, to the astonishment of all, Mall—daughter of the great Duke of Buckingham—had installed herself in it, forsaking her own grand painted chambers, with their gilded ceiling and great oak carvings, in favour of a soldier's spartan rooms.

Yet the moment Frances entered it, she knew that this small chamber had been decked out with something too costly to be bought by many, no matter how rich or elevated they were: contentment.

Mall had picked a posy of jasmine and gillyflowers from the Privy Garden and placed it on the windowsill, where a lazy bee buzzed as it dipped into each bloom in search of pollen. Sunlight streamed in, making shapes out of shadows as lovely as any painting by a great master.

Mall sat on the edge of the bed, combing her chestnut hair, humming a madrigal. She beamed and jumped up at Frances' approach, brimming with happiness, like a bloom that stretches towards the sun after a long, harsh winter. 'Tell me, why, why did I never meet Tom Howard until this moment?'

Frances smiled, her own anxiety pushed to one side by her friend's delight. 'Because if you had, you would never have been allowed to marry him. You have only done so because you have wealth of your own, and are so high and close to the King that none dare stop you. And even then it is because you are a widow and past childbearing.'

'Thank you for that reminder. How know you I am past childbearing?'

Frances' eyes widened. 'Do you have your

flowers still?'

Mall threw a pillow at her. 'Yes, I do, thank you, young mistress.'

'Would you go down that road again?' Frances realized that she was shocked at the idea that one who was nearing forty might willingly entertain the thought.

'Do not worry, I have no plans for such. I would rather use rue oil and parsley than have another child, though I worry Tom might wish for one, young as he is.'

'Do those remedies also forestall a child being planted?' Her own mother would never have thought of telling her such things—indeed, would have striven hard to keep them from her ears.

'No. For that you would need greater protection. Some gentlemen sheath their yards in cloth or sheep's gut.' She laughed at Frances' expression. 'Though I am of the view such things are an armour against enjoyment, and a mere cobweb against danger. And, typically, gentlemen hate such devices. Perhaps we should ask my lady Castlemaine, though dear Barbara favours producing the bastards, then attributing them all to the King, whether they are his or no. I hear even he challenged the paternity of the last one, until the sweet lady claimed she would dash its brains out if he did not recognize the child as his own.'

This talk of the King reminded Frances of why she had come. How could she have forgotten for a moment, even in the face of Mall's new happiness?

'Mall, I need your counsel. The King has sent the Duke of Richmond to the Tower!'

'Has he indeed? On what charge?'

'Some cause to do with neglecting his duties in

Dorset for the Crown.'

'And is it true?'

'I know not, yet I doubt it. It followed on so hard from that other business.'

Mall looked at her narrowly. 'What other business?'

'The King came upon us at Master Lely's studio. The Duke had commissioned a picture in little, of me. I thought he ought not to have it, that it was not fitting, and we struggled for possession of it when the King came upon us.'

'And now the Duke finds himself in the Tower. Well, weep not. My brother Buckingham has been there twice at least, once under Cromwell for marrying the daughter of Fairfax; the next for unseemly quarrelling in parliament. He came out none the worse for it.' Mall sat on the edge of the bed. 'I see your difficulty, though. If the King has truly sent Charles Stuart to the Tower for fear that you favour him, then it will make His Majesty think doubly so if you plead for his release. And yet the King is a just man, not given to arbitrary action. Indeed, many believe he should be far harsher with his enemies. You must find a way to appeal to that sense of justice without fanning the flames of his jealousy.'

Frances left Mall and stepped out into the glorious spring sunshine, feeling anything but joyful. This was her fault and her doing. No one else's. She should have closed her mind against the Duke as soon as he remarried. She might criticize Lady Castlemaine, but as Barbara herself had pointed out, why was she so much better? The only answer would be for her to make a genuine sacrifice.

And now she would have to seek an audience with the King.

She sought him first by approaching a Gentleman of the Bedchamber who, knowing the King's preference for her, was happy to inform her he thought that His Majesty was with the Queen.

The Queen, however, since the day felt almost like summer, had gone with a number of her other ladies out onto the lead roof outside her chamber where there were benches and pots of flowers, and all were listening to delightful songs being performed by a company of Italians moored upon a barge on the river beneath.

'Her Majesty missed you,' whispered Jane.

'I am looking for the King and was told he would be here,' Frances whispered back.

'He is in the Privy Garden with the Chancellor,' Jane replied. 'He left not ten minutes since.'

Frances slipped away before the Queen could notice her and ran back through the Vane Room and down the King's back stairs into the garden.

The King stood, surrounded by his dogs, setting his time by the sundial there while he and his Chancellor discussed the Dutch war and the perfidy of the French.

The Chancellor sat on a bench, his gouty leg propped up in front of him. He looked round at Frances' approach. She had always liked the old man and prized his honesty, even admiring the fact that, amongst so many rogues and lickspittles, he had never learned to polish his counsel to make it palatable. 'And here is Mistress Stuart come to beg for the release of the Duke,' he announced in his usual blunt way. 'I have already told His Majesty that this imprisonment looks like spite, but no doubt I will be sent away with a flea in my ear. Here, you try, mistress—perhaps with your pretty face you will have more luck.' And then a thought struck him and he continued teasingly, 'Of course it is your pretty face that caused the problem in the first place . . .' He rose stiffly and hobbled off, saying that he hoped His Majesty would find time to come to Council since there was a war to prosecute.

The King calmly finished adjusting his watch. All was quiet and peace here in the Privy Garden, with only the sound of a songthrush hidden in a lilac bush, the buzz of the bees, and the gentle shushing of the wind in the trees as if they were singing a lullaby to some goddess' newborn babe. It was hard to believe that war and pestilence lurked outside the gates.

'Majesty, I . . .' she began.

'As my Lord Chancellor informs me, you have come to plead for the Duke of Richmond.'

Frances decided the less she said, the better. She simply nodded.

'The question is, why? He is beneath you in every way. He drinks. He is a handsome enough fellow, but so is Rochester, or Buckley, or indeed Buckingham, yet you do not sigh for them.' The King shook his head at the bitter mystery of love, yet Frances had no intention of explaining that the other Charles Stuart's teasing made her laugh, that she liked the solidity of his body and that there was something in his sleepy grey eyes that ignited a passion she had not felt before. 'I am a rational man, and yet for you I behave irrationally.'

Frances decided it was time to interrupt. 'And all know you to be fair also, Majesty. That is why this act seems unmerited to all who hear of it.'

She waited, hardly breathing, unsure if the Duke would be released or she would end up in the Tower with him.

The King sighed as if the decision he was coming to might be against his own best interest. 'You are right. This act was arbitrary and I am not proud of it. The Duke of Richmond will be released.' He paused. 'Perhaps his lady could ensure he fulfils his duties as Lord Lieutenant. The need will be greater as the war takes firmer hold.'

She bowed her head at the stark reminder that the Duke's conduct was not her business, but his wife's.

'Thank you, Majesty. I am sure the Duchess will be deeply grateful for his release.'

She made to leave, but he caught her wrist and pulled her harshly to him. 'I am still waiting, Frances. I am a patient man, but none has ever tried my patience as you do.'

She knew not what to answer and was grateful that his favourite bitch, Fymm, spied a squirrel and chased it madly across the garden, barking so loud that windows opened on the floor above and the King released her.

In her bedchamber she threw herself onto the bed, fighting tears. She had secured the Duke's release and yet had no right to feel any pleasure in it. That, by entitlement, belonged to his wife. And yet, if she knew that lady, it would be anger and recrimination that waited on his table, not a welcoming feast at his return. And who could blame the Duchess, if she knew the truth?

Frances caught the baleful look of the parrot upon her.

'What a piece of work is man?' the bird enquired in tones of mournful bafflement.

'As for you, Bird, with your sharp eyes and your clever comments, you remind me too much of he who gave you to me. It is time you had another home and I thought of him no more.'

She covered up the cage in an old chemise and, before the bird could protest, marched down the wainscoted hallway to the tiny chamber where Mary Lewis had been billeted.

'I have brought you good news—the Duke is to be released. And also a friend to share your quarters. He is good company and will liven up your life with his wit and wisdom.'

'I am glad about the Duke. He has always been kind to me.' Mary held up the cage. 'May I truly keep him?' A smile of sheer delight lit up her homely features. 'I have never been allowed a pet. My mother thinks all animals dirty creatures and just more mouths to feed.'

'Here are his nuts and grains. Feed him.'

As she handed over the food Frances felt a sudden pang at severing the connection.

'Farewell, Bird.'

The parrot surveyed her consideringly.

'Not farewell, Duchess. Until we meet again.' He made a bowing gesture with one wing, as if for all the world he were a Court gallant.

Mary laughed, enchanted. 'See, he calls you Duchess, comic creature, when you are but Mistress Stuart.'

'Indeed.' Frances felt a feather of chill brush over her skin. 'For a dumb beast he is full of surprises.'

She was about to seek out the Queen and

344

discover her duties for the day when she turned quickly to Mary. 'I am greatly relieved at the news of the Duke's release, and yet, Mary, I would not have you think I had any hand in it.'

Mary Lewis, with that quick wit that sparkled behind the plain exterior, nodded swiftly. 'Indeed, I would never have thought you did, and will certainly convey as much to Cobham.'

But when Frances had left her chamber Mary stroked the parrot's ruffled feathers. 'Yet what has she confided to you, Bird, on the subject of the Duke of Richmond?'

The bird surveyed her beadily, considering the question at length, before finally offering a view. 'Remember Charlie Stuart!'

'It is injudicious advice like that, I fancy, that has led to your change of address. Poor Frances. To be desired by a king yet love another woman's husband! Well, I will keep her secret, and yet I hope *I* never fall in love.'

The parrot, acclimatizing itself to its new owner with a wanton lack of fidelity, squawked in agreement.

* * *

The Queen, Frances discovered, was eager to leave London and take the waters once more in Tunbridge Wells.

'Will all her ladies be going with her?' she asked Jane La Garde.

'To begin with, only the Countess of Suffolk and some of the older ladies, for the rest she wishes to stay and adorn the Court. Catherine Boynton hides in her chamber lest she is chosen and must

345

leave her Dick.' Jane dropped her voice. 'To be honest, though the Queen says she wishes to take the waters, we believe it is fear of the pestilence that sends her scurrying, yet she dares not admit that to the King. His Majesty seems to feel no fear. Remember how he touched all and sundry for the King's Evil, even that old man who rubbed his sores in His Majesty's face?'

'Is the pestilence increasing then?' Frances suppressed a shudder of fear.

'Inside the palace all talk is of war; outside it is the distemper they dread more.'

Frances smiled bitterly at the thought of staying and adorning the Court. Yet she knew this was how she must play her part. She must be gay as a painted butterfly and convince the King that the Duke of Richmond was neither enemy nor rival— indeed, was nothing at all to her.

To this end she got out her most lavish gown, wrought from fourteen yards of finest grosgrain in the shade of bird's-eye yellow that brought out the freshness of her skin and complemented the sheen of her tumbling hair. She asked her tire-woman to fetch the pendants that the King had given her for her Valentine.

'You are as lovely as the first day of spring, mistress,' announced the tire-woman with a rare poetry.

'Thank you,' laughed Frances, enjoying the sight of the dazzling young woman who looked back at her from her looking-glass.

First she would sup and then join the company in Lady Castlemaine's apartments.

Barbara, with her natural instinct for show and ostentation, had installed the Italian singers from the barge in the gallery of her eating room, from where they serenaded the company beneath like angels on a cloud. Lit by countless candles, the scene did indeed seem heavenly—were it not for the outrageous cut of the ladies' dresses, baring almost their entire breasts, and the shouts of the drunken gallants as they won and lost at Basset, while Barbara continually refilled their glasses either to celebrate or to console.

A great pile of gold coins sat in the middle of a green baize table where the Comte de Grammont presided like a grand and balding emperor. He was second to none at relieving the rich of their money, and Barbara's guests seemed to win or lose with equal abandon. She thought for an instant of Walter and trusted that he was too small a prize to be of any real interest to de Grammont.

'Come and talk awhile, Mistress Stuart.' Frances turned from the gaming table to find the King, his hand outstretched to her so that she had little choice but to take it or humiliate him. She placed her hand in his and followed him to an alcove that contained a window seat looking down upon the river.

'Am I forgiven for my jealousy?' he enquired with an expression so modest and friendly that she had to reciprocate.

'Indeed.' She gave him her sweetest smile. 'There was no cause for it, Your Majesty.' She fingered the pearls in her ears. 'I have not thanked you for your generosity at Valentine's Day.'

'And yet I heard the rumour that you wanted not to accept them, save that your lady mother insisted upon it.'

Frances flushed a delicate pink. There was little

doubt who would have spread that rumour.

'I am sorry, sire. It is just that they were of such great value.'

'A great deal less than I have spent on other ladies.' He took her hand and kissed it. 'Worry not—it is what I like about you, even when I find it most frustrating. You cannot be bought. That is why it will be the greatest pleasure of my whole life when you come to me willingly.'

To her astonishment she was rescued by the least likely of champions.

'Your Majesty,' Chancellor Clarendon's voice doused the King's ardour like a bucket of water thrown over a dog in heat. 'A messenger has come from the Duke of York. We are called to the Council on some important matter of the war.'

Chapter 17

Frances smiled gratefully at Edward Hyde as the King took his leave.

She knew the Chancellor was a sworn enemy of Lady Castlemaine, and the reason her husband Roger Palmer had been made an earl in the Irish peerage was because the Chancellor had refused to seal the patent making him an English earl, or endorse any other preferment that allowed its profits to go to Barbara.

The Chancellor smiled back. His round face was lined with pain from his gout and he walked heavily on a stick, but some of his honest cheerfulness occasionally shone through. 'I had better leave before the King discovers the meeting is not as

348

pressing as he thinks.' To her amazement the Chancellor winked. 'If the Queen had died, there were those at Court who thought you would make a fitting successor, even though you brought no portion of Tangiers and Bombay. You would bring honesty, a quality that should be prized above gold, but in this ungodly place is valued as lightly as a whore's refusal. I did not wish to see that quality abused, even by the King.' He sighed the sigh of a man who had long waited for the attention of his monarch. 'Though if you succumbed, some might argue that the King would turn his mind to other matters, so mayhap I do myself a great disservice.'

'I thank you for it all the same.'

He smiled, not unkindly. 'You do not wish to offer yourself for the sake of the nation then?'

'I think the nation can survive without my assistance,' she replied.

Yet she saw that he was only half-joking.

'May I offer a word of advice? The King may countenance your refusal of his advances, but he will not accept a rival.'

'Yet my lady Castlemaine is not the most faithful of companions,' she replied, knowing he was right, but unable bear the pain of his logic.

'You are not my lady Castlemaine.'

However, the King had much to occupy him in the coming days. According to Tom Howard, the Dutch war was not progressing well.

'The King storms to and fro in his closet, railing against the Dutch that their damned blockades are destroying all our trade. Worse, he says they are spreading word through all Europe of the contagion that stalks London, so that our English goods begin to be shunned even in the places we may still reach.'

'We at least will be safe from it,' announced Catherine Boynton. 'Her Majesty insists that all her ladies must move to lodgings in Tunbridge Wells and thence, if the pestilence continues apace, to Hampton Court or Salisbury, where the King will later join us. London is beginning to empty for fear of the plague.'

Frances thought at once of her father and mother, and of course of her sister and brother. Perhaps the threat would at least mean that Walter was removed from the capital.

When she sent word to her mother at Somerset House, the reply did not resolve her worries. She and Sophia, as well as her father, were removing to Paris, along with all the Queen Mother's Court. Walter, her mother wrote, had persuaded them that he would be better staying in London under Frances' watchful eye.

'How can I watch over him when I will not be here myself?' Frances demanded of the empty air. She scribbled a reply that it would be far better for Walter to accompany them to Paris, and despatched a messenger to take it to Somerset House with all speed.

Despite the rumours of the growing threat, Mary Lewis received a commission that her mother insisted she must fulfil.

'*A riding habit? She wishes you to take delivery of her riding habit?*' Frances could hardly credit that the Duchess of Richmond would send her young daughter out into the plague-ridden streets of London on such a mission.

'It is a very *special* riding habit,' Mary answered, with a humorous look that belied her young years.

350

'Moulded in Paternoster Row from the finest cloth, in a shade of red, embellished with much silver lace.'

'I had better come with you,' Frances replied. 'I may not be a Londoner, yet at least I know the lie of the streets better than you do. I wonder if we should take a wherry or a hackney coach?'

'A wherry,' advised Cary Frazier, who was perfuming some gloves nearby. 'My father says at least there is only you and the wherrymen. You will not have to encounter the populace and risk catching their infection.'

Although Frances held no very good opinion of Dr Frazier's medical advice, this at least made sense, though there were many who believed the contagion came not from other people but from a miasma in the air, and carried flowers and nosegays against it.

The wherryman at Whitehall Stairs greeted them with a cry of 'Oars, east!' and afterwards harangued them with a list of doom and disaster that encompassed the spread of the contagion, the fecklessness of drunken gallants who used his services and skipped off without paying, the paltry reward of pubic-spirited wherrymen and the incompetent organization of the war against the Dutch, ending up with the rumour that the King had already fled London and left them all to die.

'As to that, wherryman,' Frances pointed out tartly, 'we have just left the Court but half an hour since, with the King in good cheer and very much in command.'

'Aye,' grumbled the man under his breath, 'for the moment. You mark my words, they'll all be off like rats from a sinking ship before the summer

351

heat arrives. No doubt about it, the playhouses will be closed soon on account of the pestilence, and that'll be an end to my trade. Here you are, mistresses, the tide was in our favour, Pudding Wharf and Stairs. That'll be fourpence and a free prayer thrown in!'

They disembarked and walked up the slippery wooden stairs, heading northwards towards Paternoster Row. The differences were marked even since her last sortie. Now all walked down the middle of the road, despite the mud and the mire from the channels full of ordure, fearful of going near the houses. The City of London was still free of the shutting-up that was happening in Covent Garden and St Giles, safe as yet behind its high walls. And yet there was fear in the air. All the traders now washed their money in vinegar as the wherryman had, some reaching out to take it on long poles so as to keep a distance from their customers. Many chewed tobacco, which was much vaunted as a plague preventative, or garlic, while others carried flowers or smelt strongly of vinegar, which they sprinkled on their clothes.

Paternoster Row, near to the great St Paul's, once famous for making beads and rosaries, was now home to dozens of mercers, silkmen and lacemen. Despite the fear of contagion, the dark, narrow street was filled with the coaches of the gentry almost blocking up the whole roadway, while their coachmen passed the time trading insults and wishing their masters and mistresses would complete their purchases and return, so they might retreat safely to their homes.

At the far end of the street they caught sight of the sign they were seeking, the coveted hand and

352

shears designating the shop to be that of a master tailor.

It was very much à la mode for ladies of the Court to have their riding garbs made not by dressmakers, but by men's tailors, and indeed these tightly tailored outfits were the envy of the world. Even French ladies, who despised all else about the country, came to England for their riding habits. The fashion was for men's fitted doublets, in red brocade, embellished with gold thread, worn over a waistcoat, tied at the neck with a waterfall of Brussels lace—the whole worn over long skirts that could be draped side-saddle and worn with tricorne hats or velvet caps adorned with ribbons or feathers. Some ladies even wore periwigs under their hats, so that their masculine silhouette outraged critics, who protested that from the waist up they could be taken for men.

The riding habit the new Duchess of Richmond had bespoken was a particularly vibrant shade of vermilion, so bright indeed that they almost had to shade their eyes when the tailor shook it out for their approval.

'She will certainly cut a dash in that,' Frances remarked.

'Or blind the huntsman and stun the hart into submission!' Mary added, and they both dissolved in laughter.

The tailor shook his head at this levity and arranged to pack the habit away in a large box, which they had difficulty in carrying. So much difficulty that, as they left the shop, they bumped into an old woman and all but knocked her to the floor. She seemed well enough dressed, yet she had a curious kind of scarf wrapped around her neck as if she had to wrap up against the cold, even though it was a fine day.

'We bid you sorry, mistress,' Frances put out a hand to help her up.

As she did so she noticed a curious reaction from the passers-by. They backed away from the old woman, as if nothing would make them come within six feet of her.

Finally a gentleman called to them, panic making his voice high and wild. 'Keep your distance, young mistresses, can you not see she has the contagion upon her?'

The old woman's scarf blew in the breeze and they saw for themselves the telltale swellings beneath her ears and in her neck and, without a word spoken, crossed themselves with the sign of God the Father, the Son and the Holy Spirit, and in unison murmured 'Amen'.

*　　　*　　　*

Three days later they were on the road for Tunbridge Wells. There had been muttering amongst the Queen's Portuguese servants, and especially among her many priests, when the Queen told them they were not to come, and a general sigh of relief from everyone else. The priests fanned the flames of Catherine's religious ardour, which meant long hours on their knees for her ladies, mumbling prayers and telling their rosaries, until they fervently wished the King had chosen a Protestant bride.

'She is a different lady when they are left behind,' whispered Cary Frazier.

Frances agreed. Given free rein, the Queen's natural gaiety and joyousness flourished and she was good company, sweet and generous, forever suggesting frolics and jaunts, yet never keeping her ladies up inconsiderately late at night.

Tunbridge Wells, Frances marvelled, might be but thirty miles from London, yet it was as if they were leaving hell, or Purgatory at least, and arriving in Paradise. Untouched by the chilly finger of the plague, the small town seemed festive, with its string of pretty painted houses. And all around them was the glory of an English spring.

Kent had always been the garden of England and this year spring had come early and was unusually hot. In every garden and orchard the apple trees frothed with blossom as if they had been draped in white lace. The birds, with no thought of war or pestilence, sang their clear and ancient songs.

And since most gentlemen had stayed in the capital, a sudden devil-may-care mood took hold of the Queen's ladies and they shucked off their silk slippers and ran races in the green grass near the springs, and played at leapfrog and Blind Man's Buff beneath the shady canopy of the chestnut trees. Jane La Garde revealed a talent for telling fortunes and sat with each lady's hand in her lap in turn, predicting the future that each of them wanted to hear.

To the Queen she foretold an heir to the throne; to Catherine Boynton a rich life at Court and that she would one day become 'My lady'; she predicted that Cary Frazier would become a respectable housewife, which much annoyed her. When she took Frances' hand in hers, a little cloud settled upon her forehead. 'You will indeed get what you desire, yet for a fleeting moment only, and you must take the moment in both hands and hold it fast.'

Frances stared at her, taken aback, then jumped up, glad that Jane was but playing a game and had no true knowledge of prediction.

And yet, one aspect of her foretelling seemed to be coming true. The Queen was happier than any of her ladies had yet seen her. She rested well, ate well, and a bloom seemed to come over her that rivalled that of the blossom on the trees.

Frances and Cary watched her one morning as she laid her white petticoats out on the bushes to dry. She had maids to do this, yet seemed to take great pleasure in performing the task herself. Unaware of their observation, Catherine stretched in the sun and stood, eyes closed, drinking in the bright rays, and all the while stroking the swell of her small stomach.

Cary Frazier gasped. 'Think you the Queen . . .' She hesitated.

'. . . is carrying a child?' Frances finished for her.

Frances wished strongly that this was the case. The King would be so happy, and so would his people. The fear of the succession finally allayed and England healed.

All her ladies noticed that when the musicians who had accompanied them from London began to play, the Queen sat by and watched, refusing all entreaties to join in the dancing.

Quietly and subtly they all watched and waited, holding their breaths. They did not have long to wonder.

As June beckoned, and the skies blazed the brightest blue that any could remember, and the weather was so warm that Cary stripped to her shift and swam, the Queen beamed and sang all day

356

long.

They picnicked one night on cold hare pie and gooseberry syllabub, washed down with cold wine, and told tales of love gained and lost, and what they most desired if anything could be granted them.

Later, when they were asleep, Frances woke to a strange and eerie sound. The cry was so harsh and high that she decided it must be that of a vixen fighting with another in the woods beyond. But as she listened she knew that it was no animal, but the despairing cry of a woman.

She threw on a robe and padded swiftly towards the Queen's lodging, to find that Cary Frazier had had the same thought.

The Queen sat on the edge of her bed, her hands covered in blood where she had tried to staunch the flow, the most desperate look in her eyes that Frances had ever seen.

She opened her bloodstained hands and there, in the cup of her palm, a tiny being lay—not boy nor maid, yet clearly a human soul, no more than three inches long.

They found a cloth and gently took the slip of humanity from Catherine's bloody hands.

At that the Queen seemed to wake from her nightmare. 'The babe must be baptized or it will never join the Lord God Almighty in Heaven.'

'Then we will baptize it here and now!' Frances dimly remembered that, in extreme cases of need, the sacrament of baptism could be performed by anyone, lay or priest.

'We need water.' Cary looked around the room, yet there was none there, water not being considered a safe drink. 'I will go to the spring and get some.' She ran through the orchard that separated them from the chief spring and scooped some water into a goblet.

Yet that seemed all she was capable of and, on her return, she sat on the bed next to the Queen and hid her face in her hands.

Frances took the goblet of water and poured it over the tiny dead child, repeating the words she had known from her childhood. 'I baptize thee in the name of the Father, the Son and the Holy Ghost.'

Catherine turned towards them, her eyes beseeching, desperation ringing through her voice. 'I wish none to know of this. Above all, not my husband the King. I cannot bear the pity, the looks and the whispers that would follow.'

Gently, Frances put down the babe and cleaned Catherine's hands.

'Yet what of your condition, Majesty?' She gestured to the blood on the bedclothes. 'You may need physic.'

'The King plans to go to Hampton Court. We will go there tomorrow. My duenna, the Countess Penalva, will assist me. She has great wisdom.'

Frances hardly dared ask the next question. 'What of the babe?'

Catherine sobbed, then with a huge effort of will she calmed herself. 'Bury it, with all my prayers and thanks. Erect a little cross above. And please, on your honour as my trusted women, tell no one.'

Frances nodded. 'I will send a tire-woman to sleep at your door and listen, should you desire aught in the night.'

'Thank you,' she smiled faintly at Frances' consideration, understanding that such a servant would ask fewer questions than one of her ladies.

Outside her apartments Cary Frazier clutched Frances' arm so that she almost dropped the forlorn bundle. 'It might have been a future King or Queen of England.'

Frances nodded. 'And now we bury it.'

They found a spade in a woodman's hut near the springs and dug a tiny grave, deep enough to protect it from discovery or the depredations of animals. 'I know not the words of the funeral rite,' faltered Frances, a tear sliding down her cheek. Yet she must say something, no matter if it were not the true words of the ritual. 'Eternal rest grant unto this babe, O Lord.'

They both bowed their heads in silent prayer.

The Queen's ladies were delighted at the news they were to move to Hampton Court, since country pleasures, delightful at first, were already beginning to pall. They missed the playhouse, the buzz of gossip and the convenience of the haberdashers and milliners in the New Exchange, as well as the presence of gentlemen's company.

Yet they tempered their pleasure when they saw that the Queen had lost her gaiety and was quiet and subdued. They exchanged enquiring looks, yet through some feminine intuition and protective loyalty none spoke of it, suspecting a wound that lay too deep. Instead the Countess of Suffolk became brisk as a busy hen and pecked them all into packing up their possessions, so that by the end of the day they were ready to leave.

On the very morn of their departure, Jane La Garde came and whispered in Frances' ear that Mary Lewis was ailing and had asked for her.

'Mary, sweeting,' she called into the chamber, since it was still in darkness, even though the hour was well advanced. 'Are you not packed up? The coaches are outside waiting for us.'

She sniffed the air, her nostrils assaulted by a strange and unfamiliar scent.

When there was still no reply she guessed Mary must be sleeping. Perhaps if they wrapped her in a blanket she could slumber her way through the dull journey and wake refreshed at Hampton Court.

Frances knelt down on the matting next to the narrow truckle bed where Mary slept and shook her gently. 'You must wake, Mary dear, or we two will be left behind.'

Mary was indeed asleep. Her wiry nut-brown hair fanned out on the pillow and the lacing of her chemise had come apart, revealing the skin beneath. The heavy drapes that shut out all the sunlight stirred in the noonday breeze and a shaft of light illuminated the bed as if it were onstage.

Frances gasped and recoiled.

Red blotches, the size of a christening cup, marked the tender skin of Mary's chest, and her breath, when Frances leaned towards her, smelt rank and rotten as a sewer.

With halting fingers Frances untied the laces and opened the girl's chemise still further.

Beneath Mary's armpit she felt a swelling, with a hard pus-filled centre, and almost cried out the dread words 'Lord Have Mercy Upon Us!'

Outside the lodgings she could hear the horses neigh and paw in their eagerness to depart, their bridles clanking, the other ladies chattering in the ordinariness of the summer's afternoon.

And yet here, in this small chamber, Frances pondered what to do in this terrible dilemma.

If she told the other ladies, fear would run

through the assembled gathering as if a ghost had risen from the grave. The nearness of the Queen to the contagion would start a panic.

Should she send a message to Mary's mother to journey here at all speed? Frances hesitated, torn, for would the Duchess drop her concerns and come? No.

There was only one solution. The nature of Mary's distemper must be hidden. The Queen's leaving was a blessing, since it would remove her from harm's way and make the thing much the easier, without the presence of her ladies clucking around like hens when the fox approaches.

Frances paused: was her planned action the height and depth of wickedness? She had already suppressed the news of the Queen's miscarriage, and now she contemplated hiding a victim of the plague. At what risk to others and herself?

She thought of the houses in St Giles and of the anguished cries of the people shut up and condemned to death. And shutting-up was indeed the fate that would await bright, witty Mary, if Frances let it be known what distemper ailed her.

Yet, if she were to suppress the truth, one hard consequence followed. She would have to stay and nurse the girl herself.

Frances turned and caught sight of a looking glass on the wall. A lovely young woman stared back, with fair tawny hair and clear grey eyes, and skin that held the fresh, unsullied bloom of youth. A young woman who danced more gracefully than all the other ladies, whose seat upon a horse outdid all rivals', who loved to build houses of cards, to go hawking and feel the wind on her face; who longed to live in the mellow manor house she had drawn countless times before she ever saw it. She closed her eyes, trying not to think of the stories she had heard of victims covered in sores, eyes bulging, escaping from their houses and running out into the street from the unbearable pain of their swellings.

She could not have the life she desired, yet at least she might do some good.

She closed and locked the door, summoned a groom and gave him a message for Jane La Garde, the kindest and least suspicious of all the ladies. Mary was indeed ailing, she said, and Frances would stay with her a while until she rallied, then follow on as soon as the sickness abated. Frances had but one request. That her old nurse be summoned from Somerset House to come and aid her.

As she watched and waved at the departing line of coaches, Frances asked herself what she must do now. Apart from pray.

She was on her knees when the groom knocked on the door. 'I thought you might like to know of the Duke of York's great victory at Lowestoft, mistress. He has shown the Dutchman what we are made of, and sent him home with his tail between his legs. You can hear the guns pounding, standing on the streets of London. There are bonfires everywhere celebrating the victory!'

Frances thanked him and closed the door. She had never felt less like celebrating in all her life.

When Nurse arrived next day, a little older and stiffer, yet delighted to be needed, Frances told her the terrible truth before she even entered the sickroom.

'If you prefer, you may stay in lodgings in the town and return to London tomorrow on the coach.

None would think the worse of you for it.'

Nurse sniffed loudly at such a lily-livered proposal. 'I have had my threescore years and ten. What use is a crone such as I to the world? It is you I would want to leave this place. I will tend the maid.'

Frances hugged her, moved almost to tears.

'I will indeed leave. Yet only for a short time. I wish to visit your friend, the Widow Wyatt.'

'It is the Almighty you have need of, not an apothecary.'

Frances held out her hands, comforted by Nurse's familiar presence. 'I will leave the Almighty to you, and choose the apothecary. Mayhap they could work together.'

'Now, child, no blaspheming. All things are possible with God. Yet if you are going to London, mayhap you could find word of your silly brother Walter.'

'Walter? Surely he is gone to Paris with the rest?'

Nurse shook her head, anxiety clouding her eyes. 'He would not go. Ran off. Said he would be better off with you.'

*   *   *

The thought of Walter alone in the plague-ridden city made her blood stop in her veins. She must do what she could to find him.

For greater safety from being questioned or accosted, she decided to don her man's riding habit and vizard as she had done before.

She had been on the road four hours without mishap when she reached the turnpike for Woolwich to take the ferry across the river to

London, and here she stopped, amazed. The whole river as far as the eye could see was packed with small craft on which were loaded panniers and bags, furniture and people. It seemed that half London's citizens were deserting her for the safety of the country. And she the only one out of a thousand who was travelling northwards, back into the city.

In Woolwich she settled her horse at the livery stables and took the common tilt-boat since she would be less noticed, and would not have to put up with the banter of the wherryman. In this she was not in luck, for the master of the tilt-boat seemed to have been brought up in the same school.

'Are you sure you want to go in to London now, young sir?' he queried, studying her with interest. 'Does your mother know you make the journey into the city? Is it whores or an alehouse you seek, for you'll find those in Dartford or Sevenoaks aplenty, and safer too.'

Frances pulled down her vizard and handed over her money, which went straight into the vinegar jar.

As they crossed the river they passed the King's gilded yachts lying against the wall of the dockyard. The tilt-master followed her glance. 'Aye. And I'd bet he'd like to be aboard one of those and off away from all the troubles that beset him. The victory at Lowestoft was short-lived enough. It has been going from bad to worse for our navy. Those damned butterboxes. They should stay in Amsterdam to count their gold and poke their fat, ugly women! Some say it was them who sent the contagion over to ruin us.'

They passed Greenwich and on towards Limehouse, where London truly began with its sight of the Tower and London Bridge. Frances stared intently as they passed Traitor's Gate, wondering how the Duke must have felt when the Serjeant-at-Arms had him conveyed there.

The thought came to her that if she could not find Walter, she might ask the Duke for his assistance in seeking him out.

By London Bridge the weather changed from hot to sweltering. She left the boat at Three Cranes Wharf and began her walk up towards St Mary le Bow. Here, too, the streets were jammed with coaches and carts vying with each other to leave the city.

Indeed, in the last weeks the whole of London seemed entirely changed. Then only a few houses were shut up, but now Frances saw that whole streets were chained and silent, either because their owners had left or because they had been shut up against the plague, with that fatal red cross. Now only the watchmen remained to keep looters out of the empty houses and stop the occupants escaping from those that had been boarded up.

Even the very air was silent. The bells that had tolled continually for the many funerals had ceased, there being too many dead to give funerals for. All the hawkers and traders who called their wares and were so much a part of London were quieted by the pestilence or by fear of it.

She stopped outside the church of St Mary le Bow to read the sign pinned to its door. Frances shuddered, realizing it was a Bill of Mortality hideously illustrated by skulls, skeletons and grave-digging paraphernalia, listing the deaths that week due to London's dreadful visitation.

The few people she saw on the street were

queuing for passes from the Lord Mayor to leave the city, or were searchers with their white sticks, rooting out the dead for one groat per corpse; and, more terrifying still, the self-styled plague doctors, clad in leather coats with their huge hats and beak-masks filled with spices, intended as a protection, but which rendered them as frightening as the contagion itself.

From an upper window Frances could see a child leaning out and begging to be released from the house of death in which it was entombed.

On the corner of Cheapside she stopped to read a mass of posters offering 'the only true plague water', 'infallible preventive pills' and a claim that made her smile bitterly: 'the royal antidote against all kinds of infection'. How the King, with his rational and scientific mind, would have raged at that, had he but known of it.

As she turned down the street to the widow's shop she saw a great crowd gathered, staring as one upwards into the sky.

A young woman was in the centre. 'Look,' she pointed above her, 'do you not see? It is an avenging angel with a fiery sword in its hand, come to visit the plague upon us for our wickedness!'

They all nodded and mumbled their agreement. One man dared dispute the vision, and the others turned on him, raining him with blows.

It was then that the woman's gaze fixed on Frances.

'Wait a moment,' she accused. 'You are no man!' She tore off Frances' hat and vizard. 'Are you not the King's doxy?'

'She is, too,' a scrawny, bandy-legged youth challenged, pushing his face right up to hers. 'I worked as scullion in the palace kitchen, and would lay an angel I saw you there.'

'Shameless whore,' accused another.

''Tis because of you, and the rest of the King's concubines, this contagion has come to pass!' screamed an old woman.

Frances felt them closing in on her, when Widow Wyatt, hearing the disturbance, came out onto the street and dragged her inside.

The dark herb-filled shop felt like a sanctuary, and Frances realized she was shaking.

'It is a fearsome time.' The kind woman shook her head. 'Even those who are free of the distemper behave as if they have lost their senses. Yesternight they banged on my door demanding free cures, as if I had any such. The quacksalvers and the charlatans make such preposterous claims that they are angry at me, since I do not. Still,' she winked at Frances, 'the dead cart has not come for me yet, and for that I must be grateful.'

'I saw a plague doctor on the street. Do they do aught to help the afflicted?'

'Hah!' the widow spat on the ground. 'I would as soon turn to a plague doctor as to an executioner! Though the latter would be cheaper. It's my opinion they but blow on the flames. Once they call in the plague doctor, you can be sure the victim will never wake until the last trumpet sounds.'

Frances slumped down, feeling suddenly forlorn and desperate. Had she risked all this for Mary, to no avail? And what of Walter, alone and without friends in this plague-riddled place? 'Is there nothing that can be done then? I have come on behalf of a young girl to try and bring some hope to her at least.'

Widow Wyatt looked her in the eye.

'A plague doctor would bleed her or apply leeches, and would certainly sell you Venice Treacle, thereby hastening your young friend towards her grave.' She handed Frances a cup of spiced ale to help revive her spirits. 'One physician I trust above others believes in giving spirit of hartshorn, then sweating out the disease. I will gladly make you some, yet from my own observation there is but one cure.'

'And what is that?

'The buboes of those that survive the contagion always come to a head. If your friend's do not do so, you will have to try and lance them. It will not be easy or pleasant. And afterwards apply a poultice of Unguentum Terebinthinae. 'Tis an ointment of oil of turpentine. I will mix you some now. And keep her warm while the fever rages.' She stroked Frances' face gently. 'And pray also.'

The widow busied herself with mixing the remedy. When she opened a large phial, a strange rancid odour filled the shop with its powerful fumes and, despite herself, Frances shuddered.

'And you have confidence in this remedy?'

The widow laughed, a strange sound in that melancholy time. 'You can do as the quack doctors do, if you prefer. Shave the nether part of a live chicken and strap it next to the bubo until the bird dies. Keep doing this until at last a chicken lives and you know you have drawn out the poison.' She patted Frances on the shoulder. 'Or you could use my turpentine poultice. I know which treatment I would prefer, were I the victim.'

Frances nodded, feeling that if indeed it was herself who ailed, she would trust the widow over a clutch of plague doctors.

'I will do it.'

This time, when she was back on the street, Frances kept her vizard firmly down and strode as fast as she could towards the river, passing the stinking carcasses of cats and dogs, slain in their thousands for fear they spread the disease, and a crazy-haired old man urging London's afflicted citizens that it was the hour to repent, for the Kingdom of Heaven was near at hand.

She had just reached Thames Street, but a few yards from Three Cranes Wharf, when she stopped, rooted to the spot by the saddest sight she had seen so far. In a tavern doorway a young woman lay dead of the pestilence, and at her breast sucked a living child.

She thought for one mad moment of scooping up the babe, yet knew it too might carry the distemper and, instead of helping Mary, she might bring back even greater destruction. She made the sign of the cross on its tiny forehead and ran along the wharf, crowded with jostling people carrying their great bundles of possessions, and onto a wherry bound for Woolwich, and thence to Tunbridge Wells and to Mary.

Chapter 18

Nurse had done a good job with their lodging. So thick were the fumes of rosin and incense that they smothered any smell of sickness.

Mary's fever was still high and she tossed and

turned, mumbling in her delirium.

'None have coming knocking on the door suspecting her affliction?' Frances asked anxiously.

Nurse shook her head. 'What said the wise woman?'

'She gave me medicines. Yet I have a task ahead that will require all my courage. She says Mary will only survive if I lance the boils under her arm and in her neck.'

Even though she was stoical by nature, Nurse flinched.

'Will you hold her for me? It is the only way. Let us do it now while she is sleeping.'

Frances had been given two implements like sharpened knitting needles by Widow Wyatt, and these she now drew out and placed on the bed. Next she opened the oil of turpentine and that strange, rancid odour filled the air, making her cough and splutter.

While Nurse held Mary's shoulders, Frances took out the leather gloves and the mask against infection that the widow had given her and went swiftly to work. There were three buboes, two in the neck and one beneath the arm. The neck was easily dealt with, but the protuberance under Mary's arm was hard and crusted. Mary screamed as Frances tried again and again to lance it.

At last it gave and the foul-smelling poison gushed out.

As soon as it was spent, Frances quickly applied the poultice and tied it on with strips of torn petticoat.

'Let us move her to the chair one moment while I gather up the bedding and burn it. All we can do now is hope and pray.'

370

Frances bundled up the soiled sheets, still wearing her stout gloves, and took all out into the small green patch behind their lodgings. The oil of turpentine that had fallen onto the linen made it burn with a satisfying ease, and soon all was ashes.

By the time she returned, Nurse had lifted the slight body back onto the bed.

Like a relentless undertow dragging at her feet, dog-tiredness swept over Frances until she knew she must lie down.

'I will watch her,' Nurse reassured her. 'Time now to sleep and hope. You have done a great deal already.'

'Desperate diseases must have desperate remedies. There is that about Mary which touches my heart. Besides,' she took the old woman's hand in hers, 'we had not so soft a life in France, you and I, that we cannot face a little risk and hardship.'

Nurse stroked her face, as if suddenly Frances were a child again. 'You are not like those other ladies, and never will be.'

Frances smiled tiredly. 'I sometimes wonder if it were better for my own good if I were.'

The old woman sighed. 'Keep your faith, child. You will find contentment at the last.'

But this piece of advice was lost on Frances. She had laid herself down upon the servant's pallet next to the bed and was already asleep.

The groom who had told them of Lowestoft returned and bent Nurse's ear with news that for four days London had held its breath, listening to a great gun battle in the distance, until the news of another great victory was claimed. But it did not stop the flow of the rich, he said, who now in ever-increasing numbers left the city to the poor and the plague.

*　　　*　　　*

By the end of that sweltering month it seemed that the whole of Whitehall had moved to Hampton Court, followed by a mile-long train of coaches and carts loaded with their belongings, while the King travelled by royal barge by way of a visit to his ships in Greenwich.

Forty miles away Mary's life dangled on a thread between life and death. On the third day when she had still not recovered, Frances began to give up hope.

A messenger arrived from the Queen requiring Frances to come and take up her duties at Hampton Court.

'Yet how can I leave Mary?' Frances demanded.

They turned to consider the small figure laid upon the vast bed.

'Look, look!' Nurse gasped. 'She wakes!'

Gingerly, as if after a long and dreamless sleep, Mary opened her eyes and sat up.

'Am I yet alive or are you two angels of the Lord?' she asked faintly.

Frances ran to her bedside. 'The Lord does not suffer such assorted angels as we two! You are indeed alive, sweet girl, and praise Almighty God for it.'

'How long have I been ill,' Mary asked wearily, 'and with what manner of distemper?'

Frances and Nurse exchanged a swift glance, knowing it were better that she knew not the terrible truth.

'You have had the spotted fever, just as the

Queen did when she was in such grave danger, but the worst is past now. You are weakened and have lost much weight. You must sit and rest, and fatten yourself like a gourd ripening in the sun. It is time you went home to Cobham and sampled the delights of country life.'

'Delights! My mother is so mean she will have me on half-rations and sack some poor servant, since she can use me to do the work in their stead.'

'Not with Nurse there, she will not. I will ask Nurse to accompany you for your convalescence. She is more than a match for your mother, believe me.'

And so it was that Mary Lewis went unwillingly home to remain there under Nurse's protective wing until she was fully healed, having exacted promises—somewhat unwillingly given, for reasons Frances would not admit to—that Frances would come to Cobham as soon as the Queen could spare her.

She also sent a letter for Mary to deliver, asking the Duke, should he go to London, to make enquiries after her errant brother Walter.

Though Frances thought her secret hidden well, Nurse knew exactly why she was so reluctant to visit Mary at Cobham Hall.

'Fear not, child,' she whispered as she and Mary took their leave. 'Each man—or woman—is the architect of their own destiny. You have resisted the King because you wish for another life. And one day you will have it, as God is my witness.'

Frances smiled at the old woman. 'Then I wish God would hasten to provide. The King, when he is determined, is a hard force to resist.'

Her words, as it turned out, were prophetic. His

Majesty, having missed her so long, redoubled his attempts to win her.

Despite war and plague, the Court was as gay as ever at Hampton Court. Parliament might have been prorogued until September for fear of the pestilence, but at Hampton Court with its charming walkways, parterres and fountains, green lawns amongst the profusion of June roses, masquerades were still enacted, music played and picnics planned.

The sudden death of one of the King's guards of the plague reminded the gayest amongst them that London was but a stone's throw away, so they moved—bed, coach and carved chair—to Salisbury, where Frances found that she among all the Queen's ladies was billeted in the royal lodgings.

'At least Mr Chiffinch is not here to tip the King the wink as soon as you are abed,' whispered Cary Frazier.

But Salisbury did not meet with the taste of either the King or the Queen. It was subject to great winds and streams of water flooded across the main street, trapping them inside and making the King restless and melancholic.

Frances tried to divert him with the strange dream she had had the night before, when she had found herself in bed with all three of the French ambassadors who had followed the Court to Salisbury. The King found the tale so hilarious that he summoned the ambassadors to hear it from her own lips.

'Fear not,' Frances informed the astonished gentlemen, who were not sure whether they should be scandalized or amused, 'I am sure it was but a symbol of the close relationship between our countries!'

But she did cause a somewhat deeper scandal the next day on the Bowling Green. The Queen was very fond of playing bowls or hunting every day after dinner, and Frances often accompanied her. On this sweltering day of July the backbiting Comte de Grammont came to watch them.

Frances, suspecting him of leading her brother astray, had little love for the man. The feeling was more than reciprocated.

'How pleasant,' he commented, when the Queen was out of earshot, a look of calculated spite lighting up his powdered features, 'to be a young lady desired by the King, who can amuse herself with playing bowls while the common people die of pestilence a hundred miles away!'

The Count, she knew, cared not a pinch of snuff for the common people or whether they lived or died. Thinking of Mary and her brush with death, she smiled and carelessly dropped the bowling ball on his silken toes so that he howled and hopped, causing so great a commotion that all gathered round and heard Frances' reply.

'Indeed, Count,' she flashed, suddenly beside herself, 'and what do you know of the pestilence? Know you that that it causes the breath to stink, that the buboes drive sufferers so mad with the pain that they run into the street, in spite of the watchman, and jump into the river?'

De Grammont shook his head, forced into a rare silence.

'Then talk not to me of running away from the pestilence, for it is a nearer friend to me than you think.' She turned on her heel and left him, while the other courtiers wondered in low voices how

Mistress Stuart knew so much of the contagion.

De Grammont, for his part, hopped furiously away, calculating the while how he might get his revenge on this upstart girl with the dangerously outspoken ways that she hid under her innocent air. It was then that he remembered her brother. It was time to renew his attentions.

Word of her encounter must have reached the King, for he sought her out throughout the palace, his dogs snapping at his heels, finding her at last in the Queen's Bedchamber, where she was arranging a great bunch of pink roses.

'Well, Mistress Stuart,' he teased, 'you have the Court all abuzz, laughing at de Grammont. Not a useful enemy to make, as he has a poisoned wit about him.'

'Let him say what he will,' Frances went on calmly dealing with the roses.

'He says you boast of that which you cannot possibly know.'

Frances shrugged.

'Yet how did you come by so intimate a knowledge of the distemper?'

'I nursed a young friend. With God's will, she survived.'

A look of horror came upon the King. 'Of the plague? Belle! You might have caught the contagion and perished.'

'Aye. Yet the person I nursed was young, and dear to me, and her own mother neglected her. Without help she would not have survived. Besides . . .' She stood up and, in her red heels, stood almost eye to eye with His Majesty, knowing it must be a rare experience for one who was two yards high. 'I have no husband, or babes, and am

376

not like to, since none dares court me.'

'Are you blaming me for that?'

'Whom else should I blame? Who would dare to anger the King by making an honest offer to the woman he pursues?' she demanded angrily.

'I love you, Frances Stuart, to my own distraction and beyond.'

Before she knew it, she found herself pushed backwards onto the Queen's great bed.

Frances felt his hot breath upon her neck and his fingers tearing at her lacing.

'Well, this is a pretty sight indeed,' a harsh voice mocked behind them. They turned to find Barbara, whose advancing pregnancy served only to whip up her anger. 'One moment Mistress Stuart is an angel of the Lord laying her healing hands upon the sick, and the next she is tasting the delights of temptation and, from where I stand, putting up little resistance.'

'Impudent jade!' the King flashed back at her, his eyes glittering with cold anger. 'If you stumbled to the floor and Goodness helped you up, you would steal its purse and accuse it of Lechery. Begone, woman, and leave us alone.'

'I will not!' Barbara stood her ground. 'It is time you saw that Mistress Innocence here would betray you in the blink of an eye if a gentleman of substance offered for her. She accepts your embraces, yet they disgust her. How is it, Majesty, that you are the only one who does not see it?'

Frances could see the hurt in his eyes and wished to shout that he did not disgust her—indeed, she liked him a great deal, yet could never love him as he wished. Better to let him think Barbara correct in her assumptions.

Frances thought for one moment that the King might strike Lady Castlemaine.

Yet before he could do so, Barbara swept her cloak back to reveal the great belly she had been trying to disguise beneath swathes of blue satin. He drew back his hand. He was not the man to hit a woman, above all when she carried a child, whether it was his or not. 'Leave us,' he shouted. 'Insolent woman! Go!'

By now the commotion had brought the Queen and her women running in.

'Come, Mistress Stuart,' the Queen took her hand, 'let us go hawking before the sun goes down and it is time to dine.' And as they walked down the great staircase, leaving the King angry and frustrated, the Queen whispered to Frances. 'Do you know what the French ambassadors are saying? That Mistress Stuart is the rising sun, and that my lady Castlemaine must watch her step or she will lose the best rose in her hat. They mean the King, of course.' She looked at Frances, her dark eyes honest and without guile. 'I have reason to trust you, Mistress Stuart, and to thank you also. If my husband had to choose between you and my lady Castlemaine, I would ten times rather it were you.'

'Yet, Majesty, I do not wish to make such a choice.'

The Queen stroked Frances' face with her child's hand, as if they both knew that women, even if they were queens, did not truly control their own destinies. 'I know. And I hope you do not have to. I will always help you if I can, remember that.'

Frances nodded. It was pathetic how little power this kind queen had in her own Court. All authority and patronage radiated from her husband the

378

King. Had she been a different person—more like Barbara, in fact—devious and manipulative, eager to build castles of influence, things might have been different. As it was, she lived on scraps dropped from the kingly table, and Barbara begrudged her even those.

Anger flashed through Frances at the unfairness of it and she resolved that, if her own chance did come, she would leave this place and build a life where she ruled her own kingdom, however narrow its sphere of influence.

For the moment they abandoned stormy Salisbury and moved to Oxford, where the Court took over the colleges, as it had done in the time of the civil war.

*   *   *

Charles Stuart, Duke of Richmond, read again the letter that Mary had given him from Frances. When he had finished he held it against his lips, staring out over the parkland that surrounded Cobham Hall. Already the leaves were falling from the trees, and soon the landscape would be as bare and bleak as his own soul. Usually he loved to see the bones of nature emerging, the soft mole-velvet of the ploughed fields, waiting to be seeded for next year's crop. Yet this time he could not avoid the echoing deadness within. He had loved his first wife and mourned her deeply when she and their child died. But this marriage had been the great error of his life.

And yet, what had Frances so aptly told him? That he had made his bed and must lie in it. And that meant making the best of it and forgetting

Frances. Now she asked him to get involved by looking for her brother.

He shrugged. It was possible she asked him for this favour out of simple friendship. And in friendship he must respond, putting from his mind all thoughts of what might have been.

And it was in this spirit that he called for his coach and turned his six horses towards London.

To his amazement, the Duke found a London that was fast restoring itself. Yet there seemed madness in the air, as if Londoners had decided all risk was over and they might allow the few remaining victims of the plague to walk freely amongst them, even shake their hands or embrace them.

The merchants who had shut themselves up on their own ships moored in the river were bringing their families back and opening up their houses in the city.

The alehouses and tippling houses were suddenly full to the brim with laughing men, women and children.

'Come on, me lord,' a scoundrelly-looking man addressed the Duke as he glanced round the Leg of Mutton in King Street in the hope of seeing Walter. 'Let us drink to our deliverance.'

The Duke grinned and threw in three guineas. 'Let the next be at my expense!'

'And your very good health too, me lord.'

His next port of call was Lincoln's Inn. Yet the Inn was almost entirely closed up, lawyers proving more cautious than the rest of the populace, and less eager to return and minister to the needs of their clients. The gatehouse-keeper's wife did helpfully suggest, however, that she thought young

380

Mr Stuart was staying in the parish of Camberwell, courtesy of a fellow-student whose father was the vicar there.

A brief ride across the river took him to St Giles' Church, where a fair-haired young lady opened the vicarage door and informed him that her brother Ezekiel and his friend Mr Stuart were out hawking, and that he had indeed been staying with the family for some months.

Charles Stuart thanked her gratefully, remarking that he was surprised they had stayed so near to the city in these terrible times.

'My father said it was our duty,' replied the girl. 'He was shocked that so many men of God fled at the first sign of danger, yet that was when their flock needed them most.' She surveyed their guest and decided he was kind and sympathetic. 'It was terrible, sir. There was no one to visit the dying or say prayers over the dead. Father was the only minister left in three parishes.'

'He must be a brave man indeed.'

'He said God would keep him safe, even in the midst of pestilence.'

The Duke found himself liking and admiring the sound of the vicar of St Giles.

'And the young men—your brother and his friend—how do they amuse themselves?'

'Hawking, tennis, riding if they can borrow the horses, playing cards . . . though my father has greatly discouraged that. He even banned the two fine gentlemen they play with.'

The Duke found himself greatly interested. 'These two fine gentlemen, is one of them elegant and charming, dresses in black with a fair periwig?'

The girl nodded, as serious as an owl. 'He ever

tries to charm my father, but I do not think my father truly likes him.'

The vicar was clearly a man of sense, immune to the louche attractions of Lord Rochester. 'What is your name, by the way?'

'Hannah, sir.'

'Well, Hannah, if that gentleman makes an arrangement to meet Walter and your brother, could you send a message to the Duke of Richmond at the Palace of Whitehall, hard by the Bowling Green?' He handed the girl a bag of coins. 'On behalf of Walter's sister, I know she would wish to contribute to his keep. Send the message with a chair-man or hackney coach, if you do not have a servant to spare.' He imagined there was not much extra for luxuries in this generous household.

'Shall I tell Walter you came to look for him?'

'Just that a messenger called from his sister Frances. She would very much like to hear from him. And remember about the gentleman.'

She nodded gravely.

'Goodbye, Hannah.'

'Goodbye, sir.' She shut the door. The Duke imagined her returning to read Latin poetry or translate some Catullus. The vicar, he rather thought, was the kind to educate his daughters as well as his sons.

At least Walter was safe. That, at least, would be a huge comfort to his sister. He would write and tell her at once.

* * *

'The wretch!' Frances gasped when she received his message. 'The selfish, horrible little wretch! How

could he make us suffer all these months that he
might be dead of the plague in some attic and none
of us know it?'

She realized her face was wet with tears, and
acknowledged for the first time how relieved she
was at this news. And how grateful to the sender.

'Have you heard?' Mall whispered to her next
morning. 'We may be returning to Whitehall at last!
The Bills of Mortality are declining and the King
has received word from the Duke of Albemarle,
who has stayed in London throughout to keep
order, that the pestilence is all but over. Tom says
all those brave clergymen, doctors and apothecaries
who ran off and left the sick are creeping back.'

Frances thought of Widow Wyatt and wondered
if she had remained in London or had also
abandoned the city to its fate.

Now that he had heard from the Duke of
Albemarle, the King was all eagerness to return.

'Not yet!' the Queen begged him. 'Let us be truly
sure the city is safe before we return there.'

Her ladies suspected the Queen had another
reason to wish to stay safely in Oxford: that she was
pregnant once more.

When the child miscarried again, her grief was
pathetic to witness.

His Majesty, not knowing of his wife's previous
loss, told her he was simply glad she could conceive
at all, and treated her with great tenderness.

Mall and Tom were amongst the first to go back,
and the King appreciated the gesture. Yet it was a
sad and changed place that awaited them. There
were plague pits in many corners of the city and
some houses remained closed up, but the bells were
beginning to ring and the hawkers returning to the

streets.

Mall, descending from her coach, put a hand on Tom's shoulder. 'Listen! Have you ever heard a sweeter sound than that?'

'Dumplings, ho!' . . . 'Buy my dish of great eels!' . . . 'Lily-white vinegar!' . . . 'Newborn eggs, eight a groat!' The cries, so long silenced, had begun to echo through the rapidly filling streets.

'Now we will go back to our house and see who has thieved and taken advantage and who has been honest and loyal to us.' Despite all, Mall was in a great good humour. London was finally getting out of bed to greet a new day.

Frances longed to return also, but had to stay with the Queen. Her heart went out to that honourable lady, with her new loss, especially since Lady Castlemaine was so obviously with child.

But soon the Queen's desire to be near her husband overcame her loss and fear and by March she too planned a return to Whitehall. At long last Frances could sense optimism in the air. Spring was taking hold, the plague had gone and the great beating heart of London had started up again.

And so, with mounting excitement, they packed up their great train of coaches and started their journey back to the capital. A few small knots of Londoners watched and waved, please to see their Queen return again, while one or two spat on the ground at the perfidy of the great, who had abandoned them to their fate that they might save their noble skins.

The first night back in the palace Frances flung open her window and listened to the bellman calling out below, 'Maids in your smocks, look well to your lock, your fire and your light, and God give

384

you goodnight, at one o'clock!'

While Frances leaned out of her window and breathed in the familiar sooty London smell, the Duke of Richmond was opening a message he had just received from Hannah.

My Lord Rochester and the Comte de Grammont had reappeared in the life of young Walter Stuart.

Tomorrow night, Hannah diligently wrote, they had promised him some great and alluring excitement. Her brother Ezekiel had counselled him against accompanying them, but Rochester had written a witty poem of invitation, and Walter, having spent some quiet months with the kind and generous family of the vicar of St Giles' Camberwell, was ready for an adventure.

'For what truly can befall me?' he grinned at Ezekiel. 'I have no money to lose at cards. I can expect no inheritance, so none will lend me money against my future fortune. I may drink too much sack or canary wine, but that is worth the price to exchange some witty words with the famous Lord Rochester.'

Ezekiel tried to remind Walter that he had, quite rightly, formed a distrust of that corrupt, yet charismatic gentleman, but to no avail.

He would go.

So it was that the Duke made an excuse to his wife and, donning a cloak and borrowed periwig to hide his distinctive hair, and taking only one servant with him, rode the next night towards Camberwell. Here he waited in an alley not fifty yards from the vicarage until the two noble gentlemen arrived.

As the night wore on and a cold, dank mist descended, the Duke began to wonder if

Hannah had been mistaken. The lights had been extinguished all through the house, save for the one candle that the law demanded be left in a downstairs window to light passers-by on their way. Perhaps Walter had joined the household for prayers and gone to bed.

Just as he was stretching and patting his patient horse, the Duke heard the sound of muffled laughter. A hackney coach had stopped at the end of the road containing five or six revellers, who whispered and clinked their bottles. A downstairs curtain moved, near the lone candle, and moments later Walter Stuart emerged.

Two things struck the waiting Duke. How touchingly young Walter looked, and how very like his sister. Both shared that graceful upright carriage, and a striking freshness that came not from innocence, which could be a cloying quality, but from a likeable directness, which had time neither for pretension nor for calculation.

Walter climbed into the coach.

The Duke hesitated a moment. What if Rochester's motives were innocent and he took the boy merely to some drinking den full of poets and actors, where no true harm would come to him?

Yet Rochester's motives, in his experience, were rarely honest or straightforward.

The Duke followed at a discreet distance as the hired coach progressed to Camberwell Green and thence to the Elephant and Castle, and afterwards by way of Newington Causeway to Borough High Street. Here he breathed a sigh of relief. They were heading for the Bankside.

Since the hour was so late, the bull- and bear-baiting would have ceased and all the playhouses would be closed. The stewhouses alone would be open for business, the whores and harlots yawning as they prepared for another long night.

The Duke dismounted and tied his horse to a post by the Bankside Stairs. He had an inkling where Rochester and de Grammont would be taking their young protégé—a notorious whorehouse known as the Cardinal's Hat in Cardinal Cap Alley. He had to admit, he and his roistering friends had frequented the place in his youth, either to drink late into the night or to have a woman.

So what was their intention in bringing Walter here? An avuncular gesture? The gift of a whore, to initiate him into the pleasures of the night?

Yet the only gift Rochester would enjoy giving, the Duke suspected, was one that would give Walter the pox. The whole Court knew of the mercury baths administered to the Earl by one Madam Fourcard in Leather Lane, to alleviate his syphilis. The Duke could see how such a gesture might appeal to his warped sense of humour. Or his desire for revenge.

Already the Duke could hear the approaching group of revellers and slipped into the back entrance of the Cardinal's Hat. A motley group of gentlemen sat around in various stages of drunkenness and undress, many oblivious to where they were or whose breast they pawed.

'Greetings to you, my lord,' a fruity voice welcomed him. 'A long time since we've seen you here. I hardly knew you in the wig.'

A toothless middle-aged woman in a dingy cambric dress stepped out of the dim light.

'Lucy Loveless!' he greeted her.

'Loveless by name, and I intend to keep it that way, having seen what love has done to all you gentlemen.'

The Duke thought quickly. The last thing a young man like Walter would wish was to be publicly rescued. He could just imagine the story spreading through the Court like lye leaking from a washing vat, and rendering the boy a laughing stock. He would have to think of something more subtle.

'Lucy, might I ask you a favour?'

'Will you pay me for it?'

'Need you ask? A certain young man will arrive in a whisker, in the company of Lord Rochester.'

'Oh, him.' Lucy spat on the floor. 'No self-respecting whore'll touch him. His yard's as rotten as month-old meat. And smells as bad, too.'

'He will have a young man with him. A very young man. I want you to take the young man by the hand and tell him that his shot has been paid by a well-wisher. Then ply him with strong waters until he knows not if it is day or night. In the morning say all was well, that he rode you as if for England and St George, and send him happy on his way.'

The Duke handed over a handsome tip and slipped back into the alley, hoping no one had noticed him, just as there was a great banging on the door as the merry group of gentlemen demanded admittance.

* * *

Frances, knowing nothing of her brother's adventure, was simply glad to see him well and happy. He was even talking of returning to his studies. The Duke himself seemed strangely reticent on the subject of Walter, and it took a lot of clever worming by Mary to discover what had truly happened and to write it to Frances in a letter.

Frances was touched and grateful beyond measure.

'Oh, what a clever scheme!' She seemed unmoved by all this talk of whores and stewhouses, or even by the Duke's prior acquaintance with them. 'To outwit Rochester and save Walter's face when he could so easily have been disgraced and humiliated.' And then there was the news that Mary had persuaded her mother to let her return to Court in a few weeks, now that she was fully recovered.

As spring warmed into a gloriously hot summer the Court noticed a curious change in the King, which greatly alarmed them.

This energetic, enthusiastic man, who not only ruled a realm riven by competing interests, but found time for his twin passions for science and women, while at the same time trying to fend off the commercial depredations of the Dutch, was gradually succumbing to a restless melancholy.

All noticed it, from Barbara Castlemaine to Chancellor Clarendon. And all knew the cause.

The Queen planned masques and masquerades in Greenwich with fireworks and his favourite music, to no avail.

Lady Castlemaine attempted to counteract it by trying more tricks in the bedroom.

Chancellor Clarendon adopted a more direct approach. He went to see Mistress Frances Stuart and told her that she was depriving the King of his sanity.

The rapidly ageing Chancellor, crippled by gout, hobbled into her chamber just as she readied herself to visit the Queen. For once he did not have a beadle before him bearing the mace of state, as he usually did on all occasions, for which ceremonial he was often derided.

'Come, sit down, Mistress Stuart.' He patted the window seat next to his ample form. My poor legs need a respite already.'

Frances had always liked the Earl for his uncompromising honesty and for the occasional twinkle in his eye, which made his harsh words palatable. He might be the focus of a dozen plots to replace him as Chancellor, but he truly cared about the King.

'I make it a rule never to interfere in the King's affairs of the heart.' His eyes crinkled suddenly, realizing this was not entirely accurate. 'I try to stop the depredations of The Lady, it is true, so that there is some small sum left in the country's coffers once she has raided them, yet that is all. If the King wishes jewels and titles for his mistresses, that is his affair, though I doubt he gets good value for them. I am silent as the grave. Until this moment. He knows not that I have come here. Indeed, Lady Castlemaine thinks she is my enemy, yet her anger would be as a breeze next to the whirlwind of the King's if he discovered, and yet here I am.' He took her hand in his gnarled one. 'The King suffers as I have never seen him suffer. He could command you. Yet he does not. He asks you; he entreats you. Could you not take pity on him, for the state of the nation?'

Frances got to her feet, snatching back her hand. 'I do not resist the King, as some surmise, because

390

I shine with virtue like some beacon of holy light. I do so because I wish another life!'

'And this other life,' Chancellor Clarendon enquired with surprising gentleness, 'is there any prospect of achieving it? Is it with some other gentleman who dares not offend the King?'

'It is more difficult than that.'

'Ah. So it is not simply the King who stands in the way of your happiness?'

'No.'

'Could you not take pity on the King, then, at least for now? Until this other life becomes a possibility? I know maidenhead is not so easily restored . . .'

'I care naught for maidenhead!' Frances flashed. 'It is not my maidenhead I struggle to protect, but my honour. If I love another man, by climbing into the King's bed I cuckold him, and this I do not want to do.'

Clarendon watched her, weighing up her words without mocking them. 'And yet, from what I divine, you may never have this other man whom you think you love.'

This was the cruel and painful truth. A fact she could not avoid.

'Then I will have no one.'

'Mistress Stuart, I pity the King. Of all your sex he has chosen a lady whose heart is made of basalt.'

'It is not so!' Tears began to blur her eyes. 'My heart is not stone. It beats fast, it leaps and melts like any other's. Yet honour is what makes a person most themselves. If I give the King myself without honour, I cheat both him and myself, and the man I truly love as well.'

Clarendon rose to his feet. 'Mistress Stuart, I both

like and admire you. His other ladies have bled the King and our country dry. They have shown greed and rapacity and he has never been able to refuse them. You have asked for nothing. And yet, for all his weaknesses, I pity the King on his bed of thorns.'

Yet the King did not have long to languish on his bed of thorns, for another challenge, almost as great as the last that had engulfed London, was waiting in the ovens of Thomas Farriner, supplier of ship's biscuit to the navy, in Pudding Lane, and would at any moment burst into malicious and destructive life.

Chapter 19

'It is most unfair!' Cary Frazier scolded Frances. 'We must all wear black for the Queen's mother passing, yet you look so much better in it than we do. We seem like crows on a line, yet you are made for the colour.'

'Made for black! That is hardly a compliment,' Frances responded with spirit. 'As if I were to be a widow before even I am a bride!'

'No, no.' Jane La Garde, misunderstanding the banter, tried as she often did to make peace. 'It is only that Frances is so fair, and her hair shows up so well against the darkness of the cloth.'

'Yet fair hair is not fashionable, as my sister Sophia likes to remind me. And I look well in black because I am a giantess who is not dwarfed by the colour.'

They were readying themselves for Sunday worship, and ever since Queen Catherine's mother had died a few weeks ago, all her ladies were sentenced to dress in the deepest black, with no jewels, feathers, flowers or adornment of any kind.

'Did you see how dull and plain my lady Castlemaine looked without her jewels and her face patches?' Cary enquired, her eyes lighting up with satisfaction.

Before Frances could reply, the Countess of Suffolk entered the Queen's apartment and clapped her hands. 'Bring your fans, ladies. Even at this hour outside it is as hot as noon. I have never known aught like this summer.' She began fanning herself energetically. 'And I fear the minister plans a lengthy sermon . . .' They all sighed and moaned loudly. 'It will be good for your souls. And when the King falls asleep, as he always does, no whispering or laughing. It is for the maids of honour to set the lesser ladies a good example. Come!'

Obediently they followed Lady Suffolk to the Chapel, ignoring a crude sally from a group of gossiping gallants lounging against the wall on the subject of which lady they would take to bed, if they were the King.

The Countess had been right about the minister's sermon being lengthy, but not about the King falling asleep.

In fact the King glowered angrily at him, since the man had chosen his text from the Thirteenth Book of Revelation, reminding the congregation that the number of the Beast was 666 and that, since this was the year 1666, all had expected dire catastrophe.

'People feared that in the year of our Lord 1666 there would be pestilence, war and fire,' thundered the minister with all the passion of a Solomon

Eagle. 'And already we have been visited with the first two: pestilence and war! How long before this sinful Court is visited with its third punishment?'

The minister glared accusingly at the assembled courtiers, and even at the King himself.

'Fool!' murmured the King to the Earl of Clarendon, sitting next to him. 'What possesses the man, with this talk of further catastrophe? Has no one told him that the more you stir, the more it stinks! Have we not just recovered from the plague, and now he talks of worse to come?'

A flurry at the back of the church made the King glance round. A Groom of the Bedchamber approached with a message that Mr Pepys of the Navy Office needed an urgent word.

Glad to escape the ill-judged sermon, the King strode out.

'Thank you, Mr Pepys.' He shook the hand of the navy official, clad in his Sunday best of satin robe and white silk neckcloth, his face all red from running in the hot weather that had lasted into September. 'You have saved me from a tiresome sermon, praising the Lord that though we have suffered war and pestilence, we are so sinful we may be visited by fire!'

Mr Pepys looked as if a ghost had walked across his grave.

'Yet it is true, Your Majesty. It is that which I have come to tell you. A great fire has begun in the city, hard by Thames Street. In the shop of a victualler to the navy. The Lord Mayor plays it all down. A woman could piss it out, he says, yet I have seen with my own eyes that it lights up the city like a match in a tinderbox.'

'A fire! Now we have had it all. Order Bludworth

394

to blow up all the houses in its path. We must stop this fire before the flames take hold. The city is already on its knees.'

While Mr Pepys hastened away, the King summoned his brother, the Duke of York, and they departed together to inspect the extent of the disaster for themselves.

Gossip that a fire had broken out was already spreading through the congregation almost as fast as the fire itself. Knots of worried courtiers gathered at the end of the service, all concerned about their homes, those of their family and the precious goods they had stowed away hither and thither, and how far the flames would reach.

'Do not be anxious. The fire is well within the city walls,' announced the Countess of Suffolk briskly. 'We have a house down by the river, and my husband sends word that the fire will soon be put out. They have these new fire engines that the city liveries have paid enough for, after all.'

News came from an unexpected quarter when Mary Lewis, having known nothing of the dangers she risked when she set out, arrived unexpectedly by water from Cobham.

'Mary! Mary, are you safe? Did you pass the city and see the fire?'

Mary looked pale and tired. She nodded. 'I must have seen three hundred fair houses all on fire, and people running in the streets breaking open the wooden pipes with axes to get water for their buckets. Others were running around seeking boats. One of them jumped aboard our tilt-boat, even though we were going in the wrong direction.'

'But why are you here? And alone? I did not think you were coming for some days yet.'

For reply, Mary sat down and began to cry quietly. 'It is my mother. I know she has been harsh to me in the past, yet recently she seemed to soften somewhat. Mayhap at last she saw the value of a daughter, even a plain one like me.'

Frances knew not what to think. The resentment of the Duchess towards her daughter still burned brightly, and yet she could see the love Mary bore her, despite all she had suffered from her heartless parent.

'She sickens. They think it is the quartan fever or an ague. None seems to know what to do. With every blood-letting she seems weaker.' Mary jumped up and clung to Frances, her thin body shaking with sobs. 'She is all I have. No brothers or sisters. The Duke has been kind to me, kinder than my mother. And yet, she *is* my mother. Could we go to your apothecary? You said it was through her good offices that I survived the spotted fever myself.'

Frances looked away, a mass of conflicting emotions besetting her. There was the danger of going to the city at all to seek out the widow, when part of it was on fire. And then what reason had she to put their lives at risk for the sake of a harpy who had shown little kindness to those who deserved it most, even her own daughter? Beneath these considerations was another, more dangerously submerged thought, one that made her ashamed of even thinking it.

If Margaret were to die, the Duke would be free at last.

And yet it was that very thought that made her see she had no choice. For the sake of her own conscience, she must do all she could to save the

396

Duchess.

'Please, Frances,' Mary begged, her small face white with strain, 'let us at least try your wise woman.'

'If what we hear is true, she may have fled the fire.'

'If she has fled the fire, then I will go back to Cobham and pray.'

Frances nodded, for she had to give the child this much hope at least. 'We will go.' She hesitated. 'How is the Duke?'

'He looks after her well despite their differences, though she thanks him not at all. And he drinks too much wine.' She shrugged, a small smile lighting up her pinched face. 'But then who could blame him? My mother would drive any man to drink!'

'Come. If we go, we must go soon, before the fire takes further hold.'

The first wherry they hailed was reluctant to carry them anywhere near Three Cranes Wharf. 'All are afeared, mistresses. Thames Street is full of storehouses holding tar and pitch, then there's the timber and coal all kept thereabouts. And the Star Inn, hard by, be full of hay for the ostlers. I'll take 'ee as far as I think is safe and no further, on my life.'

Even on the river bank here, almost two miles from the conflagration, they could detect a strange acrid smell, stronger even than the usual London stink. It was a powerful stench of burning ash mixed with rosin and turpentine, and brandy and pepper from the burning warehouses. In the distance, round the bend in the river, there was a glow, as if a giant red sun was about to rise beyond the horizon. The effect was one of unease, as if some great unnatural event was waiting to unfold.

They travelled all the way in silence, watching the flames come nearer.

The King passed on the royal barge, his brother the Duke of York at his side, his harsh features burnished by the light, his face expressionless, waiting to see what new disaster had befallen his capital.

As the barge approached Queenhithe he jumped down onto the stairs. A group of city dwellers was already trying to put out the blaze in nearby Thames Street, but to no avail. 'Good men!' he shouted and delved in his a pocket for a handful of sovereigns to encourage them.

A moment later Frances saw how he was taking charge himself, organizing fire posts and drafting in soldiers to aid the civilians in their terrible task, with the Duke of York to command them. They saw him disappear into the stables behind the Star Inn to emerge upon a fine white horse. The beast reared up in shock at finding itself in such a crowd, with flames crackling all around, and seemed as if it might bolt with England's monarch on its back. Yet when he spoke to it softly, the animal calmed down and seemed afterwards unmoved by the shrieking of terrified women and the thundering of carts as they passed by, laden with belongings.

At Blackfriars, where Frances and Mary finally alighted, the fire had not taken so fierce a hold. They were able to find their way through the crowds heading for the river, and the chains of blackened men passing leather buckets and swearing that the river was so low, due to the parched summer, that the pumps had failed.

All the merchants in Paternoster Row, where

Margaret had sent them for her riding habit, Frances noted, were moving out their goods. Plate and gold were being shipped to the Tower and all their other valuables into the nave of St Paul's Cathedral, where they hoped the stone walls, and the protection of the Lord, would keep them safe.

'The Royal Exchange has caught!' shouted one merchant to another. Frances sadly remembered the silk mercers and haberdashers in their elegant galleries that she had visited with such delight when she first came to London.

God be praised that Widow Wyatt's house at the sign of the unicorn was so far untouched. And yet an angry crowd milled outside and started pulling a foreign-looking young man with long, dark hair from inside the shop.

'String him up from the sign!' directed a young woman. 'The watchman saw him throw a package in here to start a fire. It is the French and the Papists that are behind this destruction, as sure as I am a stout Protestant.'

The crowd all laid their hands on the lad, ignoring the widow's shouted protest that he was her assistant and the package was harmless.

Had it not been for the Duke of York passing with a troop of guard, the young man would certainly have met his end.

'Leave him alone!' commanded the Duke, instantly recognizable as a man of authority even though he wore no uniform. 'This is not the work of the French or the Papists, but the parched weather that has burned us up all summer without a drop of rain.'

'He would say that, being more or less a Papist hisself,' muttered a whiskery crone, yet they obeyed

399

him and dispersed all the same.

'*Mistress Stuart?*' he demanded in amazement. 'What in the Devil's name are you doing so far from Whitehall, and in this danger? Does the King know you are here?'

Frances shook her head. 'We do not tarry, but young Mary here came for help from this apothecary for her mother, who ails.' She pointed to the shop and its terrified occupants.

The Duke of York shrugged. 'The best physic is no physic at all, if you ask me. Come on, men! We must carry buckets to the Royal Exchange and save what we may.' They rode off into the strange orange light, which made all glow as if it were the hour of sunset.

The surly crowd, seeing her familiarity with those in authority, made a grudging path for Frances and Mary to the apothecary's shop.

'We came to ask if you would consider a commission,' Frances demanded of the widow, closing the door and leaning on it. 'To go by water with Mary here nearby to Gravesend, and there nurse her mother, who is ill of an ague or the quartan fever. We will pay you well for it.'

'I would have said I'd stay here till I was burned out.' Widow Wyatt shook her head, looking suddenly old. 'But that mob might come back and we'll both be strung up, so yes, I'll go, though I can make no promises that I can cure your mother.' She indicated the row of vast jars and bottles at the back of her shop. 'Yet I will come on the understanding that you help me store my jars in the church.'

So it was that they helped her carry her great ceramic jars of essences and oils and powders to the nave of St Mary le Bow, jostling and being jostled

400

by the crowds of merchants elbowing each other for the last bit of hallowed space in which to store their unhallowed goods.

When they were done, Frances took a bag of coin she had saved from her *bouge* of Court and handed it to Mary for the journey, and for any needs the widow might have. They waited as Widow Wyatt selected a cordial, syrup of poppies and an evil-smelling bark from the Fever Tree, which she said the Jesuits swore by in their treatment of the ague, though she herself did not stand for any religious mumbo-jumbo.

They walked as quickly as they could down the narrow streets, whose jettied house-fronts were so close that the fire did not even need to pause and take breath, but could spread unstoppably from neighbour to neighbour.

At the river, they parted.

'The widow will do her best for your mother. And I will pray for her also.'

They stood for a moment in the midst of the shouting and the flames, and Frances saw in Mary's eyes that she understood the height and depth of Frances' sacrifice.

Since their arrival but an hour ago, the great Thames had filled up with even more boats and lighters laden with the goods of fleeing Londoners. The small craft nearest them was filled nearly to sinking with a husband and wife, four children, all their great bundles and at one end, almost unbalancing the whole, a pair of virginals.

As Frances watched, a pigeon flopped down to its death at her feet. She looked up and saw that in every window, even though the houses were ablaze, pigeons stood on the ledges, paralysed by fear, until at last the flames licked at their feet and feathers and they thudded one by one down from the sky as if they had been shot. Everywhere was the stench of burning houses, the shrieking of women, cracking timbers and the deafening toll of warning bells from every church that still stood.

When her own boat was loaded, Frances set off upriver. Even on the river great flakes of burning debris rained down on them from the sky, setting light to everything, their possessions and the very clothes they wore, until it seemed as if the water itself were ablaze. Frances looked out in terror and fear at the golden, burning river of fire, as if some biblical retribution was indeed being visited on the capital and its citizens.

Even the hinges and locks on London's prisons had melted, the wherryman told them with relish, and all the prisoners had escaped.

In the distance, through the outline of falling buildings, they saw that the roof of the gracious church of St Mary le Bow—whose great bells declared anyone born within their peal to be a Londoner—had just caught fire, and the widow's jars and bottles with it.

*   *   *

'It would fair break your heart,' Mall sighed, a catch breaking her voice as she listed the damage that the King's surveyor had just presented to the King. 'Fourteen thousand houses and eighty-seven churches destroyed, St Paul's Cathedral among them.'

As Tom pointed out solemnly, in three days the most flourishing city in the world had been reduced to a ruinous heap, the streets only recognizable by the mangled remainder of the churches that had once adorned them.

And yet, Frances conceded, the King had shown great courage and leadership, ordering more buildings to be blown up to create fire-breaks, and sending food to the thousands who had fled and were camping out in Moorfields, the village of Islington, the Piazza of Covent Garden and as far afield as Highgate.

Yet despite all the action taken, it was only when the wind changed direction and disappeared that the fire finally abated.

Most men subjected to pestilence, war and fire might succumb to regret or melancholy, or even ask themselves if the soothsayers were correct—had the licentiousness of Charles' Court truly provoked this devastation? Was London indeed a latterday Sodom and Gomorrah, visited with fire and brimstone by the wrath of heaven? Yet the King was a rational man, and no believer in divine retribution. He was also firmly practical, and only a few days had passed before he called in his surveyors again and began to start planning a fine new city.

Despite the heavy financial blow wrought by the fire, and the rumours of invasion by both the Dutch and the French, eager to take advantage of England's plight, the King kept up his spirits and began to think about a peaceful negotiation to end the war, and a new start for the nation.

It was in this optimistic spirit that an idea came to King Charles.

'Once peace is concluded, I desire a medal to be struck in silver with myself on one side and Britannia ruling the waves upon the other,' he

403

decreed.

Yet who could personify the freshness, beauty and strength of Britannia?

Hardly Lady Castlemaine with her soiled reputation, or the Queen, who was, after all, Portuguese. There was only one woman suitable for so great an honour in Charles' eyes.

And so it was that, as soon as the ashes had settled, Frances found herself travelling to the Royal Mint to have her likeness captured by one Jan Roettier, the King's master engraver.

She had been greatly moved by the King's request. To be the face of her country was an honour that went deep, especially at such a low point for England. If Charles believed such a medal would cheer the nation in this, its darkest hour, she would be overjoyed to agree.

Especially as the whole idea had put Barbara's nose so out of joint.

'It is only to bribe her into his bed when other means have failed,' Barbara told her friends, her violet eyes narrowing. 'Now he appeals to her vanity. Yet she will pay a price for it, as I live and breathe.'

The fact was that Frances was grateful for the diversion. Left alone, she could not but wonder how fared the Duchess of Richmond in her distemper, and whether the widow had helped her to survive it. Posing for Britannia would be an uplifting new experience. The Queen, ever generous, even though she may have felt a pang of envy, readily spared her.

Arriving by water through the Traitors' Gate, Frances felt a shiver of apprehension. How many people had come within these walls, from Thomas

404

More to Queen Elizabeth and the sad Lady Jane Grey, wondering if they would ever leave again? Her thoughts also flew to the Duke of Richmond, confined here for his feelings for her, which the King could not forgive.

The Royal Mint was situated in a long, narrow structure that ran along three sides of the compound near the postern hard by Little Tower Hill.

And what woman would not be charmed to find that the Mint's chief engraver, Jan Roettier, a personable man of thirty-five, was smitten by her from the first? Especially when he found she was a young lady who was actually interested in the process of making coins and medals.

He led her reverently past the new screw presses and rolling mills, which had recently begun to replace the old hammered coins.

'We can now make thirty coins in a minute!' Roettier informed her enthusiastically.

'And how many could you make before?' Frances asked, watching one workman sitting at the base of the machine flicking struck coins out of the press and inserting new blanks.

'Less than half. Now imagine, perhaps one day it will be your face that is pressed into the coins of England!'

Frances laughed. 'I am happy just to appear on the King's medal.'

'First I must do the limning of your face.' They had arrived at a small room at the end of the building nearest the river, where the light was good. He gestured to a screen. 'If you could change into the smock hanging up behind, I would be most grateful.'

Frances gulped when she saw quite how sheer the smock was. She slipped it on, to find every curve of her body outlined, and in the chilly sunlight of the winter afternoon her nipples stood blushfully to attention.

When finally she emerged it was to find that a stool had been placed in front of a screen, painted all in white, making her feel like the target in a shooting range.

Seeing her discomfiture, Jan Roettier reached out a hand and led her towards the stool as if they were dancing a Coranto. She then arranged herself on it, grateful that she was so tall that her sandalled foot touched the ground, and she did not have sit there with her legs dangling like a fat little sparrow on a perch. Roettier contemplated her in silence, then reached forward and tweaked the smock so that her left shoulder was exposed.

'Mistress Stuart, I have had a long apprenticeship in capturing likenesses and I appreciate a thing of rarity and beauty when I come across it. Believe me, it does not happen often.'

'In that case I hope you succeed in capturing my rare and beauteous likeness for the King's medal.' She laughed back at him, and Roettier was joining in when the door opened and a small dog ran in, followed immediately by its owner, His Most Royal Majesty King Charles II.

Frances and the engraver fell silent, mostly from the unexpectedness of his arrival.

'Do I intrude on a private moment?' he enquired.

Roettier dropped a low bow. 'Indeed no, Your Majesty. I was merely telling Mistress Stuart that, from my wide experience, she was a suitable subject for a medal.'

Charles laughed. 'I bet you were, you dog. And, odds fish, indeed she is as well. A rare and unspoiled beauty has Mistress Stuart—and I should know, for I have tried my damnedest to spoil it!' The King laughed heartily at his own joke, then sighed. 'Sometimes I think she is the only innocent thing in my whole Court. So mind your conduct with her, Master Roettier. You are not in Antwerp now, man. We have ways in this country of dealing with our coiners for transgressing. We can have their engraving hand cut off and nailed above their place of work. Aye, or they might face the ordeal of the hot iron, so conduct yourself well.'

Noting the man's frightened face, Charles took mercy on him. 'Fear not, that was back in the Dark Ages. Nowadays we let them off, if their handiwork is good enough. Have you seen the Great Seal Mr Roettier is working on for me, Belle? When it is finished, every law passed in the land will bear Mr Roettier's handiwork. Now, leave us a moment, there is something I wish to discuss with Mistress Stuart.'

As soon as they were alone, the King came and stood in front of her. Without warning he slid her sheer smock further down her shoulder until the breast was revealed. His lips were suddenly on her neck, his breathing thick and heavy. 'Listen to me—stop this empty resistance.' He looked into her cool grey eyes, and a kind of madness came over him. 'I will give you anything if you surrender! I will make you a duchess and send all the others packing, my lady Castlemaine amongst them. You shall have estates, jewels, titles, all! I keep Barbara only because you will not grant me the last favour, and without that release I will go mad.' He took her face in his hands and twisted it painfully towards his. 'Yet it is not release I desire, but love. If only you could love me, Frances Stuart!'

'Yet you know I cannot.'

His eyes fixed on hers. 'Yet if you cannot give me your heart, I would settle for your body.'

There was a sharp knock on the door and Mr Roettier entered, announcing that he must start his work before the light failed.

'Damn the light!' was all the retort he obtained from His Majesty. 'Think about it, Mistress Stuart. I will give you one week to come to me willingly. After that if it must be unwilling, so be it.'

It was a silent hour that followed, as Jan Roettier sketched the lovely face of Frances Stuart, pondering in jealous silence, and a certain shameful envy, how it might feel to be a monarch so powerful he could command his subjects to submit themselves to him, body and soul, whether they wished to or not.

*   *   *

'He will not do it. I would wager a hundred angels he will not do it.' Mall turned to Tom, tangled in the sheets next to her. 'What think you, Husband? Will the King truly force Frances to succumb to him?'

Even though the sun had long been up, they were both lying in the great bed in Mall's chamber, a bowl of luscious fruit next to them, which they had begun to eat before being distracted by other pleasures.

'He is no tyrant in other matters,' Tom shrugged, the sun's rays lighting up his naked flesh, 'yet in this

408

who knows. He has been patient a long time.'

'And is that how you men overcome resistance,' Mall drew a finger across his chest teasingly, 'by giving a week's notice of enforced surrender? What pretty behaviour!'

'I am not a king,' Tom replied, smiling lazily. 'If I were, I would not wait a week.'

'You would take what you wanted on the spot?'

He leaned towards her. 'And give no quarter.'

Mall laughed, delighted.

'Oh, cease, you two!' Frances, coming into the bedroom, joined in the laughter. 'Just as well you are not King.' She sighed, serious again. 'I have come to a conclusion.'

The sudden decisiveness of her tone made them sit up. 'And what is that?' Mall asked, pulling the sheet about her.

'I have not been fair to the King. I have tried to be firm in my rebuttal, and yet betimes I have let him think all is possible in the end. He is right. I have dallied with his affections too long. The truth is, I have kept my innocence, but lost my honour. Now I must make up my mind. Am I willing to share his bed? If I am not, then I must leave this Court and find myself a husband. Any husband who is not blind or deaf, but has his hair and teeth, will do for me.' She smiled at the couple in the bed, who had been startled into silence. 'Indeed, any gentleman with fifteen hundred pounds a year who would take me in honour would suffice.'

'Forgive me,' demanded Mall, leaning up on one arm. 'Is this the same Frances Stuart who would not surrender, even though she was could be a duchess, and now will settle for a paltry fifteen hundred pounds?'

'That was as a mistress. This will be as a wife. At least I will have a chance of a proper life. And I will need to throw the net wide, since who will dare take from him the apple of the King's eye?'

Mall snorted. 'Then find yourself an old man. Better to be an old man's darling than a young man's slave.' She stroked Tom's arm lasciviously. 'Though there are advantages . . .'

A knock on the door made her jump, as if it were the King himself.

While Mall and Tom slid, laughing, from the bed to dress, Frances opened the door to find Jane La Garde outside in the passageway. 'Frances! I am so glad I have found you. I have looked all over.' There was a strange, suppressed excitement about her that Frances had never seen before. 'A visitor is below in the Privy Garden who needs to see you with great urgency.'

'Who?' Frances wondered if it were her mother or sister, or perhaps Mary. Yet why would Jane behave in this manner, as if she were the possessor of some great secret, if it were one of them?

'He said I must not tell you.' Jane flushed as red as the taffeta bed hangings, as if even this was more than she had meant to convey.

'I will come presently.' Frances shut the door and leaned against it, filled with a sudden premonition of what was to come, and a great rushing began in her ears, as if she stood beside a tumbling waterfall and might fall headlong into it at any moment.

Chapter 20

On that cold winter morning the trees of the Privy Garden were bare and withered, every green thing was dead. And no birds sang.

There seemed only one living, breathing being in that whole place.

He stood, leaning against the sundial. The slanting rays of the sun lit up his russet hair like the halo on an angel. When he turned she saw that his clothes were mud-streaked and his cheeks whipped into colour by the long ride.

Charles Stuart, 3rd Duke of Richmond and 6th of Lennox, was no romantic hero from a picture book. He lacked the swagger of his uncles, those royalist heroes who had strode so gaily into battle. Yet his gaze held both warmth and humour, and at this very moment regarded Frances with so much long-suppressed love that she could only run to his arms.

At the final minute she checked herself. 'Your Grace of Richmond, how does your wife? Is she recovered?'

The Duke straightened up his long body. 'Mary and I wish to thank you for your good offices in sending the apothecary to us. The woman did all she could to help us in our affliction. Yet I am afraid my wife died four days since, and was buried yesterday in her family vault. Mary stays on at Boarstall and sends you her fond wishes.'

Frances' heart leapt. 'I am sorry for your loss.'

A beat of silence followed into which unspoken words fought, thick as soldiers warring on a battlefield.

'Poor Mary!' She saw that at least with Mary as the topic of their discourse they were on safe ground. 'How does she fare?'

'Well enough. Her mother took her to her bosom at the last and was able to own how much she loved the girl.'

'I am so glad!' She could see what a rare gift this must have been to Mary, starved as she had been from infancy of a mother's love. She remembered that it had been Mary who diligently discovered how the Duke had rescued Walter.

'I wished to thank you for saving my brother from a humiliating fate.' She hesitated, feeling suddenly conscious of his nearness. 'Had I suspected where Lord Rochester was taking him, I could have gone and given the woman in question a piece of my mind for corrupting his innocence!'

The Duke smiled. 'I am sure the ladies at the Cardinal's Hat would have greatly appreciated your opinion. Yet perhaps your brother would rather not have had so much attention drawn to the situation?'

'You are right of course. He would never forgive me.' Frances bit her lip. 'Does Mary stay long with her mother's family?'

'That depends,' he looked at her, his expression clear and direct, as if he was emerging from a dark tunnel and could at last see ahead, 'on many things. She would like to return to Cobham, but it would not be proper without a chaperone.'

Frances laughed, then stopped herself, since it seemed unseemly. 'So you have a need for a chaperone for Mary in your house?'

'I do indeed.'

'And what are the qualities needed in this

412

chaperone?'

He smiled slowly. 'She must be beauteous.'

'I see.'

'And able to sing French songs.'

'Indeed?'

'And to ride fearlessly.'

'A hard bill to fulfil.'

But the Duke had not finished yet. 'She must also have good dress sense, so that she may school Mary in the ways of dressing as a lady of fashion.'

'I'm sure Mary would expect no less.'

'Her dancing must be light as a feather in springtime.'

Emotion flooded through Frances. Hope. Fear. Relief. 'Yet where will you find such a paragon, think you?'

The look in his eyes made her pulse begin to race. 'I hoped I might be looking at her.'

'Not myself? Since surely I would need a chaperone of my own?'

'Unless you were my wife.'

Frances wrapped her coat tighter against the cold, her breath stilled upon the morning air. 'Is it not too soon after your wife's death for such thoughts as that?'

'It was common knowledge that my wife and I saw not eye to eye.' Frances knew this to be an understatement. 'Few will raise an eyebrow if I wed again.'

'Except one.' The cold hand of fear took hold of her heart. 'And he could do much to stop it. Are you sure you dare risk his displeasure?'

'Mistress Stuart . . . Frances. I have considered this. The memory of my sojourn in the Tower is still fresh enough.' He laughed disparagingly.

'Rats and mice are not the cheeriest bedfellows. Yet my life without you has been empty indeed, as I have learned to my great cost. There can be few chains heavier than those I have carried this last twelvemonth.'

She had no chance to argue further as his arms had enfolded her and any protest would have been addressed to the velvet folds of his coat. Instead she returned his kiss with a passion that would have startled the King.

'Let us marry then,' she declared at last, emboldened by his clear love for her, and the offer of a proper life away from the treacherous maze of Whitehall. But a sudden cloud blighted the clear horizon. 'Yet I have no dowry to bring you. Any I might have expected would have come from the royal purse, as attendant to the Queen, and I think that as likely as Yuletide in July.'

The Duke laughed bitterly. 'I did as my uncle bid me and married for the sake of my estate, and look where it has led me. Let Cobham fall down around us, yet we face it together.'

He pulled her to him once more.

She knew full well the risk they ran. The Earl of Clarendon had reminded her that the King would brook no rival. He might go to any lengths to stop the woman he so desired from wedding another man. For he would understand, as she did, that this would be no marriage of convenience, where the bride might slip direct from her marriage bed into the King's and her husband look the other way.

This marriage, conceived in love, and strengthened in adversity, would be the end of all the King's hopes and pent-up desires. Frances would be lost to him forever.

414

And yet there was a nearer risk to their contentment, and one of which neither was aware.

Not twenty yards from where they plotted their escape, Barbara Castlemaine stood behind the heavy brocaded curtains of her apartments near the Holbein Gate watching the lovers, a gleam of satisfaction in her eye. So the angelic Frances, who had denied the King so long, was ready to throw caution to the wind for another.

Barbara knew the intense pain this would cause the King, and felt only delight. Frances had threatened her position and caused her more concern than any other woman in the land, and now she was about to pay for it.

Yet in this, Barbara found herself on the horns of an uncomfortable dilemma.

It was clear that Frances and her admirer, poor fools, thought themselves deeply in love. That Frances could have spent almost five years at the Court of Charles II and still believe in such a fairytale was ludicrous beyond belief, yet she had always been a strange girl. Barbara's first instinct was to expose their love and see it smashed like a log under the woodman's axe. Yet, delightful though that might be, how would it serve her purposes?

The safer course would be to let them quietly elope, since even the King could not rescind a legal marriage. And yet to do so would deprive her of the role she wished to play in Frances' destruction. She wanted the King to witness with his own eyes his betrayal by the woman he loved, since that would cause him the greatest suffering. And now she must ponder how to achieve it.

As soon as Frances and the Duke, love's idiots,

had said their fond farewells, Barbara put on her cloak and slipped downstairs.

The person she sought to assist in her endeavour was Mr William Chiffinch, who had not long since taken over from his brother Thomas as Page of the King's Backstairs and who, along with Mr Progers, the King's groom, knew more about the secret assignations, the cuckoldry, the love affairs and betrayals amongst Whitehall's courtiers than anyone in the palace.

When she sought his assistance, with the promise of favours and rewards, the gentleman was only too happy to oblige.

From his apartments near the King's own Mr Chiffinch controlled which ladies, both clean and unclean, were permitted to go up to the royal bedchamber, and expected to profit greatly in power and influence from doing so.

Yet not lately.

Frances Stuart had been bad for business.

The King's obsession with her had greatly reduced his interest in the myriad other women whom Mr Chiffinch provided. Indeed, the merry monarch had in recent months grown so melancholy he had lost interest in bedtime activities at all.

Barbara knew of this better than anyone since, to her great annoyance, she had had to use every one of her whorish tricks to fan his flagging enthusiasm, and had cursed Frances under her breath as she did so.

To Mr Chiffinch, the King's current condition was blasphemy, and he knew who was to blame. Indeed, it was a source of relief when Lady Castlemaine came to him. She might be a

416

termagant, rapacious, greedy and self-seeking, yet these were motives Mr Chiffinch understood and knew how to deal with.

Far harder to understand, and more threatening to the way things worked, was Frances, who had used neither her beauty nor the King's strong desire for her to her own advantage. What use to anyone was an attitude such as that? Mr Chiffinch would be more than happy to keep watch on her, and to inform Barbara if she had any unscheduled visitors.

He bowed low to Lady Castlemaine.

'She has too long ruled the King's heart, yet caused him only suffering.'

'Indeed,' Barbara nodded her head. 'It is our bounden duty to relieve him of her.'

A servant appeared behind them with a silver tray of goblets and a bottle of brandy. 'At long last, a return to business as usual!' he offered, and they both drank a toast.

*   *   *

It struck Frances that if you had a secret, as she and the Duke of Richmond had, the Restoration Court was the perfect place to disguise it, since every person you encountered possessed two faces and showed only one, usually not the true one, to the world.

There were those she liked and trusted: Mall, her father, Mary and perhaps Jane La Garde; and strangely enough, Queen Catherine, who might in the judgement of some be likely to hate her. She was not so sure about her mother and Sophia. And of all these, Mall was the one she trusted most, so it was to Mall that she turned now, to enlist her help and advice.

Mall was at her toilette when Frances knocked on her chamber door. Frances was relieved to find that Tom was on guard duty, since the fewer who knew of her errand the better.

Mall sat at her dressing table, which was draped in a rich Turkey rug, on which her jewels were carelessly arranged, studying her reflection in an ornate Venetian looking-glass and combing her long hair with a tortoiseshell comb.

Frances was glad her friend had found happiness at last, even if it scandalized the conventional. Mall had been born into one of the greatest families in England, seen her father murdered, and loved those she should not as well as those she should. She had been a loyal wife and a loving mother who had lost her dearest son, Esme, whose death had ironically caused Frances' own beloved Charles to become the Duke of Richmond. And only now, in the autumn of her life, had she found a love that made her truly happy.

'I have a great thing to ask of you, Mall.' Frances' eyes fixed upon her friend's face. 'I will understand if you refuse and bear you no ill will. Yet you, of all people, who have found love at last, will understand why I make this choice. Now his wife is dead, I intend to marry the Duke of Richmond.'

Mall swung round to face her. Frances noticed the marks of love upon her neck. 'And he will take the risk? Even after his holiday in the Tower?'

'He will.'

'And he truly realizes the weight of the King's anger that may fall upon him?'

'He had three weeks as His Majesty's guest to ponder it.'

Mall sighed, understanding better than any the mountains and ravines that still lay between Frances and her happiness.

'And what of a dowry? Cobham is a fine house, as I recall, and yet there was little money in the coffers to maintain it.'

'He will take me dowerless.'

Mall whistled. 'It must be love indeed.'

Frances smiled. 'That and the lesson in unhappiness he has learned from the late Duchess.'

Mall laughed. 'Yes. I can see she would be a good teacher in the perils of marrying for money. And this favour you wish of me. I can guess what it is. You wish me to intercede for you with the King?'

Frances threw herself into Mall's open arms. 'If only you would! There is no one else. None who could understand, as you can, how empty a life is without love.'

'And yet, my dear girl, that is how all but the veriest few live. In this Court people would the more readily accept ambition as a reason to marry than love. Love is the stuff of assignations and affairs.' Sadly she stroked Frances' fair hair. 'In our world love and marriage are not usual bedfellows.'

Mall pulled her robe tight about her and considered the matter further.

'And yet, the man you hope to marry is a duke, the highest rank in the English nobility beneath the King. He is not part of the King's coterie, and so may have made fewer enemies. The marriage is not disgraceful to your honour and the King's rank, as it might be if you married some simple squire and raised your brats in a hovel. He is a cousin to the King, if not a near one, and a noble Stuart besides. For the moment say nothing, be gay, behave as ever

419

you do. Go the playhouse and be seen. I will wait for the best moment to try and plead your case.'

When Frances had departed, Mall sat looking into the glass, yet seeing nothing.

It was not so long since the King had asked for her help in getting Frances into his bed, and she had refused. Now Frances asked an even harder thing of her. To beg the King to let her marry another. Yet did the King truly love Frances, or was it simply that she, of all the ladies he had ever pursued, resisted him?

Frances did as Mall advised her. She took extra care in her dress and made a great show of chatting so happily with the other ladies that some of them wondered if she was to become Queen after all. Cary Frazier whispered behind her hand that she had heard rumours the King loved Frances so entirely that he might divorce Catherine and put her on the throne instead. Yet beneath it all, Frances thought of little else but when Mall would break her news to the King and how he would receive it.

'Let us go to Mr Dryden's new play, *The Maiden Queen*, at the King's House!' Catherine Boynton suggested. 'I hear there is a new actress taking all by storm by the name of Nell Gywnn, who used before to be an orange girl.'

'But Catherine,' Jane La Garde reminded her, 'on a Friday? It is Lent, remember, so there will be no play today.'

Catherine clucked in annoyance. 'Let us ride out, then, to Hyde Park. The weather warms at last and I have seen buds on the trees there.'

The usual assembly of fops and gallants, ladies with vizards covering their faces, and the occasional brave beauty who rode unmasked, risking the depredations of sun or wind, rode around the Ring, waving and nodding at each other.

Frances smiled graciously, and offered her hand to various acquaintances. Her heart jumped in her chest when she spied the Duke, riding on a fine grey horse, trotting towards her. Discreetly she gestured that he should break away from the others and meet her under a tree some few yards off.

'I had not heard from you since we came to an agreement,' he whispered. 'And feared on reflection you might have changed your mind.'

The look she gave him, long and loving, reassured him that she had not.

'My friend Mall Howard has promised she will approach the King. She is his old childhood playmate and will plead our interests as none other can. All we can do now is hope and wait.'

He glanced around, making sure they were not observed, then swiftly kissed her hand. 'I am ready for whatever you may ask of me.'

Cary Frazier chose that moment to come and search for her, and the Duke doffed his hat and rode swiftly off.

'Was that the Duke of Richmond?' Cary asked, a sly expression creeping into her eyes. 'He seemed in a great hurry to be away. I suppose he does not want to be seen talking alone to the lady the King loves, or he might lose his head!' She laughed loudly at her own joke, but Frances felt a shiver that was nothing to do with the sharp weather. She knew the King would never act as Great Harry had done with Anne Boleyn, and send vaunted rivals to the scaffold or to suffer the axeman's blade, yet there were other things he might yet do to blight

421

their happiness.

She hoped Mall would speak soon, since waiting to know the King's reaction was hard indeed.

She did not have much longer to suffer such indecision.

Two days later Mall, who had been greatly concerned to find the right moment, decided to beard the King coming out of the royal box at the theatre. The new actress, Nell Gwynn, was playing the part of Florimel and seemed to cause the King such delight that he slapped his thigh, looking merrier than Mall had seen him for many a long month, after all the trials and tribulations that had befallen his kingdom.

When the play finished and the jig that ended every performance was drawing to a close, Mall waited for him to emerge.

'Your Majesty,' she dropped a low curtsey. 'Might I have a private word?'

'Odds fish, Mall, why the formality?' he replied, his dark eyes flashing with rare good humour. 'How many years have we shared our friendship, you and I?'

'Since we were babes, Majesty. And that friendship is precious to me indeed. And what I have to tell you may risk that honour, yet I have undertaken to tell it nonetheless.'

'God's blood! What news is this, so dire it could come between childhood friends as we are?'

Down below, the theatre was still busy and deafening, the seats and galleries thronged with noisy courtiers and their ladies, shouting apprentices and bawling orange girls. The stench of sweat and piss from gallants too careless to make for the house of office rose in waves, making even the stout-hearted Mall wish for a breath of air.

'Might we take a turn in Your Majesty's coach?'

Charles stopped and picked up Fymm, the one of his many spaniel dogs that accompanied him everywhere, and shooed away his flock of attendants. 'I am at your service, madam.'

Once they were inside the royal coach, Mall was struck silent, a situation as unusual as if all the birds in the sky had stopped their twittering before some terrible event in the natural world, and it struck the King as just as ominous.

Charles watched her curiously, leaning his long, lean frame back against the plush upholstery. 'Does all this silence and secrecy touch on your marriage and how far your brother condemns it?'

Mall, taken aback that her brother still cared, laughed hollowly. 'No, it touches Your Majesty more than myself. I come on behalf of Mistress Stuart.'

Imperceptibly the King's countenance stiffened.

'Indeed? And what has Mistress Stuart to convey to me that she cannot do it herself?'

Mall screwed up her courage. There was no gain in being other than honest and direct. 'Mistress Stuart begs your Majesty's permission to accept an offer of marriage from the Duke of Richmond and to leave the Court.'

The King swung round as if the whole carriage had lurched on some violent and unexpected bend. 'The Duke of Richmond is a sot! He has the wit of a yeoman and the carriage of a bumpkin squire.'

Mall ignored these unfair jibes. The King, obsessed as he was with Frances, could hardly be expected to list his rival's virtues. 'He is no witty gallant who writes plays and poetry, like Lords

423

Rochester and Buckhurst, it is true, yet he is a decent, honourable man.'

'And I am not?' he turned to her, his face pale with anguish. 'Mall, how can you intercede for him when I begged you myself, in friendship and trust, to show her how much I longed for and need her in my bed?'

'I did so, Majesty. Yet if you force her to succumb, you will kill the thing you love! That is your dilemma.'

'Mayhap it would be worth the price.' He turned away, staring out of the window. 'I wish to hear this from her lips.'

'Have you thought, Majesty, that mayhap she cannot give you what you want?'

'Yet I have seen it. She is no frozen soul. There is passion there for the unlocking.' He beat his forehead suddenly with his fist. 'Yet, Mall, this breaks my heart, that she wishes to marry him!'

Mall reached out a hand, moved to the soul by so much raw emotion. Of all the countless ladies Charles had encountered, it seemed only one had broken through the shell of his cynicism. Charles adored women, and endlessly sought their company. Sometimes, as in the case of Barbara, he allowed himself to be dominated by them. Towards his sister, Minette, he showed himself capable of great tenderness. To his wife he exhibited unusual sympathy for her disastrous barrenness. Yet only Frances held the key to his heart.

'She must come tonight and tell me this herself. Then I will consider my decision. Convey to Mr Chiffinch that he is to show her to my apartments after we have supped. I will forgo my usual entertainments. Tell her!'

424

Mall sighed. 'I will, Majesty.'

They had reached the Holbein Gate and Mall got out to go in search of Frances.

At last she found her in the Queen's Closet, sorting out Her Majesty's many gloves. She looked up when Mall entered, her clear eyes full of questioning.

'I have done my best,' Mall whispered, so the other ladies could not pick up their conversation. 'He requires your presence in his apartments after supper. Mr Chiffinch will show you up.'

Frances busied herself with applying attar of roses to a pair of grey suede mittens. 'Was he very angry?'

'With me, not you. He feels I have betrayed him.'

'You have no inkling if he will let me go?'

'He is hurt and angry. He does not understand why you refuse when he offers more than he has offered any woman before.'

Frances held her head up. 'Then I will have to convince him.'

Mall held out her arms. 'I will pray for you, if the prayer of a bad woman can tell with God.'

All noted the blackness of the King's mood at the supper table. The sweetest Italian singers could not move him. The wits failed to raise a single smile and eventually shrugged and turned away. His Majesty barely touched his favourite dish of oxtail, not even noticing the eager dogs that yapped impatiently beneath the table hoping for the bones when he was done. Even a visiting astronomer, whose latest theories he had listened to eagerly, failed to register his interest. The only enthusiasm he showed was for the grape, which was an unusual thing in him. He more often left the ordering of the second or third bottles to his rowdier courtiers, but tonight he broached the wine deeply.

Barbara Castlemaine took in the glittering eyes, the restless manner and the short temper and guessed what might be happening. The silence of Mistress Stuart, sitting far away at the end of the table, hardly speaking a word, confirmed it.

'Eat something, Majesty,' she murmured maliciously, 'or all will say you pine away ignominiously for the lady. Already they laugh at you behind their hands. To think the dullard Duke of Richmond will reap the pleasures the King has sown. They whisper amongst themselves how sad it is that all this time you have spent breaking in a ready horse and it is the Duke instead who will ride her.'

'Leave the table, impudent jade!' To the horror of all and the great delight of The Lady herself, he raised a hand as if to strike her.

Barbara simply laughed.

Chapter 21

It struck Frances with a shiver of concern that the King's new bedchamber was conveniently isolated from the busy rooms in Whitehall Palace.

He had moved not long since from his apartments overlooking the Privy Garden to the grand Volary Lodgings, named for the nearby bird court, facing onto the river. Within the lodgings there were two bedrooms, she knew—one to which he invited dignitaries who, rather to their surprise, might find the monarch receiving them

426

while he was still in bed or in the act of getting dressed or going to sleep. There was a withdrawing room, a library, a closet and, to one side, the laboratory where the King conducted his scientific experiments. There was also a smaller, more intimate bedchamber.

It was to this last that she found herself being led by a poker-faced Mr Chiffinch.

The king was not yet present and as she warmed her hands at the large fire, she saw they were shaking. What did he intend? To force her to submit and batter through her long-held virginity?

And if he did, what would be lost? Not her honour but his.

She thought of the Duke and how he had suffered imprisonment in the Tower for her sake. She could endure an equal ordeal. Some instinct told her that if the King forced her to yield, he would let her go after. Yet would the Duke take her, knowing the price she had paid in this most personal and private intrusion?

And in that loneliest moment of all her life, she knew that he would.

The sound of a step behind her made her turn.

The King stood watching her, his expression a mixture of tenderness and rage, as if the wolf looked on the lamb and saw, for the first time, the creature's newborn loveliness.

His gaze veered to the bed. 'I could compel you, you know,' he said in a voice so low she barely caught the words.

'I admit it.' She held her head up. 'Yet the fact you will not do so is what makes you the man you are.'

'And what man is that?' he asked bitterly. 'One

427

that other men laugh and sneer at.'

'Only those who prize dross over gold.'

'Yet I do not see the gold you perceive in the Duke of Richmond.' He pulled her roughly against the stiff brocade of his royal robes. 'What can he give you that I cannot?'

'An ordinary life.' She looked into his eyes, her own direct and honest, since there was no point dissembling. 'You and I both know what it is to lack a home of our own. I yearn to look out of my windows and see a green park, to manage a household, have babes about me, make up physic in my stillroom . . .'

'You are too rare for these things!' He turned angrily away. 'Any yeoman's wife can bake and brew. I have offered you what I have offered no woman before. I could still divorce the Queen . . .'

'Yet I would never wish to take her place. Majesty, I beg you, let me leave the Court and live in honour.'

'Honour!' he spat the word out as if it were blasphemy. 'Is this why you guard your maidenhead with sharp spikes of icy virtue? To keep your precious honour?'

'Honour is naught to do with maidenhead, sire. I could surrender that a hundred times and still have honour. Honour is to live life according to one's own lights. It is why you choose to be tolerant when it would be easier to be narrow; why you are generous to those who have done you service; why you have, in your own way, been loyal to the Queen when many would have you discard her.'

'You say these things make me honourable. Some would say they make me a fool.'

'You are no fool, Majesty, and will never be

428

remembered as such.'

He stared silently out over the dark river, lit only by the glimmering lights of the wherries that still plied their trade even at this hour. 'I have loved you to madness, Frances Stuart . . .' His voice tailed off sadly and she thought now he would let her go. But she was wrong. He turned to face her, his face set in stone. 'And for that reason I wish to know that you will be properly provided for. I am not satisfied that the Duke of Richmond has the funds to do so. I will appoint Chancellor Clarendon to look into the matter and report back to me.'

The bitter taste of despair came into her mouth. This was a delaying tactic, she knew. Knowing it would be impolitic to refuse the match outright, the King was strewing other obstacles in her path to stop her marrying.

Frances curtseyed.

'You may leave now.'

As she turned away she heard the rustle of silk, and a heavy cloying perfume that she knew at once filled the chamber. Barbara Castlemaine, in her undress, had come to reassert her dominion.

As she glanced back she saw Barbara already undoing her laces, and caught the murmured words which, being Barbara, were not of love, but of self-interest. 'You make a mistake in your choice of Clarendon. He will wish her to marry the Duke of Richmond, so there is no chance of Mistress Stuart wedding you and giving you heirs that will bar his own grandchildren from the throne.'

'Barbara,' the King demanded wearily, 'do you ever forget to politic?'

'Never,' Barbara replied, slipping to her knees as she unlaced the King's breeches.

From the muffled sound of her voice, Frances guessed what distraction she was deploying and left before she heard the King's reluctant release.

*   *   *

Frances awoke the next day with the strangest sense of being in a yellow haze. She had to sit up and shake herself to discover if she was dreaming.

In fact the haze turned out to be a vast bunch of daffodils so enormous that they disguised from view the person bearing them.

'These are for you, freshly picked at sunrise.' Mary Lewis' smiling face finally emerged from behind the bouquet. 'They are from your parkland. The Duke says to tell you a million more await their new mistress.'

A lump rose to Frances' throat, so overwhelmed was she at this vision.

The thought that she might have her own house with daffodil-filled gardens was wondrous in itself, yet even more delightful was knowing that she might share it with a man she loved, and who wished to make her happy.

Yet there were many holes in the road towards such contentment. Indeed, the picture was so lovely that she could not bear to think of it, in case it was dashed away from her.

'Mary!' Frances jumped out of bed, ashamed at how late it was, and embraced the girl, flowers and all. 'If only it were so, yet the King has not yet given his permission. But I should not talk of my hardships. I was sorry to hear of your own loss.'

'If you were, you must have been the only one!' She saw with relief that Mary was smiling ruefully.

430

'My mother had not the gift of making friends. The whole house breathed a sigh of relief when she departed.'

'Yet you yourself must have mourned her passing?'

'Thanks to your affection, I found the courage to stand up to her and she did embrace me at the last. Yet she had not a warm heart like you. Oh, Frances, we have such plans for your arrival! The Duke has called for his mother's linen to be washed and put on the beds, he chivvies the servants to clean the house till it gleams, and even harries the hens to lay more eggs for your breakfast table.'

Frances laughed with pleasure at this foretaste of such unfamiliar delights, yet was terrified that it was a deal too presumptuous.

'More's the pity, but the Duke had better spend less time with the hens and more with his steward. The King has asked the Chancellor to study his inheritance and report that he is a fit provider, and the estate not too encumbered.'

Mary's face fell. 'I do not think there is much in the coffers. The Duke wished to build a banqueting house for you, but Mr Payne—he is the steward—sniffed and asked, "How will we pay for it, Your Grace?" Yet the Duke, ever the optimist, insists we will find a way. If I had to choose between my pinchpenny mother and your carefree duke, I know which it would be.'

Mary saw the look of concern in Frances' eyes.

'I am unfair in my description of life there. The Duke knows his limitations.' She smiled at her friend. 'It will be only a *small* banqueting house!'

Later that day, after Mary had left for her return to Cobham, this time taking Nurse with her as chaperone, word arrived that the Chancellor had indeed requested that the Duke of Richmond and his steward visit him next day at his great mansion, Clarendon House, hard by St James'. All of London knew the meaning of this. The King was looking for reasons to prevent the marriage and had hit upon the Duke's unsteady finances.

Frances stood by the open window of her chamber. Spring was coming to the capital. Even through the usual fumes from the dyers and brewers, the sugar-boilers and chandlers and the countless cooking fires, the sun had penetrated and was dappling diamonds of light across the river. All around birds twittered to each other that the winter had departed. A dove flew by with a twig in its mouth and settled on a rooftop opposite to build its nest in the eaves.

Apprehension took hold of her. Would the birds of the sky be allowed their own fragile homes and not she, because the King loved her?

She sprang up, unable to sit demurely in her chamber, or help pull on the Queen's perfumed gloves, while her whole future was being decided by Lord Clarendon, only half a mile away.

Frances had always been fond of the Chancellor.

Even when she was a young girl in Paris his familiar figure, forever sounding off against the more decadent members of the Court, and reminding Prince Charles that he would one day be King, had been a reassuring sight amongst the tattered Cavaliers, so many of whom who had lost their honour and their dignity.

And when the King did finally achieve his throne, it had been the Lord Chancellor who had been the fiercest critic of Lady Castlemaine.

432

He had helped her once; would he do so again if she went to him and pleaded their case?

Her old nurse's saying jumped into her mind that 'each man is architect of his own destiny'. Not pausing to lose her confidence, she donned a vizard, took her cloak from its hook and ran quietly down the back stairs through the Pebble Court towards the row of sedan chairs that stood beyond the Banqueting House. She left no message for the other ladies. The fewer who knew of her destination, the better. Gossip flew faster than mud under the wheels of the night-soil cart in this city.

The chair-men deposited her outside the gates of the Chancellor's new mansion near Piccadilly.

''Tis said it's the greatest dwelling in London bar Whitehall Palace,' commented one of the men, leaning on the sedan chair and gazing up at the colonnaded exterior with its rows of great floor-length windows, so different in its elegant proportions from the remnants of the Tudor city around it.

'He's feathered his nest all right,' grumbled the other. 'Maybe he paid for it with money he got for selling Dunkirk to the French.'

Londoners were still angry at the government, she knew, for handing Dunkirk back to King Louis, and they had made the Chancellor a scapegoat for their ills.

'Aye,' ruminated the other. 'Folk blame him for the Queen's barrenness also, though I can't see as that's his fault. And they do say,' the man dropped his voice confidentially, 'that he built this palace from the stones that was intended for the repairing of St Paul's.'

'What a farrago of nonsense!' Frances countered

with spirit. 'My Lord Chancellor is a beacon of honesty compared to most.'

The two chair-men took her money and watched her curiously as she approached the front door of the magnificent house, wondering who this lady was who so freely spoke her mind.

'What a decaying age we do live in,' one muttered to the other, 'when women think they can have opinions.'

'Aye,' agreed the second. ''Tis all the King's fault. His sense is all in his breeches, so they say.'

If the Chancellor was taken aback by her unexpected arrival, he did not show it.

'This is an unusual pleasure, Mistress Stuart,' Lord Clarendon greeted her as he was wheeled in the special gout-wheelchair that the King had devised for him. She gazed round admiringly at his vast withdrawing room, lined with gilded portraits of poets and writers.

Frances wondered if she should speak formally, maintaining the usual protocols where nothing was ever mentioned directly, or throw caution to the winds. An instinct about the old man before her told her she could open her heart. 'My Lord Chancellor, you have always been a good friend to the King.'

'I have done my best. Yet there are many about him who poison him against me. The Duke of Buckingham mocks me for my old-fashioned notions. The Lady tells the King I work only for my own advantage.'

'Yet the King knows, of all his counsellors, you are the one who speaks the truth.'

Edward Hyde, Earl of Clarendon, looked suddenly old and frail, a mere shadow of the unbending statesman he had once been. 'They mock me to the King. They say, "Look, here comes your schoolmaster to tell you what you must do."' He sighed heavily. 'I do not think the truth is what the King wishes to hear.' He looked at her, his filmy eyes clearing. 'And in this case what the King wishes to hear is that the Duke of Richmond cannot support you and will not make you a suitable husband.'

A groom arrived with a tray of wine. The Chancellor's gout clearly did not stop him imbibing, even at this early hour. 'I have seen the ladies come and go. You were the best of the lot. Indeed, I wish you *had* married the King. Yet the Queen did not die, and I would not support divorce, as the Duke of Buckingham counsels so eagerly.'

'Even if I could marry the King, I would not desire to do so.'

'Yet why do you choose the Duke of Richmond?'

'Despite all the risks, he dares to offer me his hand and heart without need of settlement or dowry. Besides, I must leave the Court. The King is ever more eager in his pursuit of me, and perhaps what people say of me is true, that I have all but prostituted myself to him. This is my only honourable course of action.'

'Ah,' the Chancellor repeated cynically, 'honour. What is that?'

'Will you help us? We both know this is but a ploy to stop the marriage.'

The Chancellor delved in the side of his wheelchair and pulled out a small painting. Frances was amazed to see that it was a miniature of her own portrait, dressed as the goddess Diana.

The Earl held it up.

'I have ever loved this picture. All that was best

about our Court when it was first restored is here. Beauty. Elegance. A new freedom. You look out, clear-eyed, hopeful, like the doe in a forest glade.' He slipped the painting back down the side of his chair. 'I would not have you hunted. I would have you get your chance to run free, away from this Court that has become corrupted, from a king who has lost his own honour. Yes, I will help you.'

*　　*　　*

The word delivered to the King from his Chancellor, the Earl of Clarendon, was that while Cobham Hall was indeed encumbered with debt, it was no more so than half the noble houses in England, and that since considerable rents were due to the Duke from his tenants both in Kent and Scotland this very week on Lady Day, all in all there were no pressing financial reasons why the Duke and Mistress Stuart could not be wed. What was more, the Chancellor added, perhaps provocatively, was that since the Duke was so nearly related to the King, there would no problem with the standing of his credit since the King could not in honour allow him to be ruined.

When he heard his Chancellor's verdict the King kicked out at Gypsy, his black lurcher, and shouted at a Groom of the Withdrawing Chamber for spilling his wine.

The Court watched, awed, and waited to see what His Majesty would do next.

'What did you expect?' demanded Lady Castlemaine as they sat down to supper. 'I told you the Earl of Clarendon had his own agenda. Besides,' she leaned in to his ear, 'you have not heard the whole. The wags have it that he counselled her to hold onto her Duke, for she will find none other of his rank prepared to take her.'

The anger and disappointment etched on the King's face gave her the greatest satisfaction.

'Dismiss the old fool! You have others who can give you better counsel now. You have kept the man near you too long, out of kindness. This is how he repays you.'

To her great fury, the King seemed submerged in melancholy.

'Come,' she chivvied. 'You are not some tragic play-actor on stage in Drury Lane. Order him to return the Great Seal at once. There are others worthier of it.'

The King turned, his dark eyes glowing with anger. 'Be quiet, impudent woman. It is not the Chancellor I am concerned with!'

His gaze fastened resentfully on Frances, who had placed herself discreetly at the other end of the long table, with the Queen between them for safety.

Barbara drew back from his tone as if she had been struck. How could he still yearn for that little bitch when she treated him thus?

'We must have music!' ordered Queen Catherine, picking up that the mood needed to be lightened around her dinner table. 'Sing us some sweet French songs.'

A fair-haired young boy appeared on the dais next to her and sang like an angel, his pure voice rising as a skylark soars towards the sun.

To Barbara's intense irritation, the music seemed to soften the King's anger towards Frances, as if he could remember the time when it was she who sang the French songs so sweetly.

Tempted to rise noisily, despite the King's

437

continued presence, and storm from the hall in search of better company, she noted that Mr Chiffinch stood in the small alcove near the passage where the grooms and scullions carried food from the kitchens, signalling discreetly to her. She slipped from her seat.

Mr Chiffinch bowed and gestured to a large tapestry depicting the eviction of Adam and Eve from the Garden of Eden.

Barbara followed him behind it. 'I am very sorry to interrupt your ladyship at the table,' Mr Chiffinch whispered. 'Yet you requested that I keep my eyes open on your behalf.'

Barbara nodded, excitement mounting. She knew the King's Page of the Backstairs would not pull her from the hall, when all were dining with the King and Queen, for naught.

'I thought that you would wish to know that Mistress Stuart has a visitor.'

'Indeed, you interest me greatly, Mr Chiffinch.'

'The Duke of Richmond arrived not ten minutes since, in a great rush, swathed in riding capes. He tossed the groom an angel to water his horse. It seems he had ridden in some haste to see the lady and was deep disappointed she was not present in her chamber.'

A smile of victory lit up Barbara's half-closed eyes. She could almost scent blood.

'Thank you, Mr Chiffinch. I am very interested in your news indeed.'

The sweetmeats were arriving by the time she sat down again at the table.

With renewed appetite, Barbara tucked into the vast spread of green plum cake, almond blanchmane, rose sorbet with fresh apricots from the King's hothouses, accompanied by a glass of extremely alcoholic orange cordial.

Having finished, she turned to the assembled crowd and clapped her hands. 'Your Majesties, ladies and gentlemen, I would be honoured if you would grace my apartments with your presence for music, cards and gaming.'

Given the high quality of Barbara's music and the bottomless fountains of wine provided, this suggestion was greeted with universal approval. Even the fact that it was Lent did not deter the crowds.

The Queen, who had taken to the joys of the gaming tables with surprising enthusiasm for one who had such a narrow Catholic upbringing, was one of the first to her feet.

The King, seeming to forget her great sin, reached out his hand to Frances. 'Come, Mistress Stuart, join us for a hand at Basset and a glass of wine.'

'Sire, my head pounds as I were inside the bell of St Mary le Bow.' This was indeed true, though in the usual way she would ignore it.

Looking convincingly pale and wan, she curtseyed to the Queen. 'Might I be excused my duties to Your Majesty for the rest of the night?'

The Queen readily assented.

Behind her Barbara smiled maliciously. 'Poor Mistress Stuart,' she offered in a tone of unusual sweetness, 'perhaps you ought to retire and recover your spirits.'

Frances nodded, alert at once to Barbara's unwarranted generosity, yet eager to escape the endless evening for the quiet and peace of her chamber.

'Thank you, your ladyship, and indeed that is what I will do.'

Her first inkling that she had unexpected company was from the chambermaid who was clucking outside the door like a rooster protecting the henhouse. 'Oh, mistress, mistress, I am sorry, but there is a gentleman in your chamber. I did not know whether to summon a guard from the guardroom. Yet he walked in with such assurance, as if it were his own apartments, that I knew not what to make of it!'

Frances, taking in the riding cape carelessly flung on her gilded leather chair, and knowing at once to whom it belonged, could not prevent a smile. 'Worry not. I will deal with the gentleman. You may go to bed.'

The girl was just about to obey when a sudden memory of Barbara's unwonted consideration came back to Frances and made her suspicious.

'No, stay awhile. I have changed my mind. And let me know at once if you hear approaching strangers.'

The girl nodded. 'I will indeed, mistress.'

The maid sat down, clearly relieved she had committed no unforgivable misdemeanour in allowing the gentleman entry.

Frances entered the chamber quietly and closed the door behind her.

The familiar figure turned, his eyes lighting up with delight at her arrival. He took both her hands in his, as if they were about to dance.

'What, no gift of daffodils today?' she teased, her spirits soaring at the sight of him.

'They wait for you at Cobham. They will live longer to enjoy your company if I do not gather

440

them.'

She laughed at his absurd whimsy.

'Yet, I did not come empty-handed. See what I have brought you this time.'

He led her to the window. A huge moon hung in the sky, seeming so near she could almost reach out and touch it. 'Black Dick, who works for me in the fields, and has little sense in his head according to his fellows, but seems to me to have more than most, says it is a blue moon. It seems nearer and brighter, he says, than at other times, and brings good luck.' He turned her towards him. 'You can see why I value his good sense.'

She had no chance to reply since his mouth was on hers, and his arms held her tightly against his body.

When finally he released her, the teasing tone was back in his voice. 'I am solvent enough to wed you, it seems.'

She knew not if it were the worry at their situation, but Frances' head began truly to pound unbearably. 'I wish all this were over, and the Court could forget you and me and our little doings.'

'It is never a little doing where you are concerned. Lie down, I will stroke your head. It is a trick my old nurse used, when I was a boy, to chase away the dragons and snakes I fancied coming into the chamber.'

Frances lay down on the canopied bed while the Duke sat beside her and began to stroke her eyelids gently. 'And I thought you so brave!' she protested.

'A man can be brave on the battlefield and still shrink in the bedroom.'

'Not with the right company, I hope,' she replied flirtatiously.

'Is this the Mistress Stuart so famed for her maidenly innocence?'

'I never claimed such!' she protested as he leaned over and kissed her again.

Outside in the corridor a great commotion began and the door was flung open.

The King stood on the threshold, with the weeping chambermaid a step or two behind him, his face as pale as an avenging ghost. 'So this is why you cannot bear my company and must retire alone to your chamber.'

Frances scrambled quickly up, forgetting her headache, and even to whom she spoke. 'Why should I not entertain the Duke of Richmond when he at least makes me an honest offer?'

For an instant she thought the King would strike her. Instead he turned his fury on the Duke. 'I could have you thrown in the Tower again for this! And not for three brief weeks.'

He caught sight of the window, with the moon shining in, where they had stood but a moment ago, and a kind of cold madness overtook him. He made as if he would take hold of the Duke's collar and run towards the open casement and eject him bodily into the Thames.

'Sire! Stop!' Frances summoned all the dignity of which she was capable. 'He is your subject. He cannot fight back.'

The look of a rabid dog left the King's eyes and he released the Duke.

'Go!' she begged him.

'I cannot leave you in such circumstances.'

Frances shook her head. 'I am in no danger here. It will go better for us both if you leave. I will send you a message tomorrow.'

He recognized her logic, yet the stiff, unbending lines of his gait as he departed told her of his extreme reluctance.

The King stood by the window, as still as a statue. 'If it were not for my position, I would have thrown him in the river.'

'And had a good man's death on your conscience out of jealousy.'

'You have driven me to this.'

'Oh, pish!'

He looked astounded at her sudden lack of respect.

'I have driven you to nothing. You only want me because I refuse you. You are like a child who envies another's toy.'

'Mark to whom you are speaking.'

'I do. Our great King.'

The King considered her. 'You are not yourself.'

'I am more myself than I have been in my whole life. You see what a harpy you would possess if you bedded me? All this talk of grace and innocence. Pah! You would be well rid if you released me.'

He took hold of her wrist and held it so tight it pained her. 'I do not intend to release you. The Duke of Richmond is henceforth banished from my Court and all his duties are in abeyance.'

'Majesty . . .' she began.

'Do not dare to plead his case.'

Even though she was so angry, Frances had to fight back the tears. Women showing weakness always moved the King, yet something in her resisted playing for his sympathy when she longed to hit out.

Instead she stood up proudly, her eyes almost level with his. 'Perhaps you should go back to her who sent you.'

If his anger had been softening, now it flared again into fire.

'Step carefully or I may banish you also.'

'I would welcome it.'

'Indeed, you would, so you might play house with your doltish duke! Then I will do the reverse, I will insist you stay here at Whitehall.'

'Then I shall petition the King of France to let me return and join a convent.'

The King laughed bitterly. 'And offer God your long-preserved virginity? A fitting use for all your beauty! Yet at least you would drive no more men to madness.' She looked down and saw there were red weals marking the pale skin where he had gripped it. 'I will leave you to offer yourself to God. But mark this, I will never relent in the matter of the Duke. I would rather you went to your convent than marry him.'

Abruptly he turned from her and departed, leaving Frances to her despair.

In her mind's eye she saw the daffodils at Cobham fluttering in the night air, their beauty and promise a bitter reminder of her fading dream.

Chapter 22

'Frances! Frances! Get up!'

She woke to find Mall standing by her bedside. 'All Whitehall is abuzz with the tale of the King's coming to your chamber last night and finding you with the Duke. Is it true the King almost flung him into the river?'

444

Frances sat up wearily. 'Barbara Castlemaine brought him. She must have been spying on me, for none knew he was here. I did not even know myself until I returned to my chamber and found him there.'

Mall shook her head. 'What a heartless trollop she is. She could not bear your rivalry, so she must expose you by hurting him the most she can.'

'And now the King has banished him from the Court, yet makes me stay here, however much I long to leave.'

Mall considered the position. 'You must throw yourself on the mercy of the Queen! She has much to thank you for, remember. She knows you consider her, and there was that business of the child. You are her maid of honour, I am sure she will speak for you to the King.'

Frances dressed hastily, throwing her nightgown onto the floor and reaching for her smock, revealing her bare arm as she did. The red weals from last night had discoloured into an ugly yellowish-blue. Quickly she pulled on her gown so that Mall did not catch sight of them.

They found the Queen finishing her morning prayers.

'In Lent, Her Majesty likes to say her rosary as well as going to daily mass,' sighed Catherine Boynton who, like her other ladies, felt the Queen's religious devotion could be a trifle onerous for those who waited on her. Especially the ladies like Catherine, who wished to spend every spare moment in the arms of her young man, rather than those of God.

'Her Majesty will see you now.'

The Queen was in her closet, the small room

where she kept her prayer stool and her rosary beads. It was as plain and spare as a monk's cell, the only adornment being two paintings of the Virgin Mary and the Queen's favourite saint, Teresa of Avila.

'Were you named for St Teresa, Mistress Stuart?' Catherine asked, referring to Frances' middle name.

'I am certainly the only Teresa in my family.'

'You are honoured to be named for a saint. It means she will intercede for you in times of need.' The Queen smiled gently. Frances wondered whether she knew about the fracas last night and, if so, whether it had wounded her, or was she now so used to her position that she rose above such things.

'I am at such a time now, Majesty.'

Catherine put down her beads and turned to study Frances. She was older than her lady-in-waiting by six years, yet she possessed a childlike quality that made her seem much younger. Part of it was her physical size. The tip of her head just reached Frances' shoulder. She noticed that the Queen had started to wear her hair in puffs, which Frances herself had made fashionable.

'And what would you wish the saint to help you with?'

'I wish to marry the Duke of Richmond, Your Majesty, and gain permission to retire from the Court.'

'Am I so stern a mistress that you wish to leave me?' Catherine asked teasingly.

'You are a delightful mistress. I have been honoured to serve you.'

'And I have had cause to be grateful to you.'

446

A silence hung between them, in which the lost baby and the King's pursuit of Frances hovered like ghosts.

'Yet I long for a home of my own.'

The Queen sighed so deeply that Frances saw, for the first time, how lonely she must sometimes be. Far from her homeland, forced to learn a strange language, shocked by the values of the Court, having to turn a blind eye to her husband's indiscretions while knowing how unpopular she was because she could not give the King and his people the thing they most wished for. 'Are you asking my permission to leave?'

Frances nodded.

'Even if I agree, my husband will take it harder. He does not like to be left. He cannot see that any other existence could rival the wit and excitement of his Court. I remember when the Duke of Newcastle, his old tutor and a man he greatly admired, wished to live in the country, the King spoke not to him for three years. What was the King's response to your own request?'

'To banish the Duke, Majesty, and command me to stay at Whitehall.'

'That is what I would expect of him, even if it were not for the other matter.'

They both knew what the other matter was, and that out of discretion they need not spell it out.

'I have told him that if I cannot marry the Duke I will seek permission to join a convent.'

The Queen laughed softly. 'I cannot see you in a convent. Your hair is too fair and your taste in clothes too good. You would have them throwing away the veil and changing their habits in a trice.'

Frances smiled, putting a hand up to cover her

447

face, her sleeve falling away as she did so.

The Queen's expression swiftly changed. She took hold of Frances' arm. 'Did my husband make those marks upon you?'

Frances nodded reluctantly.

The Queen seemed to grow suddenly in stature. 'It is time there was an end to this madness. St Teresa and I will talk to my husband and plead on your behalf. He will only see me, but I am sure she will be present also. Perhaps you should pray to her for her intercession.'

So it was that for the very first time Frances Teresa Stuart prayed to her saint and namesake that she would be allowed the freedom to choose her own path in life, and have at least a chance of happiness.

'Amen,' whispered the Queen, quietly echoing her prayer. 'I will do my best for you, Frances.'

*   *   *

Charles, Duke of Richmond, stared out of the window of the sunny Tudor tower at the park below. The day was new-minted, the sky a perfect optimistic blue. Deer roamed among the narcissi and wild daffodils that surrounded Cobham Hall, the mellow brick mansion where Queen Elizabeth had stayed in the first year of her reign. The park, farms and woodlands he had inherited spread out lush and smiling as far as the eye could see. As he looked towards Cobham Mount he could picture the famous oaks whose vast circumferences were more than twenty feet, and beyond towards the chestnut tree that locals called the Four Sisters, for its four branches that spread out like arms.

448

All that Cobham lacked was its longed-for mistress.

'I cannot kick my heels here when she bears the King's wrath alone,' he insisted to Mary. 'I must go back to London and face the anger of the King.'

'If you do so rash a thing,' Mary warned, 'you will find yourself in the Tower before sunset and how will that assist your cause?'

'Easier to raise the Devil than to lay him,' endorsed Nurse darkly, looking up from the wool she was winding onto a card.

'Yet what if the King harms her? And all the while I am skulking here?'

'He will not do so. I often witnessed his character at Court. He is no Bluebeard.'

'You did not see the fury in his eyes last night. I thought he might kill me there and then.'

'Yet he did not.'

'No.'

'You should eat, Your Grace,' counselled Nurse. 'I will ask the clerk of the kitchen to bring bread and cheese.'

The old woman rose stiffly.

'Nurse, stay seated,' Charles insisted. 'I shall go myself. The diversion will do me good.'

The parrot, which had been calmly watching the scene from its perch, suddenly woke up, eager to be included in the general imparting of wisdom.

'Give a man enough rope and he'll hang himself,' it commented sagely.

The Duke laughed out loud, glad of the break in the tension. 'As for you, Bird, I shall find a piece of rope to hang you myself.'

The parrot put its head on one side and weighed up the danger of this threat to its general well-being.

'Foolish Charlie Stuart,' it pronounced pompously and tucked its head beneath its wing to sleep.

*   *   *

The Queen was as good as her word. She went to seek out the King in his new laboratory, and he was so surprised at this unwarranted intrusion into his private space that he forgot to object.

She had already passed through his chamber and closet, marvelled at his many maps—especially the one of Portugal—stopped to inspect the model ship, so accurate in its every detail that it had taught him more about his navy than any previous king had known, and had arrived in His Majesty's laboratory just as Mr Boyle was giving the King a demonstration of his air-pump.

All around them were signs of the King's passion for everything scientific. An experiment designed to challenge the theories of the alchemists was laid out upon wooden benches; a part-dissected toad lay pinned to a board, next to a thing so horrible the Queen almost fainted away when she saw it: a pickled foetus sent to the King by Dr Elias Ashmole.

'Your Majesty, I have not had the honour of welcoming you here before,' her husband greeted the Queen with the slightest air of hauteur, which she instantly disarmed by her reply.

'Aye, and you wish me anywhere else but here now!'

The King smiled. 'Naturally you are welcome.' He pushed Fymm under one of the benches with his foot, since she was barking rudely.

'Even your dog protests,' Catherine commented. 'Yet I needed a private word. I am afraid it could not wait.'

'Indeed, then perhaps you might leave us, Mr Boyle?' His dark eyes, usually so affable and courteous, seemed as forbidding as the frozen ocean, and the lines around his mouth—always a notable feature—as deep as furrows in a winter field.

'This business of Mistress Stuart—' she began.

'Are you sure this is a matter you wish to discuss?' he interrupted dangerously, 'since it touches upon you also.'

'Perhaps that is why I would welcome it.'

'Speak, then.'

'It will not sit well in the country or the world for you to play the tyrant and refuse this marriage.' This was a Catherine he had not encountered before, level-headed and cool. 'After all, there will be little doubt about why you forbid it.'

The King sat down, listening to her silently.

'Is the fact of this marriage so important?' the Queen enquired. 'As I recall, my lady Castlemaine's marriage did not deter your marked attentions.'

'That was different,' was his terse response. 'Lady Castlemaine did not profess to love her husband.'

'It is the love then, not the marriage, that irks you so?'

'I am not overly fond of either. Besides, how can she love such a fool?'

'Perhaps he is not such a fool as you think. He is not a polished courtier like your friend Lord Rochester, and it is true he avoids Court life. Yet there is a story I heard among my maids that it was

451

the Duke, not your noble poet friend, who came off best in some matter of the lady's brother.' She studied her husband, her head held high. 'Besides, for good or ill, we love with our hearts, not our heads.' There was a wistfulness in her voice that in his anger the King did not notice.

'Yet he is dull. An oaf!'

Catherine smiled gently. The Duke had not seemed either dull or oafish when she met him. Indeed, there had been something about his tender manner that had moved her. 'Do not they not say in your country "Please the eye, plague the heart". Perhaps the Duke of Richmond will not plague her heart.' She paused. 'And in that she will be fortunate indeed.'

He took her hand in his, unexpectedly moved. 'Have I been so bad a husband then?'

She looked at him steadily. 'I have looked the other way because I knew I could not satisfy your appetites, yet that does not mean I have been blind and dumb.'

The King picked up a newfangled thermometer and played with it, saying nothing. At last he turned to face his wife.

'If the Duke can provide me with a statement of his monetary affairs and evidence that a proper settlement can be made on Mistress Stuart, I will agree to the match.'

Catherine kissed his hand. 'Your Majesty, you have done a good thing.'

The Devil crept into his smile as he considered the matter. The Queen was right. He had done a good thing. And yet he was pretty well sure, no matter what the Chancellor might have said, that the Duke of Richmond had not the funds to provide the settlement he was about to request of him.

When the Queen relayed the news to her, Frances wanted to run and laugh and sing. Even though it was late, she summoned a link boy and requested he wait while she wrote a letter to be delivered to Cobham first thing in the morning.

'My dearest Lord,' she wrote, the blood drumming in her veins. 'The King has at last given permission that, if certain conditions are met, we may be wed at last. I am the happiest woman imaginable. Please come post-haste to London that we may lay our plans together.' She folded the letter and sealed it, writing 'His Grace the Duke of Richmond and Lennox, Cobham Hall in the county of Kent', and handed it to the page to post.

Then she waited, hugging her joy to her breast like a child with its hidden sweetmeat.

*   *   *

The King, up early as usual the next day, was astonished to see Lady Castlemaine out of bed before her usual midday levee, taking the air on the roof outside her apartments next to the Holbein Gate. Close inspection revealed that she was not yet dressed, but wore her smock with all her bosom showing to allure unsuspecting passers-by.

'Good day, Your Majesty.' She leaned on the balustrade, looking down into the Privy Garden, the valley of her breasts beckoning invitingly. 'I hear the Duke of Richmond is reprieved. Are you not concerned to seem a laughing stock at this reversal?'

For answer the King speeded his step.

'Do not listen to idle gossip,' he shouted up to her.

Barbara watched the fast-retreating figure, trying to gauge what his words signified. Was he playing one of his two-faced games, and meant not to let Frances marry after all?

The usual life of the Court engulfed them. Ambassadors arrived, suitors queued in the galleries hoping to catch the ear of the King, plans unfolded for the rebuilding of the city, which was happening at an astonishing pace, members of the Council bickered with each other and lobbied against the Chancellor, and the King and his advisors continued to negotiate a peace that would finally end the expensive war with the Dutch.

Frances waited, unable to pick up the threads of her life, hoping and praying for news from Cobham.

'Why have I had no word?' she asked Mall anxiously as they broke their fast together in Mall's chamber.

'There is no point in the Duke coming back until he has this settlement the King requires,' Mall reassured her, pouring Frances a glass of small beer and offering her a plate of meats that the groom had just brought from the kitchens.

Frances looked out impatiently at another fine spring morning. The sun was breaking through the mist on the river and countless small boats rowed up and down, laden with supplies for the city's rebuilding or carrying Londoners about their business. Already the jagged holes in the burnt-out skyline were filling up with fine new buildings where the yawning gaps had been left by the fire.

'Why does he not send Mary at least with some news?' Frances demanded, pacing up and down,

454

too anxious to settle to her usual tasks.

'Perhaps you will hear today. Now come and help me choose which gown I should wear to the playhouse tonight. The blue or the amber?' Mall held out both gowns.

'The blue. No, the amber. *I* do not know! Whichever becomes you most!'

'What a helpful response. I could almost wish your suitor had indeed changed his mind.'

She instantly regretted her words, seeing their effect on Frances. 'You do not truly think he has had a change of heart?'

Mall shook her head. She did not voice the one true concern she had, that the Duke, famously short of funds, could not raise the necessary guarantees for the settlement. She had lived at Cobham Hall herself and knew how ruinously expensive great houses were to run.

On the third day after Frances had sent her message they were walking down by the Bowling Green, marvelling at how the King managed to despatch his business and discuss state matters while playing bowls at the same time, when the conversation amongst the large group of wits and courtiers suddenly stopped.

A tall figure with familiar russet hair, formally dressed in a coat of blue velvet, the feathers of his hat fluttering in the breeze, strode through the crowd towards the King. He bowed low and presented the King with a scroll, tied up with wine-coloured ribbon.

'Your Majesty,' the Duke announced, 'here are the financial undertakings you requested of me.'

'Can you not see, Your Grace,' enquired the King coolly, 'that I am more concerned with

455

playing a game of bowls than the no-doubt-pressing question of your nuptials? You may hand the paper to the Lord Chancellor, who will, when he has respite from the affairs of state, no doubt read it and comment.'

The Duke knew he was dismissed. He bowed formally and withdrew.

As he walked away Lord Rochester could be heard commenting loudly of him, 'Midday already and he is not drunk. That must be counted a miracle wrought by love.'

The King laughed loudly and Frances saw the Duke's hand reach for the dress sword at his side.

'Indeed, sir,' the Duke replied, his voice soft and dangerous, 'from what I have heard of you, you wake up drunk.'

Frances hurried forward and pulled him into their group. 'Hush. Lord Rochester only says such things to provoke.'

'Then he has succeeded,' muttered the Duke furiously, his grey eyes flinty as a mountain rock-face.

'If every gentleman called out Lord Rochester when he insulted them, there would not be seconds enough in the whole of London,' Mall pointed out. 'He even insults the King.'

'And His Majesty treated my submission with such contempt!' Charles' fury was burning brightly. 'I do not trust him in this. It is my belief that he no more means to let us wed than he does to see me become a Dutchman.'

Mall sighed. 'You could be right. He has certainly seemed in a great good mood of late, which ties not with letting Frances go. I wonder what plan of action you should follow?'

'I have one already.'

Frances and Mall turned to him 'And what is that, pray?'

He dropped his voice. 'I have had enough of play-acting. I have arranged for a coach-and-six to carry you to Cobham tomorrow night. I will meet you at The Bear at Bridge Foot and after that we may be married with all speed.'

Frances' heart lurched. At last she could truly think of escape and life with the man she loved.

'My Lord,' Mall begged, deeply alarmed at this development. 'Consider the danger. How the King will react to an elopement. Frances, for both your sakes, do not pursue so rash an action!'

'Yet you yourself were married in secret,' Frances reminded her, 'and had not the approval of the King or any other; indeed, you acted against the wishes of both your brother and your daughter. And yet you are the happiest couple at Whitehall.'

'It was not the same. I wish it were. Tom was not carrying off the woman the King loves above all others.'

But the Duke would not be turned from his course. 'If we stay here, the King will find another reason to stop us marrying, and another after that. This is our only chance of happiness. Frances, beloved girl, will you meet me and agree to come?'

Chapter 23

'Come and sit by me, Mary,' Nurse chivvied. 'You have stood at yon window since the day broke. I am sure we will hear some news by and by.'

Mary climbed down from her lookout at last. She had spent all yesterday watching from the diamond-shaped window at the very highest point of the south turret, from where, she had convinced herself, she would get the first glimpse of a coach as it turned from the turnpike onto the narrow lane to the Hall.

Beneath her, parkland and fields stretched away into the distance. There were bells summoning the faithful from the surrounding villages, weary from their week's labours, to celebrate the Lord's Day in Cobham Church. Most of the Duke's servants would be amongst them. But of the Duke himself there was no sign.

'Yet what if the King has prevented them!'

Mary contemplated this disaster. Instead of living here with her beloved Frances and the Duke, who teased her and had taught her to ride astride like a gentleman when none was watching, and played card games with her as Nurse snoozed, she would have to return to her mother's family in Boarstall. They wanted her there no more than she wished to go. Even her inheritance was so meagre they would not move mountains to acquire it. Plain as she knew herself to be, and unlikely to win a husband easily, her role would once more be one of unpaid servant, without benefit this time of at least being near her mother.

Hiding her face in her hands, Mary began to weep.

This was so unlike her that even Nurse was unnerved. Mary was such a cheerful, resilient child, on the brink of becoming a capable young woman.

'Come, come,' Nurse comforted. 'Hope is a good breakfast, if a poor supper. Until we hear to the contrary, let us make ready for their happy return.'

Mary made herself cheer up and began to consider how they should best do this.

After they had finished their morning bread and ale, she went to tease the clerk of the kitchen about preparing a suitable wedding feast, even if it was made of cold meats and pies, which should be standing by in readiness for when the Duke and his intended Duchess finally returned.

She was touched to find that the servants had already been infected with the Duke's enthusiasm. The plate had been cleaned with horse tails and stood gleaming in the cupboards, the windows shone brightly, the oak of the table smelled of beeswax and every fire was ready to be lit.

Mary laughed to see that even the brass of the parrot's perch had been polished until it shone.

'Morning has broken,' the parrot informed her.

'Indeed it has, Bird, and truly I hope this is the morning that brings them home safe to Cobham.'

*   *   *

Frances did not know how she would get through the long day and evening until she slipped away to meet the Duke at The Bear at Bridge Foot.

She was so close to her heart's desire, and yet there was still so much that could go adrift. She would not be able to breathe freely until the ring was on her finger and the King was persuaded to look for love elsewhere.

Pretending all was normal, on this of all days, would have taken the talents of the most skilled actress in Drury Lane. The morning service seemed twice as long and the sermon doubly dreary.

459

Catherine Boynton begged for her company to the shops in the Strand, which were already emerging out of the ashes and boasted the newest fashions from Paris. Jittery though she was, Frances still managed to notice a little hat with a red feather that was irresistibly becoming and buy it.

London, she noticed through her preoccupation, was becoming as busy as ever it had been, with building works on every corner and the new constructions in brick, to replace the old Tudor city whose timber had burned so fiercely.

Whitehall buzzed like the hive it was, with courtiers and lawyers, members of parliament and servants, wits and gallants, all like busy bees vying with each other for the brightest pollen.

In the afternoon she was grateful for the diversion when the Queen announced she would ride in Hyde Park.

They had already ridden twice round the Ring, greeting all their acquaintances and stopping to exchange the latest gossip, when they saw the King riding towards them on a great white horse, surrounded by his usual circle. At once the carriages and mounts all parted to let him through.

He stopped and bowed to the Queen.

'Good afternoon, ladies. Your Highness. I have come to extend you all an invitation. I am having a little gathering tonight to hear a play-reading and would particularly welcome your attendance. Ten o'clock in the Privy Chamber.' He seemed to Frances to look at her alone when he said this, and she struggled not to let her face give away her alarm. Had he discovered her plan and now, at the final hour, intended to subvert it?

The ladies all nodded in acceptance.

460

'Strange,' murmured Cary Frazier, 'I have never been bidden to a play-reading by the King before this, have you, Jane?'

'No, and I am sure it will not be half as fun as attending at the theatre, where they have all the scenery, and those great machines to make ships and seas and clouds and rain and all sorts of magic. Still, it is an honour to be bidden by the King, is it not?' She looked at Frances uncertainly.

Frances' reply was lost as the weather, fine until this moment, took a sudden turn for the worse, and a great booming wind almost knocked them from their mounts, forcing Frances to hold on to her hat. Even the weather seemed to be conspiring against the lovers.

They raced back to Whitehall just ahead of the threatening storm.

Was the Duke's coach, with its six horses, already braving the same winds on its journey through the falling darkness, Frances wondered, towards Bridge Foot in Southwark?

When she gained her chamber she found that her tire-woman had laid out her best gown of golden silk. As she stepped into the dress the thought struck her that she would have to slip away directly from the play-reading in the Privy Chamber, with no chance to return for a bag of clothes. At first this distressed her, being a normal woman who liked her fine things about her, and then the thought came: because of this, she would go to her new life entirely free of her old.

She leaned in to fasten her pearl necklace with its matching pendants, feeling the touch of the pearly warmth against her skin. As she did so the moon came out from behind a blustery cloud, flooding the room with pale light, reflected in the lustrous perfection of the pearls in her ears and around her neck.

Yet these had both been given to her by the King. And she knew that if she truly wished to start a new life, she must leave them here, tokens as they were of her old existence.

Tonight all began afresh, a clean slate for their love to write upon.

She released the catch on her necklace, unhooked the pendant from each ear and laid them gently upon her dressing table.

The Privy Chamber, where the play-reading was to take place, was crowded by the time she reached it and there were few seats remaining. Then she saw Mall waving to her and that she had saved the elaborate gilded leather chair next to hers.

She glanced at Frances as she sat down, but all she said was, 'A wild night for adventuring.'

And Frances, holding her gaze, replied, 'Indeed. Yet a full moon to guide lovers' footsteps.'

'Or to light their pursuers.'

Tom Howard, in the seat beyond, leaned suddenly forward, laughing. 'I did not know you two enjoyed riddles so.'

'Oh yes,' Mall replied. 'Nothing we prefer to a puzzle.'

Tom shook his head. 'Will I ever understand the fairer sex?'

Mall simply smiled.

When he had gone to fetch them all a glass of canary wine, Mall slipped Frances a small package. 'Do not open it here. It contains some guineas and a small trifle I bought in Venice, which the ladies there carry to defend their honour, though from what I hear with little success.'

Frances' heart skipped. 'You think there may be danger then?'

Mall smiled and waved at a gentleman who was watching them curiously. 'We live in dangerous times.'

Tom was returning with their wine, so Frances slipped the package into her sleeve, where the folds of her smock easily disguised it.

The play was one of inordinate length and little wit, yet even if it had been the most humorous hit, with every role played by the cream of London's actors, she would not have attended to it. All she could do was wait. And as the hour of midnight grew nearer and all around were yawning, and indeed some falling asleep, she felt Mall's elbow in her side. 'Go. Quick, while that fool actor is droning on.'

'Yet what of the risk to you?' Frances whispered.

'I am Buckingham's sister, the King's playmate and a woman. He will not harm me. You will find a cloak and vizard in the Vane Room next door. Go!'

Frances needed no further encouragement. While the audience climbed to its feet and applauded, more from relief that it was over than appreciation, she slipped out and walked quickly past the knot of servants and courtiers who yawned outside the chamber door.

In the Vane Room she found the cloak Mall had promised and slipped it on. Then she ran between the Queen's Apartment and the King's Bedchamber and out onto the lead roof above the river, where the King and Queen had sat to watch the comet. From here a set of little-used steps ran down, skirting the Shield Gallery and on down to the Privy Stairs. A row of wherries waited here for the entertainment to finish, rocking up and down dangerously as the strong wind rendered the river more like the open sea. Frances hailed the first, whose oarsmen rowed swiftly towards her, eager to get off the river and home to a warm fireside.

'Where to, mistress?' enquired one of the wherrymen.

'The Bear at Bridge Foot as fast as you may row.'

'You are late enough, mistress, if you hope to see Jacob Hall perform in the grounds there,' he commented as he began to turn the small boat round. 'I reckon he'll be inside by now, don't you, Benjamin,' he enquired of his fellow-oarsman, 'being bought a glass of wine by the ladies?'

Frances, who had known nothing of the spectacle, was relieved that it prevented the men from asking why she went there, yet it also filled her with anxiety. Would the presence of a great crowd give them cover or make their discovery more likely?

The two men laughed at their wit, and went on pulling the oars as though the river were as flat as a millpond. Yet Frances held tight to the side with both hands, feeling the water soak her face, and the wind cut into her cheeks, wondering if she would end up this night in a watery grave instead of a bridal bed.

'Did you hear the sad tale of what befell the landlady of The Bear, but a few months since, mistress?' the man called Benjamin enquired with relish.

Frances shook her head.

'Throwed herself into the river and drowned,' revealed the other wherryman, robbing Benjamin

464

of his dramatic denouement.

'And she a fine-looking woman too, that used to be mistress of the White Horse in Lombard Street.' Benjamin tried to recover his ground, shouting above the wind. 'Do you know the White Horse at all, mistress?'

'Is she likely to, Benjamin, it being as rough as all hell?'

Frances shivered, wondering what would make a fine-looking young woman drown herself.

'They say she had the green sickness, mind.' Benjamin clearly felt his drama needed some explanation. 'And we know the cure to that. The attentions of a husband!'

By now the reassuring sight of London Bridge was approaching in the distance and they could hear the race of the water as it hit the great buttresses that held it up.

Instead of the usual steps up from the river, The Bear had its own great landing stage, since it was here that the tilt-boats stopped on their way to and from Greenwich and on to Gravesend.

Frances stood up shakily, with one of the wherrymen helping her to keep her balance as she climbed from the rocking boat onto the landing stage.

Pretending more confidence than she felt, she walked through the grounds towards the tavern. She had stopped for a moment to take stock when a strong arm took hold of her, a hand covered her mouth and she found herself pulled into a kind of arbour.

'Hush, beloved!' The tender words belied the strength of his grip, and it took her an instant to see that her assailant was indeed the Duke.

'Charles,' she breathed at last. 'Thank God it is you!'

She could say no more for his lips were on hers.

'I wish I had known Jacob Hall performed this night,' he told her, when eventually he let her go. 'Or I would have chosen some quieter place of assignation. The inn bursts with ladies and gallants.'

'Yet none of them knew you?'

He shook his head. 'I kept to my room. I thought it wise to command one, and it has proved useful indeed. Best you go there now, at the top of the stairs. I left the door ajar. And keep your hood up and your vizard on. Talk to no one. I will send a boy as soon as the company leaves and we can get on the road without being known.' He kissed her one last time, as if he could not tear himself away. 'Almost there,' he whispered and the words, in the wild empty night, sounded like a prayer.

'Hush!' She put a finger on his lips. 'Do not say it.'

As she felt her way into the back entrance of the tavern she thought of the play-reading and how it must by now have ended, and how Mall would have to make up some story to fob off the King, and Frances hoped desperately she had found one that was convincing.

She was halfway up the staircase when a violent burst of wind blew the clouds away from the moon and all of a sudden it was light almost as day. Mall's words that it could be light to pursue lovers came back to haunt her and she shivered, rubbing her arms to keep them warm. And as she did so she encountered the package Mall had slipped her, which she had clean forgotten.

She pulled it out of her sleeve and examined

it. It was a silk handkerchief tied with ribbon, in which there were two objects: a bag of coins and a small knife, no more that five inches long, richly embellished with mother-of-pearl.

A voice behind her startled her so much that she all but dropped the knife.

'A curious place to encounter you, Mistress Stuart. A tavern at midnight, and you unaccompanied. Anyone would think you had come to meet a lover.'

Frances found herself looking into the triumphant eyes of Barbara Castlemaine.

'I came to watch the rope-dancing,' Frances, her heart pounding, offered by way of explanation, 'yet found I was ailing and needed to lie down an instant.'

'And you happened to have a room. How useful.' Barbara stood barring her path. 'I too came to watch the dancing. I have a room also, since I soon expect a visitor in the shape of Mr Hall.'

Frances made as if to pass her, but Barbara put out her arm, blocking the way.

Without further consideration, Frances took the knife from her sleeve. 'Then you will go up to your room now and wait for him.' She held the knife against Barbara's ribs, hoping and praying Barbara could not sense her fear.

At least she had the physical advantage. Frances was five inches taller than Barbara, as well as both younger and fitter. Barbara's life of luxurious excess had finally begun to catch up with her.

Barbara gasped, but began to walk up the stairs with Frances close behind her. Once in the chamber, Frances glanced at the bed, but it was too wide to be of use. Instead, still holding the

467

knife, she untied the cords that held back the great curtains and made Barbara sit upon a large and heavy carved oak chair. She secured her to the chair by wrist and ankle.

Barbara, meanwhile, watched her with triumphant lazy amusement. 'This will make such a story to tell the King. Indeed, I would lay a purse of angels that he would long to be here with us, if he knew.'

'Yes,' Frances agreed, smiling while she tightened the knots. 'I recall this is the kind of game you enjoy, my lady. But you will not be telling him of it just yet.'

She pulled out the silk handkerchief that had wrapped the knife and coins and quickly, before Barbara could guess what she was about, tied it around her mouth.

A whistle from out on the landing told her it was time to leave. 'Do not worry for your gallant, Mr Hall. I will instruct him to leave you here an hour or two.' Frances clinked the coins in the purse Mall had given her. 'These guineas should keep him and his admirers happy for a while. I only hope he is in a shape to show his skills by the time he comes to untie you. And do not think you will be heard if you bang on the floor, for it is very wild and noisy below. Goodnight, my lady—and, I hope, goodbye.'

She closed the door and ran down after the waiting boy, stopping only to find the handsome Jacob Hall and hand over the purse of money. 'You are to let my lady sleep awhile so she may gain her strength for later.' There was a loud cry of 'Aye-aye' from the assembled gathering. 'She sends you these guineas that you and your friends might toast her health as loudly as you wish, for you will not wake

468

her.'

At that, one of the gallants who crowded round Jacob, his wig askew and his smock all unlaced, began to drum on the floor. 'A toast! To my Lady Castlemaine. The greatest whore in London!'

Jacob Hall looked for a moment as if he might defend his mistress' honour. Instead he took a long draught from his tankard of ale and bowed. 'Excuse me, sir. The greatest whore in Christendom!'

And while they all laughed and ordered another round of sack and canary wine, Frances finally made her escape into the coach-and-six and into the eagerly awaiting arms of the Duke of Richmond.

*   *   *

When the play-reading at Whitehall Palace finally ended, half the audience was fast asleep. Mall had slipped Jane La Garde into Frances' seat to cover for her absence, and none had so far noted it.

The applause that greeted the last scene was genuine enough, for all longed for it to finish.

The King clapped loudest of all.

'Yet where is Mistress Stuart?' he quizzed Mall as he passed.

'She took to her bed half an hour since,' brazened Mall.

'Did she indeed?' he held Mall's gaze suspiciously. 'Then I envy her good fortune. Not one of the dramatist's greatest.'

He swept from the chamber followed by his yapping spaniels and a gaggle of courtiers, just as the coach-and-six bearing the Duke of Richmond and his intended wife turned out of the liberty of

469

Southwark onto the turnpike and towards Cobham and a new life.

Chapter 24

It was the perfume that woke her. A sweet, heady, powerful scent that filled the entire room.

Frances sat up, dazed, not knowing for a moment where she was, and saw that every table, mantelpiece and even the windowsill held jugs and vases brimming with white narcissi.

And then—the wondrous, glorious realization that they had done it, they had escaped!

To her embarrassment she saw that she was clad only in her smock, and that her gown lay across the back of a carved chair, with her shoes and stockings next to it on the floor. Tentatively she climbed out of the bed to explore her surroundings. The room was a great square one, richly furnished, with wainscotting on all the walls in the manner of folded linen, and a great candle-holder hanging from the ceiling. But its chief attraction was the huge oriel window, with a cushioned seat in front, that gave onto the parkland beneath.

Frances sat down and looked out at the clouds of daffodils that painted great patches of yellow under the trees, and at the red squirrel and deer that roamed happily side by side, ignoring the cock pheasant that strutted its showy, exotic colours nearby.

The last thing she could remember was falling asleep in the coach as it jolted over rutted roads, anxiety and exhaustion finally overwhelming her.

Yet who had undressed her and left her clothes so neatly arranged on the chair? Had it been the Duke's hands that had unlaced her?

A knock on the door rescued her from these imaginings and Mary skipped in.

'You are awake at last!'

'Was it you who filled the chamber with flowers?'

Mary nodded.

'I woke up wondering if I had found myself in some celestial paradise.'

'I picked them, yet it was at the Duke's suggestion.'

'Where is he? And how did I get from the coach into bed, so that I awoke this morn wearing only my smock?'

'He carried you here and I did the rest. Do not worry, your maidenly modesty was not outraged.'

Frances laughed out of sheer happiness. 'Maidenly modesty be damned! So where has my hero and rescuer hidden himself when I wish to thank him?'

'He is below with the minister. It is your wedding day, Frances!'

Frances jumped up and folded the young girl into her arms. 'I am so glad you are here to witness it, Mary. I will have neither father nor mother, nor even my sister Sophia or brother Walter. You will be all my family!'

The thought struck her that she had left empty-handed, without even a change of clothes to be married in. 'Well, I shall be a plain and practical bride, for I brought naught with me. I must be married in the gown I wore in the wherry and the coach.'

'It is a glorious gown and brings out the clearness

471

of your eyes and the gold of your hair,' Mary consoled her.

'And draws attention from my excellent Roman nose!'

'I have made you a few adornments,' Mary said shyly. 'Put on your gown and I will fetch them.'

'Mary . . .' Frances called after her. 'Bring me a comb at least. I refuse to be wed with hair like a haycock!'

She slipped the gown over her chemise and did up the tiny pearl buttons that fastened it, wondering if her disappearance had been discovered. Barbara would never admit to the indignity that had befallen her, but she would still stir the midden in any way she could and make it stink.

Mary came back bearing a cushion, on which lay a circlet of spring flowers and a nosegay tied up with pink ribbon.

'I shall be like the Queen of the May!'

'They are ready below.' Mary placed the crown on Frances' head.

Tears sprang unbidden into Frances' eyes at the thought that her mother and father, and all the rest of her family, did not even know she was taking such a step. She reminded herself of Nurse's adage that each person must be architect of their own destiny, so she wiped her eyes and picked up her nosegay.

'Are you ready?' Mary asked.

Frances nodded and followed her down the wide wooden staircase, with its ducal crowns carved into the newel posts, towards the Great Hall.

She was touched to see that the whole household had assembled, from the scullions and Black Dick, as well as Roger Payne, the Duke's steward, and

Henry Flaxney the understeward, down to the grooms, cook and tire-woman.

And at the end of the hall, in front of the vast fireplace, in which blazed a cheering fire, stood her husband-to-be, smiling with such pride that suddenly she knew not a moment's doubt, no matter what the future might have in store for them.

He reached out a loving hand. 'The flowers become you more than any jewels.'

The minister enquired who would be giving away the bride.

When Roger Payne stepped forward another wave of sadness assailed Frances that it would not be her own father who gave her away, and yet the delight in her bridegroom's eyes soon stilled it.

'Dearly beloved,' began the minister. 'We are gathered here in the sight of God, and in the face of this congregation, to join together this man and this woman in holy matrimony.'

When he arrived at the fateful question of whether any person present knew of any lawful impediment, Frances found herself glancing towards the door, as if a fanfare might blow at any moment and the King burst in.

Yet no impediment was raised. At last the minister turned to the Duke.

'Charles, wilt thou have this woman to thy wedded wife, to live together after God's ordinance in the holy estate of matrimony? Wilt thou love her, comfort her, honour and keep her, in sickness and in health, and, forsaking all other, keep thee only unto her, so long as ye both shall live?'

Twenty people held their breath, waiting.

'I will.'

473

And then it was her turn.

'Frances, wilt thou have this man to thy wedded husband, to live together after God's ordinance in the holy estate of matrimony? Wilt thou obey him, serve him, love, honour and keep him, in sickness and in health, and, forsaking all other, keep thee only unto him, so long as ye both shall live?'

Before she could assent a squawk made everyone start and look behind them. The African grey parrot jumped up and down, fluffing up his feathers and declaring, 'I will! I will!' while all in the room cried with laughter.

'So, Reverend,' the Duke requested straight-faced, 'I hope this does not mean I have married the parrot?'

'Or that the parrot has married me,' teased Frances.

'The bird remains unwed,' confirmed the minister, entering into the spirit of this unusual wedding ceremony.

The rings were then exchanged and the vows completed, to general rejoicing, and no small relief to both parties.

As a final act the Duke delighted the assembled gathering by kissing his bride in full sight of all, while the parrot cocked his head and uttered with some satisfaction, 'Good old Charlie Stuart!'

They then repaired to the dining chamber, where a wedding breakfast had been laid out under Mary's strict supervision and was now enjoyed by all, from the Duke and his new Duchess down to the humblest undergroom.

Mary had discovered that Simon, the bird-scarer, was a dab hand with the fiddle, and after the dishes were cleared they ran through every country dance he knew until they were all fit to drop. Upon which the Duke announced that they might have the rest of the day off, while he and his wife retired, despite the early hour.

So it was that, somewhat to their embarrassment, Frances and her bridegroom were escorted up the great staircase with much banging of saucepans and whistling and stamping, to their bedchamber where a jug of mead, famed as the newlyweds' drink, awaited them.

'Here,' shouted Mary, producing something from her pocket, 'we must fling the stocking!' She handed it to Frances, who threw the stocking over her head into the laughing crowd of spectators, where it was fortuitously caught by Mary herself.

'You'll be the next then, Mistress Mary!' teased the steward as they finally departed, leaving the bride and groom alone together.

Charles strode over to the window and closed the crewelwork curtains.

When he turned back Frances stood waiting, naked as Eve in the Garden of Eden, with the crown of flowers still upon her head.

She reached up to move the circlet, but he stayed her hand. 'I had thought you a duchess, but I see you are a queen.' The words, casually said, made them think of the King and what they had both risked for this longed-for moment.

And then his mouth was on hers and she thought of nothing but him as he lifted her and carried her to their marriage bed.

'With my body I thee worship,' he whispered as he laid his body onto hers.

She clung to him then, exulting in his touch, tiny darts of pleasure coursing through her body, until at last she exploded into a starburst of amazed fulfilment.

From the floor beneath came a distant squawk of 'Good work, Charlie Stuart!'

*   *   *

When news of the elopement reached the King, his anger was of biblical proportions. He ran out of the meeting where they were negotiating with the hated Dutch Ambassador and went straight to her chamber, his dogs snapping at his heels.

He found that Catherine Boynton, Cary Frazier and Jane La Garde had got there before him. They stood, startled and anxious as hens in the hen house after the fox has been, amid the chaos of Frances' possessions.

'We hear she has fled to Cobham to wed the Duke,' explained Cary hesitantly with one eye on the door.

'She has left all she owns behind,' added Catherine.

'Even her gowns and her trinkets.'

'And all of her jewellery,' Jane added hesitantly, 'asking that we might return it to the givers.'

The King strode across to the dressing table and picked up the pearl necklace he had presented to Frances. With a great wrench he snapped the string and the pearls catapulted round the room in all directions. The ladies watched in frightened silence as he flung each pendant earring down and ground it into the floor, as if he imagined it were the Duke's face.

'Did none of you know of this elopement?'

They shook their heads in silent unison, and even

the bold Cary Frazier knew for once to hold her tongue.

As he angrily departed, Lord Cornbury, the Chancellor's son, had the misfortune to be arriving on an errand from his father.

'What business have *you* here?' the King snarled. 'If you seek Mistress Stuart you have missed the boat—she has eloped with the Duke of Richmond.' A thought struck him and he leaned up close to the bewildered peer. 'Or perhaps you knew that already? Perhaps the Earl your father supplied the horses and dressed himself as coachman that he might aid the lovers.'

'Your Majesty, I knew nothing of this and neither did my father.'

'Indeed?' sneered the King.

'I thought Your Majesty had agreed to the match, if not exactly given it your blessing.'

Charles looked at Cornbury as if he would like to set the dogs on him, and not his own gentle spaniels, but the slavering bear-hounds kept for bear-baiting, who were ready to tear a beast limb from limb.

'Tell your father from me that he has not heard the last of this.'

'Your Majesty, as God is my witness, he has not heard the first of it, either.'

But the King was in no mood to listen to reason.

Barbara, when he dragged her away from the gaming table to listen to his rant, could not resist a chance to stick the knife in. If she could not sabotage Frances' marriage, at least it offered the chance to ruin the Chancellor.

'I told you Mistress Stuart was not the angel she professed to be. And of course Clarendon is up to his ears in it. All the Court talks of it.'

The King paced up and down the Matted Gallery while Barbara watched him, half an eye on the Queen's ladies who had gathered in the Privy Garden in twittering groups, Mall among them, talking in envious tones of Frances and the Duke.

In one thing Frances had been right: Barbara had not mentioned the incident at The Bear to anyone.

'I would wager a hundred guineas Mall Villiers had a hand in this,' Barbara accused. 'She is a bold woman, especially since she married Tom Howard and looks like the cat that got the cream. And she is thick as fleas on a dog's back with Mistress Stuart. It was she who made excuses for her last night. You should find out what she knows of this.'

'I will indeed,' replied the King, much struck.

'And, sire,' Barbara was never one to give up an advantage. 'It is time to take the Seal away from that old fool Clarendon. He has had his day and clutters up the Council with his own schemes instead of pressing yours.'

Charles sighed heavily. 'As usual, you are right, my lady. Until this moment I allowed my loyalty to stand in the way of my judgement. But I will never forgive him for this. It touches too near to my heart. He will indeed have to go.'

'Believe me, I will watch him leave and dance a jig as I do so.'

The King studied the woman whose bed he had shared for so long, and with whom he had fathered so many children. There was not an ounce of the kindness in her that he had found in Frances Stuart.

Yet Frances had betrayed his love and his trust, and he must forget her.

But first someone must pay.

*   *   *

Mall had been awaiting the summons and when it came it was almost a relief. Tom had had no peace with her, for he told her she had been murmuring all night that she had betrayed the King, her childhood friend.

Tom had half-persuaded her to seek an audience with him for herself, when the messenger came to request her presence.

The King was in his hothouse admiring his white camellias with his gardener by his side.

'I imagine you know whom their perfect purity brings to mind?'

'Yet Frances is neither perfect nor perfectly pure!' Mall had intended calm apology, yet could not help herself. 'She is simply human.'

'The other night at my play-reading, did you know she intended to flee with the Duke?'

'Yes.'

'Then why, since you claim to love me, did you not prevent it?'

'I believed Frances had a right to happiness that not even a king may overrule.'

'A right!' Charles crushed the perfect bloom he held and flung its petals to the ground. 'What right do any of us have to happiness? I must rule a kingdom and be tied to a woman I did not choose and whose bed I share from duty to produce an heir. Do I not have a right to happiness also?'

'Perhaps. Yet Frances has chosen to attest her love before God and forgo all others, as the state of matrimony ordains. It behoves all of us, even kings, to respect it.'

'You did not used to be so sanctimonious about marriage, Mall. I remember the love you bore my cousin Rupert, though you had a husband of your own.'

'I was young and foolish. It has taken a whole lifetime to find a man who has taught me the true meaning of love. You will soon find another to beguile you as Frances did.'

'No!' the anguish in his voice cut through the hot afternoon air. 'I loved her, Mall.'

Knowing the risk she took, Mall still took it. 'Yet she did not love you, and to force her into your bed would have been dishonourable.'

'You are cruel.'

'I am honest. Let her go and know you have done a good thing.'

'The Court will not be the same without her.'

'No.'

'I will never forget her.'

'No more you should.'

Yet if he did not find love again, Mall mused, he would soon find consolation. They said Nell Gwynn, the new actress, was both pretty and witty. Perhaps she would invite Mistress Gwynn to sup when the King was present.

*   *   *

The Earl of Clarendon had won back the King's good opinion many times before, but not on this occasion. The cut had gone too deep. Yet he clung onto his position and his great house in Piccadilly until at last his son and his son-in-law, the Duke of York, persuaded him he must return the Great Seal, which was needed to stamp all the laws of the land—and leave the country before his impeachment was proven and he lost everything.

He did so with a heavy heart and a sense of being deeply wronged.

Barbara, as good as her word, stood out on her balcony, wearing nothing but her smock, to watch the one man who had resisted her power face his final defeat and humiliation.

'My lord!' she called down to the gouty old man. 'I would not have let you off so lightly. I wish you had been quartered and your limbs hung up on the city walls.'

'Madam,' Clarendon shouted back, 'I do not wish you so cruel a fate. I merely wish you old.'

*   *   *

Frances stood in her parkland surveying the new building, with its classical pilastered columns and arched stone entrance, which was emerging with extraordinary speed from the old manor house of Cobham.

John Webb, a nephew and pupil of the famed Inigo Jones, was directing the venture most efficiently, and Frances enjoyed the challenge of adding her own ideas as to how it could be done without too much outlay. Yesterday he had shown her a pile of old bones and oyster shells that the workmen had dug up, with all the pride of an archaeologist unearthing ancient Rome.

Since the Duke and his new Duchess were unwelcome at Court, her husband had decided to make Cobham the hub of life in Kent, with his wife the shining star at its centre.

481

Having never had a home of her own, Frances found she was made for the life of a chatelaine. Simply walking through her own house gave her enormous pleasure, as did stopping to admire the fireplace with the fierce Saracen's head carved above it, testifying that its owners were once Crusaders; checking that all her sconces and chandeliers were well supplied with candles; or standing in front of the poignant inscription in Latin, which proclaimed that 'Each Man Makes His Own Shipwreck'. What must have happened to Cobham's occupants that they wished to create something as sad as that? And yet, how close to a shipwreck her own life had come.

Most of all she loved simply living here. She liked the scent of fresh linen in her linen cupboard and the sight of the rows of glass bottles in her stillroom. She had a knack, she found—never given rein before—for choosing her tapestries and furniture with taste and style and creating a charming atmosphere.

When she had told Mr Webb she wished the bedchamber painted the colour of a pigeon's breast, he had looked back at her in horror. And yet now he admired the colour so much that he recommended it to all his lords and ladies.

She also found she had the skill of handling servants, of being friendly and yet firm, and getting good work from all. Valued only as an ornament until now, she took a deep and surprising pleasure in making herself useful.

And when she was tired of domestic bliss, there were the new delights of the bedchamber.

Mary, meanwhile, was turning into a young woman before her eyes. Soon she would be thinking of a husband of her own.

Charles, for his part, was tender to his new wife, and protective. She had not told him yet, but her flowers had not arrived this month. She would wait until the next month's courses were due and she was certain of her news, since she knew how greatly he desired an heir.

Not a day passed, in rain or shine, that she did not thank God for her good luck. Sometimes she missed her friends at Court, and yearned for the latest play or fashion from Paris, and told herself she did not intend to be a country wife forever, never visiting Court or city, yet a true and loving marriage suited her well.

Her mother had forgiven her at last, seeing no doubt the advantages of having a daughter with a large house, who had become a duchess. Next month Mall came to visit the house that had once been hers.

She had not seen the King, and was told his anger with her burned brightly still. And yet he had done a strange thing. When the war with Holland had finally ended, Charles had issued a medal to mark the peace. Mall had sent Frances one and she stood with it in her hand.

'See, Mary,' she laughed, astonished that the medal used the image of herself, engraved months ago by Jan Roettier. 'Here I am depicted as Britannia with my shield and spear, sitting astride the rock of England, ruling the waves!'

She had taken nothing with her when she left the Court, and wanted nothing of her old life. Yet this disc of silver gave her great happiness.

Frances, Duchess of Richmond and Lennox, was not yet twenty-one and she had made her life's great choice, in the face of the fiercest opposition. She had been loved by a king and now she would live on forever as Britannia.

It would make great tales to tell her grandchildren. Yet for today, her home, her husband and her household beckoned. And she was truly glad of it.

Behind her, in the golden light of the afternoon, the Duke held open the door to the house she had drawn so often in her imagination and never dared hope would one day be hers.

Frances smiled and walked through it and into her future.

Postscript

The Restoration Court was fascinated by the question: did Frances Stuart ever surrender to Charles II? No one could believe that he loved her obsessively for five years and that somehow La Belle Stuart resisted him, no matter what inducements he offered her.

The gossipy Pepys, while admiring her beauty, could not decide if Frances was a 'cunning slut' holding out to be Queen or a virtuous woman. In the end, when he heard the story of Frances returning her jewels to the King, he decided it was 'the noblest romance' and that Frances was the greatest 'example of a brave lady that ever I heard in my life'.

John Evelyn, a more high-minded commentator, also believed she was honourable. It was also widely discussed at Court that Charles might divorce the Queen and marry Frances.

People in her own time had difficulty believing that she would choose the Duke of Richmond over the King and suspected she married him for expediency's sake, yet the letters Frances wrote to her husband tell another story.

'Oh my dearest, if you love me, have a care for yourself,' she wrote three months after they were married, ending the letter, 'I find I am the happiest woman that ever was born in having the heart of my dearest Lord, and the only joy of my life, which I will rather choose to die than lose.' Even given the vivid seventeenth-century language, the sentiment is clear. Frances loved her man.

485

They were always short of money and her husband sought various diplomatic missions. While he was away Frances kept him chattily in touch with the progress of updating their house, Cobham Hall. One of her letters has a delightfully modern feel: 'I hired the painter you mention to paint the Bed-chamber. It is now almost done . . . If you did but know how hard it is to get workmen at this time, and how lazy those are which are here, I am sure you would be of my opinion.' Some things never change!

Mall Villiers (finally Howard) lived contentedly with her 'Northern Tom' and, despite the gap in their age and status, they were described by one contemporary observer as 'the fondest couple that can be'. Tragically, Mall's daughter died at twenty, having only just become a bride herself.

Mary Lewis married and had a daughter whom, tellingly, she named Frances.

Catherine Boynton finally got her Dick, as well as a £4000 dowry from the Queen. Since he has gone down in history as 'Lying Dick Talbot', perhaps the bargain wasn't such a good one.

Lord Rochester married heiress Elizabeth Mallet, whom he had earlier kidnapped, and continued his louche life, dying of syphilis at 33, despite the attentions of Madam Fourcard and her mercury baths. He is still remembered for his lyric verse, and even more for his pithy comments about the King.

Barbara Castlemaine was one of the great survivors. After ten years of her reign, the King made her Duchess of Cleveland when he moved on to a new mistress. She kept an increasingly dubious string of lovers—from actor Cardell Goodman, who would demand 'Is my duchess come?' before agreeing to start the play, to the scoundrelly 'Beau' Fielding, whom she married at 63, only to find he was married already. She died poor after marrying off her five royal bastards to various minor scions of the aristocracy.

Sophia Stuart married Henry Bulkeley, Master of the Royal Household, who had an unfortunate penchant for duelling—often to protect Sophia's rather racy reputation. There was even gossip that, some years later, she might have become the King's mistress! She became an ardent Jacobite and followed King James II to France after he was ousted from the throne, where she spent the rest of her life. She proved a prolific mother with two sons and five daughters, all of whom survived her.

Frances herself was not so lucky. She was definitely pregnant four months after her marriage, and there is a touching letter in the British Library from the steward of one of her husband's Scottish estates offering congratulations to the Duke and Duchess. 'The news of her Grace's being with child will make all your Grace's vassals mad; some of them have come to me almost 100 miles only to be informed of the certainty. It is looked upon here as no small miracle to hear so great brutes as they be so heartily zealous for both your Graces.'

But that pregnancy was not to last, and there is no mention of any others. Sadly, the 'great brutes' who had walked a hundred miles for news of an heir were destined to be disappointed. This must have been an enormous sadness to Frances.

But a greater sadness faced her. After just five years of marriage her beloved Duke, away on a mission as an ambassador in Denmark, was tragically drowned after drinking too much wine. Some months later his body was returned to England and to Frances, in a ship whose hull had been painted black and which bore dramatic black sails, to be buried in great state in Westminster Abbey. Gossip at the time had it that the King might have sent him to Denmark deliberately so that he could approach Frances again, but this is highly unlikely. By this time the King's eye had lit upon one Nell Gwynn, among others.

The King did eventually forgive Frances, mainly because the year after her marriage she was struck down with smallpox and, as Pepys speculated, 'all do conclude she will be wholly spoiled.' In fact her beauty emerged largely undimmed, but the shock was enough to make the King soften towards her.

After her husband's death Frances lived on at her beloved Cobham, but it must have seemed empty without her Duke. Money and legal considerations meant that eventually she sold her interest to her sister-in-law and moved back to Whitehall, but this time as an independent woman.

Despite being courted by a number of suitors, she never married again. Perhaps Frances, having tasted a happy marriage, preferred not to risk an unhappy one. And perhaps, after being so long pursued, she had had enough of men!

She lived a long and slightly eccentric life, becoming known for her passion not for kings and courtiers, but for cats and cards. She became a lady-in-waiting again and gave evidence in the 'Baby in the Bedpan' scandal under James II, when his queen was suspected of smuggling a male baby into her childbed when an heir was desperately needed.

Frances also amassed a considerable fortune

through sensible investing, which on her death she left largely to her nephew, Lord Blantyre, with instructions to build a house in her native Scotland to be named, with characteristic individuality, 'From Lennox Love to Blantyre'– Lennox being her beloved husband's ducal name.

She also left two large portraits of herself and the Duke, with his fine russet curls much in evidence, which were to be hung in the house and are still there to this day. Some time later the family shortened the rather extravagant name to Lennoxlove. By one of those extraordinary twists of fate, I was married at Lennoxlove almost exactly three hundred years later.

It was during Charles II's reign that Frances' image as Britannia was used on English coins, and she remained there for more than three hundred years, until 2008. Pepys thought it a generous gesture on behalf of the King, but perhaps he had a lot to apologize for.

On her death Frances requested an effigy be made of herself, life-sized, 'as well done in wax as can be'. By another of those twists of fate, the effigy is now on display in Westminster Abbey Museum, having recently been rescued from a loft, and stands next to the equally life-sized one of Charles II.

In a delightful example of history coming to life, between the two figures, standing proudly on its perch, is that of her parrot, an African grey, which lived with Frances for more than forty years and died only months after she did. It is, the museum informs us, the oldest stuffed bird in England, and possibly the world.

Maeve Haran, London

Acknowledgements

With thanks to the staff of the British Library for access to the letters between Frances and the Duke of Richmond; to genealogist Jenny Thomas for extremely useful advice; to Terry Curran, Estates Manager of Cobham Hall, and Sylvia Hammond, the very helpful guide and Cobham expert, for her generous contributions of time and information; to the National Archive of Scotland for Frances' will, which to my joy and amazement could be downloaded; to Dr Richard Luckett, Pepys Librarian of Magdalene College, Cambridge, for his tour of the library and the unforgettable experience of holding Pepys' diary; to the engaging staff of the Keeper of the Muniments of Westminster Abbey Library, for a wonderful and unexpected glimpse into this hidden gem . . . and for pointing out the effigy of the parrot! To my agent, Judith Murray, for her advice and friendship; and to Jenny Geras, a brilliant editor whose judgement greatly enhanced the telling of Frances' story; and lastly to my family, who have to put up with hearing fascinating seventeenth-century facts until they want to scream.

A list of sources

The following books have been invaluable in recreating the period:

My Dearest Minette: Letters of Charles II to his Sister, ed. Ruth Norrington, Peter Owen 1996; *The Memoirs of the Comte de Grammont*, Folio Society 1965; *Lord Rochester's Monkey*, Graham Greene, Bodley Head 1974; *Samuel Pepys: The Shorter Pepys*, ed. Robert Latham, Penguin Classics 1987; *King Charles II*, Arthur Bryant, Longmans 1931; *The England of Charles II*, Arthur Bryant, Longmans 1934; *Postman's Horn—An Anthology of the Letters of Later Seventeenth-Century England*, Arthur Bryant, Longmans 1946; *King Charles II*, Antonia Fraser, Weidenfeld & Nicolson 1979; *A Gambling Man: Charles II and the Restoration*, Jenny Uglow, Faber 2009; *Restoration London*, Liza Picard, Phoenix 1997; *A Journal of the Plague Year*, Daniel Defoe, Everyman 1953 (originally published 1722); *Old London Street Cries*, Andrew W. Tuer, Scolar Press 1978; *Ladies in Waiting*, Anne Somerset, Weidenfeld & Nicolson 1984; *Royalty Restored*, J. Fitzgerald Molloy, Dodo Press 2008; *Van Dyck and Britain*, ed. Karen Hearn, Tate Publications 2009; *Sixteenth- and Seventeenth-Century Miniatures in the Collection of HM The Queen*, ed. Graham Reynolds, The Royal Collection 1999; *The English Housewife*, Gervase Markham, ed. Michael R. Best, McGill Queen 1986; *Clarendon's History of the Great Rebellion*, OUP / Folio Society 1967; *The Honour of Richmond*, David Morris, Ebor Press 2000; *The Great Fire of London*, Stephen Parker,

Sutton Press 1996; *Chivalry & Command: 500 Years of Horseguards,* Brian Harwood, Osprey 2006; *Whitehall Palace Official Illustrated History,* Simon Thurley Merrell / Historic Royal Palaces 2008; *The Lily and the Lion,* Philip Mansel and Robin W. Winks, Cassell 1980; *Painted Ladies: Women at the Court of Charles II,* Catharine MacLeod and Julia Marciari Alexander, National Portrait Gallery / Yale 2001; *The Funeral Effigies of Westminster Abbey,* ed. Anthony Harvey and Richard Mortimer, Boydell 1994; *La Belle Stuart,* Cyril Hughes Hartmann, Routledge 1924; *The Illustrated Pepys,* Robert Latham, BCA 1979; *A History of Women's Bodies,* Edward Shorter, Basic Books 1982; *Love and Louis XIV,* Antonia Fraser, Phoenix 2007; *Henrietta Maria,* Alison Plowden, Sutton 2001; *The King's Ladies: Charles II and His Ladies of Pleasure,* Dorothy Ponsonby Senior, Robert Hale 1936; *Cavalier,* Lucy Worsley, Faber 2007; *The Diary of John Evelyn,* Everyman 1907; *Charles II and The Duke of Buckingham,* David C. Hanrahan, Sutton 2006; *Inns and Taverns of Old London,* Henry C. Shelley, Wildside Press 2004.